a
Dream House Girls Novel
1

Follow Your Bliss

FOLLOW YOUR BLISS
Dream House Girls, Book 1

Sign up for Holly Rose's Newsletter
at https://linktr.ee/writerhollyrose

For my sweet sister, Schoener M.
Thank you for your unwavering love and support. I will always treasure our amazing childhood of playing with our Barbie dolls.

Author's Note

While this contemporary romance novel is meant to be hopeful, steamy, fun, and (hopefully, at times) funny, it does touch on some potentially sensitive themes and topics.

If you'd like to know more, you can find a full list at https://www.writerhollyrose.com/content-warnings.

Chapter 1

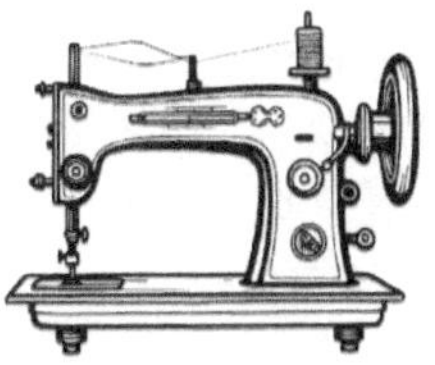

The Time Capsule

Rose

FEW THINGS PISSED ME off as much as running out of water-soluble embroidery stabilizer while sewing a fuckton of tulle after midnight. And on a borrowed sewing machine, no less.

I lifted my foot off the pedal and stared with bleary eyes at where the stabilizer ended, mocking me. This last completed seam would've earned me the right to go to bed, according to the taskmaster in my brain who desperately worried I wouldn't finish Becca's wedding and bridesmaid gowns by next month. But no, as with all things since I'd moved home three days ago, the stabilizer was against me, too.

To hell with it. I was an expert. Even on Mom's sewing machine, surely I could finish without the seam slipping out of the tulle. I gently pressed the pedal and went six inches before the seam pulled out all the way back to the stabilizer.

"Motherf—"

The "Sisters" song from *White Christmas* emanating from my phone drowned out my cursing. At least my sister's shitty timing kept me from rage-ripping $200 worth of silk tulle I couldn't afford to replace.

I took a deep breath. "Hey Lily, did you get home yet?"

"Rose! Thank God."

So much drama in three syllables. I huffed a laugh. "Are you having a real crisis, or a Lily crisis?"

"A real crisis! Do you remember the time capsule we buried at St. Dorothy's summer camp?"

"Girl, that's so random…" While my brain searched back fifteen years, I pushed my chair back three inches until it hit the side of my childhood bed. I bit back a choice *fuck*. I had to find my own place before I lost my mind. "I've traumatically blocked most of middle school, but yeah, I remember it. Why?"

"I need you to go dig it up."

"Lily…*what?*"

"I need you to dig it up."

I laughed. "No, you want me to trespass on Archdiocesan property and vandalize it. Not happening."

"The church was deconsecrated, and it's for sale, so no one will even notice. Becca called earlier, insisting I wear my half of the 'best friends forever' necklace she gave me to all her events and the wedding, but it's in the time capsule, and I need it for the couple's shower tomorrow night."

I scoffed and picked my work back up. "Lily, that's a ridiculous ask. No way."

"Please, Rose, I *need* it for tomorrow night. And I'm stuck in Portland till tomorrow. My flight got canceled, and they can't get me on another one till morning."

This was definitely a Lily need, not a normal one. "Just…tell Becca the truth."

"No, no, no," she said forcefully. "She loses her shit if every wedding-related thing doesn't go exactly the way she envisions it."

"I get it. I've dealt with more bridezillas than I want to remember, but she'll have to hold onto her shit like a grown-up. Or do it when you get back. You have to call 811 before you dig. What if I hit a water main or something?" Why was I thinking through the logistics?

"Please, Rose? Can't you go do this one small thing for me? It's in the middle of the garden at the foot of the St. Dorothy statue. They wouldn't have buried it near pipes or wires, and it's already nighttime there, right? Nobody'll even see you. I *promise* I'll pay you back big time. I said I'd help you find an apartment, right?"

"Lily, no. I have enough problems without being slapped in handcuffs or with a million-dollar fine."

"Oh, I know," she went on, completely ignoring me. "I can talk to my friend who works at Chateaux Marseilles. Maybe she can—"

"That new luxury apartment building on Metairie Road? Honey, you know I left New York City because I'm broke, right? And besides, you already promised to help me find the termite-infested shack in my price range. No takesy-backsies."

"We'll find you something that's *not* termite-infested," she huffed. "I'll find some options for you next Friday."

"That's a whole week away. I need to escape the daily Mom-and-Steve show before I swear off sex forever." I reached for my purse on the other side of the wardrobe moving box stuffed with dress designs. "And my old room is too tiny to make Becca's bridal gown, eight bridesmaid dresses, and one flower girl's dress. Fuck me, it's so many." I wanted to cry every time I remembered.

"Just get me the necklace from the time capsule, and I'll pay you back. I gotta go. My Lyft's here. I'll see you tomorrow night at the shower, okay? Bye!"

"Wait—" The line went dead. "Annnd, she's gone." I started digging in my purse for my lip balm, cackling to myself about how she thought I was actually going to dig up a time capsule on someone else's property.

Spool of thread, spool of thread...matchbox from Punk Decay, the dive bar where Isaac, the guy I was seeing, played back in June—*ouch!* I sucked on my finger. Found that pin cushion I'd lost earlier. Ooh—travel-size Febreze. I sprayed a couple of spritzes into the air and twisted my body through it. Almost as good as a shower.

Lip balm applied, I went through my dress to-do list to see if there was anything I could get done until I got more stabilizer in the morning and final measurements at the couple's shower at night. I read the same sentence twice before admitting defeat.

The front door to the house opened, and Mom and Steve's gentle laughter filtered down the hall and through my closed door. I smiled, stretched my back, and snipped the excess threads from the petticoat. This house needed thicker walls, but they were so stinkin' cute together. So happy. It made me miss Isaac.

Well, I missed the *idea* of him more than the man himself. I hadn't had a serious relationship in nearly ten years. Not since—well, it was too damn late at night to think too hard about Michael the Asshole. He hardened my heart for the perilous world of dating at the tender age of nineteen, proving what Mom taught us from the day we were born: don't get attached because men don't stay.

Michael had been a Level Three relationship: the nope-not-ever-again-with-anyone place where the L word lived. Since him, I'd only had Level Two relationships or below. Level Twos—friends who fuck—were harder to come by and a lot more fun, but messier to end. Level Ones like Isaac were only about sex. And when they ended, there were no hard feelings.

I rolled my eyes toward an inevitable breakup with Isaac who was skittish about long-distance plans and had barely texted since he'd been on tour the past two months. Seeing someone or not, I was somehow always alone.

Rose Guidry, Proprietor and Designer of Sweet Roses Bridal: her love life will never interfere with your wedding day, guaranteed.

Mom's bedroom door opened, and within moments, loud moaning reverberated through the wall.

I chucked my scissors onto the sewing desk in a huff. Jesus, not again.

Ohhh, Dahlia.

For fuck's sake.

Steve, I need you to fuck me, Mom begged. His answering, guttural moan made me dry heave.

"Oh *hell* no," I muttered. I threw down the petticoat and grabbed my purse, but since there was no fucking room to move, my foot twisted in my Hello Kitty comforter. I faceplanted onto the plush mauve carpet, banging my elbow on Mom's antique dresser. The rhythmic squeaking of their bed made me a frantic squirrel, and I jumped to my feet like a prize fighter. Heart racing, I burst out of my room with my purse and phone in hand and ran to the kitchen, grabbing keys from the hook. I was out of my childhood home in under three minutes and standing beside Mom's Camry.

They weren't used to having anyone in the house, but that didn't make it okay. I'd have to unpack this bullshit with my therapist when I found a new one.

The streetlight in front of the house buzzed against the backdrop of crickets chirping. Literally every house on my street was dark. I was stuck for another hour, at least, and I wasn't even wearing a bra.

Now what? Even this late, the humid, relentless, August heat was sending rivulets of sweat down my back. One of the things I hadn't missed about New Orleans. A car whooshed down Power Blvd., the cross street at the end of the block. Somewhere, an owl *whoo whoo'ed.*

"Guess I'm digging up a time capsule," I said to no one.

I snuck into my own backyard like a thief, took the pointiest shovel from the shed, and set out for St. Dorothy's. As soon as the AC blasted the sweat from my face, I peered into the rearview mirror. Confirmed: I was a trash gremlin. When was the last time I washed my hair? My knees manned the steering wheel down the residential street while I pulled out my bun to finger brush some order into my mass of curls and corralled them back on top of my head.

Less than ten minutes later, I parked on Mimosa Street under a sprawling magnolia tree. My headlights swiped past the for sale sign posted in the churchyard, a red "sold" sign stuck diagonally across its top right corner. Lights from inside the church filtered through the stained-glass windows onto pallets of construction materials covered with tarps.

Shit. Maybe I shouldn't do this.

But...still no movement by the church or the rectory, so bad decisions were a go. Lily would owe me the biggest fucking favor I could think of. It might even be bail. No. If she has to bail me out, that *still* won't be the big favor.

I slipped out of the car, stashing Mom's keys in my shorts pocket as I quietly shut the door. I crept to the trunk where I'd stashed the shovel, and with the tool of my impending crime in hand, I stole through the bushes like a lunatic toward the statue of St. Dorothy that was, thank God, still marking the spot.

It was as hot as the hell I was going to for digging up someone else's holy property. Not like the bridal fashion world would miss me, as many rejections as my designs had gotten from my dream firms. Termites swarmed around the streetlights, and I slapped away eight mosquitos before I made it to the statue. I pulled down on the legs of my short shorts. They barely fit me anymore, but most of my other clothes were still on a moving truck somewhere between New York and New Orleans, not due for another two days.

Sweat dripping down my back, I estimated three feet out from the statue where the time capsule was buried—one foot each, Father Dorio had said, for the Father, the Son, and the Holy Spirit. Crazy, the things that stuck in your mind.

X marked the spot mercifully between two scraggly azaleas. At least I wouldn't have to dig up any plants. With any luck, no one would notice the area had been dug at all. Light from a decorative post lamp in the church yard vaguely lit the area without putting a spotlight on me, which was helpful since the only light I had was my phone.

Thrusting the edge against the weedy garden, I stepped on the shovel's shoulder to drive it in. Why did Lily drop the necklace into the time capsule in the first place, and what cosmic bullshit made it my problem?

Five shovels in, I was making woefully little progress, and my un-bra'ed boobs were a menace. I paused, peeking at the church through the trees. All still quiet on the lot, and no one had passed in the street the whole time I'd been here. Like Mom always said, the only people out at this time of night were drunks and skunks. Stone cold sober, I knew which I was.

About a foot in and two feet wide, I leaned against St. Dorothy cursing my recent lack of exercise and how easily I gave in to my sister's demands. Maybe I should've just told Becca about the necklace. Maybe she would've had a good laugh over it.

Maybe not. The deranged look in Becca's eyes when I suggested she might want a lace wedding dress—when clearly, she was a bride who needed silk chiffon—still haunted me.

"Fergalicious" blared from my phone in my back pocket. I dropped the shovel and fumbled my phone out, dropping it into the mud. Ripping off one of my gloves, I shut off the sound. My heart pounded so fast and hard I could barely read the preview. It was Heather, texting me again to try and get me to move back in with her and our friend Abby. I put a muddy hand to my chest.

My fellow Dream House Girls, so-called for the wreck of a rental we shared in college, were the sweetest friends a woman could ask for. But I couldn't accept more of their help. They sent me off in style when I left to "make it big" in New York. How could I go back admitting such defeat, especially when I'd been shit about keeping in touch?

I wiped the sweat from my face with the inside edge of my tank top and shoved my phone back in my pocket. My racing heart felt like an anxiety attack, and I didn't need another one of those right now. I deepened my breathing and started a mental list. First, the capsule, then the necklace, then shove it all back down in the ground. Find a cheap apartment; finish Becca's dresses; keep trying to get hired by an established brand, while launching a whole dress business with no idea where to start; then pay bills.

Damnit. Listing out my mess was *not* helping my anxiety.

Jason

Big Dick Tools.

I reread the email to be sure I wasn't dreaming. Big Dick Tools wanted to meet with me at their Florida headquarters to talk about a sponsorship. I laughed out loud alone to myself, hefting a full laundry basket on my hip.

I scanned down the email on my way to the couch. This could be the big break I'd been waiting for to finish my renovations, and they approached *me*. Sure, I made a point across all my social media channels to talk about how much I loved their tools, and I'd started tagging them to get their attention. But this proved that all my hard work building my goofy-ass brand had been worth it. Every splinter, every late night building bookcases or editing videos.

But my sense of accomplishment faded quickly. I had no one to tell about this. If I was still with Kasey, I'd be working that godawful bank job to support her through med school. That door was so firmly shut, it'd disappeared over the eighteen months I'd been back. I was still too chicken shit to reconnect with my friends. My siblings would tease me mercilessly, like they already did anytime my work came up. Mom already hated everything about—

Her number took over my phone's screen. God, was she psychic?

No. No way was I willfully submitting to another one of her insomnia-fueled reviews of my life, no matter how well-intentioned. I tried to go back to the email, but I bungled the hamper and my phone, accidentally answering her call.

Shit.

"Hey Ma, can't sleep?"

"You know me so well, Jason. How are you doing tonight, baby? I missed you at dinner."

"Yeah, sorry I couldn't come by. I had to baby the finish on a four-poster bed I'm building for a client. Did y'all have fun?"

"It was lovely, but I was so happy to get back home. I finally got a chance to catch up on your videos for the week."

I set the laundry basket down and rolled my neck, knowing full well where this was going from the disappointed tone of her voice, pretty much the only tone I heard anymore. "It's just marketing, Ma. That's all it is."

"But the furniture you make is beautiful enough to be the star of the show. *You* are beautiful enough. You don't have to pimp yourself out with those shirtless videos."

"Pimp myself out?" I chuckled. "How much wine did you have at dinner tonight, ma'am? I don't think I've ever heard you use that word before." Maybe my gentle teasing would bring out her more playful side.

She chuckled too, but it didn't stop her from pushing. "You know what I mean. You're never going to find yourself a respectable young woman if you don't respect yourself."

I pinched the bridge of my nose. "I respect myself just fine. Having my shirt off is part of the schtick of my account. My followers love it." Fuck it all, I was going for it. "And listen to this: I just got an email from a national line of tools. They want to talk to me about a lucrative sponsorship." I couldn't keep the pride from my voice. "They're talking about paying me to feature tools I already use on my accounts, maybe even star in some of their ads."

"Wow! Really? That's amazing!" Her impressed tone was such a relief. This was maybe the most excited she'd ever been about my social media ventures. Sure, she shared every non-shirtless post and seemed to pull people out of the woodwork to buy custom furniture from me, but she would sleep better if I had a "real job."

"What tool company?" she asked. "Craftsman? Black & Decker?"

I cringed, all pride punctured. "Big Dick Tools," I rushed out.

"Jason, you're not going to work with *those* people, are you? If your account was more respectable, maybe you could get more respectable sponsorships. Bob Vila never had to take off his shirt."

"Ma, I'm twenty-eight. If I want to post pictures of myself without a shirt on social media, I can do that." I paced, wrapping the drawstring of my shorts around my fingers.

She sighed. Heavily. "Of course, you're all grown up and don't have to listen to anything your mama says. But most respectable people don't get paid for making half-naked videos. When Rebecca saw your account, she said it was sinful how you were sharing your body with the world. She had to block it. She was too embarrassed to even look at it."

"Mom, Ms. Rebecca also says that when church music distracts you from praying, it's the devil."

"Okay, I admit that's a little much. But she said it in front of her daughter. And Misty might start thinking you're not very serious about her or the church, that you're trying to catch a bunch of other women."

I'd been thinking that I might be ready to date again, but it was unreal and unfair how my family equated my finally taking pride in my health and appearance again as me planning to sleep around as much as possible. The truth was that I hadn't been with anyone since I left Kasey, and I planned to stay celibate until I found a woman I could see myself settling down with. I was even halfway through an eight-week attempt to not take matters into my own hands, thanks to a church group I got suckered into joining. Not that I'd tell my Mom *that*.

"I don't care what Misty thinks. We're not dating. We're not even friends."

"You're not dating *yet*. You have to give her more of a chance than that one time you took her to dinner. I don't know why you never asked her back out again. She's such a beautiful, religious girl."

I breathed out heavily, trying to figure out how to explain this to my mother. Again. "I only took her out because you and Ms. Rebecca were so pushy, but the date was a disaster."

An understatement. At the end of a miserable date, Misty subjected me to twenty handsy minutes of refusing to get out of my car unless I agreed to come inside and sleep with her, even after I told her I was celibate. I finally lured her out with the lie that I'd go inside and think about it. But once her feet hit her porch, I jogged back to my car and drove away. Mom thought I was exaggerating.

"She's not the one for me." I wanted to add, *she's the one* you *want me to be with*. Or *she's the love child of artificial flowers and the cardinal sin of lust*. But I kept my mouth shut to make Mom happy. Because I still felt so goddamn guilty.

"You're just not used to classy women who like to take things slowly."

I took a deep breath, stretching my head back. My stomach churned. Discussion of my ex—my biggest mistake and reason for all my guilt—incoming.

"Please listen to your mama, for once. I told you that Kasey was bad news, and you didn't believe me. She did such a number on you. I want you to be happy, Jason, but I'm afraid you wouldn't know true love if it walked up and slapped you in the face."

A laugh choked out from my throat. "God, I hope my true love wouldn't slap me in the face. That's abuse, Ma."

Mom's chuckle made me smile. I'd missed her so much while I was gone. And knowing that she loved me no matter what, and that she only wanted the best for me, made these phone calls and her overbearing nature a little easier to take.

She was right about at least one thing. Kasey tried to cure me of my spiritual side, to iron out all the beautiful, miraculous mysteries I saw in life with her science-only way of thinking. I hadn't exactly been a good church boy when I met her, but leaving her had been like opening the door to my heart again and finding the world was bright with colors, not just black and white.

My gaze drifted up to the wood-strip cathedral ceiling of my converted-church home. Spiritually, I was a lot like it—strong foundation, good bones, but under constant renovation as I evolved. After I came to my senses and came home, there hadn't exactly been church hymns waiting here for me. But my own personal faith was. And my family was.

Unfortunately, they all still thought I wasn't capable of making my own decisions about work, my life, or my love life.

"I wouldn't want anybody to slap my beautiful boy's face. I love you, you know that, right Jason?" My mother's fearful, heartbroken tone warbled back into these conversations, and it made my chest hurt. I'd done that to her. Broken her heart, and she'd taken me back in anyway.

"I know Mama. I love you, too."

"I just want you to have a good woman who puts you first and lives a faithful life."

The last thing a woman needed to do was put her partner first, but I wasn't revisiting that old argument again. "I know you're just looking out for me." I stood up and stretched my back, yawning and looking out one of my few non-stained-glass windows. It was past midnight, and I was ready to go to sleep.

Something moved on the edge of my property. I looked closer.

"Alright, my sweet boy. I'm going to bed. Got to be up early to help your sister get ready for her couple's shower. Good night, honey. I love you."

A light switched on in front of the St. Dorothy statue and switched off immediately. But it'd been on long enough for me to catch sight of someone digging in my azaleas.

"Alright Ma. Love you too. Good night!"

I hung up and looked out the window for a minute, my phone's keypad open in case I needed to call the cops. The person paused a minute, stuck the shovel into the ground, and pulled down long hair from a bun on their head. With the street light casting a silhouette from behind, that was definitely a very shapely woman digging something up in my garden.

Phone still in hand, I grabbed a bright flashlight and went out to investigate.

Chapter 2

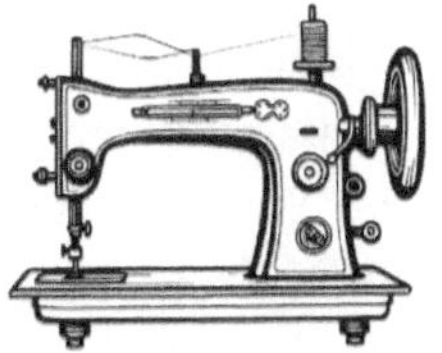

The Bucket List

Rose

How far the hell down was this time capsule? Covered in mud, bitten up by mosquitoes, completely soaked through with sweat—why? Just....why was I here? The hole before me was big, but not nearly as big as the favor Lily would owe me.

I jammed the shovel into the earth again. What should I ask her for? Photographs of my dresses for my website I still had to build? Too small an ask. I could probably talk her into doing that for free, anyway. Kick her boyfriend out of her apartment so I could live with her? As if that would happen. And why would I want to live with her constant judgment?

"I don't know what I'm looking at, but it seems pretty shady."

I whirled in a panic at the voice as a flashlight lit me up from behind. A ripped, shirtless man leaned against the statue of St. Dorothy, flashlight pointed off to the side so I could look up into his—oh no—very familiar face.

I knew this man. Or I knew that boy, a long time ago. Time must've had a crush on him. Why was he so goddamn hot? My brain and mouth were slow to catch up with the situation and even slower to attempt a response.

I tried not to let my gaze dip below his eyes. But in a spectacular fail, I clocked the mountain range across his chest, veins down his muscled arms, the stretch of delectable yumminess below his belly button that made my lady business actively clench, and athletic shorts hanging low off unreasonably toned hips. My hormones were Christina Aguilera and her "Dirrty" background dancers.

Isaac, with his sickly Victorian goth mystique, did *not* look like that naked. I sucked my tummy in and pulled down on my short shorts.

He cocked his head and narrowed his eyes. "Wait, aren't you...? Rose Guidry? Is that you?"

He took a step closer. Yep—Jason Soniat. Becca's little brother.

Fuck me, he'd grown up.

"Jason? Ohmygod hi!" I pushed a curl out of my face, no doubt smudging even more dirt onto it. Unbearable heat from inside and out made my face as hot as a crawfish in a boiling pot and probably twice as red. I crossed my arm across my braless boobs. "What're you...did Lily...are you here for the necklace too?"

But no, it didn't make any sense that Lily would've called Jason to help me. And by the confused, pissed look on his face, that was not why he was out here.

He shook his head, brows furrowed. "What necklace?" His gaze followed the flashlight's bright spot into the hole and over the piles of dirt around it. "Why are you digging a hole in my garden?"

His irritated tone tightened my chest and sent my heart racing like I'd been called into the hot principal's office. New kink unlocked. We stared at each other, and I gripped my shovel with white knuckles. "*Your* garden?"

"Yeah. This is my property." He gestured at the mess I'd made with a deeper frown. "What are you doing out here?"

"I'm so sorry, oh my God I'm so embarrassed I didn't know this was your—Lily asked me to come and dig up the time capsule we buried in summer camp because she put the other half of her best friends forever necklace Becca gave her in it." *Big breath.* "Because Lily's in Oregon until tomorrow and if she doesn't have it at the shower tomorrow night, Becca's gonna *kill* her..."

My voice petered out as he pursed his lips and scratched the back of his head. Surveyed my vandalism in total silence.

I swallowed hard. I would die right here in the mud of hot face, tachycardia, and wretched cringe, and Lily would owe a debt to my ghost. A fancy casket. Maybe a marble tombstone with an awkward statue of a weeping angel putting her foot in her mouth so everyone would remember me accurately.

"A time capsule? Um..." He turned and looked back toward the church, then back to me. He sighed, and his frown smoothed out into straight-lipped resignation. "Hang on. I'll grab a shovel and help you."

"Oh no, no, no. I wouldn't dream of asking you to help me."

"You didn't." He wedged his flashlight onto the statue of St. Dorothy between her basket of roses and flowing robes. "I'll be right back." He walked off toward the old rectory.

Goddamn that ass. Fuck. Me.

I resumed digging, whisper-cussing myself out. "What the fuck? Why are you such a horny dumbass?"

My crush on Jason started in science class on the first day of sixth grade. And the last time I saw him—oh God, prom. He took me to my senior prom. Nobody else had asked me, and I was so desperate to go that I let Lily ask Becca if one of her brothers would take me. Even though they went to a different high school, and I hadn't seen them in years.

I'd asked for Jason.

And bless him, he went with me, even though he had a girlfriend at the time. But he must've been so miserable all night—I was so shy and quiet back then. Becca must've owed him a favor as big as the one Lily owed me now.

Jason came back with a shovel and a bigger work light on an extension cord. Ohmygod he'd actually been serious about helping me dig up his yard.

He handed me a cold bottle of water, and the condensation dripped down my arm to my elbow, splashed on my flushed chest. "You must be dying out here."

The cold water bottle and the visible sweat on his muscles made my nipples pebble and my throat extra dry. "Thank you." His skin looked smoother and more luxurious than mulberry silk. I bet he exfoliated.

"I didn't know there was a time capsule here." He dropped his phone in his pocket, and it dragged his shorts even lower on his hips. Holy smokes.

I downed half the bottle before answering him. "There used to be a plaque for it." I set my bottle on the statue's base and walked around to the opposite side of the hole for a new spot to dig.

Then I tripped over my own feet and slammed into him with a yelp, grabbing his shoulders with my dirty gloves.

He threw his hands up at the last second, and one landed squarely on my boob.

"Oh God!" He immediately moved his hand to my waist with an "I'm so sorry are you okay?" as he helped me steady myself.

But he wasn't fast enough to stop the cascade of hormones whizzing straight to my vagina.

"Yeah. That's the most action I've gotten in two months," I said. Painful heat shot up my face as he stared at me for a full second.

He cleared his throat and coughed. "Me too," he admitted, his face reddening.

Now all I could think about was his hand on my boob. I couldn't meet his eyes. "Yeah," I said in a small voice. "The plaque is...well it doesn't seem to be here. Anymore."

He set his big muscles to work, digging twice as much and fast as me. Neither of us spoke as we dug. I wanted to be digging my own grave. What could I say to him after that? I couldn't very well ask him when he got so freaking hot. And for the love of chiffon, I wouldn't mention the eighth grade spin-the-bottle debacle.

"Did you really buy St. Dorothy's?"

"Yeah. I couldn't pass it up. Repurposing old buildings was my main interest when I went to school for architecture." He paused to wipe sweat from his brow. Eyed his shoulders and brushed off the dirt I'd put there. "I always wanted to live in a converted church."

"Why's that?"

"I love the bones of it." He gestured toward the old church. "The steeple, that amazing bell tower. Churches are built to last, and you just can't replicate the original stonework, the stained-glass windows, the vaulted ceilings. Plus, all the utilities are there." He leaned closer to me on the handle of the shovel as if to get me to share his vision.

I froze like a deer in headlights, my next big breath taking in the lusty, masculine scent of soap heating off his toned body. I bet he tasted as good as an orgasm felt.

"I'm so sorry. You're gonna need another shower." I curled into myself. I shouldn't be allowed to talk to people.

He glanced at me kinda sideways. "No worries. I love the creative challenge of putting everything into place in a new way. Not to mention save a community building from being demolished to build another soulless neighborhood of duplexes with no trees."

His excitement was infectious. Or maybe that was his pheromones? Regardless, I'd always loved this church. As a child, I sat in the pews on Sundays looking up at the rafters and spent so many days after school running through the brick arches in the back. I was glad it was in such sexy, rough-looking hands. I mean, such good hands.

Cheese and crackers, Rose, remember Isaac? I was with Isaac.

But...window shopping was okay, right?

Jason turned to me as if remembering himself. He smiled sheepishly and went back for another shovelful. A mosquito landed on his large, smooth shoulder, and I swatted it off. He looked at his shoulder and back up at me.

"Mosquito," I squeaked.

"Thanks. Hey, are you sure we're digging in the right place?" He dove the shovel in again, and it pinged against something hard. He looked up at me, dark eyes sparkling. "I think we found it!"

He dug around the edges of a stainless-steel cylinder, hefting it out of the dirt. "This is almost exciting, like a treasure hunt."

"God, I'm glad you think so."

He chuckled and pulled the cylinder from the mud, knocking the worst of the mud off. "Your time capsule, m'lady. Let's bring it to the porch so we don't lose anything in the dark."

"Bless you. You're my knight in shining..." He wasn't wearing a shirt. "Flesh." I winced. Too weird, Rose, too weird.

He set the time capsule down onto a piece of plywood stretched across sawhorses and pulled off his gloves. Even more handsome in the incandescent light of the porch, his eyes were the big brown I remembered, the kind of warm eyes I wanted to curl up in. His dark, thick hair was curly and out of control in the best possible way, loose around his ears.

"Hmmm. Looks like I'll need a wrench—hang on, I'll be back."

He went inside the church, and I took off my mom's gardening gloves and sat them on the workstation, studying the time capsule. Eight bolts on either end. This was gonna take a minute, and here I was with still no makeup on, in a tiny tank top—with no bra—and shorts that barely fit anymore. And he was going to have to see me in the light. I pulled my hair down and back up again, adjusted my clothes. Lily was going to owe me the freaking world.

Jason

I walked back onto my porch with my favorite toolbox. The pretty yard vandal smiled at me and went back to studying the time capsule. When did I last see Rose? It had to be her prom. She'd worn the tightest black dress and barely spoke a word except thanking me profusely the whole night for taking her.

Wrench acquired, I set to work on the time capsule's bolts and threw a quick up-and-down glance at her. Her thick, dark hair was a messy bun on top of her head, and frizzy, corkscrew curls poked out wildly at the nape of her neck. Mud smudged her pretty pink cheeks and the colorful tattoo of roses on her upper arm. That was new. She fidgeted with a pink crystal necklace that kept falling into her cleavage, which was generous and also mud streaked. Jeez, how did I accidentally grab her boob?

I tried to avert my eyes from her chest, but she kept pulling up on that tiny tank top and drawing my attention to how her nipples stood proud of the fabric. My shorts were suddenly tight.

Kind of like my pants on prom night.

My body was only on edge because I hadn't been this close to a beautiful woman with that little clothes on in a long time. I flexed my thigh muscle really hard and held it, trying to make the blood flow somewhere else. It was a trick I learned off the internet a couple of weeks ago, and it didn't work too bad. But even abstaining from self-pleasure was harder than it had been a few minutes ago.

Pun intended.

I flashed her a smile. "Did you wear all black just to sneak around in my yard and dig this up?"

"Yeah, I went full stealth mode for my wild Friday night," she laughed. She casually brushed dirt off her chest and pulled the ripped hems of her short shorts down, as if wishing they were longer. I sure as hell didn't.

"Also, most of my clothes are still in transit from New York."

I glanced at her again just as a mosquito landed on the pale, soft swell of her breast. I reached out on instinct but froze before I touched her. "You have a mosquito on your..." I pointed.

"Oh!" she exclaimed, slapping at it. "They're eating me alive."

"You must be delicious." My cheeks heated even more than the August night called for. Why did I say that? I was thinking it, but why say it out loud? I bit my lip and started on the sixth bolt.

She laughed nervously. "I guess so."

What did I know about her these days, besides that she was making my sister's wedding dress and standing in the wedding? "New York. Fashion internship, right? Becca mentioned you were moving back home."

"Yeah, that's right."

I nodded, starting on the last bolt. Another memory of her popped into my head, from my eighth-grade end-of year party. Pretty Rose, sitting wide-eyed across from me in a circle of classmates, where the bottle I'd spun pointed unmistakably at her. Crawling toward each other at the center with friends whooping all around us, her long curls hanging down, lips parted, eyes determined.

I dropped my wrench to the workbench, the cylinder unbolted.

"Thank you so much," she murmured. I carefully emptied the contents of the capsule on the plywood as she rifled through it. A few stuffed animals, a bracelet, lots of folded up pieces of loose leaf, a rolled-up newspaper...

"There!" She grabbed a pink enamel and gold half-a-heart necklace. "It's a little dirty, but I bet my mom has jewelry cleaner."

I dropped a few items back into the capsule, but a Polaroid of a dozen campers caught my eye. There in the center was middle school Rose. "Oh wow, look at you!" Just as I remembered her—wide-eyed with her long curls everywhere.

She leaned in toward me, the heat magnifying her rosy scent. I smirked. Of course Rose would smell like roses.

She grabbed the photo from me, groaning. "Oh wow, look at those bangs. Let's put that back in the time capsule, shall we?"

I shifted through the papers. What did people think was important enough to put in? "A poem for the future, a prayer, and oh, what do we have here?" An index card with Rose's name on it. I'd hit gold. "'Rose Guidry's Bucket List'?"

"Oh my Lord, let me see." Her hand snaked out for the card, but this was too good to hand over without reading it first.

I held it up over my head, laughing. "No, I wanna read it."

"Give it!" She swiped for it but was too short to grab it.

I started to read it.

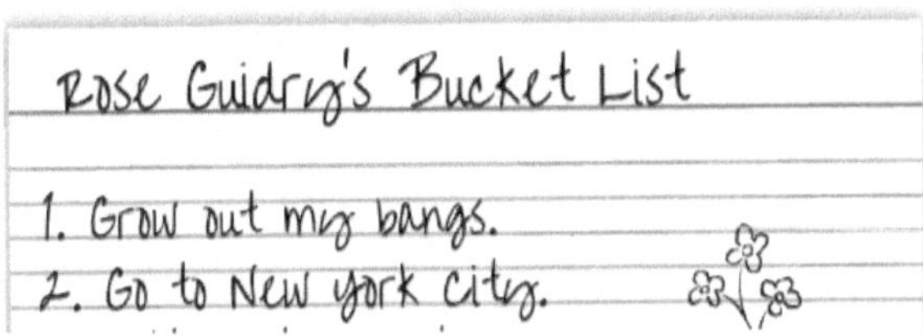

"It's mine, Jason. Give it!" She jumped for it, chest-bumping me and knocking a sharp pain into my chin with her head.

"Ow!" She ducked her head with her hand over it. "I'm going to die the minute *after* I kill my sister," she growled.

What was I, a little kid with a crush? "I'm sorry. I'm such an ass. Are you okay?"

With a triumphant cackle she made a sneak attack for the card, but I whipped it above my head again. "Ahh, you almost got me! Waltz with a cute guy, go to Paris...how many of these have you done already?"

"I don't know," she shot back, "because you won't let me see it!"

I peered into her narrowed, angry eyes. "Okay, I'll let you see it if you don't take it and run. Deal?"

My heart stumbled as she glared back at me, her full, rosy lips turned up at one end. Her dark blue eyes were almost purple in the porchlight. Stunning. She'd always been cute, but now she was fucking gorgeous.

"I did help you dig up my property in the middle of the night."

"Girl. It's not even one." For a moment, she only stared back. "Fine. Okay. Deal."

A corner of my mouth quirked up. Did she call me *girl*? "And I'm gonna hold it while you read it so you can't run off with it."

She shrugged. "Whatever. Can I see it now? What mortifying things did twelve-year-old me write?"

I brought the list down to her level and leaned in with it.

She slipped her hand around my forearm and gripped it, probably so I didn't take the list away again. Thank God it was dark out here, or she'd see exactly what that simple touch was doing to me.

"Okay, I grew out my bangs." She ran a finger with chipped purple nail polish down the list, as if trying to find all the worst ones before I could. "I've lived in New York City."

> Rose Guidry's Bucket List
>
> 1. Grow out my bangs.
> 2. Go to New york city.
> 3. waltz with a cute guy.
> 4. Go to Paris.
> 5. Make J.S. fall in love with me.

But I found it first. "Number five: 'Make J.S. fall in love with me.' Who's 'J.S.'?" My heart rate went up with my eyebrows as I met her wide eyes.

Her face, already bright pink from the heat, turned a vibrant shade of red as she removed her hand. Her breath hitched.

It was totally me.

I couldn't stop my slow smile. Didn't somebody tell me she had a crush on me when we were in school together? This and her deer-in-headlights stare just might be confirmation.

That was kinda...cool. I felt my smile spread wider.

"It wasn't you," she blurted. "That was, oh, what was his name?" She scrunched her eyes shut and pressed her fingertips to her brow.

"Jonathan Santos. Yeah. Huge crush on him in middle school." She crossed her arms and fixed her eyes on me.

"Oh yeah, Jonathan Santos." Sure it was. "The first openly gay boy in our class."

She shrugged, her stare daring me to challenge her. "The heart wants what it wants."

The church's clock chimed one o'clock. She broke her gaze and started shoveling everything back inside the capsule. "I've kept you up long enough. Thank you so much, really. Is it okay if I come back tomorrow to bury it again?"

"Nah, don't worry about it. I'll seal it up and bury it for you."

"Are you sure? I've already put you out enough."

"Yeah. I don't mind." I stuck her bucket list back into the capsule and experimentally laid the silicone seal back over the mouth of the cylinder. "I probably ought to clean this first and let it dry so it seals back right."

Kasey had sanded me down a little each day so I wouldn't snag under her thumb, but the last few minutes with Rose had me feeling like a fresh-hewn cut of wood, full of splinters and promise. And I didn't want it to end.

"Do you want to come in and cool off before you go?" I asked. "Let me get you some more water."

"No," she said forcefully. "Absolutely not."

She didn't have to turn me down with such vehemence, but okay. I crossed my arms and nodded as if I agreed that was best.

She downed the rest of her water and tossed it into a nearby trash can, then edged toward the steps looking positively miserable. "You already took me to my prom because your sister made you, *and* you helped me dig up your yard. I've imposed on you enough for one lifetime."

I laughed. "My girlfriend at the time was pretty mad when she found out."

She covered half her face with her hand. "I'm so sorry."

"No worries. She was kind of mean anyway."

"Oh good! I mean, not good. But. Yeah. Um. I have some third quarter moon manifestations to do anyway. Goodnight. Thank you again!"

Ooh, that's right. She was a "godless Guidry girl," as Mom called her and her sister. Even if she hadn't shot me down so hard it stung, Mom would never approve of me dating her.

She took three steps off my porch.

"Rose! Your gloves!"

She turned around and met me at the edge of the porch, took them without meeting my eyes, and then headed straight across the yard toward her car.

I leaned against a porch column, trying not to notice the sway of her ass in those short shorts. "Shovel!" I shouted.

She pointed her index finger up in the air, sharply changing her trajectory to pass by the statue.

"See you tomorrow night, Rose."

She waved without looking back, got into her car, and was gone.

Chapter 3

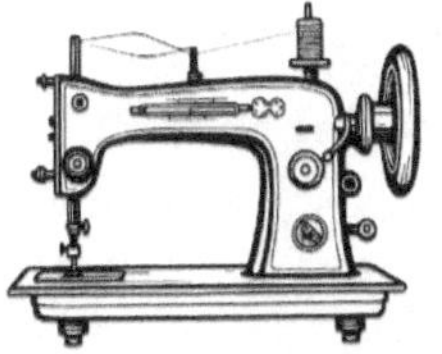

Salty Virgins' Club

Rose

"So you understand now why you owe me your first born?" I clasped that damn BFF necklace around Lily's neck while she cackled at my story. She was late as usual, and I'd been standing around the outside of the venue like a creeper. I smoothed the netting on my dress's skirt down, one of my own design.

"I'm so sorry, baby. I had no idea Jason bought the church. Here. Hold this."

Not even a thank you as she passed me two heavy bags with her photography equipment. "Why was the stupid thing in the capsule in the first place?"

Lily laughed harder as she shut her trunk. "She told Finn LeBlanc I liked him, and I was pissed. I put it in with this snotty letter telling future Becca how I bet she regrets her actions. Oh—did you bring the letter too? I'd love to read it."

"No! I was too busy trying not to get arrested for trespassing and vandalizing. Is that a T and V? Or maybe it's a T and D—trespassing and digging."

"Pssh Jason wouldn't have done that. He's so sweet! And you're standing in his sister's wedding." Her pale green eyes got big. "Did you swear him to secrecy about the necklace?"

I exhaled a sharp, audible scoff from the back of my throat. "Yes, while I was in the middle of my T and V I remembered to beg him for secrecy. No, I didn't think about it."

"But that's such a great story, oh my God. I wish I could tell Becca. She'd think it's so funny." She lifted a tripod from the sidewalk, and we walked in together. "We always wanted you to marry one of her brothers so she could be our sister."

That forced a short laugh from my chest. "Where were y'all on that when I had a crush on him in middle school?" But also, no way would that've worked. He was a popular jock, and I was a shy nerd. I spoke maybe five words to him the whole time his locker was under mine, eighth grade year. We barely made conversation at prom. Thank God I could avoid him for most of tonight while I checked final measurements on bridesmaids.

Our heels clicked on the polished marble floor on our way into the cozy ballroom Becca's mom rented for the night.

"Well, you're both all grown up now." Lily nodded toward where Jason stood using a selfie stick to take photos of himself with an elderly couple.

Okay, *damn*, he looked fine in that suit—impeccable fit—and it was pretty dang adorable how he was pressing a kiss to the top of the older woman's head.

"Maybe now's your chance," Lily said softly. "He's pretty cute, right?"

"I'm seeing someone. Besides. I'm not interested in anybody who uses a selfie stick, thank you very much."

"Don't be so quick to judge. Selfie sticks are just a tool."

"You're just a tool," I muttered under my breath as Lily squealed at Becca's approach and I set one of her photography bags onto an empty table.

"Guidry girls!" Becca danced up and hugged Lily, then me. "Rose, your dress is gorgeous. Did you make it?"

"Thank you, I did." I put the second bag down, and when I turned back around, Becca's fiancé, Brad, and Becca's mom were greeting Lily. I liked to pretend Becca was my friend too, but I barely knew these people. I was only in the wedding because she had to replace a bridesmaid who would be too pregnant to fly to New Orleans next month.

Brad hugged me. "Great to finally meet you in person!"

"Mom," Becca said, "you remember Lily's little sister Rose, right?"

"Yes, of course. The dressmaker." Becca and Jason's mom adjusted her glasses higher up her nose to assess me. Her dark eyes, the same shape and color as Jason's, glanced at the tattoo on my bare arm, my crystal pendant. Her smile faltered and became *Polite*, but she still came in for a slight hug. "Thank you for stepping in. Becca couldn't bear for someone in the bridal party to walk unpaired down the aisle."

"Hi Mrs. Betty." Great. Let me add another mom who didn't like me to my collection. Why were so many of them like this? I was a delightful mess.

"How long have you been making dresses, Rose?"

Translation: *Are you sure you're good enough to make my Becca's wedding dress?*

"Oh gosh, I've been sewing and sketching dresses since I was able to hold a needle and pencil. And I just finished up an internship at Lovelace Bridal in New York City." *Boom*. Big name-drop.

Her eyebrows went up in grudging respect. "Well, if the dress itself is anything like the sketches Becca showed me, it will be just beautiful. I was just asking Becca the other day..."

Jason's presence moved into the edges of the group like warm sunshine, greeting Lily with his brother, Alex. I tried to catch pieces of what he said while answering Mrs. Betty's questions about sourcing fine fabrics.

"Hey, Rose." Jason came around Lily, smiling, our shared time capsule secret dancing in his big brown eyes. "It's been such a long time!" His dimples deepened as he came in for a hug.

His arms came low, so mine went high around his neck, my breasts pressing against all those muscles. My cheek brushed his beard as I murmured into his ear, "Thank you again and please don't tell Becca." He *winked* at me as he left the hug, and heat shot up my face. Curse my pink skin. I had to be red as a lobster. Again. And now I'd smell like his panty-dropping cologne all night.

"Hey Rose." Alex gave me a half-hearted, bored sort of hug. Closer to my height, the youngest Soniat was the one I knew the least about, save for their parents. And I think there was an older brother off somewhere else?

"Rose, how do you like being back home?" Becca asked.

"Girl, I'm not gonna lie. It's been rough. I'm three days into apartment hunting, and I can't find anything in my price range. So, I'm stuck living with my mom and her boyfriend. And let me tell you, the walls in that little house are so thin—"

Mrs. Betty literally clutched her pearls as Lily laughed and Jason snorted. I bit my lip. I had to stop being so blunt when so many people were squeamish about sex.

"Oh, Steve, um, Steve snores like a freight train. Yeah. So, I'm desperate for a new place. I'd live in my car, if I had one." I laughed awkwardly. Way to sell yourself to the crowd, Rose.

Becca turned to Jason. "Wait, this is perfect timing! Aren't you ready to rent your apartment at the church?"

Nooo. No no no. My pulse was a tiny tribe of cannibals pounding on my ear drums, and I was on the menu. Jason nodded, smiling but not meeting my eyes. Yeah, he clearly wanted nothing to do with that.

"Oh, that's okay," I blurted, to save him. "I'm sure I'll find something soon. I have headphones to drown out my—Steve's snoring." My face had to be a darker pink than my dress, and Jason's eyes were sparkling with held-back laughter.

Did I have to add Becca to my shit list?

Jason

At Becca's suggestion, Rose's already-red face had gone wide-eyed and still, *still*, she wasn't fooling me that Steve's "snoring" was anything but code for loud sex. I could listen to her put her feet in her mouth all night.

"It's just the old rectory." I was damn proud of that "just the old rectory," but I was downplaying it now, both to bail Rose out from something she obviously wasn't interested in and to head Mom's disapproval off at the pass. "And I'm not exactly ready to rent. We'd have to share the bathroom and the kitchen until I get those built in the church, so..."

Mom bristled beside me. Her next phone call was already playing in my head: *you can't let that Guidry girl move into the rectory and share your bathroom. Lightning might strike her when she walks into the church! And what will Misty think?*

Although, a seamstress would be a quiet neighbor, and at least I knew she wasn't a serial killer or anything. "If you're interested, you should come by tomorrow to see it."

Rose's eyebrows went way up. "So, we'd be, like...roommates?"

"Don't worry about all that tonight, dear." Mom put her arm around Rose's shoulder and started walking, physically removing her from the conversation. "What I want to know is, what did Becca pick for the flower girl's dress? She still hasn't shown me..."

Mom's voice faded as Rose's big eyes glanced back at her sister, who walked along with them and Becca.

Alex chuckled beside me. "Mom's gonna give you so much frickin' grief if you let a woman move in with you, especially one as hot as Rose, especially one of those 'godless Guidry girls.'"

I shook my head, but my eyes followed Rose across the room. She pulled her iPad out of her bag and fumbled it, nearly dropping it. Adorable. "She says that shit around you too? I thought it was just me."

"Mark my words. If Mom comes over one day and finds some pagan altar in your house, she'll freak the hell out."

I heard Alex, I really did, but I couldn't take my eyes off Rose. She'd been beautiful, all sweaty and mud-streaked last night, but tonight she was luminous in that petal-pink dress, long dark curls falling around her creamy shoulders and arms. That sexy tattoo of roses rambling down from her shoulder.

Annnnd now Mom was introducing her to Misty. Fantastic.

"Your girlfriend'll have a problem with it too." Alex grinned at me behind his drink.

"Stop. You know Misty's not my girlfriend."

Misty said something to Rose, and they looked directly at me. Both caught me watching them, then Misty touched Rose's arm, recapturing her attention.

Alex snorted. "I think you need to have that conversation with *her* then, because she looks like she's claiming her territory, bro."

It was hard not to compare the two women since they were standing side-by-side. Misty was all thorns, all sharp angles in her personality and body. Like a drama-seeking beauty queen, she wouldn't be caught dead in anything less than full stage makeup and hair-sprayed perfection, and she thought the world owed her whatever she wanted. And what she wanted was to cultivate her devout religious persona while banging anything that breathed in the shadows. She was loud and pretty, and she turned a lot of heads.

But never mine.

Rose, like her namesake, was effortlessly beautiful and velvety. That strapless dress was all feminine beauty, showing off her ample cleavage and voluptuous curves like petals. Her skin was a temple treasure, and I'd devotedly perform whatever sacred rites would grant me the honor of touching her. Fuck, how would it feel to draw a finger, or my tongue across the length of her collar bone?

But firmly, no. Alex was right, and that almost never happened. Rose was like cheese fries at Lee's Hamburgers—amazing in every way, but something I should stay away from.

"But damn, Rose grew up fine as hell, huh? She was so awkward in middle school, remember?"

Alex wasn't helping.

"Shy at her prom, too." Seeing her last night unlocked more memories. When Becca asked me to go to Rose's prom all those years ago, she said she'd offered Rose a choice between me and Alex. I'd been flattered until prom night. She barely talked to me, barely wanted to dance. She either didn't want me there after all, or she was really shy. But she was kind enough to pretend not to notice when I got a boner the one time she agreed to dance with me.

Alex clapped a hand on my shoulder. "On second thought, now that Mom's got Mark married off and Becca *almost* married off, she's been pushing pretty hard at me and Bess to get married. So, you should definitely let Rose move in. That'll put the Eye of Sauron on you instead, and with all that"—his eyes tracked Rose down and back up—"temptation around. Who knows, you might even end your dry spell."

"Yeah. I don't know." Getting involved with anyone casually was too risky for my bruised heart. But also, the next woman I date should probably come Mom-approved if I wanted any peace at all.

Misty's laugh rose above the soft music and din of conversation, and Alex tossed his head toward her.

"How's Misty's salty virgins' club going?"

I rolled my eyes. "It's called the Single Adults Living Truth group—SALT. And yeah, it sucks. It's not at all what I signed up for."

"I still can't believe she took over your group. Girl's obsessed with you."

Alex may not have been wrong on that one, either. In a classic example of no good deed going unpunished, I'd excitedly joined a church group that volunteered to help around the houses of elderly parishioners with small repairs and accessibility renos. But Misty learned that the other members of my group were all single and talked everyone into combining our group with hers. The days we worked on houses were fulfilling, but the nights we met to plan were a nightmare.

I still think she did it to get access to me and so I couldn't block her phone number without missing the info I needed for volunteering. But I had her in my contacts as "DO NOT ANSWER," and that'd already saved me a few times.

"Mom's thrilled about me being in a church singles' group," I said. "She thinks I'll find a good, churchgoing wife there."

Alex laughed mid-sip, coughing on his drink. "Bro, you can't let Mom keep you under her thumb like that. You have to—"

"I know," I said, drowning him out. If there was one phrase I never wanted to hear again in my life, it was "under her thumb." Kasey's favorite thing to say to me about Mom still made my shoulders tense and my gut twist.

"I don't get it. Why don't you want to go out with Misty? She's hot, down to fuck, and Mom would award you son of the year if you married her best friend's daughter."

Dad walked up, saving me from answering Alex. "Hey Jason, I didn't see you come in." He hugged me then leaned back, adjusting his glasses as he peered at me. "You wouldn't believe who I ran into yesterday when I was inspecting a house out in New Orleans East. Jack Kumar."

My heart sank. "Oh yeah?"

"Yeah! He's doing well. Busier than he can manage." Dad folded his arms, nodding and leaning into his story. "I told him you were still looking for a good architecture firm to put down roots in. I told him about your church reno, and he said they could use your experience on an adaptive reuse project they have coming up—converting some office building downtown into a couples' resort. So, I gave him your number, and he's going to call you sometime next week."

This again. "I appreciate it, Dad, but I'm not looking to work anywhere. I like what I'm doing, and I don't have time to take on anything else."

"I know you're doing well, but a full-time job would give you security. Benefits. A retirement plan." He clapped a hand on my shoulder. "Do me a favor and go meet with the guy. See what he has to say. It can't hurt to get more information."

"But can he work there shirtless?" Alex ran a hand through his short, dark hair, laughter gearing up in his voice. "At least shirtless Fridays, and he wants to be in the firm's man candy calendar. They can call it 'Kumar's Kuties' with a K, and all proceeds will go to rehabilitating the wild Jason back into a professional workplace."

I rolled my eyes and held my tongue. Calling him out on making fun of my work would only make my little brother double down and get dirtier. Alex guffawed at his own joke, and Dad shook his head.

"I love you, son." Dad put his arm around Alex. "But you're a mess."

"Hello, gentlemen." Becca came up to us with her keys out. "I forgot my planner in my car. Would one of my favorite brothers go get it for me?"

"Mark will, but it'll take him a while to catch a plane from Chicago," Alex joked.

"On it." I grabbed Becca's keys, eager to walk outside and escape my family for a few minutes.

Okay, longer than a few minutes, as guest after guest arrived and went in, including Rose and Lily's mom, Ms. Dahlia. Becca didn't mention her planner was in the back cargo space under a pile of wedding magazines.

Planner acquired, I was three steps back into the hall's foyer when a woman's soft, stunned voice met my ears from around the corner.

"Are you serious?" Rose's sweet voice was unmistakable, and her hushed, shocked tone made me stop short.

Her mom's excited *Yes!* was drowned out by Lily's laughing and squealing. "Mom! Oh my God! When did he propose? Your ring is gorgeous!"

Oh. I should step back outside. The door was quiet, so I could probably get away with—

"Last night! We went to…"

Ms. Dahlia spoke more quietly, and I couldn't catch the words. I turned around to leave.

"But you said you'd never get married again, after Dad." Rose pressed. "The three of us are Team Marriage Is a Sham. Fuck the patriarchy! Remember? But now you've just…changed your mind?"

I paused, my heart kinda sinking at Rose's vehement words despite none of that being my business. But it was an odd take for a woman who designs wedding dresses for a living.

"Well, honey, no. I grew, I guess. And changed. And Steve's nothing like your father." She laughed derisively. "Believe me. We love each other very much, and we're excited to make this commitment. There's nothing like having your partner in your corner, and being married means a lot to us."

"Rose," Lily sputtered. "You're not the one getting married. Just be happy for her!"

Rose's murmured, *I am*, didn't convince me one bit.

"I was going to tell you tomorrow, but I couldn't wait. And Rose, it would mean the world to me if you'd make my dress. And yours and Lily's. And my friend's daughter, Emma, will be the flower girl."

"Of course, Mama."

I smiled. That one was genuine. And sweet.

"Did you set a date?" Lily asked.

"So, about that. It's important to Steve that his brother, Matt, stands as his best man—you know he doesn't have much family. But Matt's flying out to the Gobi Desert in November to start filming his latest wildlife documentary—tracking the migrations of some kind of camel that's on the brink of extinction because of climate change. He'll be there for over a year, and we don't want to wait. So...we're getting married in October."

"*This* October?" Rose's low lament contrasted with Lily's squealing.

"I'm so excited! We'll help you with everything," Lily said. "You won't have to worry about a thing." A phone rang, and she paused for a second. "Becca's looking for me. Let's do breakfast tomorrow morning, and we can start planning everything."

"Perfect!" Ms. Dahlia replied. "Oh wait. Rose, aren't you apartment hunting in the morning?"

"Um...yeah, but I'll just do it after."

"Great!" Lily said. "I'll be at your house at nine..." Their voices faded with their footsteps.

Rose wasn't marriage material, and that officially closed that door. I felt bad for her, though. I didn't know anything about making dresses, but that sounded like somebody asking me to add four more custom library walls to the ten I already had to make. Within the next six weeks. Maybe I should offer her that apartment. She needed a win, and maybe a friend.

I built up momentum like I'd been walking for a minute and turned the corner. Rose was leaning up against the wall, arms crossed, staring at the floor. She looked up and turned her head away from me, wiping her face.

"Hey. Everything okay?" I asked when I got even with her.

She nodded, unspooling a soft tape measure from a concealed pocket of her dress. "Oh yeah, I'm good! I'm so good I'm finger-lickin' good." She shut her eyes for a moment as if screaming internally, then smiled brighter. "I'm gonna go measure some women."

"Do—" But she strode quickly ahead, not hearing me or not wanting to. Okay. Maybe her disinterest in the apartment was about me. I should keep my mouth shut.

She stopped short and whirled around, making me almost run into her. "Do you really have an apartment to rent?"

I gulped, unable to crawfish under that soft gaze. Her eyes were still bright with tears. "Yeah. Let me give you my number. I'll be home all day tomorrow if you want to come see it."

A few minutes later, we'd exchanged numbers and Rose was leading a bridesmaid toward the women's restroom. At least I'd offered, and maybe she wouldn't want it.

Becca appeared beside me. "Thanks, Jason." She took her planner but looked down at her phone. "Have you been watching that tropical storm in the Caribbean?"

"Yeah," I said, still distracted. "They're saying it's probably heading to Texas." And a good thing too, since I was going to try to get to Florida in the next couple of weeks to talk to the Big Dick Tools people.

"Poor Texas. But I selfishly hope we're in the clear on this one." She snapped her phone off. "I'm sick of evacuating every other week, being gone overnight for no reason, then coming back to all the housework we left behind. Ooh look, here comes the food!" She danced off toward Brad and his parents.

I smiled. Now they were a great match, and as the frosting on top, his family and ours were close *and* went to the same church. That's what I wanted: a great match for me who was also a great match for my family. I'd have to keep looking.

I rubbed at the empty ache in my chest and scanned the room. Straight ahead, Misty was watching me. I half-smiled and made a sharp left toward the buffet table.

'Cause Misty was *not* it.

Chapter 4

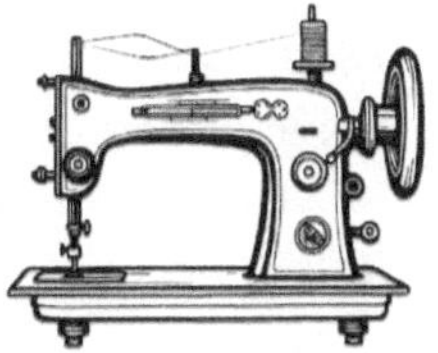

Sweat & Sawdust

Rose

In a shocking turn of events, it was nearly ten, and Lily still wasn't here. I should've known better than to make plans to see Jason's apartment at eleven, since Lily Time was at all times at least an hour behind everyone else's.

But at least it gave me time to talk dress designs with Mom. After the bombshell she dropped on us last night, immersing myself in the familiar discussions—Chantilly lace versus romantic eyelet lace and sweetheart versus V-necklines—was ironically a welcome distraction. Yawning over my coffee, I scribbled notes about Mom's preferences of silhouette and veil.

Her hand landed on my wrist, stopping my writing. "Are you sure you have time to make my dresses? I know you're nearly done with Becca's, but October's so close."

Why did I lie to her about my progress? I smiled reassuringly and put my hand on hers. "Mom, I will *not* let you get married wearing someone else's dress. It's fine. I got it." I took my hand away, but she didn't budge.

"Are you...okay with this?"

Hell, no. "Yeah, I can get it all done."

"Rosie, that's not what I meant. Are you okay with me getting remarried? You didn't seem as excited as your sister last night."

Lie, lie, and lie. "No, I'm fine! I want you to both be happy. It just surprised me, is all. I didn't know y'all were even talking about it." And lie some more to make it look like I wasn't anti-marriage. "It's about time he put a ring on it."

Mom laughed, and Lily walked through the door. And for the first time, her late arrival was a win for me.

"Good morning! I brought buttermilk drops from Tastee Donuts."

"Hell yeah," I murmured, pulling one of the crackle-icinged, spherical donuts from its box. "I forgive you for being late. You know these are my favorite," I said around a mouthful.

"I know!" she sang. She grabbed a mug and sat at the table with us. "Sorry I'm so late." She launched into a story about her boyfriend and her dog, but I caught sight of the clock and stopped listening.

"It's okay. I just told Jason I'd be there to look at his apartment this morning, so I need to leave in like thirty minutes."

"Oh good! I'm glad you're going to look at it! Okay." Lily pulled out a fat notebook and opened up to a page full of notes. "Let's get down to business. What day are you looking at in October? And where do you want to have the ceremony?"

"Hotel Maison De Ville had a spot on the twentieth, so we grabbed it yesterday."

My mouth dropped. "Girl, you move fast!" That was exactly two months away. Between Becca and Mom, that made two wedding dresses, two flower girl dresses, and ten bridesmaid dresses. And only three-and-a-half of Becca's bridesmaid dresses were close to being done. But I had no car and just enough money for a few months' rent and food. And at some point, I'd have to start building my business, even though I had no idea where to start. Either that or find a real job.

I hugged myself, rubbing my shoulder tattoo. At least Jason might be solving my living situation. He was such a nice guy. Last night, after we'd been paired to walk together down the aisle, he'd even talked his mom out of making me cover up my tattoo for the wedding. I wouldn't have minded, but she didn't exactly ask nicely and everyone was staring.

And if I rented his apartment, it'd be the third time in three days he'd been my knight in shining flesh/suit/whatever he was wearing today. If only he would Kool-Aid Man through the wall right now and save me from this discussion about wedding vows.

He could totally pull off that costume. Then he'd *really* be a thirst trap.

Nope. I had Isaac, and Jason had—how did his mom put it? A "lady friend." But it was weird how every time Misty put her arm around him or touched him, he scooted out from under her. Maybe they were in a tiff. Hopefully she wouldn't give him trouble if I moved in.

An alarm chimed on my phone. "Sorry, lovely ladies. I have to go." I gathered my things, dropped kisses on both their heads, and grabbed another buttermilk drop for the road.

At eleven sharp, I pulled Mom's Camry back to the scene of my T and V. But this time, I wasn't dressed for a crime. One extra fluff-up of my hair, which was still in good shape from last night, and one final check that my lipstick was perfect, and I was ready to make a good impression on my potential landlord. Because after the ridiculously low price he'd texted me last night, I was determined to love whatever holy shack Jason had to rent me.

Following the high-pitched machine screel of a saw to the porch, I found him cutting wood and (pity) wearing a shirt this time. I waved for his attention. He looked up and smiled, then turned off the saw and removed his ear protection and goggles.

"Hey, good morning!" He met me at the foot of the stairs, and we shared an impromptu should-we-hug routine ending in an even more awkward hug. "Sorry. I'm probably all sweaty and covered in sawdust."

His soapy, musky scent had me weak in the knees. "Sweat and sawdust smell so good on you, I think one of my ovaries popped out an egg." Adrenaline kicked through me with a wave of heat to my face as he threw back his head and laughed. "I mean it didn't because I'm on the shot." Fuck, that's worse. I hid my face in my hands. "I—I mean you smell fine. Maybe you should talk the words now."

His laugh petered out. "Well, I'm glad I don't stink. Come on. Let me show you the apartment."

I ducked my head and followed him down the sidewalk to the old rectory door, appreciating the way his jeans hugged his ass and how his muscles moved under that red T-shirt. Delicious, but I had to stop thinking of him as climbable. He had a girlfriend—er, lady friend—for God's sake. I was seeing Isaac.

Maybe this was a bad idea. Seeing him every day would be intimidating. Unnecessarily tempting. Would it be awkward if Isaac ever came to visit? Honestly, both sides of that coin were unlikely. Jason wasn't interested in me, and Isaac? Him visiting was as likely as Mrs. Betty getting a tattoo of the devil on her forehead.

I followed Jason inside the old rectory. He closed the door behind us and fanned his shirt out in the air conditioning, lifting the hem and wiping sweat from his face. I dragged my eyes kicking and screaming away from his sweaty stomach to the pale gray walls of the sunny room. Actually, wait—this was gorgeous. New, wide plank dark wood floors, wide windows. I loved the smell of fresh paint.

"So, this would be your living room. Everything's freshly renovated—"

I put my hand on his arm to stop him. "Wait. You did all this yourself?"

His eyes went dark, and his Adam's apple bobbed. "Yeah. Um, everything but the wiring and the plumbing."

"I remember this room. It was a dark, wood-paneled cave with like...gold shag carpet." I walked a few steps away, whirling around to take in the whole room. "Oh my God, there's even crown molding. What's this color on the walls? I wish I could be the person who names wall paint and nail polish."

"Oh yeah? What would you call it?" He stooped to pick up a canvas drop cloth, shook it out from its haphazard folding, and started carefully folding it up.

"Hmm." I crossed my arms and tapped my lip, eyeing up the room. "Diana's Moon. What's it really?"

He grinned. "Tender Gray, but it's Diana's Moon now." He laid the drop cloth over his arm and started off down the hallway, stopping halfway down. "The kitchen's at the end of the hall, and here's the bedroom." He stepped inside and flipped on the light. "The rectory was designed for two priests to live in residence, but their rooms were so small. So, I took the wall down in between to make a bigger bedroom, bigger closet. I also attached the bathroom to it to make it a master."

As I entered the room, he went into the bathroom, tossed the drop cloth over his shoulder, and started washing his hands.

This room was much the same—spacious, fresh, and bright. I hadn't even seen the kitchen yet, but this place would fetch him a lot more than he offered me. I couldn't accept his charity.

My worried face appeared in the bathroom mirror beside his, and he looked up at the movement.

"You like it?"

I took a big breath, wrapping my hands around my arms. "Jason, I can't take this apartment."

"You don't like it." His smile flatlined as he pulled a hand towel off a hook and dried his hands. "That's okay."

I laid my hand on his arm to reassure him. "Oh God no, it's gorgeous! Look at this penny tile, and fuck me. Is that a jetted tub?"

He laughed. "Yep. It's a Kohler jetted tub."

"Jason, this place is *pa-la-tial* compared to the closet I lived in with two other women in New York City. It's a hundred times nicer than the fancy cookie-cutter apartment my sister wants me to look at that I couldn't afford. I can't take it because what you offered me for rent has to be a pity deal."

He turned toward me. His eyes met mine, and the bathroom shrank into an intimate space. God, his shoulders were broad. I bet he could fuck me standing in the middle of a room. My face went hot, and he stepped backwards into the bedroom, the drop cloth draped from his crossed arms like a shield. Did he feel that too?

Stop, Rose's body. You feel nothing.

"It's not a pity deal. Promise. Like I said, you'd be renting the apartment a few months before I'm ready, so until I get my kitchen and bath built out in the main church, I'll have to use yours. I can use the half bath in the church most of the time, but I'll need this one for showers. Come see the kitchen before you make up your mind."

I followed him out into the hallway, but stopped and looked longingly back down the hall. "The living room would be a perfect studio for my dressmaking. Would it be okay if I used the place as a business?"

He flipped the light on in the kitchen. "Yeah, do whatever. But there's another room next to the living room I forgot to show you. It's full of my junk right now, but I'll move it out so you don't have to lose your living room to work. I know how important it is to have a workshop. Frankly, I don't know why every house isn't built with a dedicated workroom. I'm building one into my house here."

"That's brilliant." Hands on the back of a chair, I looked around the kitchen. It clearly hadn't felt the magical caress of Jason's foxy hands, but it was clean. "My mom always wanted a workroom, back when she taught sewing classes in our garage, before she went back and got her graduate degree."

His brows lowered. "Oh yeah, isn't she a couple's therapist?"

I cackled, rolling my eyes. "No. She's a sex therapist. I can tell you all about orgasms, but nobody in my family knows shit about relationships."

His dimples divoted in a big smile, and he scratched at his beard, casting his gaze around the room as if he wasn't sure where to look after that statement. "I haven't had time or money to renovate in here. Stove's old, but everything works. The refrigerator's new, and so's the vinyl floor and the wall paint. I'll renovate it when I have a functioning kitchen in the main house, so at some point, you'll have to use my kitchen," he joked. "There's a hookup for a washer and dryer there"— he pointed to an alcove with open accordion doors—"but I haven't put them in yet. Bring 'em if you have 'em, but if not, you're welcome to use mine in the church until I get you a set. Is that okay?"

"Yeah. I don't care. The kitchen's great." I put my hands flat on the table and leaned toward him. "But if the rectory's this beautiful, you have to show me what you've done in the church." I bit my lips together. I'd pretty much invited myself into his personal space, and maybe that was weird. "I mean, you don't have to—"

"Yeah, absolutely!" His pleased surprise made me smile. "I'd love to show you. Nobody ever comes around. Come on." He held the kitchen door open for me and led me through the familiar brick arches in the courtyard.

Maybe I shouldn't have invited myself into his house. That's not a normal renter-rentee thing to do. And now we were walking side by side without talking. This silence was painful.

"My mom's the main thing most people remember about me. She's amazing, but geez, imagine being sixteen at Lakeside Mall with your mom, and having college kids point at her and say, 'I had sex with that lady!'"

He completely stopped, hand on the door, and glanced down at me. He looked totally confused and more than a little alarmed. "Wait, what?"

"She teaches human sexuality at the University of New Orleans," I blurted, laughing nervously. Why must I fill silences?

He laughed again, and I joined in as he led me into his house. At least I was making him laugh today?

"Maybe lead with that next time."

"Noted." I stepped all the way in, turning every which way to take in one of the most beautiful homes I'd ever been in. The old church was so much like I remembered, but also not at all. The vaulted wooden ceiling was still there, but he'd cleared the pews and laid down fresh wooden floors—a few pews sat along the far side wall as if hadn't wanted to get rid of them but didn't know what to do with them yet. The deep altar area, set up on two stacked platforms, held a console table with a record player. A cozy living area anchored the middle of the great room with rugs and sofas. Fresh tile and paint graced the foyer, as well as a few doors that hadn't been there before. Above the foyer, over the choir loft, the sun shone through the stained-glass window of a dove and cast everything it touched in shades of blue and orange.

It was clean and elegant with a mostly white and wood palette, but rustic and comfortable with pops of gray-blues and bohemi-an-type rugs in reds and yellows. Soothing, gorgeous, and comfort-able. "Wow. I'll never live anywhere this beautiful. Did you hire a decorator, or are you just naturally good at everything?"

He smiled. "I'm naturally an obsessive learner and Pinterester. I'm thrilled you like it. I never get to show it off, and the more I sit here with my decisions, the more I second-guess myself." He pointed toward the foyer. "I put in a fresh half bath, and I added an office for myself. Where the altar used to be will be the kitchen. One day."

"Wow." I turned to where he stood against the wall, his thick arms folded across his chest. He bit his lip as if worried what I would think.

"Jason, this is...*so* beautiful. Not that the rectory isn't beautiful too, but this room is like therapy. It's *elevated*. Like I might come knocking on your door just to sit in here and be calm."

"Thank you! It's nowhere near done. Come see where every-thing's going to be." He led me to the altar where he explained how the kitchen would be laid out. The dining room beside it, in the area where priests used to get ready for mass, already held a fine-ass dining table and chairs.

I ran my hand along the tabletop. "This is gorgeous. Did you make this?"

His almost-proud smile was so tentative and humble I wanted to hug him. "Yeah. Even did the upholstery. It's amazing what people will teach you for free online."

I pulled a chair out to peer at the seat, which was smoothly and uniformly done in the palest vintage gold velvet that I would never have thought should look this amazing with everything else. "I'm so impressed! You did such a professional job. It's so neatly done."

"That's high praise coming from someone with your talent." He walked across the room toward a fireplace with a deep hearth perfect for sitting on. The chimney was so well integrated it looked original even though I knew better.

"I put a fireplace in. It was a bitch, but I learned a lot about brick-work." He laid his hand on the mantel. "I thought about sanding this down, but I can't decide which way I like it."

I stepped beside him, inspecting the unsanded piece of wood. "Oh, I like it rough."

He huffed a soft laugh, and then I heard what I'd said.

I snorted. "For the mantel, too."

He pointed up to the choir loft over the foyer. "I'm sleeping up there for now and building a bathroom up there. But I can't decide if I want it to be the master bedroom, or if I'll make it a lounge area slash guest room."

"Where else would you put a bedroom?" I looked around. It was just one big, open room. "And you can't be planning only one bed-room."

"No, I'm going to have at least four, maybe five with the master."

"Where's that all going?"

He smiled. "Come see." He brought me back across to the altar and down a now-open hallway to the old community room, completely empty down to an unfinished concrete floor.

"Oh wow." My voice echoed in the two-story room. "I completely forgot this existed. We used to have our camp plays here."

"Oh yeah? This'll be the rest of the house. I just have to decide if I want the master back here or on the choir loft. I love sleeping up high under that window, but one day when I get married and have kids, I can't imagine I'll want to be that far away from them."

As if having a girlfriend wasn't enough, Jason was marriage-minded. I tossed him and his panty-soaking smile into my friend bin.

"My cousin's house has the option for a master downstairs or upstairs. You could do both and keep your options open."

He nodded. "See? You get it. That's what I'm leaning toward, too. But I've designed this part of the house about a thousand ways on paper, and I still can't figure it out."

"It's so exciting that you get to completely design how your house will look. I used to love drawing out blueprints for all my Barbie dolls' houses when I was little. I've always been obsessed with house plans, for some reason."

"Well good, maybe you can help me figure this shit out." He flicked off the light in the community room and headed back into the church. "Because I can't make up my mind."

"Oh, I doubt I can help. I just like to play. But Jason, this is going to be so amazing when you're done. It's already so beautiful. Talented doesn't begin to cover it. I'm really, so amazed at what you've accomplished." I stood on the altar, looking around. *Don't say it, Rose. Don't, say it.*

"But doesn't it freak you out to live in an old church?"

He stopped beside the record player and frowned at me. "What do you mean?"

I gestured down the middle of the church, where the aisle used to be. "So many dead bodies went up and down this aisle during funerals. And just the whole supernatural aspect of it. It doesn't freak you out a little, that the place could be haunted? Especially sleeping up on the loft. This old place must make all kinds of noises."

He stared at me. "Rose, I'd—I'd never thought of that until this moment." He mussed up his curls and crossed his arms. "Well shit. I'm not gonna sleep at all tonight. Thanks a lot."

I put my hands briefly on his crossed arms. "I'm sorry! I'm sure if it was haunted, you'd know by now. I could do a smoke cleansing for you if you want. Anyway, it can't be worse than hearing my mom and her boyfriend go at it in the next room."

He grinned and shook his head. "I absolutely never know what's going to come out of your mouth."

I smiled back weakly. "It's a questionable talent."

His dimples locked on my hormones, and "Dirrty" was in my head again. "It's kind of charming. So do you want to rent the apartment?"

"I really, really want to. But it's worth so much more than you're asking. Are you sure?" I bit my lip. If he said no, I might cry. If he said yes, I might cry.

He shrugged. "I don't think a stranger would want to share a kitchen and bath with me, or vice versa. You'd be doing me a favor. Really."

"Okay. If you're sure, I'll take it. Thank you so much!" I rushed him, throwing my arms around his middle and squeezing. "You don't know what this means to me."

His arms came briefly around me with a back pat, and when I pulled away, my hair caught in his beard. He stuck out his hand. "Then it's a deal."

"Deal." I shook his hand. "Is there a rental agreement?"

"Not yet. We can draw something up together. That okay? I'll pay for electricity, gas, and water. Anything breaks, it's on me. What am I missing?"

"I'll have people coming in and out for fittings and other appointments. Is that okay?"

"Yeah, and that workroom I mentioned has a separate door, so your clients can enter there instead of your living room."

"It sounds perfect. And the timing couldn't be better. My little pile of stuff is supposed to be coming from New York tomorrow morning."

He dug in his pocket and handed me a key. "This goes to your front and back doors, and here—let me text you the code to the door outside the workroom. It has a keypad."

"Okay." Oh shit. I scrambled to get my phone out of my pocket before he texted, but it was too late. The song "I'm Too Sexy" by Right Said Fred blared loud for us both to hear, and my face went hot.

I murmured *thanks* and shut it off, meeting his twinkling eyes. He glanced down to my phone with pursed lips, trying to hold back a laugh, which he lost control of.

Curse my love of assigning songs to contacts. The moment I got in the car, I was changing that to the theme song for *Friends*.

"Okay, roomie," he said. "I'll see you bright and early tomorrow."

"The brightest!" If I didn't die of embarrassment first.

Jason

A half-block away from home, I leaned over panting, hands on knees. I hadn't even made it five miles this morning after fitful, scant hours of nightmares about ghosts running up and down the loft steps.

And the rest of the night trying not to think about Rose. I pulled my water bottle from its pouch and took a long draft. She sure liked to touch, didn't she? Jesus. Over and over. She had me so amped up I had to use a drop cloth as a shield so she couldn't see what even those spare touches were doing to me. Then surprise-hugging me. My self-abstinence wasn't going to last much longer with her around.

Fuck it, I'd just walk the rest of the way home. I had so much to get to today, not least of which was planning what questions I had for the Big Dick people. I'd taken their first available appointment—next Friday—so I had almost two weeks to obsess over it. It had to go well. Working with them was my only way to turn that vast, empty community room into a two-story home. If only the worries Mom put in my head about being associated with them weren't warring with the excitement of a dream coming true.

A moving truck pulled out from my driveway and passed me on the road. Rose must be all moved in. Even though I'd always planned to rent out the rectory apartment, it felt weird to be a landlord. And now that I was, I had to douse my attraction to Rose—even though she apparently thought I was sexy. I grinned to myself. As intriguing as that was, what really puffed out my chest was her reaction to all my hard work.

My followers on all my social media platforms loved everything I did. Every step of the way through renovation they cheered me on, raved over my finish selections, and sent me more than a few marriage proposals. My family had been by a few times and been impressed. But man, Rose's admiration hit different.

She'd looked like a Disney princess discovering a new castle with her long, curly hair, graceful movements, and expressions of wonder. And every time she touched me, my body completely lost it—instant shivers, instant arousal.

But I closed that door firmly in my mind. Despite what seemed to be a mutual attraction, none of that mattered. She wasn't marriage-minded, my mom didn't like her, and she was my renter. Three strikes. She probably had a boyfriend—a bonus strike four.

I entered the back door, the one I told Rose I'd exclusively use while I was using her kitchen and bathroom. Footsteps and shifting noises emanated from the direction of her hallway and living area. I grabbed a water from the fridge and called out a good morning.

"Morning! I'm back here!"

I followed her voice to her living room, which was a sea of boxes, several open but unpacked. Styrofoam peanuts littered the floor.

"Rose?" I peeked around the boxes.

A blanket with a cat flying a rocket ship covered a mound in the middle of the room. Half the blanket flopped down to reveal her lying on a giant bean bag chair. I jumped and pressed my hand to my pounding heart, still skittish from my night in the now-surely-haunted church.

"Jesus, Rose, you scared the shit out of me. What are you doing?"

She pressed her fingertips under her watery-looking eyes. "I'm so stressed out. There's too much stuff, and it's everywhere. My mom even sent over all my stuff from her attic. I don't know how she talked the movers into taking more than they originally agreed to." She covered her head back up with the blanket. "She probably promised them a bunch of free sex toys."

Her voice was muffled. Surely, I didn't hear her right.

"What?" I asked. But no. As much as I wanted to pull that thread, that's not what was important. Nor was that appropriate as her landlord. "Let me know if you need help moving furniture or anything. I've got a bed frame to finish filming, so I'll be in the workshop."

The blanket flopped back down. "Filming? Is that some kind of woodworking technique?"

"Filming for my social media channels."

"Oh, is that why you take so many pictures of yourself?" Her eyes widened. "That was so rude. I'm sorry." She stood up and folded her blanket, dropping it into a box. Another tank top and short shorts today.

"Where have you seen me take a bunch of pictures of myself?"

"At Becca's shower. The selfie stick usage was a little unhinged. What do you do online? You said you're an architect, right?"

"That's what I studied, but it's pretty tough to break into."

"So, what do you do? And how did I miss asking you this?"

"I build custom furniture—bookshelves, tables, beds, cabinetry, even decks. That kind of thing. There's a huge market locally for handcrafted furniture, and between that and the money coming in from my social media sponsorships, ads, affiliates, merch, et cetera, I'm making more than I would as a beginning architect in Louisiana."

"Really," she said, more of a statement than a question. "That's amazing. I already knew you were crazy talented, but you must be really smart, too. My roommate in New York was always after me to start an Instagram account for my designs. But I…" She took her long hair down from its bun and put it back up again. "I'm so overwhelmed. I have a ton of gowns to make, my serger and sewing machine are still in boxes, I don't know where anything is. And I don't even know where to start with my business." Her voice wavered as she stacked a small box onto an already-high stack then wiped under her eyes. "I'm trying really hard not to cry in front of you right now, and even harder not to have an anxiety attack."

Shit—I'd had more than my fair share of those. "Hey, it'll be okay. Just take it one step at a time. It's the only way I can handle things. And go easy on yourself. You only moved in this morning. Let me help you set some things up." I pointed to a headboard. "Want me to move this into the bedroom? I always set my bed up first when I move into a new place."

She looked back at me, deflating. "Thank you. Yes. That would be amazing."

I sat my water bottle on the windowsill and hefted the full-size headboard with her pushing her box spring down the hall after me. "Between the windows?"

"Perfect." She set the box spring against the wall and left again.

I set the headboard in place and spotted a metal bed frame leaning in the corner of the room. I grabbed it and started setting it out. "Do you have the hardware for your bed?"

"Yes!" She rummaged through boxes while I set everything out and pulled the plastic off her mattresses.

"So do you only make wedding dresses?"

"And bridesmaid dresses." She came back with a bank envelope jingling with screws and a small, pink toolbox. "Here you go. I'm only taking customers by word of mouth right now, but I've been trying to get picked up by a major player in the business on my way to starting my own label. Holland Lane is my dream firm, but they won't give me the time of day. I could open my own boutique, but there's so much involved with starting a brick-and-mortar. I'd have to find a manufacturer to work with, make all the patterns, find a retail spot to rent—and I don't know how I'd survive in a local-only market. It's all so overwhelming, but I have bills to pay right now, you know?"

She was actively wringing her hands, looking around at the boxes as if not really seeing anything.

"You can make money with your brand without producing wedding gowns. Like you could…make T-shirts or stickers about sewing to sell online. Better yet, post sewing or design lessons, or even sell classes on sites like CraftClass. I'm working on a class for them right now. Or even just build your platform and then the right people will come to you."

She stared at me blankly. "Can we add making money on the internet lessons to our rental agreement? I'm completely lost, but it sounds like you know what's up."

"Yeah. One of the biggest things I've learned is how important visibility is. Like I saw online the other day that a shoe designer hit it big after some famous actor found him on Instagram. Wait—who was in the news the other day because he got engaged to that singer? We went to middle school with him. He works for that millionaire?"

"Oh, Sam. Sam Cooper. Yeah, he got engaged to PJ Lane."

"Weren't y'all friends? Reach out and see if PJ will let you make her dress. Your platform would explode with that kind of visibility."

She waited for me to step out of the bed frame and laid her box spring down. "Girl. I'd hand-weave the fabric like it was the freaking Middle Ages for that opportunity."

I stopped and narrowed my eyes at her. "Is there a reason you keep calling me 'girl'? It doesn't bother me, but it does confuse me."

She put her hands on her hips, her small smile slightly challenging. "Nobody bats an eye when somebody calls people 'bro,' or 'man,' even if the person they're talking to identifies as female. So why can't 'girl' be the universal?"

"Huh." I nodded. "That makes sense. I like it." And it made me smile inside every time she did it. I wanted to hear the story behind each of her quirks—the direct questions, the double entendres, all the touching that was making me insane. I bet she had a compelling explanation for them all.

"But PJ," Rose continued. "She has a bad rep as a diva. I'm sure she's only interested in the celebrity designers who are probably already knocking down her door. Why would she want something from a nobody like me?"

I shifted her mattress into place on top of the box spring. "Why would you self-reject without even trying? I haven't seen your designs, and I don't know anything about wedding dresses, but you must be pretty good to get that fashion internship. And Becca raves about your work all the time."

She smiled and shrugged, pulling a sheet set covered in unicorns and rainbows from a box and tossing me a pillow. "I appreciate it, but PJ's too high profile. I'd have to build a following before she'd even look at me, right? So sure, maybe goals. But I'm at the bottom, so that's where I need to start."

"Do yourself a favor." I went around the bed and took the fitted sheet from her, pointing at a round ottoman in the corner. "Sit there, go to Instagram right now, make an account, and grab your handle. What's the name of your business?"

She pulled her phone out, settling onto the ottoman cross-legged, her shorts riding high up her inner thighs. "Sweet Roses Bridal. My friend, Heather, already made me a logo, I just haven't done anything with it."

"That's a perfect name. Wait, Heather Aucoin, from middle school?"

She nodded. "Yeah. Graphic design is one of her many talents."

"I remember her. She helped me get through algebra." I trained my eyes on the unicorns, making quick work of her bed as she tapped and swiped on her phone, its case covered in cat mermaids.

"Okay, I'm all set up. I'm gonna go follow you. What's your username? Or do I search for your real name?"

"I'm Deck Daddy. You have a quilt or something?"

She fell over sideways, cackling and throwing a leg down to keep from falling off the ottoman. "*Deck Daddy*?"

I smiled, too used to that reaction to be insulted. "It's got just the right amount of shtick, which works in my favor. But I admit it's a little too close to 'dick daddy,' which has caused more than one massive misunderstanding to come my way—and more than one massive dick pic."

She'd almost recovered from her laughing fit, but that set her off again. After a minute, though, she was sitting back up and scrolling. "Okay, okay. I found you. And, followed. Helloooooo Deck Daddy." Her eyebrows went up.

I caught my face in a mirror leaning against the wall. I'd turned bright red, for some reason.

"Wow. The women and gay men on Instagram eat you up, don't they?" She looked up. "Oh, a quilt? Yeah, lemme grab it." She stuck her phone in her back pocket and dug in another box, pulling out a comforter. It was covered in, of course, roses.

"How did you come up with Deck Daddy? It's brilliant."

"Well, I didn't get a lot of followers on my old handle, *Woodwork-ingwithJason*, until one day my reflection showed up in the sliding glass door beside a deck I built—and my shirt was off." I scratched my beard, a little embarrassed to be talking about this in her bedroom. She billowed her comforter onto the bed and sat down on it, going back to scrolling my account. "The post blew up, and one of my followers called me 'Deck Daddy,' and I kinda ran with it. So now I give the people what they want." I grinned at her, but she stared back at me. "What?"

She breathed out, returning her eyes to her screen. "I mean you were always good-looking, but goddamn. HA! One of these women tagged you, #WILF: woodworker I'd like to fuck."

I smiled at the compliment. And the hashtag. And at her blushing furiously after she said them.

So...did Rose have a boyfriend?

Nope, that wasn't something I needed to know.

"Okay, but I have to buy some Deck Daddy merch." She burst out laughing. "Oh my God, I love this shirt."

I leaned over her shoulder. "Which one?"

"This blue one." She tapped on the screen with a pink nail. "With the hammer and nails: '#nailed by @DeckDaddy.'"

"I'll give you a shirt. You don't have to buy one. What size you want?"

"Um, large. I like 'em big."

I miraculously held back a snort, but she didn't.

"They're on order, but it's yours when it comes in." Among the cardboard boxes in the living room, I'd seen a few pieces of furniture like a dresser, a desk, and a nightstand. But I didn't remember seeing any kind of worktable or sewing machine. "What do we have to do to get you set up to work?"

She stood and shoved her phone into her back pocket again and pressed both hands to her stomach. "You're so sweet, but you have better things to do than to spend all day holding my hand."

"Nah, what else is a landlord for?" I followed her back into the living room and picked up my water bottle.

"In my experience? Lying about repairs and trying to cheat you out of security deposits. Oh, do you want a security deposit?"

I swallowed my water. "No, that's okay. Seriously. What can I help you with? You have a table for your sewing machine? I cleared the room out yesterday."

"Thank you! Yes, that folding table against the wall. Let me find my sewing machine."

I grabbed the six-foot folding table she pointed out and brought it into the room, but I didn't have high hopes for it. It was mostly held together with duct tape and good vibes—literally, a sticker that said "good vibes"—and she'd wrapped the top of it in pink satin. I managed to get it open, but it was shaky as hell.

"You don't have another table?" I asked as she walked in with a box.

She shook her head. "No, Strawberry Jello's all I've got."

"Strawberry Jello?"

"The table." She set her box on it and gave it a shove, and the whole thing swayed.

"Let me see if I have another—"

"No, it's totally fine. I'm used to it, I promise." Hands pressed to her stomach again.

"You can't work on this. I could build you a table."

She paused with her hands inside the box, staring at me with a confused expression. "Jason, you're not trying to lure me into a sex dungeon with all these favors, are you? Because in my experience, when a man offers a ton of unsolicited help, eighty percent of the time he's trying to lure you into a sex dungeon."

I smirked and placed my hands on the swaying table, meeting her already-laughing eyes. "That's a high percentage."

She copied my body language and leaned in. "The other twenty percent want to embroil you in a pyramid scheme involving fish sticks and hand puppets." She shrugged. "New York City was an interesting place."

Trying to hold back a smile, I leaned in closer than I maybe should've. "Are you trying to besmirch the good name of the sex dungeon I built underneath my church home?"

She busted out laughing, and so did I. "Now I know you're lying." She pulled crunched up newspapers from the moving box. "Because if you dig down five feet in Metairie, you're probably hitting water. Seriously, you've done way too much for me already." She pulled her sewing machine out and set it in the middle of the table. It bowed under the weight. "You don't have to build me a table. And I can't afford one, anyway."

I stood back, folding my arms. "Rose, are you trying to have to buy a new sewing machine? Because that's what Strawberry Jello wants."

She breathed out and shook her head. "You should see it when I cut fabric out."

"What if I made it into a video for my channel? I've never made a sewing table. Might bring in some new followers, and then my followers might also go follow you. Winning all around."

Her face soured. "Would I have to be on camera, though? I'm not made for video."

I frowned at the exquisite woman before me. "Well, yeah. That's usually part of the draw. I guess you don't have to, but you'll get more followers if you do."

She pulled at her shirt. "I take the worst pictures. I always look like a trash gremlin."

"A what?" I scoffed.

"A *trash grem-lin.*" She enunciated, no humor to her voice as she pulled a moving box for clothes closer to the table.

"Wait, you're actually serious. I'm not saying this to make you feel better, but—" I couldn't tell her she was beautiful, even though it was true. "You look absolutely nothing like a trash gremlin."

Her cheeks pinkened as she rolled her eyes. "I wasn't trying to get you to disagree with me. Isaac, the guy I'm seeing, says I'm just not photogenic."

There he was. And he must wear magic glasses that make beautiful things look ugly. "If you posted photos or videos of yourself, your numbers would go up faster. Just saying."

She half-smiled at me. "How does your girlfriend feel about you posting all these shirtless photos of yourself?"

"I don't have a girlfriend." That came out faster and harsher than I'd meant it to.

She frowned at me. "Yeah, you do."

I shook my head emphatically. "No, I really don't."

"But I met her the other night. Misty?"

"She's *not* my girlfriend." That definitely came out harsh. "Wait, did she tell you she's my girlfriend?"

Her pretty mouth made a perfect O. "Your mom introduced her to me as your 'lady friend.' That's not mom code for girlfriend?"

I sighed heavily and rolled my neck. "Misty's the daughter of my mom's best friend. I took her out to dinner exactly once over a year ago, and only because Mom wouldn't stop pushing me. Worst night of my life."

"Well, she stood there beaming when your mom said it." She raised her eyebrows suggestively. "She wants her some Deck Daddy."

"Geez, I can't believe my mom introduced her as my 'lady friend.' Who even says that?" I leaned against the back of a rattan sofa that'd seen better decades. It crackled like it might break, and I stood back up.

She grimaced. "I'm sorry. I didn't mean to start shit."

"It's not your fault. Misty's just...a lot. She's pushy, overbearing, and doesn't understand the concept of 'no.' When I took her to dinner, she was determined to have me for dessert, and I—"

Rose snorted. "Waitwaitwait..." She grabbed her phone, scrolled for a minute, then held the phone up to me. "This what she wanted?" The post of me lying shirtless across the dining table I built.

I laughed. "I'm serious! She's such a hypocrite. In our church group, she led a whole discussion about how devoted she was to saving herself for the sanctity of marriage, which is fine if that's what you believe. But on that date, she wouldn't shut up about how good she was in bed and how she wanted to prove it to me. Despite me telling her I wasn't interested. Repeatedly."

"Ah, now it makes sense why you were treating her like she was an amorous skunk at the shower." She gazed at me with a small smile, eyebrows up. "Are you a virgin?"

I sputtered for a second. But was I surprised at her frankness? "No." I laughed. "I'm not." *Do not ask her if she's one.*

Nope. Not good for landlord-renter relations.

"Well, if you want some unsolicited advice, my mom would tell you that you're right to run in the opposite direction from Misty."

"Why's that?"

She shrugged. "Is sex important to you?"

"Yeah." My face heated up. Which is one of many reasons why the past two years have been difficult. Why the past half hour had been difficult. And now she wanted to talk about sex?

"Then it's important to be sexually compatible with a potential mate. And if you already don't like her touching you?" She wrinkled her nose and shook her head. "It's only downhill from there."

"I wish my mom thought like you did. Misty's got her fooled into thinking she's a wholesome woman of the church. Mom thinks I'm not into her because I'm not used to dating 'women of quality.'" I put that into air quotes.

She rolled her eyes. "Your parents *totally* did it before they were married."

I laughed at the sheer absurdity of that thought. But the frankness of this conversation was more than a landlord and his renter should be involved in. "I guess it's the quiet ones you have to watch for, huh?"

"What? What do you mean?"

"You. Dr. Ruth junior over there."

"Listen, you try having a mom who's a sex therapist. Do you know what she gave my girlfriends as party favors at my eighteenth birthday party?"

I edged toward the door. "I'm afraid to ask."

"Vibrators," she said, not breaking eye contact.

I rubbed the back of my neck. I needed to get out of this apartment. And into a cold shower.

"Yeah, and she didn't ask me ahead of time if it'd be okay."

"Wow. I don't think my mom's ever done anything as embarrassing as that."

She laughed, pulling ribbons and bolts of fabric from boxes. "It was fine. My friends were excited to get them. Told me I was so lucky to have such a cool mom."

I should've walked out, but I had to ask. "Why vibrators?"

"So we, as young women, could be in control of our own sexuality and not rely on someone else to find gratification." She licked her full lips and leaned over to dig in a box, giving me a clear sightline down the middle of her shirt from cleavage to belly button. "And to learn what we liked. Sexually."

What did pretty Rose like? Sexually?

I held my water bottle in a strategic line down my crotch. I had to get out of here.

"She didn't want us to fall into a bad relationship just because we were horny. Like she said she did with my dad." She stood and pressed her hands to her stomach again.

"Good for her. Hey, did you eat anything today?"

"Um…" She dug through another box. "Coffee."

It was past ten. She was going to make herself sick. "I'm about to make myself breakfast," I lied. "How do you like your eggs?"

"No, no, don't worry about me. I'm fine." She pressed her hand to her stomach again and walked behind a stack of boxes.

"I'll make 'em scrambled."

"You really don't have to—"

"With some bacon."

Her head popped up from behind a dresser, eyes lit with hope. "You have bacon?"

I laughed. "I'll call you when it's ready."

I went back down the hall and started cooking. Her morning reminded me of my first day after I got home from leaving Kasey. All my shit in boxes in a crappy little apartment, no job, no idea what to do next. I laid on my mattress on the floor that night, crying, wishing that everything in my life was different. That I hadn't messed up with my family and friends, that I'd been enough for Kasey to stay. If I hadn't doomscrolled across an Instagram ad for therapy, I don't know how I would've gotten through it. No one should have to go through big changes in their lives alone. Why wasn't this Isaac guy down here helping her? Why weren't her mom and Lily helping her?

"Come and get it!" I called down the hallway.

"Girl." Rose's voice came from behind me. "The smell of bacon already floated me down the hallway like a cartoon character."

I turned and handed her a loaded plate. "Sit down and relax. Eat. You're not gonna get done any faster by not taking care of yourself."

She grabbed a half-finished Diet Coke from the fridge and sat at the table, immediately grabbing the fork I'd set at her place. "Thank you so much."

"You're very welcome."

"Ohmygod, this is so good," she mumbled around a mouthful of eggs.

I grabbed a Steno pad and a pencil and sat across from her. "I'm glad. Listen, I've got a lot of work to get to today, but—"

She covered her mouth, her eyes big. "Wait, you're not eating?"

"I already ate, but I didn't think you'd let me make you something if you knew." I sat the pad and pencil next to her plate. "Before you go back to—"

She stood up with a shaky breath and came around to my side of the table, wrapping her arms around my neck from the side, her head against my back. "Thank you," she said softly.

I patted her arm, and she pressed a quick, warm kiss to my cheek, radiating electricity to every nerve ending.

"I appreciate you." She went back to her seat and kept eating, wiping tears from her face.

My cheeks burned. "I'm glad I could help. And hey." I tapped the steno pad. "I'm serious about the table. Sketch or list out what you need, we'll come up with a design, and then we'll start filming. Deal?"

Her answering smile made me feel like a better man than I was. "That would be amazing. You're literally my knight in shining flesh."

"No problem." I saluted her like a fucking idiot, grabbed my water bottle, and left before I indulged my sudden impulse to kiss the top of her head and tell her everything was going to be okay.

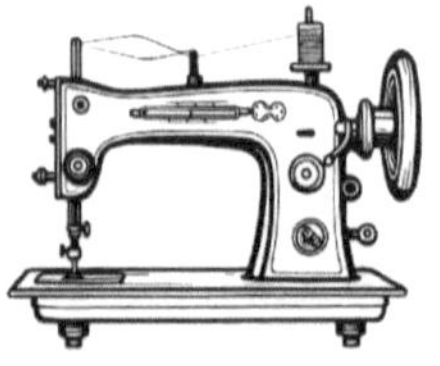

Chapter 5

Steely Dan

Rose

I MOVED IN ALMOST a week ago, but I was barely settled in. But I did get two more dresses done. I left my books, my TV, my Nintendo Switch—really all my fun stuff except my favorite vibrator, of course—in boxes while I worked on Becca's dresses so I wouldn't be distracted.

Not that Jason hadn't been a distraction. A welcome one.

I was *not* prepared that first night, when he asked if he could take a shower just as I was going to bed. He must've thought I was already asleep when he came out of the bathroom, but I was awake enough to see him walk through my bedroom *wet and wearing only a towel around his waist.*

All that beautiful, still-damp skin, smelling like his manly soap. Fuck me. He was viscerally, biologically attractive to me, like his skin was a salt lick and I was a deer.

I smoothed the pinned-out fabric into place and grabbed my shears. Deck Daddy wasn't a distraction I needed or should want. I was with Isaac. Even though he'd been out on tour for the past two months and barely answered my texts anymore.

Nope, I wouldn't think about Deck Daddy smelling like soap in a towel, or Deck Daddy all sweaty from his run helping me set up my bed and cooking me breakfast to make sure I was taken care of. Or the easy rhythm we'd fallen into, cooking together, sharing meals, and working on my table. Woodworking reminded me of sewing, turning flat raw materials into three-dimensional, finished objects. It was exciting to learn something new, and Jason made everything fun. He was so patient explaining everything, teaching me how to use his tools, laughing his sexy laugh when I said something else ridiculous. His praise and support every time I posted one of my designs on Instagram or made show-off-able progress on Becca's dresses made me start to feel like I could handle this.

Nope nope nope. He was the marryin' kind. I wasn't, and anyway, I was seeing Isaac.

The chorus of "50 Ways to Leave Your Lover" rang on my phone. Speak of the devil. I set my shears down and picked it up. Hmm...he wanted to meet on a video call tonight, after leaving me on read for the past two days. I braced my hands against the table. With our relationship only about sex, and we didn't even live in the same city anymore...what was the point? He had no interest in my life's work. I could only identify maybe two of his songs.

I dropped my head and closed my eyes. Level One relationships never had substance, and I was usually okay with that. But lately my soul felt like my bank account: sad and empty.

Something *popped* behind me. A small, hard object hit my left butt cheek, and I yelped and whirled around.

Jason stood laughing at the doorway, a Nerf gun in either hand. "I'm gonna leave this one right here." He slowly lowered one of them to the ground like we were in a hostage situation. "We have ten minutes until the sun's perfect for the last shot we need for your table."

I took a slow step toward the Nerf gun.

"*Anh-anh-anh!*" He held his palm out toward me. "I'm not done."

Hands on hips. "You're gonna get it so bad, Deck Daddy."

His cocky smile made me flush. He knew what I was about, alright.

"You only have five minutes to take me out." He cocked his electric green and orange weapon and crooked his finger at me. "Bring it on, Sweet Rose." He turned and ran.

In five quick paces I got to the gun, picked it up, checked it for ammo. Slipping the foam bullet bandolier he'd left hanging from the doorknob over my shoulder, I stepped out into the hallway and looked to my left first. Another foam bullet hit my right butt cheek.

I whirled around to see him laughing and running for the door. "Hey Soniat, leave my butt cheeks alone!" I raced after him to the back door and out onto the lawn. There—hiding behind a brick arch. I slipped behind another one and peered around the tree beside it.

The sun was starting its descent into a red-tinged sky. The world was golden, and the crepe myrtle trees edging the courtyard shed their white flowers everywhere. The wind *shushed* through the pines and oaks, and the only other sounds were the courtyard fountain and Jason's laughing.

"What do I win when I shoot your ass up?" I demanded.

"A Deck Daddy shirt."

I looked down at the red "Deck Daddy likes to screw" shirt I was wearing for the shoot. "I already have one."

"Yeah, but this is the blue one you wanted. It came in today."

"Hell, yeah." I dashed to the next arch and took aim. I shot; I missed. He howled. "That was too close!"

I ran toward him across the courtyard, firing, and he dove behind a row of azaleas. From arch to arch and tree to tree, we chased each other all around the back property in front of his double-wide trailer workshop, sometimes laughing so hard we couldn't stand up. He got me over and over, but I hadn't landed a single shot.

He walked toward me with his gun held up and turned out like he was surrendering. "Wait, wait! Time out! We have to film the last segment."

"Yeah, okay." I waited until he was within ten feet of me. "Not!" I shot his stomach, and I didn't stop, not even when he squealed and turned around. That just got me the butt shots I'd been going for.

Laughing so hard he could barely breathe, he came closer, gasping *Stop! Stop!*

He lunged for my gun, but I wasn't about to give it up. "No! No! It's mine!" I turned and doubled over it, squealing.

His arms and hard body came around me from behind, and without much effort, he wrestled it from my hands. He let go of me and stepped back, panting, jogging backwards, and gloating with both guns up over his head. "I won!"

"No!" I gasped, wiping my face. "Now I'm all sweaty and you're gonna make me go on camera?"

He laughed at me, walking toward the workshop. "You're supposed to look sweaty when you build stuff. C'mon. It's showtime."

I followed him up to the porch where he handed me a water bottle and started the camera. I was getting more and more comfortable with filming because Jason made it fun. The banter was kinda exhilarating, and he never minded when I wanted to stop and fix my hair.

He took a few minutes to check his cameras and get everything perfect. He was even more unbearably handsome in the setting sun, with his eyes pools of burnt amber and his dark curls highlighted with a touch of red. But I could only ever be a Deck Daddy fan.

In my experience, no man ever attained that level of beauty without an overabundance of conceit and arrogance. Unless, of course, you were Jason Momoa or Chris Hemsworth or Chris Evans. But guys like that didn't grow on trees.

If only. I'd be a happy, horny little farmer, growing myself a crop of hunks, some for me, some for my friends...

Jason's voice broke through a quickly-blooming, orchard-related why-choose fantasy in my head. "Okay, just like we practiced, okay?"

I nodded. "Let's do it."

We took our places on either side of my sewing table. My fingers itched to pull off the canvas cloth draped over it. Despite my begging and pestering, he hadn't let me see it for the past three days.

Jason shifted into his social media personality. "We've been hard at work," he said, "and now it's time for the big reveal." He looked at me, nodded his head, and together, we both took off our Deck Daddy shirts. He revealed his godlike physique, and I revealed a Deck Daddy tank top.

He turned to me, acting confused as he delivered his lines. "Wait, Rose. I thought we'd..." He motioned between his bare chest and me. "I thought we'd agreed to go topless."

"Nope." I set my gaze back on one of the cameras and shook my head. "That's your shtick, Deck Daddy."

He shrugged. "Suit yourself." He turned toward me and laid his hands on the table between us. "Are you ready to see it?"

I echoed his position on the opposite side of the long table, raising my eyebrows suggestively. "Just what are you about to show me, Deck Daddy?" I ad-libbed.

He turned away laughing.

"Come on! I can't wait to see it," I whined. "You haven't let me see it since we finished building it."

"Okay, okay. Here she is." He pulled the drop cloth away.

Both of my hands went over my mouth, and actual tears sprang to my eyes. The last time I saw it, it was bare wood, my standing height and with a bottom shelf for supplies and bolts of fabric. But now, the whole thing was painted white, and the tabletop was a smooth, marble-look surface. There in the middle was a decal of my logo, the stylized gown made of rose petals with "Sweet Roses Bridal" beneath.

"I wanted to get you a custom cutting mat as a tabletop, but not only was it cost-prohibitive, they wouldn't be able to handle the decal, and it wouldn't come in for forever. And I know you need this, like yesterday. So, I did some research, learned that melamine was the next best surface for a cutting table." He ran his hand along the surface. "And, well, I knew a guy who knew a guy, and—Rose, are you crying?"

I nodded, wiping my face. "It's beautiful. It's...Jason, I can't believe you made this for me. It's such a step-up from Strawberry Jello, it's not even in the same food group. Thank you so much."

I went around to his side of the table and hugged him right around his middle, my cheek against that mulberry silk skin.

"Aww, you're welcome." He squeezed me back but stepped away quickly and glanced at the camera. "I guess it's safe to say you're another satisfied customer?"

I ran my hands along the tabletop. "Yes, so very satisfied."

Jason winked at the camera. "Deck Daddy aims to satisfy. Thanks for hanging out with us while we made this sewing table for Rose of Sweet Roses Bridal. Remember to follow her, at SweetRosesBridal and follow me, DeckDaddy, while you're at it. And remember folks, it's all fun and games to go shirtless when the saws are off, but always wear protection when you use your tools."

He crossed to the cameras and turned them off. "Perfect. I think this is gonna be something my followers haven't seen before. Thanks for letting me make it for you."

I couldn't stop crying and running my hands over my table. "Are you kidding? It's perfect and amazing, and how could I ever truly thank *you* for this?"

He grinned. "Thank me by helping me take down my cameras and bring this bad boy to your sewing room. I have a church meeting to get to in about an hour."

"Whatever you say, Deck Daddy."

I set down my straightening iron and popped on a red lipstick. As hot as I looked right now, Isaac would never know I'd spent all day bent over a sewing machine, running around playing Nerf guns, and filming in the hot setting sun. Why didn't I straighten my hair more often, besides it being a pain in the ass? He liked it better, and I had to admit, it was a good look for me.

I curled up on my bed in my sexy halter top and short shorts, waiting for Isaac to call. Playing and filming with Jason had gotten me all heated up, and I was hoping to expend that sexual energy on a phone sex date. Because maybe I'd been too pessimistic about this thing with Isaac. And maybe if I looked hot enough, he'd come down to visit me.

FaceTime was ringing, still "50 Ways to Leave Your Lover." Bad vibe, but that was all my fault. I sat up, cleared my throat, adjusted my cleavage, and slid my finger across the screen.

"Hey handsome, how are you?"

He was walking on a city sidewalk, and the connection was spotty. "Isaac?"

"Hey Rose, I hear you now. What's going on?"

"A lot! I'm all moved into my new apartment, and I made so much progress on Becca's dress today. I think it's going to be one of the most beautiful dresses I've ever made. You made it back from tour? How are things in the city?"

"Good, good. We're going back out next week. Got a gig tonight, too. I'm on my way there now. I woke up with a sore throat, and I've been trying to save my voice all day, so I can't talk long."

My heart sank. "Oh. Okay."

"So, listen." He paused beside the door of Punk Decay. "We need to talk." He looked up and nodded at someone off camera.

I knew it. "Really?" I huffed, my face going hot. "That's the cliché you're going with?"

He rubbed his hand across his beard, his blue eyes catching the streetlights. "Rose, I can't do this."

"Do what?"

"Long distance. You're a great girl and all—"

"Woman."

He rolled his eyes, and I wanted to poke them. "Woman. Of course. My whole life's up here, and I don't feel strongly enough about this to string it along. I've been seeing someone else."

The hurt part of me shriveled under the heat building in my chest. "You mean you've been cheating on me?"

He shrugged. "It happened kinda fast, while I was out on tour. I really like her."

I called it. Men. Never. Stay.

"Got it." I ended the call. Deleted his contact info. Deleted my pictures of him and any of us together—except that one. I looked fine in that one. I cropped him out and tossed my phone on the bed. Stood up and paced my room.

"UGHH!" I growled and threw a throw pillow across the room. Why was I such an idiot who attracted ever stupider idiots?

He couldn't keep it in his pants. Exclusivity was all I asked of him, and it was a pretty low fucking baseline. He'd never been super nice to me, not really. So why had I trusted him? Why was I seeing him at all?

Jason wasn't even a romantic option, and in the first week of knowing each other as adults, he'd selflessly offered help at every turn, even taking care of me when he noticed I wasn't doing it myself. And he'd asked for nothing in return. Isaac once walked empty-handed up the ten flights of stairs to my apartment, right beside me, and never once offered to carry one of my grocery bags. He wouldn't even go down on me unless I "returned the favor." Tit for tat, always.

I'd tried so hard to guard myself from being hurt by men by offering them the only relationships they can sustain, but clearly that wasn't working. Here I was, hurt again. And over stupid Isaac?

No. Actually? This was for the best. I needed time to get serious about my business, and why keep someone in my life who made it harder?

My gaze landed on the ornate wooden chest I kept my sex toys in. But first, I would take care of myself. It was only eight o'clock. Jason was still at his church group, so he wouldn't need the shower for another couple of hours. I locked my bedroom door, lowered the lights, and put fresh batteries into my favorite vibrator.

If I was going to be alone, I was going to enjoy the hell out of it.

Jason

Ten more minutes, and my fifth SALT meeting would be over. Thank God. We'd already discussed which parishioners needed our help next, when we'd go, and what we'd take care of, so now it was time for Misty's two-faced bullshit. It was one of the three things I hated most about the group.

I barely listened as she led a discussion about sexual immorality and discovering God's illusive plan for you as a single person. Which would be fine coming from anyone else, but having it come from her mouth irked me every time.

She'd texted me after Becca's shower last weekend, inviting me to her house for "dinner and a BJ." I'd texted her back and told her no, and to only contact me with information about the group. Her response?

> It's so hot when you play hard to get, but I promise you'll be hard when I wrap my mouth around you

I hadn't dignified that with a response, and I was dreading getting her alone tonight. But I had to talk to her and make her understand that we were never going to happen and that she had to leave me alone.

"So, I'll close out with this, from Thessalonians." Misty stood at the front of the room at a lectern. "'For this is the will of God, your sanctification: that you abstain from sexual immorality; that each one of you know how to control his own body in holiness and honor.'" She smiled, her gaze catching on mine.

She got off on her double life, didn't she?

I looked to Reverend Paul, the former leader of our old group, because it was time for the second thing I hated. Although I never signed up for the group's picnics, mini golf, and carpooling to church, these people were more interested in those activities than helping the old folks.

"Thank you, Misty. Now let's get a show of hands." Reverend Paul put his hand on Misty's shoulder and pushed up his glasses. Poor Paul was clearly smitten with her.

Maybe if I dropped a hint about Paul, she'd leave me alone. He was a good-looking guy. Super nice.

Nah, I wouldn't do that to Paul.

"How many of you are coming to the bowling alley Friday night?" Paul asked.

I kept my hands all the way down, inwardly wincing for the reactions of the third thing I hated about this group: the women who'd sat on either side of me tonight.

A warm hand on my arm. "Jason, you aren't going?" Sina asked, her dark brows lowering.

"No, I'm going to be out of town." Thank you, Big Dick Tools.

A warm hand on my other arm. "But I was only going if you're going." Bethany smiled her winningest smile and twined her arms around mine, tossing her hair.

I unraveled my arms from both ladies and stood up. "Sorry. Busy." They'd already asked, and I'd already told them I wasn't looking for a relationship. Their constant touching and competition over me was as unwanted and disrespectful as Misty's.

I slipped to the back of the room to fill my coffee cup, yet again. I'd actually been hopeful when the groups first combined, thinking maybe it would help me reconnect with my faith and reevaluate what I wanted from a partner. But that's not why most people were here. Some clearly just wanted to hook up, others were uber-religious parishioners looking for like-minded mates, and a few were fresh from divorces and break-ups; half of those just wanted to bitch about their exes, and the others were still grieving.

My new buddy, Antoine, who also got suckered from the volunteer group into this one, joined me at the coffee counter and leaned in. "If they try to organize another painting and wine night, I'm out, bro. Maybe we should form our own group."

"I know, right?"

"What do you know?" Misty appeared beside me, encroaching on my personal space and batting her lashes at me.

"Misty! What's up, girl?" Antoine bellowed, wrapping his arm around her shoulder and squeezing her. "What's goin' on?"

She held up a clipboard. "I'm looking for volunteers to plan our next mixer." Her pale blue eyes dug into mine. "You know you want in."

I scratched the back of my head. "I can't make that one."

She ran her hand up my arm and leaned toward me, laughing as if I'd said something funny. "You're so silly, Jason! You don't even know when it is."

I pulled away as Antoine took her clipboard and diverted her attention from me. He'd been the best anti-wing man.

"I think what Jason meant to say is that he sucks at party planning. But you know who doesn't suck? Antoine."

Misty ignored him but grabbed her clipboard back. "Jason, I thought we could plan it togeth—"

Paul raised his voice above the conversations in the room. "Wait a minute, everyone, it looks like we may have to reschedule bowling." He held his hand up for attention, but his eyes were on his phone. "Did everyone see the latest projections for Tropical Storm Oscar?"

Antoine pulled out his phone and got to the local WWL weather app before I could. "Shoot. Looks like I'll be evacuating tomorrow."

"Really?" I scrolled through the latest updates. Great. Meteorologists were expecting it to take a jog east overnight, and if it did, it would hit our area a couple of days before I was planning to leave for Florida.

"Let's close our meeting with a prayer for the safety of lives in the upcoming storm." Paul herded us to the middle of the room, and after a quick prayer, the meeting dispersed and people started to leave.

When the room was almost empty, I went up to Misty and pulled her to the side. "We need to talk."

She smiled slyly and walked off to the back of the room. "I knew you'd come around. Would you use your big, strong muscles to bring the coffee urn to the sink?"

I sighed, hefted the urn, and followed her into the kitchenette off the meeting space. I set it on the counter. "Misty, I was serious about what I texted last week. I don't want you to contact me in any way except about this group."

"Oh, okay." She giggled and pulled her phone from her pocket and started texting.

"I'm serious. Are you even listening to me?" My phone buzzed, and I pulled it out. She'd texted me:

> Meet me in my car thirty minutes before next week's meeting. The seats go all the way down

"Damnit, Misty, this isn't a joke. This"—I waved my finger between us—"is never gonna happen. I don't want anything to do with you."

"Well, I've been masturbating to your Instagram photos all week, and I want the real thing." She reached for my belt, but I grabbed her hand and pushed it away.

"Don't touch me! And don't contact me ever again." I pushed past her and stormed out of the kitchenette into the empty meeting room.

On the drive home, all I could see was red. Red and her disrespectful smile after I'd pushed her off. Before I even processed where I was, I was parking in my lot. I cut off the engine and sat there for a minute with my eyes closed. I pulled out the paper with all the group session dates from my pocket and checked tonight's off. Four more.

No, no more. As long as she was going to be there, I wasn't. But wait...we had to build that wheelchair ramp for Mrs. Gerstner. I folded the paper, stuck it back in my pocket, and got out of the car. I'd get Antoine to text me her address so I could build it on my own.

I walked in from the lot. Mom was going to add this to her litany of things I was doing wrong with my life. I didn't even want to tell her why I wasn't going back to the meetings since she always thought I was exaggerating about Misty's behavior.

Halfway to the church, I noticed all of Rose's lights were on. I changed my direction toward the kitchen door of the rectory. Coming home had been so much more comforting since she'd been here.

I knocked before unlocking the door. Rose sat with her knees under her chin at the table with a carton of ice cream and a spoon in her mouth.

"Hey." She wiped a tear from her face and went back in for another spoonful.

That single tear on her face diverted all my attention. "Hey. Are you alright?" She had a full face of makeup and a low-cut halter top, and her hair, although mussed, was straightened. She looked beautiful, but I missed the curls.

She shrugged. "Rough night. How was your meeting?"

I huffed a laugh. I was pretty sure I could guess what Rose would think about the church group *and* Misty. "Honestly? Pretty rough, too."

She waved her spoon in the air. "You're welcome to pull up a spoon and a chair. It's chocolate chocolate chip."

"Three magic words." I grabbed a spoon and sat beside her, oddly relieved just to be in her presence. "Wanna talk about it?"

"I..." she paused dramatically and waved her spoon for effect. "Got dumped."

"What? No way." Who would dump this amazing woman? "I'm sorry." I dug my spoon into the carton right after her.

"Yep. Isaac was cheating on me."

"Seriously?" Now I was mad all over again. "What an asshole!"

"Right? Thank God I got a clean bill of health at my gyno check-up after I last saw him. I mean, I made him wear condoms, but I—why are men?"

I shook my head. "You didn't deserve that. How long were y'all together?"

"Three months, but really only the first month, before he went on tour. He's the singer for the Public Droids. They're a kinda shitty punk band." Her eyes met mine as she dug in the carton again. "Why was your night so bad?"

"Um..." If I told her, Rose would be so angry on my behalf. I didn't want to make her night any worse, and I didn't want to talk about it anyway. "It's not a big deal. Your night was definitely worse than mine."

She shrugged it off. "It's okay. It was only about sex anyway. I have what you call—" she held up finger quotes—"daddy issues. But I spent the evening with Steely Dan, and now I'm having ice cream. So, it's totally fine."

"Well, that's...a lot to unpack. Big Steely Dan fan?" I shoveled a heaping spoonful into my mouth.

"*Big* fan. Steely Dan's my favorite vibrator."

I choked on my ice cream, managing to swallow it down before a coughing fit.

She laughed and patted my back while I recovered. "I'm sorry. Is that TMI?"

"Nope." I laughed nervously and risked a glance at her. She was looking down into the ice cream carton, digging with her spoon. Maybe it was the perfect quarter-curves of her breasts above that halter top, maybe it was all those months of celibacy, maybe it was her cavalier mention of Steely Dan. But an image of Rose lying naked across my bed popped into my mind. Her curls were spread out, and a vibrator was between her thighs. And it was glorious.

My face heated up as I changed the subject. "Dare I ask what you mean about daddy issues?"

"Oh, you know. The old story. Guy meets girl. Guy marries girl. Guy decides he wants a divorce while girl's seven months into their second pregnancy." She pointed at herself. "That's me. I'm that second baby.

I grew up understanding that relationships don't last. So, I keep it all about sex so I don't get hurt."

"That's not fair. Why do people always say a woman has daddy issues, as if it's her fault that her dad left and caused the family trauma?"

She stopped with her spoon halfway to her mouth and looked at me for a moment. "Huh." Spoon back into motion. "Feminism is a good look on you." She smiled around a mouthful of ice cream.

"You deserve so much better. I mean first with the dig about you not looking good in pictures—which I know to be a lie, because I've been editing video with you in it all week. And now this."

She didn't meet my eyes. "I don't know what I even saw in him. He kept harping on me to lose weight. He traveled all the time. Literally all I asked was for him to be exclusive, and he couldn't even handle that."

"Wait, wait. Back up. He was harping on you to lose weight? What a dick."

"To be fair..." Her luscious mouth closed around a spoonful of ice cream. She swallowed it down and licked the spoon clean.

Felt that one in my groin.

"To be fair," she continued, "I've gained some weight in the past few years. More than I'm comfortable with."

"There's no 'to be fair' about that. You know you're beautiful, right?" The words fell out of my mouth before I could reel them back down my throat.

Her almost-purple eyes snapped up to me as her face pinkened, and she looked away. "I know," she said softly.

"I hope I didn't make you uncomfortable. I just don't understand how he could be such a jerk."

"Well. I'm not surprised, really." She dug vehemently into the carton. "All men do is leave."

I cocked my head. "That's not exactly fair, either. My ex left me. Well, technically she cheated on me, and I left her. So, she really left me first."

Her face clouded over. "I'm sorry. Did that have anything to do with your bad night?"

"No. Kinda. When I met Kasey, I thought she was the one, you know? I didn't see her red flags for what they were until I was a thousand miles away from home. But she was emotionally abusive. She didn't respect my faith or my family's. She pointed out all their weaknesses, and I'm ashamed to say I loved her so much—or maybe I loved the idea of being in love—that she pulled me into her way of thinking. Talked me into moving far away from my family, effectively separating me from my whole support system, all my friends.

"I was with her for almost three years. And I was miserable. I gained, like, forty pounds, was depressed all the time. I thought she might've been cheating on me, but I didn't confront her. She never wanted to talk about marrying me, but she came home one day with an engagement ring from the doctor she'd been cheating on me with while I'd put my life on hold to support her through med school."

"*Acch*." Her hand landed on mine. "Jason, I'm so sorry. I had no idea."

"Thanks. So after taking every STD test known to man—"

"Because you gotta."

I nodded. "Because you gotta. And thank God they were all negative. I came back home. My family took me back in. But my mom's still not over it, not even almost two years later. The meeting I was at tonight..." I pulled the SALT agenda from my pocket and dropped it on the table. "My volunteering group got folded into this awful singles' group. I'm not getting anything out of it, and...I'm not going back."

She removed her hand and went back for more ice cream. "Was it as excruciating as it sounds?"

I pushed the sheet toward her. "You tell me. Here's the outline for the sessions."

She opened it up. "SALT—Single Adults Living Truth. Oh wait. The acronym's doing double duty. 'Say your prayers.' Okay, I can get behind daily prayer. I do that. 'Abstinence is God's way.'" She stopped reading and looked up at me, her lip curled. "Of course, all this is fine if that's your thing, but it's definitely not mine." She went back to it. "'Lust is a sin. Purify yourself in God's name. Sex is to be shared only between two people married in the church.'" She broke off reading and looked up at me. "Jesus, is Roosevelt still president?"

"Right? For the record, those aren't my opinions."

"Mine either." Her eyes returned to the paper. "'And masturbation is an abomination'?" She raised her brows. "Oh shit, seriously?"

I rolled my eyes. "Yeah, that was pretty much the whole first meeting."

She snorted. "But that's not gonna stop you, right?"

I huffed a laugh, looking away and back. Oh—she was really waiting for a response.

She closed her eyes and put her head down. "Oh my God, did I just ask you if you masturbate? You *don't* have to answer that. I know I overshared myself, but..."

I chuckled. "I'm...trying to abstain for the duration of the class."

Her head popped back up. "Wait. With other people, or yourself?"

"With myself. I haven't been with anyone since Kasey."

She laughed uproariously, then looked at me not laughing along. "Oh shit you're serious. But why, though?"

I shrugged, digging out another spoonful. "Not because I think it's an abomination. They talked about other benefits, like having space to focus on self-improvement, improved mood, better focus—"

"Unless you're someone with a high sex drive, then it might make your focus and mood worse," she said, carefully spooning up a ridge inside the top of the carton.

"Huh." That would explain a lot, actually.

"There are so many health benefits to orgasms. Putting the A in abstinence is in direct conflict with T." She picked up the paper again. "'Take care of yourself.' The oxytocin and endorphins released during sex help battle depression. And did you know that a study found that men who have more orgasms when they're younger are better protected against prostate cancer when they're older?"

"Really?"

"That one needs more research, but masturbation has been associated with improved sleep and mood. Not to mention stress relief. And you're still determined?"

"I mean I'm already celibate. In for an inch, in for a mile, right? I only have four weeks left, anyway."

"Well, I don't have to get it to respect it. But thanks for coming to visit. I was just sitting here stewing before you got here." She finished off the ice cream on her spoon, but it dripped down her hand. She ran her tongue up her finger and sucked the tip of it with a smack and a satisfied sigh.

I let out a held breath and averted my gaze, rubbing my beard like I hadn't just been staring at her like a starving man.

"Welp, the ice cream's all gone, and I'm exhausted. I'm gonna go wash all this crap off my face and go to sleep." She stood up and turned toward the trash can with the carton. The two perfect curves of her ass stuck out below the torn hems of her Daisy Dukes.

Jesus Christ, she was making my abstinence ten times harder. As she washed her hands, I closed my eyes and wracked my blood-deprived brain. What did I want to talk to her about?

Oh right—the storm.

"Have you been watching the latest track for Tropical Storm Oscar?"

"Shit. No. What's it doing?"

"Yeah. Welcome home." I opened up my weather app. "We probably ought to be a little worried about it. If it jogs any more east, we could be hit pretty hard. I was planning to leave for Florida on Thursday, but I'm gonna watch the news overnight and reevaluate in the morning. I might have to leave early, and you might want to evacuate."

"Has the church flooded before?"

"No, but the electricity could be out for a few weeks, and I wouldn't want to stay around for that."

"Hmmm." She pushed her chair in and leaned forward. I kept my gaze on her eyes, but my peripheral vision was deep in her cleavage.

"Why don't you use your magical celibate bits to ask God to send this storm somewhere else?"

"Bits?" I balked while she cackled. "They're not 'bits,' thank you very much. What's the opposite of a bit?" I scrounged around in my brain. "Lots. They're *lots*."

She nodded with her eyes closed. "Yeah. Sure. Okay. Goodnight, Jason."

"Night!" I called after her. "Hey, mind if I take a shower when you're done?" A cold one.

She popped her head back in. "Nope. I'll text you when I'm out."

"Sorry I never thought about having to walk through your bedroom at night. I have content lined up for a few weeks now and I just knocked out a custom, so I'll make that bathroom in the church my priority starting tomorrow."

She smiled. "I don't mind. It makes me feel less alone." She walked off humming down the hallway, completely unaware that she'd turned my whole evening around.

Chapter 6

Looking for a Sign

Jason

MY ALARM PLUCKED ME out of an apocalyptic dream about a super-market run by alien overlords. I fumbled for the noise, my brain still in the frozen food aisle of renegades until my phone hit the floor.

I grabbed it from under the bed and tapped the screen. What were all these missed calls and texts?

The storm.

I sat up and sorted through all the notifications. The storm made that significant jog to the east overnight and strengthened into a strong category one hurricane, projected to make landfall on the Louisiana coast as a category three tomorrow morning with huge storm surges expected.

Alex already left with his girlfriend. Mom and Dad evacuated this morning with Becca and Brad to Arkansas, so Mom said I could still use the Florida condo for my trip.

Shit. A few hours ago would've been the ideal time to evacuate. I threw on a shirt and sandals. Now that I had a renter, what did I do about evacuating? Some of my big trees were ticking time bomb water oaks that I hadn't taken down yet. The kind that tipped over, roots and all, in a bad storm. I didn't have my solar powered generator installed yet. No way would I get stuck here without air conditioning, not with the one-hundred-eighteen-degree heat indexes we'd been having.

I headed toward the rectory. Last night when I walked out of the bathroom, Rose was already asleep over the covers, her body wrapped around a long pillow. I'd watched her for the few seconds it took to pull the bathroom door closed quietly, making sure I didn't disturb her. Her sleep shorts exposed her whole leg, the slant of the bathroom light illuminating a butterfly tattoo on her ankle I hadn't seen before, and the ceiling fan gently ruffled her hair in the dark. And that jerk in New York City not only dumped her, but cheated on her. How could he do that to a literal angel? I both wanted to punch him and shield her from anyone ever hurting her again.

If she were my girlfriend, I'd treat her like the goddess she was. We'd spent a lot of time together this week, and the more I got to know her, the more I desired her. She wasn't just sexy and beautiful; she was smart and fun. She made magic with silky fabrics, and she even showed promise as a woodworker. When I laid down every night after spending time with her, my cheeks hurt from all the laughter.

And my body ached from wanting her. After last night, though—I rubbed my whole face. Knowing she was single was a brand-new kind of torture. Unless she was just a shameless flirt, she was attracted to me, too. But our outlooks on love hadn't changed. I was looking for my forever, and her last relationship was only about sex. If that was all she wanted, then pursuing her was a bad idea on so many levels.

So why did she feel like home?

I stopped and knelt before the statue of St. Dorothy in the courtyard. Patron saint of florists, brides, and newlyweds. *St. Dorothy*, I prayed silently, *I don't know what I'm doing here. I really, really like Rose. She's an amazing person. I don't expect anything from her, and her friendship means the world to me. She just broke up with her boyfriend, and I'm not a vulture. She's probably not even interested. But...* I studied St. Dorothy's face, serenely smiling at me, as if encouraging me to go on. *She just feels so right. I'm having a hard time letting it go, even though I probably should. Would you give me a sign if seeing if she's interested is a good idea, for both of us? Seriously, any sign. And please keep us and our families safe in the hurricane. Amen.*

I brushed off my knees and went in the kitchen door. Music played from down the hallway.

"Morning, Rose!"

"Morning!" she called back.

"Can I come talk to you?"

"Sure!"

I found her in her workroom, cutting out fabric on her new worktable. My heart backflipped seeing her so happily using something we made together. How fun would it be to make more with her?

"Have I told you lately that I love this table?" she asked, her silver scissors slicing through silky white fabric. Her curls defied last night's straightening, poking out from another bun wrapped on top of her head.

"I'm glad!" I leaned against the wall to watch her work. She'd been the only bright spot in a week full of aggravations, like running into that costly pipe-routing problem in the choir loft bathroom construction and worrying about whether Big Dick Tools would officially offer. The plans for my community room had consumed me this week, too. I tried to make progress designing it on Wednesday, but all I got for my trouble was dozens of discarded attempts littering the floor that I couldn't bring myself to throw away.

I'd gone straight to talk to Rose about it and found her cooking red beans because she remembered me saying I'd been craving them. And she reassured me that I'd not only figure out the community room puzzle, but I'd knock it out of the park. Later that day she popped up in my bathroom construction and went nuts over my tile selections and smooth sheetrock, making me feel like the god of reno.

Such simple things, but they were things I'd been starved for.

"Have you seen the weather?" I asked. "Hurricane Oscar's coming for us. Are you evacuating?"

She glanced up from her work. "No, I don't like evacuating. My family called in the middle of the night to ask me to go with them, but I don't want to go anywhere."

"I really think we should go this morning." I stepped away from the doorframe. When did she and I become *we* in my head? "That thing's gonna be a direct hit over the New Orleans area, and I've got all these big trees—"

She sighed heavily, looking around at piles of fabric as she grabbed her pin cushion. "You can go, but I'm gonna stay. I have so much to do, and I can't afford to lose any more time."

"You can't get any sewing done if we lose power, right?"

"Fair point, but I'll get more done than if I leave, for sure. I'll be fine, really. I don't have a car anyway, so I'm kinda stuck here."

"Come with me," I blurted. "I'm already going to Florida, and I have room in my car."

"Oh my God, no! I've already used up all my favors with you, remember? And most of these turn out to be nothing. When I lived with Heather, she used to talk us into evacuating for every little storm. We'd drive to Baton Rouge or someplace for the weekend, and I'd spend the next week playing catch-up." She carried the fabric to her sewing machine.

"But what if a tree comes down on your apartment? What if the power goes out for weeks, and nobody can get in or out because of flooding?"

The hum of her sewing machine continued. "I'll be fine."

Why hadn't I watched her sew before? It was mesmerizing watching the needle go up and down, a neat seam outputting from the back of the machine. "Rose, please come with me? I don't want you to be alone if something happens."

Her fingers poised over a folded hem. She shifted her leg off the foot pedal, and the machine stopped. "To Florida? I don't want to impose on your vacation."

"It's not a vacation. I have a business meeting on Friday not far from my parents' condo. There's plenty of room."

"Won't it take forever to get there? The interstates are probably all backed up, even with contraflow."

I wasn't looking forward to driving on interstates that had all been converted to all outflowing traffic. But deep in my gut I knew it was the right call. "Yeah, it might take a long time, but I really think you should come with me. This storm could be bad."

She looked around and sighed, defeated. "Okay. I guess you're right."

"And I'd feel better if we moved all your dresses you're working on into the church. I'm gonna go throw some things in a bag. Pack up. We're leaving in thirty minutes."

I gave her fifty minutes, mostly because it took me longer than I expected. I had to pick up everything loose outside that could be a flying hazard in high winds, and then transfer Rose's garment rack, fabrics, and supplies into the church. The whole time I picked up, humid wind fluttered the trees in an unmistakable pattern that only natives to hurricane weather could discern on a gut level.

In the kitchen, I threw road snacks into an oversized bag, and then I sought Rose out in her workroom again. This time she was packing up. "You ready?"

"Almost. I packed a bag for me, but I wanted to bring some things to work on. I still need to use the bathroom and grab my iPad." She zipped up the duffle of sewing supplies, and I took it from her.

"Okay, go ahead. I'll grab your bag and put it in the car. Where is it?"

"It's on the floor in the bedroom. The purple one."

"Alright. Lock up the kitchen door for me on your way out, okay?"

"Will do!"

I spotted her purple bag on the floor, added it to my shoulder, and went to the car to wait.

And wait.

"Come on, Rose," I muttered, flipping through the photos on my phone. Thankfully I was ahead of schedule with my social media posts, so leaving town early wouldn't mean a lag. And I had photos from Becca's party, Rose's table, and a bathroom cabinet I was building. I could turn those into posts, too, if we had to stay away past Friday.

I swiped back further—Rose's camp Polaroid and bucket list, the only things I'd taken photos of from the capsule before reburying it. I meant to text them to her. Surely she'd want them, even though she rushed out that night without seeming to care and without even looking at the second half of her list. But instead, I'd printed her list out on paper and used it as inspiration to start my own.

Even though I'd started learning how to take care of myself, seeing Rose's list made me realize that the pain of losing my future with Kasey had made me stop looking too far ahead. Instead, I'd had my head down, working hard. But it was time I made a conscious effort to make sure I got what I wanted out of my one life.

I pulled the printout from my wallet. She said she'd grown out her bangs and been to NYC, but that meant she hadn't made it to Paris, had never waltzed with a cute guy. I smirked at "make J.S. fall in love with me." I was thinking about her all the time, but love? I still wasn't sure that was a good idea.

From the second half of her list, she'd definitely gotten a tattoo, in fact, several sexy ones. She'd probably learned to drive, and she was already a wedding dress designer. But had she kissed under mistletoe? Had she ever seen a waterfall?

Rose stepped out of the kitchen door and locked it, and I folded the list back up and tucked it away in my wallet. She slid into the passenger's seat with a backpack and a pillow, wafting in that sweet smell of roses and casting a worried gaze to the sky.

"Are we going to make it? It looks like some rain bands are already moving in."

I grimaced. "Yeah, they're saying on the news we have time if we head east, and if we leave...this morning. We're a little behind on that, but I think we'll be okay." I pointed at the pillow. "You know we have pillows at the condo."

"I go nowhere without Princess Sleeparella." She gave the pillow a squeeze before stowing it in the back.

"Princess Sleeparella?"

"Best pillow ever. I have a hard time sleeping without it." She fastened her seatbelt and rearranged her bag by her feet. "Sorry it took me a minute. I couldn't find my tablet, but it was in my backpack the whole time. Here, I grabbed us each a bottle of water." She picked up the end of my phone charging cable as I took the bottle and murmured, *thanks*. "Can I plug my phone in? I've only got ten percent."

"Yeah, sure. Oh and here." I grabbed a Deck Daddy shirt from the dashboard. "This is your prize from the epic Nerf gun battle. It's new, so I washed all the chemicals out for you."

She took it from me and opened it up. "Thank you! Yesss. This is the one I wanted." She hugged it and sniffed it. "It even smells like you." She sniffed it a second time.

Something warm filled my chest at her knowing what I smelled like. And liking it enough to go in for another whiff.

She folded the shirt into her lap and fished a prescription bottle from her purse. "Listen. This is a little embarrassing, but if we're sharing a condo..." She bit her lip and met my gaze. "You should know I sometimes have anxiety attacks." She shook the bottle, and the pills inside rattled. "And panic attacks. And I don't always think about taking my medicine when I get that way. So if that happens, would you help me remember?"

I nodded. "Of course."

"Thanks," she murmured, putting them away.

"Hey, your table video is scheduled to post today, so hopefully that'll bring you some new followers. I posted a teaser reel this morning."

"Oh crap, am I in it?" She opened her phone as I started out on the road.

"No, it's just video of Strawberry Jello, blueprints, woodpile—that kind of thing."

She shook her head, scrolling. "Every time I visit your page, I wonder how your super religious mom feels about Deck Daddy."

I glanced back at her. How many times does Rose visit my page?

"My mom…has a love/hate relationship with it. She's been one of my biggest customers, but she hates the Deck Daddy shtick. At least I only hear about it once a week when she catches up on my posts, or when somebody new at church brings it up. She *really* hates that."

Her shoulders slumped. "I'm sorry. That's so unfair. You're building something amazing here. Look at all the engagement you get. And yeah, a lot of them are just thirsty, but even more are praising your work or thanking you for your help. Listen to this one. 'Dude you rock. Thanks for the plans for this table. It's the first thing I made on my own and my wife thinks I'm a god now.' And this: 'Thanks Deck Daddy! Your advice on drying up sap with nail polish remover was a godsend—it's been a month, and no more ooze. Hot, talented, and brilliant' with a hot face emoji. Okay, that one was both." She laughed. "But don't let anyone throw shade on what you're doing." Her hand landed warm on my arm. "I hope you're really proud of yourself."

Her praise warmed my heart, and her touch heated my face. "Thank you." I smiled at her and slipped my sunglasses down over my eyes, which were tearing up. Damn, it felt good for someone in my life to be proud of me, no mockery even in her laughter. Rose was always in on the joke, never making me feel cheap or dumb or embarrassed.

She squeezed my arm once before slipping her hand away. "Of course. Does the rest of your family give you trouble too?"

I huffed. "Dad wants to know when I'm getting a real job to use the degree he paid for. Becca and Alex make fun of me every chance they get, and Mark thinks it's just a phase."

"Seriously? Girl, if you get paid for doing the thing you love, that doesn't make it less of a real job. Why would they act that way?"

I shrugged and shook my head. Her outrage on my behalf was refreshing—supportive without insulting my family.

"Okay, well what about your friends? They support you, right?"

I sighed heavily, using my mirrors to safely wedge my way into the stop-and-go interstate. "I haven't reconnected with most of my friends, post-Kasey. I was a real ass. Just dropped everybody because they all told me she was bad for me." Another sin confessed.

"It sucks that things happened that way. I can relate, a little. I've been kinda avoiding my friends since I got back." She didn't elaborate, but I wanted her to. "Well, *I* think your work is amazing. And I don't just mean your work as in the things you build, but your whole business."

She slipped her phone between the seat and her bare thigh—wearing those damn short shorts again—and dug through her purse. She picked out a bottle of lotion, squeezing some on her hands and elbows and filling the whole car with her rosy scent.

I breathed it deeply in, comforted that she came with me. It normally took over four hours to reach my parents' condo, but today it might take twice as long. We were one car in a massive school of fish trained to swim in neat, three-lane formation, stretching out for miles.

What would Rose think about my sponsorship offer? After Mom's scorn, I hadn't told anyone else about it, but...

I swallowed hard and took the plunge, my heart racing. "So...the reason I'm going to Florida is to meet with a major tool company. They want to talk to me about a sponsorship and maybe appearing in their ads."

"Wait, what?" She turned to me fully, putting both hands on my arm. The excitement in her voice made me laugh. "When did this happen?"

I pulled to a stop in the stand-still traffic. "A few minutes before I found a shady woman digging in my garden."

"Oh my God! Congratulations!" she squealed, throwing her arms around my neck in a quick hug.

"I mean, I don't have it yet. I have to go talk to them, and they still may not offer."

"Why didn't you tell me before? That's huge! What brand of tools?"

I rubbed my beard, laughing, expecting her to laugh. "Big Dick Tools."

But she didn't laugh. "I fucking love the name." She picked up her phone and tapped away. "We love a big dick. I don't know them, but then my toolset was a dollar store special. Here they are." She scrolled for a bit. "Jason, they look perfect for you! Huge, quality brand with just the right amount of silly." She stopped, put her phone down to her lap, and threw her head back, laughing. "Oh my God, the names they have for their tools is the best thing ever."

I laughed with her. "What is it with you and naming things?"

"I don't know," she wheezed. She looked back at her phone and laughed harder, tears in her eyes. "The Three-Way Screwdriver. Size Matters Tape Measure. Tongue-in-Her-Groove Pliers. This is brilliant." She cackled as she scrolled. "When are you going to meet with them?"

"Friday morning. They're about an hour from the condo."

"And your family's not excited about this?"

"Nah, it's only more material to make fun of me with. But that kinda money will let me finish my house."

She frowned, studying me. "Of course you love your family, and you want them to be proud of you. But you're allowed to make decisions that are right for you that they may not understand or approve of."

Her gentle words echoed what my therapist had always told me. Easy to say, easy to agree with, in theory. Almost impossible for me to do in practice.

She looked back at her phone. "They have a great mission. Responsible sourcing. Excellent reviews. Would *you* be embarrassed to be associated with them?"

Her question hung in the air for a few minutes. "No. I don't think I would."

She smiled softly at me. "Then there you go."

I smiled but kept my eyes on the road. If someone had told me a few weeks ago that I'd have to spend all this time with Rose Guidry from middle school in a car, I'd have been dreading it. But now that I knew her, I loved being with her. Like, a lot.

I risked another glance at her.

Like, so much more than I should.

We started cruising in what hopefully wouldn't be our only pocket of quick-moving traffic. The image of her lying in bed last night kept popping up in my head, her shapely legs bare, her hair mussed from making love to herself. In my shorts, it was dancing at the prom with her all over again. I had to get a hold of myself, or this would be a rough trip.

"I know what might help." She dug in her backpack and pulled out a small velvet bag with a drawstring, and from the bag, a deck of colorful cards.

"Are those tarot cards?" I'd never seen any in person, unless you count the ones behind the counter at the bookstore.

"Goddess oracle cards." She shuffled through them, looking at one at a time. "One of my NYC roommates gave them to me as a going-away gift, and I haven't had a chance to look at them." She shifted toward me again, tucking her bare foot under her other leg. "Can I do a reading for you?"

Mom would about die if she saw those, and her ghost would come back to haunt me if she knew I was engaging with them willingly. "Um...are you going to...tell my future or something?"

"No, I use them for new ways of thinking about things." She shuffled the cards some more, then chose three off the top of the deck, laying them face-down on the dash. "Maybe they can give you some perspective about the sponsorship and your family. I pulled you a *what you want, obstacles, how to overcome* spread." She turned over the first card. "For what you want, I pulled the Egyptian cat goddess, Bast, who represents pleasure." She flipped through a booklet about the size of the cards. "I'm still learning this deck...but what you *want* is...pleasure. All kinds. Daily, simple pleasures, self-care, *sexual* pleasure..."

The way she emphasized the last one wasn't helping my situation. I needed to stop thinking about her like this.

But the card hit home. "That's a little...scary?"

She raised her eyebrows at me. "Because of your celibacy?"

"No, because I've spent the past two years trying to get past all that awfulness with Kasey. Learning to take care of myself again. And I've taken on a kind of mantra. God, I know this is gonna sound so cheesy, especially coming from Deck Daddy."

She looked very seriously at me. "Deck Daddy isn't cheesy. What's your mantra?"

I breathed easier. She was the first person to see it that way. "It's 'follow your bliss.' Because I've never really done that before. I followed my anxiety, I followed my girlfriend—ex-girlfriend. But I never did what made *me* happy until I came back home and re-evaluated. And now..."

She smiled. "And now you're building the life you want."

"Yeah. I'm finally trying to make a happy life for myself."

"I think that's awesome." She turned over the second card. "So let's see what's your obstacle to all that pleasure and bliss. It's Ala, the Ibo goddess of morality and fertility." She grimaced, her eyes teasing. "I didn't think Deck Daddy had any loose morals."

"Not me, of course," I said.

"But I can see how this could relate to Big Dick Tools." She flipped through the booklet, found her page. "So, your obstacles are...making sure you're acting with integrity. Or maybe even struggling with other people's ideas of what your integrity should be, what they see as acceptable, and not feeling like you need to compromise what you believe...while also respecting their opinions."

"Ha!" I barked. "Does that card have my mom's picture on it?"

She looked at the card thoughtfully. "I don't know. Is your mom a stunningly beautiful Nigerian woman sitting on a crescent moon throne with her tits out?"

"Not last I checked." How did she pull a card that summarized exactly what I was struggling with? *St. Dorothy, where are we at on a sign? Is this it? Because I don't get it.*

"Now I want to know what the third card is. What did you say it's for? How to overcome the challenges?" The sun disappeared behind a cloud, and rain sprinkled the windshield, the tiny pinpricks of a hurricane moving in. Thankfully traffic was moving now.

"Yes." She flipped over the card, gathering all three into a stack in her hands. "How to overcome is Hathor, Egyptian goddess of joy. She's usually at the beginning of something new, encouraging you to go for what you've been thinking about. Jason! This is perfect!"

Adrenaline kicked through my system. "Really?" *Okay, St. Dorothy. I hear you.*

Her returning smile was beautiful, her eyes unabashed. "Yeah! Does it resonate with how you feel about the sponsorship? Or is there something else you've been thinking about going after?"

I glanced at her—did her eyes just drop to my mouth? Swallowing hard, I checked my mirrors and switched lanes. "Yeah, I think there is." *At least, since I met you again.*

"Then it looks like you should totally go for it." She stacked the cards back up together and busily flipped through them for a few minutes before putting them away. She yawned and stretched. "Do you mind if I take a nap? I was up late and early."

"No, go ahead." I had plenty to think about to entertain myself. Mom desperately wanted me to be who I was before Kasey, a church-going man who wanted to sit at a desk all day designing houses for other people. Alex and Becca treated me like I was still that person.

But I'd never be that Jason again. I'd been through too much not to come out the other side a little wiser. And I was happy about how I was changing. Why would I want to be the naive idiot who fell in love with my eyes closed, the asshole who valued my cruel girlfriend's opinions over my family's feelings? Or the dumbass who thought that to keep her, I had to lose them. Why would I want to move backwards?

It sucked that I was disappointing my family with who I was becoming.

But Rose wasn't disappointed.

Granted, she hadn't known me as an adult before Kasey, and barely even as kids. But she seemed to respect the journey I took to be who I was now, and she seemed proud of who I was becoming.

She sighed and shifted in her seat, her head lolling toward me with her eyes closed, long lashes on her pale, pink cheeks.

Yeah, I had a lot of things to think about. I smiled, glancing at Rose. And one of them was making my heart skip a beat.

Rose

"Rose, wake up."

Everything was still and quiet. I opened my eyes. "We're there already?"

"I wish. We're still in Mississippi."

The clock on his dash read a quarter after noon. We'd been traveling for three hours. "What? Seriously?"

He nodded. "Biloxi. Traffic was a bitch. I was gonna keep pressing on, but my stomach won out. You like pizza?"

After a bathroom break, I met Jason back at our booth where he was scrolling through his phone. "I got you a Diet Coke. And hey, our video of your sewing table went up." He grinned and handed his phone over to me. "The comments are blowing up. They're obsessed with you."

My stomach dropped. "What?" Thousands of likes. He sent it to me to approve last night before he scheduled it, and the video was super cute. I didn't even look half bad.

I knew better, but I couldn't stop myself. I scrolled down to the comments.

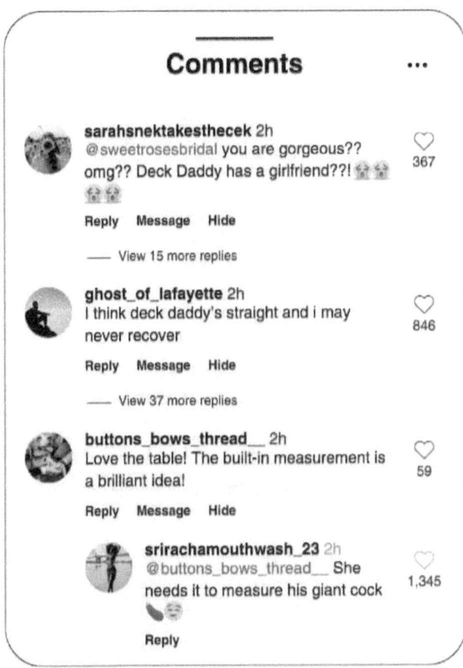

How big, exactly, was Jason's cock? Now I needed to know.

"These comments are unhinged." I raised my eyebrows at him. "Did you read these?"

He shrugged. "I know you don't need me to tell you that the internet's basically lawless and not to read the comments. But keep reading. They're not all unhinged."

I took a deep breath and scrolled down more.

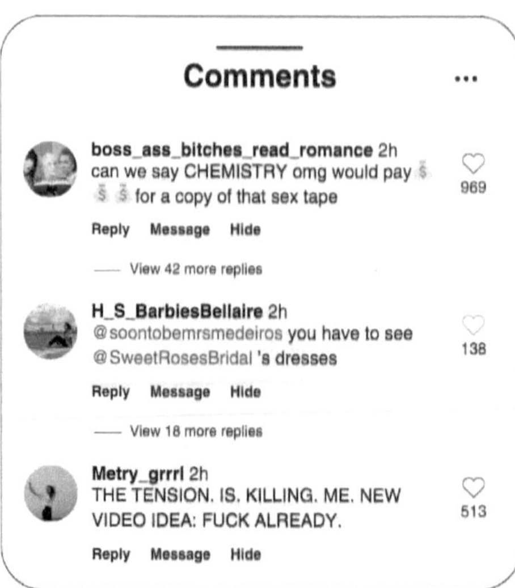

I laughed out loud. This person needed to stop reading my mind.

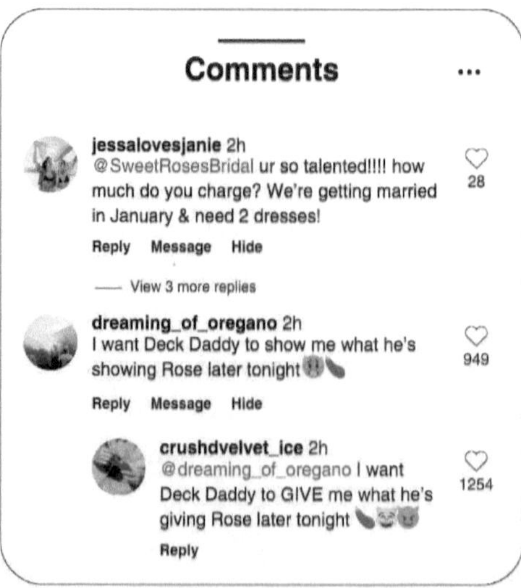

My cheeks stung with heat, and I squirmed a little in my seat. "Some potential customers," I murmured. "But Jason, all these people totally think we're doing it. There's more eggplants in the comments than in the produce section at Winn Dixie." I handed his phone back and picked up mine.

His face was all contrition. "I'm sorry. I never meant for it to—"

The server came back, and the whole time they took our order, Jason shifted in his seat, tearing off little pieces of his napkin.

"I'm really sorry, Rose," he said when she walked away, his brow furrowed over his big brown eyes. "I should've expected that, but I didn't." He picked up his phone. "I'll shut the rumors down."

"That's okay. You don't have to make a statement or anything. I'm not offended that they think we're together, and it's not like I'm surprised by internet comments." I tapped over to my notifications. "Wow, I have a lot of new followers. *Maybe* you were right, that it helps when you show your face online."

"Are you sure? I can say something. I don't want you to be uncomfortable."

I patted his hand. "Yeah, it's okay. I'm not uncomfortable. It's flattering that they think I could land a guy like you. You're sweet to care." Very unlike any other guy I'd dated.

Wait. I wasn't dating Jason.

A soft smile lit his face. "Okay, Sweet Rose. If you're sure." He popped his straw into his drink. Flattening the straw wrapper, he wound it around his finger and hummed to himself.

He was dishy, though. Nice hands, too. And now, thanks to the comments, I imagined them holding his big cock up to measure on my table.

I fanned myself and put my hair up again. "It's so hot in here. I can't believe what a great mood you're in after all that driving. If you want, I can take a turn. I'm a safe driver, I promise."

"Nah, that's okay. I'll be fine after I get something to eat. Maybe some caffeine."

We were both quiet for a moment, and I flashed back to prom night when we hadn't had much to talk about. I took another sip of my drink, scrolled through my new followers. "Oh, that's weird. Misty followed me."

He rolled his eyes. "Jesus, she's probably jealous about the video."

"Probably. She seems aggressive."

"You have no idea." He took a sip and set his drink back down. "You know, while you were sleeping, I was thinking about what you said a few days ago."

My heart sped up. "Oh God, what did I say?"

He glanced around before leaning in. "About sexual compatibility," he said quietly.

And held my eyes while he said it. Instant lady boner.

"It was refreshing to hear you say that, because for the past few months, all I keep hearing about is how awful sex and sexuality are. You shouldn't take care of it for yourself." He pointed his hands at his chest. "If you're working out and taking your shirt off on social media, you must be down to fuck anything that moves. And God forbid you do it before you're married. But all of that is such bullshit. Sex is just another way to connect with and be vulnerable with someone you love, isn't it? And I think you should fall in love *before* you're married. Why not express it then, too?"

His brown eyes were dangerously earnest, looking at me. He was downright adorable. Who knew Deck Daddy had such an emotional side?

"That's sort of what my mom says. And it depends on what you want out of life. If sexuality is important to your happiness—and it may not be. Asexuality is completely valid, obviously. But if it *is* important to you, she says a sexual connection with the person you love is important to express." I laughed nervously. "But not everyone grows up with parents who encourage that sort of thing. Not that she encouraged us to sleep around! God, I'm just digging myself deeper, aren't I?"

"No, I think you're really lucky to have had her influence. I grew up in such a repressed household. We couldn't talk about relationships at all, much less sex. You know what I don't get? My parents were fine with us watching action movies with people getting shot up, or stabbed, or whatever, but good God forbid there was a loving couple having sex. They even skipped ahead through fade-to-black scenes."

"Girl. Come on up." I patted the table. "There's room on my soap-box for you. Tell me why you can watch superheroes breaking all kinds of necks in movies but have one person kissin' a boob and suddenly it's porn."

"Exactly! I don't understand why our society treats something so natural as so dirty. Even with Kasey, I had no idea what I wanted, and no idea how to ask for it."

"So I guess what you're saying is that y'all weren't compatible. *Sexually*," I added, leaning in and whispering it as a couple with little kids were seated at a nearby table.

"No," he grimaced. "Not at all. She was kind of touch-averse, even before she started cheating on me. Which was hard for me, because I thrive on physical affection. Like, holding hands, hugging, touching. I'm sure that sounds like such a guy thing—"

I put my hand on his forearm and squeezed. His muscles tensed beneath my hand, and I flushed, imagined them flexing as he dipped his fingers into my—nope. "It's okay to enjoy physical affection, no matter who you are."

He looked quickly from my hand on his to my eyes. "Thank you," he said softly.

Gosh, his lips were beautiful. I cleared my throat and removed my hand. "Carry on."

"And Kasey didn't...she didn't like..." He looked around at the people in booths around us and lowered his voice. "She really hated when I kissed her..." he motioned around his chest.

I suppressed a shiver. It wasn't okay to imagine his mouth on my breast, especially since he was talking about another woman. I shrugged. "To each their own, but yeah, I don't get that, because I love it." My face shot through with heat, and I crossed my arms over my chest.

He laughed, coughing and choking a little on his drink. "Much less do the other thing I liked to do that she didn't. Of course, I respected all of it, but goddamn the temptation. It was hard to live with." He stretched his back, face reddening. "That sounds so selfish and completely shallow, I know, but it was just..." he trailed off, searching for a word.

"Another indicator that things between you were off."

"Yes!" he said emphatically. "Exactly."

I desperately wanted to ask what that other thing was, and it was a real testament to my personal growth re: not blurting things out that I didn't.

Just kidding.

"What's the other thing?" I asked eagerly, propping my cheek on my fist and my elbow on the table as I sipped from my straw.

He threw his head back laughing, and his face went bright red. Heads all over the restaurant swiveled toward him. He covered his mouth with his hand, eyes twinkling. "I knew after it came out of my mouth, you were gonna ask."

"You're laughing but not answering." That set him off more. I loved his laugh. I got the sense that it was disused, that he hadn't laughed this hard in a while. "What came out of your mouth, Jason? Or went into it? You're really not gonna tell me?" I shook my head. "Such a tease."

He leaned forward. "I'm trying to think of a euphemism that's PG-rated."

I leaned in, speaking quietly. "Is it thirty-four plus thirty-five?"

He frowned then chuckled, clearly having done the math. Placing his elbows on the table, he leaned in, eyes twinkling as he held my gaze. "Half."

"Ahh, she wouldn't play the pink oboe, huh?"

He cackled, shaking his head and licking his lips. But he held my gaze with those eyes. "The other half."

"Oh!" I couldn't keep the surprise out of my voice. "You like giving Australian kisses." Hell, yeah. Now I couldn't keep my eyes off his sexy mouth.

He blinked. "What?"

"You know, it's like a French kiss...but it's..." He continued to stare at me. How was he not getting this? "It's down under."

The server chose that moment to place our pizza on the table, and we giggled like guilty teenagers and murmured our thanks.

He waited for me to grab a piece before digging in himself. "But back to Misty. I'm actually repulsed by her. I'm sorry. That's so mean. But—she's pretty, I guess, if you like fake flowers. It's just that her character is so ugly. I don't even *want* to get close enough to see if we're compatible. My Mom doesn't understand why I don't want to go out with her. Alex thinks I should take what I can get from her. But sex is...it's an emotional thing for me. Not that I haven't done it casually before. But for me, there's no substitute for that kind of connection. It's so, so beautiful with someone you love. You didn't have that kind of connection with Isaac?" he asked softly.

My cheeks burned. It was one thing to talk about sex in the general way, and quite another to talk about my own sex life. "I mean I wouldn't have dated him if the *horizontal refreshment* wasn't good." I stuffed another big bite in my mouth to chew on my response to him. I thought I'd felt that way once, with Michael. But finding out it wasn't mutual had tainted every good memory with him.

"No, we didn't have that connection," I finally said. "It's hard for me to be that vulnerable. Emotionally. With Isaac—with almost any guy I've dated."

He glanced up from shaking parmesan onto his next slice. "Why's that?"

"Probably something to do with being raised by a single mom. Being told practically since I was born to guard my heart." I'd never told any guy I'd dated about Michael. I never expected them to side with me on how things ended, as if some bro bond would make them see me as less. The way Michael did.

But I didn't get that sense from Jason, and he wasn't interested in dating me. "Also...it didn't help that the first guy I ever dated seriously, straight out of high school, was so mean to me. He was my first time, my first a lot of things. I thought I was in love with him, even though

I never felt close to him. And even though he was amazing at—"
I cut off as the waitress mercifully brought refills of our drinks,
because I was about to overshare re: my breasts. She walked off,
and I soldiered on. "Honestly, sex with him wasn't...satisfying. He
was more experienced, but he still didn't know what he was doing.
He never let me in emotionally, never would commit to being my
boyfriend, not even over the two years we dated."

"That sucks." And he looked into my eyes as he said it, as if he'd
really been listening and really meant it.

"Well, it gets worse. I broke up with him because he hit on Lily."

He stopped with a slice of pizza halfway to his mouth. "What the
fuck. Are you serious?"

I brought my shoulders up in a tiny little shrug. "Yeah."

His slice of pizza held off to the side, forgotten, outrage coating his
features. "What's the matter with him?"

"I mean, I get that Lily's prettier, and smarter, and more charming
than me. Everybody likes her better. I'm used to that. But an intimate
relationship? That's kind of the one type of relationship that was
supposed to put me at the top, above everyone else. You know?"

Jason had watched me silently, concern and outrage all over his
face as I talked. Now his pizza was back on his plate and his hands
were in fists, like he wanted to deck Michael. I wanted to deck him
too.

"What a piece of shit. First off...what a piece of shit. If I ever meet
this guy, and I'm not a violent man, I might punch him in the face."

"You could totally take him."

"Second, that's not the first time I've heard you say that about your
sister, but you're selling yourself short. Yeah, Lily's okay, but you're
objectively the more beautiful sister. Alex and I both think so."

I looked down at my pizza, wholly embarrassed. "You don't have
to build me up, Jason, that's not why I told you this."

"I'm not building you up. I'm being factual."

"You and your brother were *not* comparing Guidry sisters. Don't
give me that shit."

"He had too much to drink at the shower, and he ranked the bridesmaids by hotness. You came out on top." He put a hand to his chest. "I was, of course, too gentlemanly to participate, but I'm entitled to my opinions."

"I do like being on top." I snorted. "Alex is a little shit. Where would *you* place me?" I dared to ask. "Or are you also too much of a gentleman to tell me?"

He smiled and rested his cheek on his fist—ugh, death by dimples. "Exactly where you like to be." He raised his eyebrows once.

I looked away first and laughed. My face flooded with heat, and my panties just plain flooded. Was Deck Daddy...flirting with me?

No, that was ridiculous.

"Yeah. Sure." I rolled my eyes.

"Seriously, though. Are you doing okay?" he asked. "With the break-up?"

I took a deep breath and let it out, avoiding his big, earnest eyes. "Yeah, I'm fine. Like I said, we weren't close. We weren't even friends. It was kind of...a soulless relationship. I'm more upset with myself for getting involved with him in the first place."

He smiled sadly and briefly rested his hand on mine, squeezing and releasing. The short contact zipped electricity up my arm. "You deserve so much better."

"Thank you. So do you."

After we finished eating, I stacked our plates and wiped all the drink condensation and parmesan off to the side. Conversation changing time. "I have something to show you, and I don't want you to make fun of me because I was just having fun when I couldn't sleep last night and I truly don't think it's useful but if it is in any way, yay."

I dug in my purse and half-unfolded two of the community room printouts that I stole from his stack in the middle of the night. "I went in to do laundry, but your discard stack was calling me, and I wanted to look at something other than fabric for a minute." I stopped one unfold away from the reveal.

"And I know I have some nerve showing this to someone so talented, especially when I don't know shit about construction or if anything I sketched is possible. But maybe it'll give you an idea, at least."

He finished wiping pizza grease off his hands and set the napkin on the plates. "Well don't hold back, let me see it. I need all the help I can get."

I took a breath and laid it out on the table then sat up on my knees to show him the sketch that sparked my idea. "I liked your rejects like this one, where you flipped the rectangle sideways to make the house wider than deeper. But it didn't make sense to me to have all the bedrooms on one side when you'd have all this awkward space here." I pointed to a den he'd sketched out with a balcony ringing it.

"That's exactly when I tossed this one."

"Yeah, it would be a nice room, but you'll be entertaining in the church, not the community center, right? This part of the house is meant to be more private for you and your family, right?"

"Yeah, that's what I wanted."

I took that paper away and revealed my piss poor sketch underneath that one. He regarded it very seriously with knitted brows.

"So I kept most of the high ceiling and opened it up to this breakfast area, closer to the kitchen. So now your main stairs are here by this back door, with a mudroom, but I moved the back stairs over here..." I dragged my finger to the back of the structure. "And now you kind of have this gallery area over the middle area to connect your master bedroom to your other bedrooms, to give you some privacy." I couldn't bring myself to say *to give you and your wife some privacy.* "And it allows for the library and the media room you wanted to be separated, separated. And then you get this fun upstairs bonus area, and this fun downstairs bonus area, i.e. spaces I didn't know what to do with."

He met my eyes. When did I get so close to his face?

"Rose?" He grabbed my face and warmly kissed my forehead. "I love your brain."

He released me and picked up the drawing, sitting back in his seat to study it while my third eye's orgasm radiated to every part of my body.

"I never once thought of putting a gallery here, but it's brilliant. And I can fill these bonus spaces because I'd planned on arranging the bedrooms a little differently—plus adding more bathrooms. I love the idea of the master being separated but on the same floor as the other bedrooms."

He stared at me, and I tried to pretend my heart wasn't going a mile a minute by gorging myself on the last piece of cheese bread. "Girl. You just broke my designer's block. Damnit, I wish I hadn't left the blank ones at home, because now I have all these ideas."

Sipping from my drink, I reached into my bag, where I'd stashed a handful of blank copies. I handed them and one of his drafting pencils to him with a smile.

The dimples came out to play. "Has anyone ever told you that you're the freaking best?"

I laughed and scooted out of my seat. "Have fun—I'm gonna hit the potty. I'm good with staying as long as you want to work."

About an hour and a half later, we finally made it into Alabama. Jason put on "Sweet Home Alabama" because he said it was mandatory listening whenever you crossed into the state, but traffic was still thick, and we had a long way to go.

He was singing along and in the driving zone, having captured all his new ideas at the restaurant before we left. But I was all revved up with extra sexual energy after watching him professionally sketch a house layout with those hands in such a small amount of time. And after that forehead kiss? Good lord.

Lenny Kravitz's "Always on the Run" rang out—Mom texting that she and Lily were safely in Texas with her best friend from college.

I texted her back, updating her on my situation, and pulled out my iPad to work on sketches for her wedding dress. She knew she wanted something simple and elegant, but also, in her words, "more princessy than a woman my age is supposed to dress for her second wedding." I'd started on some options for her, but I hadn't had time to work on it for the past week.

Before long, the car faded away from my notice, taking with it all residual, icky thoughts of Michael, the stress of moving and evacuating, and the increasing sexual tension between me and the cunnilingus lover over there. Fuck me, now I was imagining his face between my legs. Great. Now I was aroused and agitated again. Steely Dan was officially on the menu tonight.

We slowed down into a snarl of traffic, and I barely noticed Jason grab his phone. Taylor Swift's "Gorgeous" played from my phone, and I nearly jumped out of my skin.

His shoulders shook with quiet laughter as adrenaline kicked through my system. I fumbled to turn off the ringer, but it was Too. Late. Just like in the song, I could barely look at his smile.

"That's an improvement over 'I'm Too Sexy.' Do you have songs for everybody in your contact list?"

"Fuck you," I muttered, smiling despite my burning cheeks.

He laughed harder. "I'm sorry. I didn't mean to make you stop drawing. I love watching artists draw."

My face was about to catch fire. "Thank you."

"Are you planning a general design, or is that for someone?"

"Um…it's…" I guess I hadn't told him. "It's for my mom." I turned on the layer with the little Mom character I drew.

"Ah, your mom's getting married."

"I probably didn't mention it," I said softly, trying to remove emotion from my voice.

"Do you not like Steve? Or is it about your dad?" He asked gently, checking his mirrors as he changed lanes.

"No, nothing like that. Steve's great, my dad's somewhere in the wind. Who cares? I just wasn't expecting it. From her."

He nodded, jutting his chin out, eyes darting around like he was going to ask a follow-up question.

"I like to draw the person I'm making dresses for," I blurted before he could say anything else. "Then draw revisions of dresses in layers so they can virtually try them on before I sew anything."

"That's cool. You did that for Becca, too?"

"Yeah! I'll show you, if you want."

"Show me later. I can't really look while I'm driving."

A few moments of silence later, he spoke again. "Would it throw you off to play a driving game with me? Keep me alert?"

"Mmmmaybe not. What kind of driving game?"

His face lit up with mischief as he changed lanes again. "Maybe...truth or dare?"

I rolled my eyes. "Seriously?" If he was trying to get me to admit that I wanted to know what his cock tasted like, he'd be disappointed. Because that was a truth I'd never reveal.

"Yeah, why not?"

"How do you play it?" I asked, with a long-suffering intonation.

"You've never played truth or dare?"

"Not really."

"Alright—you can pick it up as we go. You first. Pick one: truth, or dare?"

"I have to come up with a dare?"

"No, you're picking if you're gonna tell a truth or do a dare. And then..." He tossed me a smile. "I'll either ask you an intrusive question or dare you to do something ridiculous."

No way was I picking truth. "Okay, dare."

"Ha-haa!" he crowed. "Okay let me think of a good one." He looked all around the car, at the summer afternoon sunlight filtering through the trees. "I've never played it in a car before. Ooh! I know. Moon the cars in the other lane."

"No way!" I squealed. "I'm *not* mooning *anybody*. Believe me, those days are long over."

He did a double take. "What days? You had mooning days?"

I laughed. "No, I used to be…" How could I say this? "A lot more open to public nudity."

He blinked and shook his head like he was dizzy. "Wow, okay. So since you didn't want to do the dare, you have to tell a truth, or you lose the game."

"Did you give me a dare you knew I wouldn't do, on purpose, to get me to tell you a truth?"

"While strategy is an important part of any game, it's even more important after your public nudity statement."

His dimples should be outlawed. I sighed loudly so he knew how I felt about it. "Okay, but don't forget you're next. What do you want to know?"

"Um, about the public nudity, obviously."

I crossed my arms over my chest. "In college, I made extra money…posing as a nude model for art classes."

He looked at me one too many times. In my brain, I reclined naked on a chaise, and his brown eyes traced the peaks of my breasts, licking his lips as he imagined how it would feel to trace them with his tongue.

I bit my lip and resisted squirming in my seat because he kept looking at me. "Eyes on the road, Deck Daddy."

"So wait. That shy teenager I took to prom, just a few years later, was dropping robe to pose naked in front of a bunch of strangers?" His voice was all honest curiosity, gentle surprise. No judgment.

"Maybe…yeah. It started as foreplay with my boyfriend at the time, who was in the class. And then, after we broke up—well it was decent money for sitting there doing nothing." I put my face in my hands. "You cannot tell a soul. I've never even told Lily."

"I'm speechless."

Because he was imagining me naked, or because he couldn't imagine me naked? My face heated. "It's not much different from what you do."

"I think you'll find my shorts are always on, but yeah. You have a point."

"Okay, smart ass, it's my turn. Truth or dare?"

"Dare!" he said immediately.

"Well shit. I don't have a dare picked out." Not that I had a truth, either. The only thing I wanted to know was if he was experiencing the overwhelming sexual attraction to me that I had for him, but I couldn't very well ask my landlord that.

I wracked my brain, looking around the car. "Damnit, I can't think of anything you can do safely while driving that isn't lame. It's so not fair. We'll have to play another round when we get there. Um...I dare you to...oh, I know! Compose a haiku for me."

He narrowed his eyes. "Compose a haiku? Like right now?"

"Yeah. Compose a haiku about me."

He laughed. "*About* you. Okay. That's clever, I'll give you that. Give me a minute to think."

He sat in silence for a while, tapping out syllables on the steering wheel. I went back to my drawing, trying to ignore his cute little giggles as he worked. "This is hard," he said.

"I believe in you."

He picked up his drink from lunch and slurped the last of it through the straw. He cleared his throat. "Okay, here you go. It's not my finest work, but it'll do. A haiku about Rose: *Beautiful and sweet...*"

I exaggerated an *awwww*.

"*Likes to pose naked for art...*"

I guffawed. "Hey! That's not nice."

He laughed through the last verse. "*Can't beat me at Nerf.*"

We laughed together for a minute, and I sighed at the end. "I have regrets."

"Clever, but weak sauce, Guidry. Weak. Sauce. You're gonna have to up your game if you want to get a truth out of me. My turn. Truth or dare?"

"I'm picking truth because you're just gonna give me some ridiculous dare you know I won't do."

He grinned. "You're probably right. So you're going with Truth?"

"Uh-huh."

"On your bucket list. Am I J.S.?" He glanced at me, his grin too adorable to be allowed.

Heat flooded my face. "I knew that was gonna come back to haunt me." He could already see my whole hand of cards and now he wanted his own personal time machine visit into my middle school brain? I carefully put my iPad away to buy time. The way out of this was labyrinthine, and my mind wasn't up to the task.

He probably only thought of me as Lily's little sister and his one-time classmate, so it probably wouldn't hurt to admit the truth. But I didn't want him to think I was coming on to him, especially this soon after breaking up with Isaac—not that that had even registered on a heartbreak scale. Sure, we were both single, but he wasn't looking for anything physical. And that's all I had to offer.

I guess honesty was perennially the best policy.

"Fine. Yes. I had a big crush on you in middle school. Are you happy now?"

"Yeah, I'm actually very happy right now." He smiled, checking his mirrors as he took the right fork in the interstate. "Like the whole time? Or what?"

Dimples. Outlawed. I stuck my tongue out at him. "From the first day of sixth grade, asshole. Your turn. Truth or dare?"

"I'll take one for the team and go straight for the truth."

"Okay. Did *you* have a crush on *me* in middle school?"

He winced. "Don't be mad, but I didn't."

I turned one of the vents to blow directly on my hot face, shrugging like I wasn't disappointed. "I can't help it if you have shitty taste in women."

"Or maybe next time ask me about *after* middle school."

Oh God, he *was* flirting with me. I smiled and looked away. "If you weren't driving, I'd throw something at you. In fact, from here till the condo, all I'll do is brainstorm items to throw at you later."

His dimples dug in deeper. "Truth or dare?"

"I guess truth again. Why the fuck not?"

"No, I'll throw you a softball. Take the dare."

"Okay, dare."

"Grab me a Coke from the cooler right behind my seat and pour it into my cup."

I snorted, but I reached for the drink and popped the top. "That's even lamer than my dare."

"Are you complaining?"

"No, no! Not complaining. Here." I did as he asked, handed it to him, and thirstily eyed his Adam's apple bob as he drank it. I pulled my goddess cards out again, both to act disinterested and to have something to do with my hands.

"Truth or dare?" I asked him.

"Truth."

"Did you have a crush on me *after* middle school?"

He laughed. "Yeah. I did."

"Really? When?" Because if it was now, I might be in trouble.

"Sorry, Guidry. One question per round."

"That's not fair! You asked me two questions." Maybe it was after prom?

He shrugged. "You didn't call me on it. Truth or Dare?"

I sighed heavily through my nose, but only to be dramatic. "Fine. Truth."

He licked his lips. "Was I your first kiss?"

I threw my head back laughing. "I wondered when that would come up!"

"So you *do* remember."

I nodded. "How would I not remember my first kiss? Your end of year party. In your pool house."

"So I really was?"

"Yeahp." I tapped my lips with my fingers. "My first kiss."

"Mine, too."

His quiet admission cast the whole memory in a different light. My heart had practically stopped when he spun the bottle, and it pointed at me. Our friends and classmates had whooped at the idea of him having to kiss weird, awkward Rose. Everybody knew he had a crush on Julia Roy, even Julia Roy, who had a crush on Caleb D.

"You know," he said softly, "I'll never forget what you said to me when we met in the middle of the circle. Do you remember?"

"No, but I'm sure it was something unforgivably awkward."

"You said, 'I bet you regret inviting me, now.' And I couldn't get that out of my head, the whole summer. I couldn't get *you* or our kiss out of my head all summer."

A heavy dullness sat in my chest. I had been stuck in *his* head? I never really believed it was possible for people to think about me when I wasn't right in front of them. It surprised me, every time, that I wasn't entirely forgettable.

The silence between us lengthened, only permeated by the hum of the tires on the road and the Beatles's "She Loves You" on the radio. I flipped through my cards, studying the lines of Hera, Kuan Yin, Lakshmi.

I'd spun fantasies about him for almost a year after that kiss. Him calling my house. Him showing up on my doorstep on his bike. For him to have actually thought about me was incomprehensible.

But it was also really, really cool.

"Is that why you agreed to take me to my prom?"

He shook his head. "I didn't agree to a truth."

I rolled my eyes. "I've mentally thrown a throw pillow, a roll of toilet paper, and a sofa cushion at your head already. Wait till we get there."

"So violent!" He checked his mirrors, laughing, and passed the McDonald's 18-wheeler we'd been following for too long.

"Fine then. Tell me, kind sir, would you prefer Truth, or Dare?"

"Hmmm. You seem to want me to say Truth, I guess, so I'll say...Dare."

I pursed my lips. "I dare you to tell me why you took me to my prom."

If the sudden scrunching of his nose was any indication, I wasn't going to like the answer. "Well, you know I had a girlfriend at the time."

"That was the word on the street."

He blew out a breath. "Becca was moving out, and Alex and I were fighting over who got to move out of our room and into her big bedroom with the balcony. Mom and Dad told Becca she could decide."

"Jason Soniat. You took me to prom to get a better room?"

"Kinda? I mean I had a girlfriend! But it wasn't like it was much of a sacrifice. I got a bigger room, *and* I got to go to a beautiful girl's prom."

"*Stoooooooooooop*. My big night was a bargaining chip in balcony room negotiations? And don't act like you enjoyed yourself. You were miserable the whole time."

Brown eyes under furrowed brows flitted to me. "I wasn't miserable. When you did talk, I liked hearing what you had to say. Not only that, but Jesus, you were so hot in that silky black dress, I felt like such a stud. You know what would've made it more fun? If you would've danced with me more than once."

"I danced with you."

"Yeah, but then that old song came on you liked—by The Bee Gees? And I asked you if you wanted to dance, and you turned me down."

"God, how do you even remember that? I wanted to dance with you, but I did you a favor by turning you down. You only asked to be nice." I bit my lip. More hurt was creeping into my voice than I'd intended. I stared out at the green hills of Alabama passing outside the window. Maybe I should suggest we play I Spy or Would You Rather instead. Because this didn't make sense. All this time, I'd used my prom as another prime example of me being defective. Unworthy of a man's interest. I couldn't find my own date, and I bored to tears the poor guy who'd gotten guilted into going with me.

"Maybe I wanted to dance with you," he said softly.

He was only trying to make me feel better. That's what all his flirting was. He thought I was still stinging from breaking up with Isaac, and he was pitying me. It was the only thing that made sense. The hills passed by, the sun was going down. The silence was unbearable.

"Truth or dare?" he asked quietly.

I wasn't in the mood for either, but he was renting me a fantastic apartment for cheap, helping me build my brand, and evacuating me so I didn't die in a hurricane. "Truth."

"So, all the wedding dresses. It's your life's work. But why aren't *you* married?"

I'd been asked that question hundreds of times, but his stress on the word *you* somehow transformed the question into something new. Regardless, I trotted out my old standby. "I'm just waiting for the right guy to come along."

His chin jutted out, and his brows lowered. "I don't buy that."

"What do you mean?" Why couldn't he be one of the dozens of people who were satisfied with that answer, the ones who gratefully accepted it as part and parcel of the illusion of the wedding dress designer waiting for her true love? Nobody looked below this satin-and-lace surface.

"I'm not buying it because you didn't sell it hard enough. It's a pat answer, like when someone says, 'Hey, how are you?' and you say, 'Fine,' but you just got fired and your dog just died."

I stared out my side window. I'd hidden my jaded views from too many people for too long to even be able to articulate why I wasn't married. I squirmed in my seat, exposed as a fraud and a liar. What could I even say? Because marriages don't last? Because I watched divorce tear my mother apart? Because the idea of anyone falling in love with me and staying was absurd?

He glanced at me again. "That silence means I'm right."

"You're digging awfully deep, emotionally, for a shirtless woodworker. Why are you poking this bear?"

His expression turned contrite. "I'm sorry. You don't have to tell me why."

I let the silence lengthen. I couldn't even throw the same question back at him now that I knew the story of his ex. Besides, he wouldn't understand. His parents were still together. He didn't grow up watching his mother cry *all the time*, struggling to make ends meet with two young children, all on her own. I'll always be grateful that she got help and climbed her way out of her despair, found friends and neighbors to help with us while she went back to school and found her joy in her life again.

But now she was going right back into the lion's den, and it made zero sense to me. Why would she willingly put herself at such a risk? I closed my eyes and pretended to sleep as the shadows along the roadside deepened.

Chapter 7

The Bag

Jason

"Only nine hours for a five-hour drive. Not bad, right?" I opened the door and brought the pack of water bottles straight to the refrigerator while Rose followed me in with her backpack and our fast-food haul.

"It could've been worse. Bathroom?"

"There's a half-bath right here." I pointed to the room on the left. "And a full bath in the bedroom."

She flipped on the light to the half bath off the living area, and I went back to the car for our bags, bringing hers into the bedroom. The lavender air fresheners had run out a long time ago. I opened the patio door to let some fresh air through the screens and pulled the plastic off the sofa bed. Mom was fastidious when she packed the condo up every season.

After dinner, I pulled the bedding from the vacuum bags Mom had everything stored in and threw a few pillows and sheets on the sofa for me. Rose was curled up there watching the news, but I was ready to go to sleep. I dug into my bag—where was my toothpaste? Oh, that's right. I ran out this morning and was supposed to get more today.

I rifled through all the drawers and cabinets in both bathrooms. No luck.

I popped my head back out into the living room, and she looked up from her phone. "It made landfall in Grand Isle."

"That sucks. Those poor people get it so bad every time. Hey, can I borrow your toothpaste? I forgot I'm out."

"Sure. It's in the front pocket of my bag."

I sat her bag on the bed. Square angles jutted everywhere underneath the duffle's thick fabric. What did she have in here? I checked both sides—no front pocket. Maybe she meant the inside front pocket? I unzipped the bag. It was full of...boxes. Through the clear plastic of the top one jutted the unmistakable column of a glittery pink dildo. I tried to hold my composure, but then I saw its name: The Cosmic Dick of Glory.

I laughed nervously to myself. What the fuck?

Transfixed, and more than a little aroused, I took the Cosmic Dick and other boxes from the bag—furry black handcuffs, an inflatable pillow whose box was covered with genderless stick figures having sex in more positions than I understood. A long purple vibrator dubbed the Velvet Plum Marvel with some kind of piece sticking out the side, something that looked like a ring—a cock ring, according to the box. A bunch of other things I couldn't name but was pretty sure were also sex toys.

"Hey Jason, do you wanna watch a movie?"

Shit. My face heated up as it dawned on me—I took the wrong bag. Her mom had something to do with this, for sure. Maybe these were the ones the movers were meant to have?

I shoved the boxes back inside the bag and zipped it up halfway, but then stopped. Rose was cool. She'd understand, right?

I pulled the Velvet Plum Marvel vibrator and the Cosmic Dick boxes back out. Struggling to keep a straight face, I walked into the living room with one in either hand.

"Um, Rose? I'm no expert, but I don't think anything in that bag is toothpaste."

She looked up, and all the color drained from her face. She crossed the room like a panther and snatched them from my hands.

"Oh my God! How? I told you to grab the purple bag!" She pushed past me into the bedroom.

All of my amusement evaporated. "That was the purple bag! The only other one was gray."

"No, Y chromosome, this is maroon. The other one was lavender—*purple*." She shoved the items back in and zipped the bag up, burying her face in her hands.

"Rose, I'm—I'm so sorry. I grabbed the bag I thought you asked for. I mean it felt heavier than *my* bag, but I just figured you had...girl stuff in there."

"*Girl stuff*?" Her voice rose an octave.

My face was hot. "Curling irons? Straightening...things? Aren't those also irons? I don't know."

She sat primly at the edge of the bed and put her face in her hands. "No clothes, no toiletries, no underwear. But we could have all the freaky sex we wanted." Her voice was small. "And I didn't even want to evacuate."

My dick rudely perked up in the middle of that sentence. "I'm so sorry, but I still think we made the right choice leaving." I sighed at my own stupidity. "There's gotta be a 24-hour store somewhere nearby. Text me what you need, and I'll go get it right now." I grabbed my sneakers and sat beside her, slipped one on, tying it.

She put her hand on my arm. "No, it's fine. You drove all day, and it's so late. I'll get what I need in the morning."

I bumped her shoulder. "I'm really, really sorry. And hey." I tugged on her sleeve. "You have a clean Deck Daddy shirt, at least."

She managed to smile. "True."

How to lighten this situation? "Truth or dare?" I asked quietly.

She laughed nervously. "With that bag in the room, I'm kind of afraid to take the dare."

"Oh come on! I wouldn't—"

"Truth," she said firmly.

"Would you like to borrow some of my clothes?"

She laughed out a breath she'd been holding. "To answer that question, no, I'm good. To answer the question I *thought* you'd ask, some of my friends signed me up for a sex toy of the month club for my last birthday, and my mom gives away all the duplicates she—"

"Rose, you don't have to explain yourself to me. At all." But now I wanted to know if her friends had done it as a joke. "But they weren't being mean or anything, right? Like my brother—well, that's how I currently have a Deck Daddy monthly calendar hanging in my office."

She laughed. "No. They just know I like...never mind."

I desperately wanted to know the end of that sentence, but she looked too tired and tried for me to pursue it now. "Look, I'm gonna get changed for bed, and I'll leave a clean pair of shorts on the counter, in case you want them. And the room's yours. I've got the sofa bed."

She stood up. "No, no. It's your parents' condo. I'll be fine on the sofa."

"Absolutely not. I left your bag behind, and you solved my community room problem. I want you to sleep like a queen."

"Thank you," she said in a small voice.

"Of course." I got up and went toward the door.

"Hey Jason." Her eyes were mischievous when I stuck my head back in. "Asking for a friend. Where can I get a Deck Daddy calendar?"

Her gaze tugged at mine like a physical thing, all dark eyes and thick lashes. She sucked her bottom lip into her mouth, and I forgot how to speak.

A corner of her lips tugged up. "I could use one for my workroom. Y'know, like how mechanics hang up calendars with swimsuit models?" Her eyes sparkled with held-back laughter.

Several unwordlike noises sputtered out of my mouth, ending in "yeah, sure"—which didn't answer her question at all—and I ducked out of the room.

Rose

I must've finally fallen asleep, because I woke up from one of my recurring can't-find-a-suitable-toilet dreams needing to pee.

I climbed out of bed and twisted my black denim shorts the right way again. They'd been cutting me in half. While I washed my hands after availing myself of the facilities, I eyed up the soft, stretchy-looking athletic shorts Jason had left for me on the counter.

I had my new Deck Daddy shirt on, so I might as well complete the look. Slipping them on was as much of a relief as taking my bra off at the end of the day. Why had I tortured myself when I was aggravated with him for bringing the wrong bag?

Especially when he'd been so apologetic.

The soft blue light of his phone lit up the living area through the open slit of the bedroom door. The time on my phone said it was just after two in the morning. I'd barely slept at all.

I walked out into the living room. He looked up from the sofa bed, his face and bare chest bathed in blue light from his phone. "Hey, I didn't wake you up, did I?"

"No, my bladder did. And I'm thirsty."

He chuckled. "Water's in the fridge. Help yourself."

Cold bottle acquired, I sat beside him on the sofa. He leaned his phone toward me so I could see too. The storm was moving through the New Orleans area, so there wasn't much news yet. Everyone who stayed was hunkered down waiting for it to pass and praying it wouldn't cause too much damage.

"Can't sleep, either, huh?"

He rubbed his hand across his short beard, which was a little shaggier since this morning. "No. Now that I'm a homeowner, this freaks me out a whole lot more than it used to." He snapped his phone off, casting the room into the yellow light from the kitchen. "Want to watch a movie?" He turned on a lamp and knelt before the TV stand, opening the doors and pulling out stacks of DVD cases. "Jeez, my parents have shitty taste in movies."

I laughed, coming to kneel beside him. "It can't be that bad."

He snorted. "*Speed 2. Baby Geniuses. Left Behind. Look Who's Talking Now?*"

"OhmygoshMSTK3000!" I grabbed it up from the pile.

"Oh yeah, I love these guys. *Viking Women and the Sea Serpent.* Perfect."

I curled up on the sofa bed while he started the movie. He tossed me one of his pillows before flopping down right next to me, wafting the clean, masculine scent of his body my way. He'd left his deodorant on the counter earlier, one of those Manly Old Spice deodorants with a ridiculous name, like DragonSteed or SeaDeity. I'm not too proud to say I took a whiff of it before bed then spent some time combing through his photos for crotch shots. I thought for sure there'd be a curve or a bulge that would satisfy my imagination. But less than ten disappointing photo zooms later, I closed the app and laid there too revved up to sleep for a while.

And now, sitting this close to all that inviting bare skin was extremely distracting. But before long we were laughing together at the robots' jokes. We both kept jockeying for a more comfortable position, and we finally laid with our heads close together, sharing commentary on the movie.

"Don't you wonder how some of these movies got made?" I asked.

"Yeah," he laughed, his deep voice close to my ear. "They're so ridiculous." Long minutes passed while the Viking women tried to free their men from the overlord. "Rose, can I ask you something? And if you don't want to answer it, just tell me to fuck all the way off."

His face was only a foot away from mine, and his big brown eyes sparkled in the flickering light from the TV. But he wasn't looking at me.

"Okay." My heart rate sped up.

"Actually, two questions." He licked his lips and pulled at the inseam of his shorts as if giving his package breathing room. "What's a cock ring? And do I need one?"

I cackled and sunk a little closer to him on the sofa.

He laughed stiffly, his smile not reaching his eyes. "Don't laugh! I was afraid to Google it and see something I couldn't unsee. You don't have to answer if it's weird that I asked."

"No, it's fine. You just caught me off guard." The MSTK3000 bad guys were locking Joel up again, and the bad movie resumed. "It's a sex toy—a ring that goes over a guy's cock, like at the base? They can be used just for fun, but they can also help men with erectile dysfunction."

"Well I don't have that problem," he proclaimed loudly, in true proud male fashion.

I snorted. "Of course not."

"So when you say just for fun, do you mean like, flying solo or with a partner?"

"Either. Both. Some vibrate, and some are designed with ribbed surfaces for clitoral stimulation. Which is nice, because most people with a vagina can't achieve an orgasm through penetrative sex alone."

His eyebrows rose and came together. This was clearly new information for him. "Really. So they need…"

I raised my eyebrows. "Clitoral stimulation," I supplied, nodding my head.

He shifted uncomfortably and only glanced once at my eyes. "Yeah. That."

"If you can say penis, you can say clitoris. It's just a body part. In fact, it's a lot like a penis."

He narrowed his eyes.

"Seriously! It's made of the same erectile tissue."

He pulled his pillow closer. Adjusted his shorts around his package again. I tried to see what was going on down there, but the shadows foiled me. Curses.

"But it's a lot smaller, though, right? I mean..."

I stared at him. "You think a clit's just that little nub, don't you?"

He raised his eyebrows and finally met my eyes. "It's not?"

"Oh poor, sweet summer child." I grabbed my phone and started sending him links. "There's an artist—Sophia Wallace. You need to watch her TEDx Talk because you obviously know nothing about the clitoris. The love button is only the tip of the iceberg. It's like...I don't know, like a double-wishbone shape? It's made of erectile tissue, just like a penis. But unlike one, clitoris owners are blessed with the ability to have multiple orgasms without a refractory period. It's the only organ whose function is purely for pleasure. Did you know that?"

He shook his head, eyes still firmly trained on the movie while his phone vibrated with all my sex texts.

"Here. Here's a good article on sex toys that explains how they all work, and here's a link to a reputable shop, which has even more information. Always buy from a reputable shop and not from a massive online marketplace, because that isn't something you want to buy used."

His face was bright red. "That's...a lot of information. Thank you. Fuck." He rubbed his beard. "Now you have me worrying if I've ever pleased a woman, like ever." His eyes drifted back to the TV then back to me. "I'm not a creep with all these questions. I swear."

"You're fine," I sighed, flopping back into my spot. "They don't exactly teach this stuff in school. A lot of people go their whole life without knowing what their own clitoris looks like or what to do with it. There's no way their partners can intuitively know what to do with it, either. Not that I have one. A partner, I mean. I have a clitoris."

"Hey."

I met his eyes. They were so big, and so brown, and so close to mine. Like his tempting lips.

"I'm sure there's a great guy out there for you, probably even closer than you think."

His eyes dropped to my lips, and my heart backflipped against my throat. Did he even know he did it? He immediately went back to laughing at the robots like nothing happened while I was trying to down-girl my heart back inside my rib cage. I settled in to watch the movie, but it was a long time before my pulse calmed down.

I dreamt I was having an orgasm so hard it woke me up. My eyes fluttered open. I was a little spoon. Jason lightly snored behind me, unmoving, but his thick arm had my back pulled to his front. His hand laid softly over my belly, and his massive erection pressed against my bottom, warm through our clothes.

My skin tingled all over. That orgasm hadn't been a dream. Through an effort of will unlike any I thought I possessed, I managed to not squirm back against him and pull his hand to my breast.

Goddamn, he felt *so good*.

But he didn't think of me that way. He'd be so embarrassed if he knew, especially with his vow of celibacy. Slowly, I pulled my hips forward to break the contact, but the movement woke him.

He stirred, his hand slipping across my stomach as he turned away from me. His whole body tensed, most likely at the exact moment he realized.

His hips jerked back. "Morning."

I sat up and stretched. "Morning."

"Everything okay?" he asked tentatively.

I turned to smile at him. "Yeah, I'm just—*up* now." I giggled and stood up.

"Wait, what? Christ, Rose, I'm so sorry," he slurred sleepily. "I don't have any control over my body when I'm asleep."

I didn't respond, just laughed as I walked away.

"Roooose," he called softly, dragging out the long "o" in my name.

"Yeeees," I called back, grabbing my phone. It was nearly eight in the morning, so surely there was some news about home by now. I tapped my way to our local station's website on the way to the bathroom.

"I'm really sorry. Please don't hate me."

I shut the door. "I never said I didn't like it," I called out, giggling.

"Wait, what?" His muffled voice carried through the door.

"I said, 'I know you can't control it!'" I cackled and watched the live newsfeed while I peed.

"What's going on with the storm?" Jason asked as I came out of the bathroom. He was packing up his sofa bed, still shirtless. He must be severely allergic to shirts.

Guess we're not gonna talk about his giant boner against my ass. How big was that thing? It was gonna be all I could think about today. "Nothing good. A huge electrical tower fell into the Mississippi River. Most of New Orleans has no power, and they don't expect it to come back for a week, or more."

"Oh damn, seriously?" He pulled out his phone, tapped a number, and put the phone to his ear. "My landline's ringing, but the answering machine's not picking up. Yeah—we don't have power."

I tapped over to another screen. "Entergy's outage map shows all red, all around the church. It was mostly a wind event, but it flooded in lower-lying areas. Trees are down all over the metro area, and I-10's shut down in both directions on either side of the city. This is the worst." I flopped my head back dramatically onto the sofa.

"Maybe, or maybe you're looking at it the wrong way. Ever hear that saying that the difference between an ordeal and an adventure is attitude?"

I narrowed my eyes. "Says the man with clean underwear."

"Come on." He stood by the sofa and stretched his hands out to me. "Get up, get your shoes on, and let's get breakfast. Then I'm taking you shopping and buying you some clothes."

I took his hand and let him help me up. "I guess you have a point. But you don't have to buy me anything."

"No," he insisted, his hand gently rubbing his mountainous, lickable stomach. I snapped my guilty gaze from his belly up to his eyes.

A soft smile lit his face as if he'd caught me. "I grabbed the wrong bag. This is on me."

We gorged ourselves at the Donut Hole on pancakes and bacon, then went shopping for clothes. Going shopping with a food baby in my belly wasn't the best plan, but I was able to find most of what I needed at an outlet mall in Destin—a pack of panties, a couple of shirts, and a comfier pair of shorts. Jason also talked me into a sundress and a pair of sandals for the beach, and then he pulled me into a swimsuit store full of tiny scraps of fabric posing as swimsuits.

I flipped through a rack of one-pieces, studying their construction. I'd always wanted to sew myself a swimsuit, something cute and retro, but with more coverage and support than these. No cups? No way. My boobs were way too big for that bullshit. I selected a few decent ones and a cover-up to try on.

Jason grabbed a pink, rose-patterned bikini off the rack and held it up to me. "What about this one?"

I took it from him and hung it right back up. "I don't wear bikinis."

"Why not? It would look great on you."

The woman looking at suits on the other side of the fixture smiled and our eyes met briefly. I'm sure Jason and I looked like a couple with him carrying my bags, and we maybe even sounded like one with his encouragement.

"You're very sweet," I said quietly, "but I'm not comfortable with my weight. I'd rather be in a one-piece."

He frowned, leaning an arm on the rack. "Well look, if you want, I'll help you get beach-ready."

"Mmm-hmm." If he started mansplaining how to get in shape, I swear to God. Even the raised eyebrows on the woman across from me warned, *you're on thin ice, bucko.*

I went to the next fixture over, but Jason followed me. "You know how to get a beach body, right? First, you have a body, and then—this part is critical—you go to the beach."

My eyes met the woman's, and we both smiled and shook our heads. Mollified, for now.

"I'm still not getting a bikini, funny man."

"I'm serious, Rose. You're so beautiful just the way you are."

My cheeks heated, and I couldn't meet his eyes. He was so free with compliments. He was probably that way with everyone. But it sent a thrill to my core every time he complimented me.

"By all means wear what makes you comfortable. Just don't hide your light under a bushel or whatever."

"Jason," I said sotto voce, "my stomach sticks out too much for a bikini."

His brown eyes studied me. "Why do you care what other people think?"

He was right, but I cared what *he* thought.

"Besides," he said. "You have a uterus. That's what they're supposed to do."

Now it was my turn to raise my eyebrows. "Now you know things about women's anatomy?"

"Baby." The woman across the rack leaned closer to me. "Try on that pink two-piece. Hot boy's right."

Jason's answering smile was all charm and smugness. "Thank you!" He checked the tag of one of my selections then handed me the pink bikini again, this time in the right size. "Humor me?"

I rolled my eyes and took it all into the fitting room. But I was *not* trying on the bikini. It was nice of him to encourage me, but no way would I wear one at the beach for real.

Of the one-pieces I brought in, only one wasn't a crime. It was on sale, too. I guess I'd let him get me that one.

I eyed the bikini. Maybe I'd try it on just so I could honestly say I'd done it, so he'd leave me alone about it. I slipped the bottoms over my undies, hefted and adjusted the girls into the bra cups. Okay this pattern was super cute. The dark pink matched one of the roses on my tattoo almost perfectly. The bottom was generously cut, more like a boy short than a bikini bottom.

Once it was on, I was pleasantly surprised by what I saw in the mirror. But I was still reluctant to actually purchase it and wear it on the beach.

"Sure, I'll go get you another size," the salesgirl said to the woman in the stall beside me, and then her footsteps went toward the entrance.

Maybe I'd ask her when she came back if I looked ridiculous, since the fitting room had started to clear out.

But the longer she took, the antsier I got. Was I making Jason wait too long? I examined my body in the mirror from all angles. I was either a smoke show or a smoking pile of crap.

Footsteps, and a soft knock on my door. "Rose?" Jason asked. "Find something you like?"

I slipped the cover-up on and opened the door a crack. "Don't gloat, but I'm wearing the bikini, and I think it's not half bad? But I was waiting to get the salesgirl's opinion."

"I can give you *my* opinion," he grinned, dimples locked and loaded on my hormones.

"Okay," I huffed, only agreeing because my mom treated me to a wax appointment a few days ago. "But you have to be honest. None of your smooth-talking bullshit, okay?"

"Promise," he said.

As he popped his straw in his mouth to take a sip, I stepped back and swept off the cover up.

He eyed me from top to bottom and back again, then choked on his drink, coughing, leaning over coughing, turning red-faced.

I clenched the cover-up in my fist between my breasts. "Oh my God, are you okay?"

"I'm fine *cough cough*. I just..." he cleared his throat. "Goddamn. We're getting the cover-up too, because if you cross the street in that you're gonna cause some car accidents."

My heart and my shoulders slumped. "Because I look like a train wreck. I knew it."

He leaned in suddenly, his breath warm on my ear. "No, because you look like a goddess."

He smiled as he pulled away and left, and a waterfall of shivers went down my body.

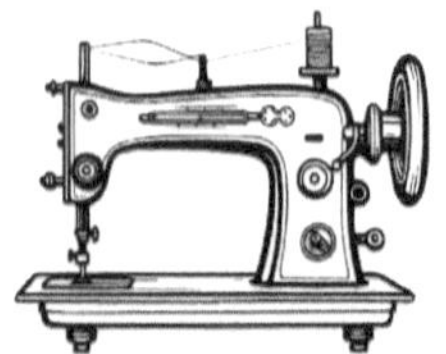

Chapter 8

Lucky Blood Orange

Rose

The beach near the condo was fairly deserted. The sand was clean, the late afternoon was warm and beautiful, and the moment we set our stuff down in a good spot, Jason whipped his shirt off, turning the heads of the few people who were already on the beach.

He opened both chaises and set them under the umbrella. "Hey...would you mind putting sunblock on my back?"

"Sure." Taking the bottle from him, I poured some into my palms and started rubbing his hard, muscled shoulders. A girl could get addicted to touching skin this warm and smooth. I wanted to rub my whole naked body against it like a cat. I took my time to be sure every spot of his back was covered, from his shoulder blades, down his long spine, along his back and sides. Down his lower back and along the low-slung waistband of his shorts where my fingers caught an upper-butt curve.

I stuck my head around his arm and smiled. "Need me to get your chest?"

"Yeah." He cleared his throat. "Please."

I was just teasing him, but damn, okay. I circled to his front and poured more lotion into my hands, giving him back the bottle. From his shoulders, I moved down his pecs and swept my hands across his nipples and his sides.

I put my palm up. "Lotion me."

He swallowed hard and poured a hefty amount into my hand.

"So, what are you going to do on the beach?" I rubbed my hands together then smoothed it down his washboard abs. Standing so close, gliding my hands along his skin...ugh, this pleasure ache was making it hard to stand.

"Uh, not much." A muscle worked in his jaw as his gaze tracked my every moment, my hand moving lower and lower down his torso. Finally, my fingers grazed that sacred space between his belly button and the top of his shorts. I held his gaze as I rubbed his lower belly all the way down to his waistband. His nipples pebbled, and goosebumps broke out all along his skin. I smirked and finished up by running my fingertips *just inside* part of his waistband before smiling sweetly at him.

"Will you get my back?" I turned around and shrugged off my coverup, revealing the pink bikini. Which I'd worn for horny reasons.

It took him two tries to get his words out. "Of course."

I smiled to myself and lifted my hair into a handheld bun. His big, slightly rough hands landed on my shoulders, rubbing the slick lotion in broad, circular strokes down my back. I shut my eyes to soak in the pleasure, not trusting myself to speak. One hand settled on the curve of my waist and grasped my hip, fingers digging in to hold me still as his other hand rocked me forward with every rhythmic stroke against my skin.

Holy mother of God. I hadn't even gone into the water, and I was *wet.* His other hand took up the same position on the opposite hip, and he slipped his thumbs in one perfect circle on my lower back. I bit my lip and held in a whimper.

"What about you?" Jason's gruff voice near my ear sent a fresh wave of chills across me.

"Uh...hmm?" Words were not possible, not the way his hand was slipping under my bikini's back strap.

"What are you doing on the beach?" Both of his hands rubbed down my sides.

"*Ohhh*," I murmured lustily, rolling it into an *um* to try and save face. "Probably just read. You?" I turned my left ear toward him.

Wait—I asked him that already.

His hands gently grasped my wrists and brought them down by my sides, releasing me but still standing close behind me. My hair whipped free in the gulf wind, and I seriously considered asking him to get my chest.

"Uh, maybe swim," he said softly. "Go for a run. Read. I don't know."

I glanced over my shoulder at him. His gaze was soft, vulnerable. Smiling, I looked away and down. "Cool."

"Okay," he chuckled. "Cool."

"Cool," I repeated stupidly.

"I'm gonna cool off in the water." He dropped the sunblock on the blanket and took off jogging toward the gulf like he couldn't get away fast enough.

I settled into a chaise, keeping my eyes on his retreating backside. The muscles on his back moved as he raised his arms and dove low into the waves. Jason would skip straight to a Level Two boyfriend with that sexy golden retriever energy. It could get so messy with me living there, though. I'd only planned to stay a few months when I moved in, but now the thought of leaving that little slice of heaven made my stomach hurt.

The thought of not hanging out with Jason also made my stomach hurt.

And the thought of him rubbing lotion on some other woman's back made my chest ache *and* my stomach hurt.

I tapped into my phone and opened up Heather's latest romance novel rec, *To Plunder a Pirate*. But my eyes stayed on Jason, and my phone went to sleep without me reading a word.

He came out of the water. From behind my sunglasses, I watched rivulets of water snake down his muscles as he got closer. My gaze tracked the hair leading from his belly button down to the generous curve of his sex in those swim shorts, and my bottom clenched thinking about it wedged between my ass cheeks this morning.

I grabbed my iPad from my bag and tapped into my working file for Mom's dress. That would keep me cooler than reading smut. Of the designs I sent her last night, she liked the mermaid silhouette best, so now I was trying to work out the train.

"Miss me?" Jason grabbed the towel and wrapped up in it, sitting in the chaise beside me and grabbing a water from the ice chest.

"Of course," I murmured. *Don't look at how cute his hair is wet.*

He shook his hair once like a dog, and seawater sprinkled all over me.

"Hey now, let's watch that stuff." I yanked the corner of his towel toward me and dried my cheek.

"I'm sorry!" He blotted at the top of my head, in my ear, tickled the corner of it into my neck.

I giggled and pulled away. "Stop!"

"I didn't want to drip on my phone." He crumpled the towel in his lap and pulled his phone from his bag.

I raised my eyebrows. "But it's okay to get me all wet?"

His dimples dug deeper as he shrugged at my double entendre and laid back with his phone.

But he'd completely broken my concentration with the beads of water still glistening on his skin. "What're you looking at that's so engaging?"

He smiled more intently at his phone, his face reddening. But he didn't answer.

"Evasive much?" I dipped my fingertips into the melting ice chest and flicked cold droplets at his chest.

"Ah!" He pretended to shiver, smiling bigger and sparing me a glance. "I'm reading."

"What are you reading?"

He chuckled and sat up closer to me, meeting my eyes. "If you must know…" He held his phone toward me with the book cover displayed. Above a photo of someone fingering a blood orange was the title: *The Thinking Lover's Guide to the Pussy.*

Fuck me.

My eyes met his, and the son of a bitch unconsciously—subconsciously?—darted his tongue out to lick his lips. Goosebumps rose all over my body, and my basement flooded in a sweet ache. "Goddamn, Deck Daddy. Is it…good?"

He shrugged, his gaze dropping to my mouth as he smiled. "I guess I'll find out at some point." He raised his eyebrows at me and went back to reading, biting his thumb and lazily rocking his leg so that I caught flashes of his toned inner thigh.

Smiling like an idiot, I swallowed hard and trained my eyes back on my screen, but all I saw was that lucky blood orange. I deep breathed through the intense need he'd triggered between my legs. Was he…was he reading that book…for me?

"What are you working on?"

It took me a second to hear him above the beating of my heart. "Um…dresses."

He scooted his chaise close enough that his body heat warmed my skin. "You're drawing? Oh! You were going to show me Becca's dresses."

"Oh yeah." I opened up Becca's file and tapped through my layers of discarded ideas to the wedding design she picked. "Will she get pissed if I show you?"

The mischief in his eyes stirred my blood. "She doesn't have to know."

I held it out to him, and he took the iPad from me, zooming in at the details at her waist, the design along the hem of the train. "Just beautiful." He handed it back. "What about bridesmaid dresses? What are you wearing?"

Oh my. The raspy way he said that, and so close to my ear, was a little like phone sex. I really liked phone sex.

I opened another file with my sister as the base. "She had a harder time deciding on the bridesmaids' dresses, but she went with this one. She loved the way the chiffon drapes off the shoulder. I liked the blush—" I changed the color with a few taps of my stylus. "But she insisted on this deep wine color. It's more purple than red."

"Why is Lily the model? Haven't you drawn yourself? Because you're gonna rock the hell out of that color. Did you know your eyes look purple sometimes?"

I smiled. "That's what my mom says." A few more taps, and I'd loaded the gown on my drawing of myself. "Here I am."

He zoomed in more on my drawing of me than on the dress. "Beautiful. You could draw professionally."

"Thanks."

"How many times have you designed your own wedding dress?" His soft smile made me feel seen, like he knew I was all about the dress even though I wasn't all about the wedding.

"Too many to count. I keep getting new ideas, and my taste keeps changing. I doubt I'll ever need one, anyway."

"Show me?"

His face was near my shoulder, and those brown eyes fluttered up to mine, warm, open, full of...hope? His eyes dropped to my lips again, and mine dropped to his.

With trembling hands, I flipped through all my attempts at drawing myself a wedding dress. "Of course, I started with princess dresses with big bells of tulle for a skirt, and then I went through my romantic phase, with silk chiffon flowers and peplums and a corset top. I love corset tops."

"Very sexy," he affirmed.

God, his deep voice could probably unhook my bikini top with a single growl. "And then my lace designs, some sluttier than others. My *Lord of the Rings* phase..." *Swipe, swipe.* "My 'wedding dresses don't have to be white phase...'" *Swipe, swipe, swipe, swipe.* "I made this one for a class. It may be my favorite. I used lace that matches my skin, so the effect is very sexy."

His mouth was close enough to kiss, and so inviting. He pulled away slightly with a hard swallow. "Do you have any drawings of dresses that you could put side-by-side with the dress itself? Instagram would eat that up."

"Yeah, I have a few. But not many good pictures of them. They were mostly taken either in my ratty apartment or in the cluttered design studio at school. The only professional photographer I can afford is my sister, because she's free, but I don't want her taking the pictures. The last time I talked to her about my work, her mouth said, 'You're making such great progress!' but her eyes said, 'your little hobby is adorable.'"

"That sucks. I didn't know she wasn't supportive. You're so talented." He sat up straighter and caught my gaze with his. "You know, a very wise woman once told me that if you get paid doing the thing you love, that doesn't make it less of a real job."

I rolled my eyes with a smirk. "Yeah. But it's kind of like making it as an actress or an artist. It's really hard, and sometimes you lose hope."

"Your sister's a photographer. That's art too."

"Yeah, but it's different. Rich people pay a ton of money for portraits. That's where she was the night you found me digging up your yard. A family hired her to photograph their granddaughter's wedding in Oregon. Flew her up there and everything."

"Damn." With his towel, he wiped away a drop of water on my thigh. "Well, I'm not a professional, but I'd love to take them for you."

Lightly swooning, I shook my head. "You don't have to do that. And I don't know where I'd find models, anyway."

"Why can't you model them? This isn't about what that asshole said, is it?" His voice had a protective edge.

Was he jealous? I didn't normally go for jealous men. But maybe I'd been reading too many romance novels because it was hella sexy on him.

"No."

"Unconvincing. Come on, let me take pictures of you in your dresses for your feed and prove to you what a beautiful woman you are."

His gaze dropped briefly below my neck, and my lips parted on their own. I was keenly aware of how close his mouth was to my breasts. His proximity and the slight, sweaty undertone of his scent set off implosions along the roadmap of my veins. "You'd really go all around town taking pictures of me?"

"Why wouldn't I want to help you realize your dream?" His brown eyes were magnetic.

I studied them with a smile. "You're really sweet, you know that?"

He looked down, blushing and shrugging. "I think I'm going for another swim." He stuffed his phone back in his bag and took off jogging to the water.

Jason

I had to get these entirely inappropriate feelings for Rose under control, but dammit I couldn't stop flirting with her.

I waded into the water and dove in for a swim. Her eyes had definitely studied my mouth as if she was considering kissing me. Her hands had *caressed* that sunblock onto my body—that was no mere application.

But Rose didn't just make my cock hard, she made my heart soft. And I needed to know if she *felt* something for me. Her baseline was so flirty, even when she had a boyfriend and thought I was with Misty. Like this morning. Liking how my cock felt against her ass, if that's even what she said, wasn't the same as being interested in a relationship.

I swam out to the second sandbar and stood in the chest-high waves, shifting my eyes along the shoreline. These past couple of weeks were eye-opening. Maybe even life-changing. For the first time in years, I was just...myself. I wasn't bending into unnatural shapes to please Kasey. I wasn't contrite on my knees trying to make things right with my family. I wasn't even Deck Daddy, the persona I think I'd created to rebel against who I'd been before and who everyone wanted me to be now.

I didn't realize how critical it was to my happiness to find out who I was away from all of that. I thought I'd been following my bliss by choosing whatever I wanted in the moment. Always wanted to live in a converted church? Buy one! Love making furniture? Make some! Shirtless photos on social media upping your follower count and engagement? Make more!

I swam parallel to the shore for a while. I'd only been following whims, completely guided by what made me happy in that moment. Because Kasey controlled my past, Mom wanted to control my future, but I got to be the lord and master of my present. And I wasn't ready to give that up. But that present had been numb and lonely until Rose came along.

While she was trying on clothes today, I'd pulled our bucket lists out again. Falling in love was the most important thing I'd written on mine, but I hadn't gone on a single date in over a year. I'd decided to be celibate to protect my heart, but maybe I'd stayed celibate out of fear. Deep down, like my family, I didn't trust myself to make good decisions there, either.

So I faced those words—*falling in love*. Approaching the dead ache in my heart with hope and compassion instead of fear and distrust pivoted me to think about the qualities of the woman I wanted to make a bucket list *with*. And every one of them pointed to Rose.

She lit me up, mind, heart, and body. She had me so sexually excited I was reading books on how to pleasure her.

I swam back toward the beach, and once I was out of the water, I jogged toward her like her presence magnetized my chest.

I wanted to trace every stunning curve of her face with my fingers. I wanted to hear every awkward thing that came out of her beautiful mouth until the end of time. To hear her undone voice whimper my name while I moved inside her.

When I reached Rose, I flopped heavily at her feet in the sand.

"The water's so warm. Come play with me in the waves."

Concealed behind her sunglasses, her eyes might be closed or trained on me. It was exhilarating not to know.

She twisted her pretty lips and mmmmed. "Nope. I'm not a fan of things swimming past my legs."

"Come on. Please come in the water with me?" I lightly pulled her ankle.

She took and released a deep breath. "Fine. Okay."

At the water's edge, the foaming waves skimmed past our ankles. "See? Nothing to be afraid of." I backed farther into the water, letting the waves break against my back and throw me off balance. "I'll be right by you the whole time."

She came in farther, and the first wave that hit her moved her back toward the shore. She squealed in delight, and it was fucking adorable.

I tapped her shoulder. "Tag! You're it!" I slow-ran further into the water until it came up to my thighs.

She called my name and followed me deeper, squealing every time a wave came in. She reached to tag me, but she yelped and grabbed my shoulders, clambering up onto my back like a sexy spider monkey. "Something swam past my leg!"

I scooped her legs behind the knees and helped her hang on. "You're okay." Nothing in the water of concern, just generic fish I couldn't name. Thrilled by her breasts against my back and her bare thighs wrapped tightly around my waist, I stayed where I was. "I've got you."

"Bring me back to the beach!" she commanded, settling her chin on my shoulder.

I delivered her safely on the wet sand, and she took several steps back up toward the umbrella. I caught her hand and pulled gently. "No, don't go. Come back! We were having so much fun!"

She dug her feet in the sand, laughing. "Noooo, I'm not going back where the fish are."

"I'm bringing you back, feeding you to the fishes." Throwing my arms around her waist, I picked her up from behind and started walking toward the water.

She squealed and wrapped her arms around mine. "NO! Jason, no!"

At the last minute, I set her feet down in the foam, and she fell against me laughing. A wave broke on the beach, bringing with it a dozen little fish swimming around our ankles. She screeched and ran back up the beach. I chased her, unable and unwilling to stop myself from falling for her.

Chapter 9

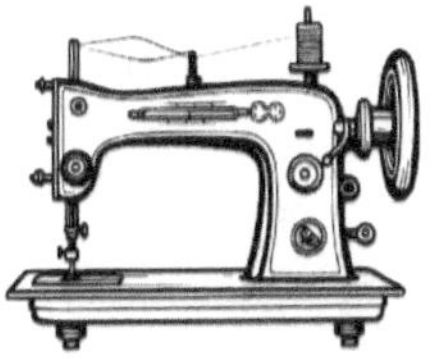

Playing with Matches

Rose

AT THIS RATE, THE bedroom's TV remote was never getting its batteries back.

After all the flirting and touching yesterday at the beach then cozying up to watch a movie at the end of the day, I'd had to give the Velvet Plum Marvel a spin in the shower last night. I tried to force Deck Daddy out of my mind, but he kept barging into my fantasy with his dimples and his giant cock. And ohhhh mama, did it get the job done. A few times. The rabbit vibrator truly was a marvel, and I was gonna have to name it soon.

And today hadn't been less titillating. Even though we didn't go to the beach because it rained most of the day, Jason psyched us up to spend the day wandering around Baytowne, eating good food, listening to live bands, shopping, and getting ice cream, and touching...oh my god, so much touching. I'd spent so much time up close and personal with him today—taking selfies, getting tickled, trying hats on each other, sitting so close together wherever we were that our thighs touched—that I'd abandoned my romance novel because real life was more exhilarating.

After dinner at the condo, I curled up on the sofa to read and return messages on my iPad. He was beside me, doomscrolling on his phone for news on his house. Thankfully, everyone we knew was safe. But because the interstate was still closed on either side of New Orleans, no one we knew had made it back home yet to let us know how his house had fared.

I was busy sending funny cat reels to Abby, but I couldn't stop glancing over at how tense his whole body was, bent over his phone.

I put my iPad down and laid my hand on his knee. "Hey."

His gaze snapping to me was a jolt of electricity zipping straight to my bottom.

"Let's do something."

His eyes flickered to my hand on his knee, and a muscle tensed in his jaw. "Like what?"

I smiled, enjoying the gutter his brain seemed to have visited. "I don't know. Do you want to go see a movie? Or go on a late-night candy raid at the grocery store?"

"Yeah." He set his phone down and put his hand over mine. "What about...have you ever been to the beach at night?"

"You know, I don't think I have."

He was smiling again. Mission accomplished.

"You'll love it." He stood and pulled me to my feet. "You don't have to touch the waves. It's absolutely magical to sit on the beach, watch the moonlight sparkle on the water and the stars break out overhead."

"Then let's go." Anything was better than having him enumerate—again—all the trees that could've fallen on the buildings of his property.

We stepped off the walkway steps into the sand, and I started to understand what he meant. It was beautiful. The sky was as black as the horizon, and the incessant crashing of waves filled the air with shushing. No one was out here but us and a group around a bonfire maybe over a mile away.

"Come on." He ditched his sandals by the steps and ran off toward the water.

I slipped mine off too and ran to the water's edge where I stood beside him and let the rolling waves kiss my feet with foam. The wind blew my skirt up dangerously high and took my breath away as much as standing next to him was.

I stepped farther into the foam. He grabbed my waist, gently pulling me back higher on the beach. "Don't go too far in. My mom always says the larger fish come out to feed at night. I don't know if it's true, but I don't want you to get gobbled up."

I laughed and put my hands on his, stepping back with him onto the beach. Without overthinking, I pulled his arms around my middle and leaned back against him with my arms over his.

My heart raced. I let my head fall back against his chest, and he nestled his face beside mine, his beard sweetly scratching my cheek. The longer I gazed into the dark sky, the more stars popped out, bright and shining from the blackness, rivaled only by the silver ribbon of moonlight dancing in the waves.

We stood in the anything-but-silent rush of the wind in our ears, sending long locks of my hair waving like flags. The ceaseless waves crashed, and as his thumb rubbed my side, my heart pounded with the unmistakable rising hope of falling. My fingertips ran soft circles on his arm.

As much as I wanted to stay in this moment forever, I wanted even more to find out what was happening between us.

I turned to him. He pulled his head back and met my gaze, his big brown eyes dark except for the moonlight sparkling in their depths. His face softened into a smile. His hand left my middle to nestle into the curls beside my face, gently pulling them back from blowing into my eyes, his thumb gently caressing my cheek and his gaze straying to my mouth.

My heart thudded as I tipped my face up to his. His lips were parted, his breath soft and sweet.

"Can I kiss you?" he asked softly.

I nodded and lifted my face closer to his. "Please," I murmured.

He closed his eyes and the distance, laying the softest kiss on my bottom lip, then barely skimming his lips against mine. It'd been the most innocent of kisses. But when he kissed me again, he *mmmfed* and pulled my face closer as if my lips were the divinity he needed. His hand tangled in my hair at the back of my head as his mouth grew hungrier, and I eagerly matched his intensity, raising up on my tiptoes to get closer. I slipped my hand under his shirt, catching smooth, bare skin across a mountain range of muscle.

I pressed the aching between my legs against the hard line between his. He softly moaned against my mouth, his hand slipping to my bottom and pulling me closer.

Soft laughter and a dog bark broke us apart. An older couple with a German Shepard hailed us. "Pardon us! Have a good night!"

I giggled against Jason's chest as he smiled and waved back to them. "Night!"

He hunched over and tucked his face next to mine, kissing my cheek then my temple.

"Let's go back to the condo," I said, eager to get him all to myself.

The moment we got inside, Jason kicked his sandals off in the foyer and dusted the sand from his feet into the catch tray by the door. "Do you want to watch Star Wars? I still can't believe you've never seen the original trilogy."

A cloud passed over my heart. We hadn't talked much on the way home, and I'd chalked it up to us both being nervous and excited to get back here and go back to making out. After *that kiss*, I wanted to sprint through *all* the bases. But...he just wanted to watch a movie?

"Um, I guess." I tucked my feet under me on the couch and adjusted my skirt over my thighs while he popped the DVD in. Every cell of my body was concentrating on figuring out what the hell was happening.

He sat close to me on the sofa, started the movie, and reached his arm around me with a smile. Okay, so at least maybe he didn't regret it. I leaned my head against him and slipped both hands onto his thigh. An invitation.

A few minutes into the movie, he reached across and rubbed at my ankle tattoo. "Why a butterfly?"

I pulled my leg forward a little so my knee was resting on his. "To remind me that even in the dark times, I'm growing, and I'll come out stronger on the other side."

His brow knitted as his fingers slipped down my shoulder. "I love that. And the roses?"

I shrugged. "I just love roses."

"Do you have any other tattoos?"

"Yes."

A mischievous smile played about his lips. "Where?"

I shrugged again, holding his gaze. "They like to play hide and seek." He blushed *hard* while I pulled his arm out straight, examining it. "Do you have any tattoos?"

"Not yet. I've thought about getting one, though."

I bent his arm, making him flex his bicep. "You should get one on your giant bicep. Look at this thing." I squeezed it. "It's as big as my head."

He chuckled. "It's not as big as your head."

"Seriously! Look at it next to mine." I held my arm against his to show the drastic difference.

"I'm just bigger than you." He put his palm out toward me, and I placed my small hand against his big one. "I'm pretty big."

I snorted. "I bet you are."

His deep chuckle made me shiver. "I mean that's what people say, right? I feel like you'd know the answer to that. I watched your videos, and I'm reading this book, but I haven't learned yet if hand size also correlates to clit size."

I giggled and moved closer. On the TV, Obi-Wan was trying to goad Luke into action. But I couldn't pull my eyes away from Jason's. "I don't know about that."

He shrugged. "If it's that much like a penis."

"Sounds like you're learning a lot." I placed a kiss right at the corner of his mouth.

His eyes sparkled as he cupped my face and moved closer. "I am. Thank you for educating me."

I rubbed my lips lightly over his. "I'm always happy to share what I know about sex with...interested parties."

"Oh, I'm interested." He sucked my bottom lip into his mouth, and all talk of the rebellion was forgotten. His hand tangled in my hair, his kisses soft, perfect.

I grasped his shoulders and pulled him down on top of me. I wanted him to crush me and fill me. His mouth burned kisses down my neck, and I lifted my knee, letting my skirt slip up my thigh.

"Truth or dare?" I whispered.

He captured my lips again. "Truth."

I swept my tongue into his delicious mouth, slipping my hand under his shirt and along the smooth, hard muscles of his waist. "What do you want to do to me?" I whispered against his lips.

He groaned into the kiss. "Rose, I'm not sure I'm ready...to do more than kissing."

Our mouths parted with a smack, and I pulled away. "Oh. You don't want to?"

"Hell yeah, I want to. But..." He sat up. Oh—he *had* been holding his hips away from me.

I pulled my hands out from under his shirt and sat up too, my cheeks heating. "Oh. Oh yeah." Why was he being celibate again? Because in my mind, this was going straight into the bedroom. "I'm sorry."

"You don't need to be sorry. *I'm* sorry. I *want* to do more with you. *Fuck.*" He pressed his forehead to mine and ran his hands up my arms. "You're the most beautiful, the sexiest woman I've ever known, and I want to do *everything* with you, but..." He pulled back and pushed my hair away from my face, searching my eyes. "I really, really like you, Rose. I'm afraid of moving too fast. I don't want to mess this up."

"Okay." I nodded, almost dizzy with desire. Thrilled that he wanted me too, but half impressed and half confused by his restraint. "I respect that." I nipped at his lip and dragged my fingertips just inside the waistband of his shorts. "But so you know, you could totally hit this right now, if you wanted to."

He closed his eyes and groaned. "I'll take that under advisement." He laid a single, gentle kiss at each corner of my mouth. "But I love kissing you. Is that okay?"

"Definitely." I dove back in for more, and he eagerly resumed exploring my neck with his mouth. I hadn't only made out with a man in a very long time, and never without knowing it could lead to more. But oh, the kissing was divine. His hand caressed my face, my back, laid flat on my bare chest above my dress. I ran my hand up under his shirt, up his chest. "Your body is so beautiful," I murmured.

"Me?" He kissed my lips and trailed his fingers down to the neckline of my strapless sundress, dipping his finger just inside to run along the upper curve of my breast. "You're like a goddess," he murmured into my lips. His kisses traveled down my neck, and he skimmed his tongue across my collarbone, making me whimper. "You're the Platonic ideal of a beautiful woman."

I moaned into a giggle, rubbing the back of his neck and down. "You're being *very* generous, but I don't think what we're doing qualifies as platonic."

"Greek philosopher—theory of forms. I'm too goddamned turned on to explain."

I grinned wickedly. "Then let's play more Truth or Dare."

He stopped kissing me to gaze at me with narrowed, hazy eyes. "Don't think I don't see what you're doing."

"Who, me?" I asked innocently, scritching my fingernails gently through his whiskers. "I'm just having fun."

Jason

How would I be able to keep my composure with Rose pressing her body up against mine, her tongue dipping into my mouth? And now she wanted to keep playing truth or dare? Like playing with matches in a gasoline plant.

Let's strike the first one.

"Alright. Truth or dare?" I asked.

"Truth," she murmured, softly biting my lower lip.

Finally, I could ask this question. "What are your favorite sex toys?"

She giggled against my lips. "Excellent question. Vibrators, sonic wave clit stimulators, and ohhh I love the things that simulate oral sex, because fuck me I love being sucked."

Fuck me, I wanted to suck her. I dipped my tongue into her mouth, wishing I was pleasuring her like I'd been reading about in my book.

"And dildos! Definitely dildos, especially if they vibrate."

My hand dropped to her bare thigh and slipped up with a mind of its own. With a Herculean effort, I moved it to her waist before it reached the edge of her panties and I lost all control. "So if it was you and me," I asked softly, "are you saying my cock wouldn't be enough?"

"Not at all." She smiled wickedly, her pupils dark and wide. "You could take a break and prolong your own pleasure by using one on me, and then I could enjoy *multiple* orgasms." A kiss at the corner of my lips.

That image made my balls ache. "What else could we do with a dildo?"

"Mmmm, I could ride it while I suck your cock," she murmured in my ear.

A drop of wetness emerged onto the tip of my cock. I tensed my thigh, stilled my hands, and tried to calm my heart.

She rubbed her lips barely against mine. "But you don't want to do that, do you?"

"God, yes, I do." I kissed her hard. "You just made me pre-cum with that image."

She hooked her fingers in my waistband. "Can I lick it off?"

My body involuntarily shivered, and I pulled my knees up a little. "Holy fuck." I laughed and grabbed her hands, shocked at my resolve. "No."

She giggled and returned her hands to my chest. "Okay, but maybe tell me where your line is so I can respect it. Otherwise, I'll probably vault right over it."

I bit my lip while her kisses tortured my neck. Even if we only used our hands and mouths to sexually pleasure each other, if she wanted more than that, I wouldn't be able to stop myself. And the idea of having sex with a woman I liked this much—especially since she hadn't even been in my life for two weeks—scared me as much as it thrilled me.

"Maybe just...no sex acts."

"Okay," she said. "Then it's my turn. Truth or dare?"

"Truth."

She murmured against my ear. "What top two of your favorite sex acts do you want to do to me right now?"

"You're going to be the death of me."

"Don't exaggerate." She booped my nose with her index finger. "I only want to be the *little death* of you."

I breathed a laugh out through my nose, kissing her neck then murmuring in her ear. "I want to be inside you."

"Tell me how you'll give it to me, Deck Daddy." Her hands tangled in my hair as she gently sucked at the base of my neck. "Dirty talk makes me so hot. The dirtier, the better."

I...had never talked dirty. But I'd also never been this wound up, and I wanted to please her more than anything. I put my lips to her ear, gently biting her earlobe. "I want to grab those sexy hips and hold you tight against me, grind so deep inside you."

Her breathy moan vibrated against my mouth as she sucked my lip. "Mmm, yes. I love a man in charge. What else?"

"I want to bury my face between your legs and feast on you. Every day, if you'd let me."

She whimpered as she straddled me. Her eyes, all pupils, gazed into mine. "Tell me how badly you want it. Tell me *exactly* how you would taste me."

She tracked hot kisses down my neck. "I'm weak, wanting to know what your pussy tastes like. I'd spread you open with my tongue, slip it inside you, drag it up and bury my face in you, suck you so hard, tease your clit with my tongue."

"Oh God, you're gonna make me come, just hearing you say it." She squirmed and whimpered but still didn't lower to my lap. Her respect for my restraint made it harder to be restrained.

"Imagine how hard you'd come if I worked you over with the Cosmic Dick and my mouth around your clit."

She scrunched her eyes, pressing her forehead to mine. "Fuck, yes." She pressed her hands to either side of my face, slipping her tongue into a deep and hungry kiss. "Yes to everything. I'm drenched just thinking about it. What's your kink?"

It was taking all my willpower not to pull her hips down to my aching cock. The sheer, molten lust in her eyes alone was about to send me over the edge. And then there was the rose perfume over her pheromones, the press of her breasts against my chest, and the thought of her pussy—wet for me—mere inches from my cock. "I think you're my kink."

She whimpered. "Tell me what you want me to do to you. *Please.*"

I hesitated. Dirty talk was harder when it was about me. "Maybe...what you said we could do."

Her answering smile was sex incarnate. "You want me to run my tongue up your cock? Take it in my mouth and suck it?"

"Yeah." Said cock was about to burst right now.

"Tell me how you like it."

I ran my hands up her thighs, afraid to answer her. The thought of her doing that to me—oh God, now her hand was slipping down my shorts and grabbing my bare ass. "Fuck, you're making me so hot." She kept her pelvis away from mine, but her squirmy, sexy body under my hands was quickly breaking my resolve.

"Tell me how to please you with my mouth," she begged.

"Take it into your tight, hot mouth. Suck me so hard, run your tongue along the slit."

"I want you to wrap your fists in my hair when I take you," she whimpered.

We devoured each other's mouths with kisses, and I would never have enough. "I swear I could kiss you all goddamn night."

"No can do, Deck Daddy. If I wake up with your hard cock against my bottom again, I'm gonna dance naked in front of you until you nail me."

I chuckled into the kiss. "I can't. I don't have any condoms, anyway."

"I'm on the shot. We're both clean."

My heart thudded into a ragged rhythm. "You want to go bare?"

She nodded.

"Holy fuck, baby, you aren't helping my condition," I murmured. I tangled my hand in her hair as my kisses dropped dangerously close to the not-celibate-anymore zone below her sundress's neckline.

"You're not helping my condition, either, with your celibacy bullshit," she teased, laughter lacing her words.

"Yeah, well it didn't help hearing you in the shower last night with Steely Dan."

"Steely Dan's at home. That was Eddie Rabbit. I stole the batteries out of the TV remote in the bedroom."

"Jeez, I might come just thinking about you in the shower with that."

"It would be entirely your own fault for laying these sexy hands on me at the beach yesterday." She grabbed one of my hands from her waist and slid it down to her ass, grabbing it with my hand.

"You mean I could've started kissing you yesterday?"

"You probably could've railed me on the porch that night you found me in your garden, and I would've been cool with it."

Her body shifted down and barely squirmed against my erection. I pulled my body further into the sofa and held her tight to hold her still. "Rose, you're making this really hard."

"So I felt." She kissed me again, panting. "I tell you what. I'm going to spend some time with Eddie Rabbit, and then when I'm a little more..." She swallowed hard. "...satisfied, I'll come back and we can kiss and cuddle. But if you change your mind, just barge in and join the fun." She kissed me hard then sashayed that fine ass away from me.

I threw my head back on the sofa, my hands over my eyes. "You're a siren. You know that, right?" My heart was pounding, my whole body was aching for her. Why would I turn down this invitation?

Her arms wrapped around me from behind, one hand sliding down my chest to my belly. I murmured *fuck me* while she whispered, "Truth or dare?" into my ear. The buzz of it shot straight to my groin.

"Dare," I croaked.

She gently bit my earlobe, and whispered, "I dare you to come watch me."

I froze. "Seriously?"

"You heard me. You wouldn't have to do a thing."

I shook my head. "If I watch you, I'm gonna want to help you out."

"I have an idea about that too." She turned my face toward her and slipped her tongue into my mouth in a kiss, then she went within my line of sight and made a big show of pulling out The Bag, dropping it onto the bed. Unzipping it. Digging around in it.

"What are you looking for?"

She didn't answer, just rifled through it then held a box out toward me with a raise of her eyebrows. The black fuzzy handcuffs.

I swallowed hard, my mouth suddenly dry. "What do you mean?"

She shrugged. "It'd be hard to join in if you couldn't reach me, wouldn't it?"

This wasn't exactly celibacy. It wasn't exactly not, though. "Okay."

She broke open the box and pulled me into the bedroom, onto the bed. "Will you take your shirt off? It'll help me get there."

I whisked it off without a second thought.

"Hello, Deck Daddy," she murmured, running her hand up my chest. "Get comfy." She raised her eyebrows suggestively as she opened up the handcuffs, stopping to read the box.

"Rose, are you into BDSM? Because I might be in over my head."

She chuckled. "I don't know yet. This is a first for me too." She held the cuffs up. "Still want to?"

I licked my lips. "Yeah."

She closed one cuff around my wrist and threaded the other through the ironwork headboard before snapping it around my other wrist. "Comfy?"

"No, not at all."

Her face clouded over, and she adjusted the cuffs. "Are they too tight? Want me to take them off?"

I leaned forward and captured her mouth in a kiss. "It doesn't hurt. I'm just all on edge. Not in a bad way."

"You can trust me. I won't do anything you don't want me to do. To you," she amended. "I'll do whatever I want to myself." She smiled and kissed me for long, aching minutes. Then she pulled back, looking a little dazed. "Okay it's really hot kissing you while you're in handcuffs."

"Yeah, I'm into it too." I kissed her again, then she moved out of reach and pulled the Plum Marvel box from the duffle bag.

"Eddie Rabbit," she said.

I watched her like a hawk. Her panties dropped to the floor from under her dress, and she took out the long, thin wand with a little piece jutting off the side and a bottle of lube, which she applied liberally to the device. She knelt on the bed before me and kissed me again. Setting her bottom down beside my knees, she laid on her back and planted one foot on my shoulder and the other on the headboard. She spread her thighs wide.

"Oh God, Rose." I could see everything. She was waxed practically bare. Her whole, beautiful sex laid wide open for my eyes alone, close enough to lean down and lick. I shifted against my shorts, trying to find release for the almost unbearably pleasurable pressure.

She pressed a button on the side of the toy, and the *brrring* vibration filled the room.

Languorously running the tip of it along her body in long strokes, she sighed and laid it against her core. For a while, she ran it in circles around her clit. Her soft cries and breaths made my own breathing ragged. Then her gasps exhaled in a series of "ohs" that got louder then stopped altogether as her foot on my shoulder sagged—did she come already? Oh shit, maybe that was just the first, because now she was slipping the whole length of it inside of her, the side projections against her clit. Good god. She sighed in satisfaction and slipped her hand inside her dress, grasping her breast. Under the fabric, her fingers teased her nipple. And *Christ*, she rocked her hips.

It was the most thrilling, most erotic experience of my life. Watching her squirm. Watching her pleasure herself. Drunk on her unbearably seductive sighs. Her foot on my shoulder flexed and moved as she jockeyed for a better position, lifting and bucking her hips. My hips shifted back and forth on their own, and I shut my eyes, forcing my body to be still. I shouldn't be watching this.

Her soft sighs got louder, and her foot pushed harder against my shoulder. "Oh, *Jason*," she moaned, and my eyes flared open. Thoughts of me were driving her?

"Rose, baby, you're so fucking hot. Oh my God, so fucking hot." I pulled at my bonds, unable to take my eyes away from her. From between her legs, from her hand inside her dress, from her beautiful face. Her eyes were closed, and she tossed her long curls against the bed. Hotter, her body more luscious than I ever could've imagined.

With the vibrator plunged fully inside her, she moved it around in circles. Moaning louder, gasping my name. She was close, and I couldn't stand it.

My right hand broke the cuff and dove inside my shorts, fisted my erection. Her eyes fluttered open, and her gaze landed between my legs.

"God yes, fuck yourself. I want to watch you."

I didn't take my eyes off her as I did what she asked, what I couldn't stop myself from doing. The slippery smacking of her body around the vibrator filled the room, and a trail of her wetness slipped down her ass. The smell of her body was a drug. She went at herself harder, faster, moaning, her whole body tensing up, her eyes never moving from where my hand worked frantically in my shorts. She cried out my name over and over, and when I saw her body contracting, I came in my shorts with her name in my mouth.

I didn't know if it was physical or psychological, but the waiting had made my release so strong. Like fireworks. And oh fuck, it was amazing.

She lay there panting for a minute, eyes closed, knees falling together. I breathed hard, heart hammering. I'd been hit by a hurricane. Breathtaking, sexy Hurricane Rose.

Her laugh was easy and breathless. "Sorry I made you masturbate."

I laughed, laid my head back. "Sorry I broke your handcuffs." I was still reeling. My hand rested inside my shorts, covered with my spend.

She sat up and kissed my lips, kissed along my jaw. "I like it when you call me baby," she murmured. Then, "I'm taking a shower." She held the key up between our faces then set it on my thigh. She had the audacity to wink at me before flouncing off to the bathroom.

I undid the broken cuffs with trembling hands. She swept into my life from out of the blue, and now she was all I could think about. Was I just indulging my high school daydreams, or was Rose Guidry my...girlfriend?

But did she only want sex? I didn't want her to only want sex. I wanted more from her than that. I wanted everything. And there it was—the only thing that held me back from making love to Rose. If I did, I might fall *in love* with her. God, I wanted that. But did she?

I grabbed a change of clothes and went to the half bath to clean up. Besides sex, what could I do to show Rose how she made me feel?

She was affectionate. She always built me up with words. She literally cried when I helped her unpack and made her that table. That, and how she was always doing little things for me, like throwing the towels into the wash before I could get to them, or leaving her old mini fridge stocked with cold water in my shop because she noticed I didn't have one. I smiled to myself. She'd left colorful Post-it notes all over my walls and tools with things like " satisfy your thirst(y fans)" and "getting warmer, getting colder" in her adorable, messy handwriting to hint at the new addition. I still hadn't taken a single one down.

So I could indulge my affectionate nature with her, do more thoughtful things for her, and...I grinned to myself. I could help her finish her bucket list. That'd definitely put that cute, open-mouthed surprise on her face. I could almost hear her touched *aww*.

But she was still going to want to have sex.

I set my hands on the counter and stared at myself in the mirror. Fuck, what a risk. The glue wasn't even dry from the last time I had to put my heart back together. But if I made love to her, and we fell in love...goddamn, what a reward.

Chapter 10

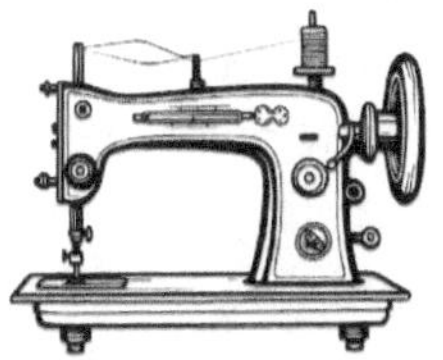

Holy Smokes

Rose

I woke up alone and disappointed that Jason hadn't come to sleep beside me last night.

I cycled through the New Orleans news outlets. We couldn't leave until after his meeting tomorrow at earliest anyway, but the interstate was still closed and the power back home was still down. Poor Jason must be a nervous wreck this morning. I smiled big. Or maybe I helped him relax last night.

I sat up, stretched my back. The condo was quiet. Maybe he didn't come to bed because he regretted what we did last night. I bit my lip and pulled my knees under my chin, stretching my Deck Daddy T-shirt down over my legs till it covered my feet. Maybe I'd talked him into going too far. Although I wasn't *exactly* responsible. I grinned. The whole thing had been so erotic, the dark look in his eyes as he watched me.

I didn't regret last night, but I might if he was weird about it. Or, shit. If he apologized and distanced himself from me, I'd have to find another place to live. I rubbed my face and took a deep breath. If that's the case, I'll kick my own ass.

I blew a breath out. Only one way to see if we were cool or if things would be awkward.

I walked out into the living room in my T-shirt and panties to find him already at his laptop at the kitchen counter.

"Morning," I said. "Are we still going to Seaside today?"

His eyes scanned down my body, and he smiled brightly before answering me. "Morning, beautiful. I want to if you want to." He closed the lid on his laptop and walked up to me, pulling me into his arms and placing a kiss on the top of my head while he rubbed my back. "I made coffee."

I smiled, wrapping my arms around his middle and breathing in his scent. Not only was it not awkward, he almost made me feel *cherished*. That was new.

"Do you still want to go to Seaside? I was looking for other things to do, and I found a state park nearby. They have a waterfall, and—"

"Are you trying to trick me into hiking?" I yawned, my words slurry and sleepy against his chest. "'Cause it sounds like you're trying to trick me into hiking."

He pulled back and smiled at me. "I just thought it'd be cool to see a waterfall, that's all."

"I mean, if you've seen one, you've seen them all. You've never seen a waterfall?"

"I've seen a couple. Have you?"

"A few. Niagara Falls, Ruby Falls, Bridal Veil Falls in Yosemite. I mean, with a name like that, I had to see it."

"You're waterfalled out. Duly noted. Seaside it is." He leaned in to kiss me, but I put my hand over my mouth.

"Morning breath."

A corner of his mouth tugged up. "As if that would stop me."

"Don't say I didn't warn you." I stood on my tiptoes and met his lips, fell into deep kissing until my bladder started knocking on my brain. "Jason. I have to pee."

He squeezed my ass with both hands. "Then go pee and get ready."

Two hours later, Jason was fangirling around a housewares shop in Seaside, a nest of shops and activity in a horseshoe around a green space and an amphitheater.

"Do I really need these retro orange juice glasses?" he asked, carefully sitting a couple of them in his basket. "No. But they look just like the ones my grandma had when I was a kid, and I can't pass them up."

I smiled. This shop gave us the first five minutes out today that he wasn't obsessing over his meeting with Big Dick Tools tomorrow morning. "As long as you're enjoying your retail therapy." I checked the price tag on a cute ceramic cheese and crackers tray I absolutely didn't need. I was usually too rabid for cheese to make it look pretty first.

"Retail therapy?" he asked.

"Yes, and now I've broken the spell. How are you feeling about your meeting tomorrow?"

He eyed the glasses in his basket, then added two more from the display. "I'm really nervous. What if I get there, and they say, 'No, we've made a horrible mistake'?"

"You're looking at this the wrong way. Sure, maybe they just want to get eyes on you and make sure you are who you say you are and you're not a psycho or anything. But I really think tomorrow's meeting is for *you* to see if you want to work with *them*. They reached out to *you*, which to me means they've already done their research and it's a done deal as far as they're concerned. All you need to do is walk in, be your charming self—"

He interrupted me with a smile and a peck on the lips.

"—and get a feel for whether you want to work with *them*." I shrugged. "That's how I see it. And if you don't like something, walk away."

"No way would I walk away. This is everything I've been working toward. Without this, I'll never be able to turn my community room into a house."

"I don't believe that. If this isn't your way, then your way is coming."

He nodded and looked around, as if taking my words in. "That's a good way to look at it."

"I think that's how the universe works. It closes doors that aren't for you, and opens ones when you least—ooh, look at that!" I made a beeline across the small store to look at a wooden wall shelf for sale. Whitewashed and slightly distressed, the back was pointed at the top with glass panes like a church window. They had it styled with tarot cards, incense holders, big hunks of amethyst, quartz, and other witchy knick-knacks. "It reminds me of your house."

He nodded, studying it from all angles. I smiled. That must be how I looked when I tried to figure out if I could sew something I saw in a store. "That is cool." He flipped the price tag. "Oof—that's a lot for such a small shelf. I could totally make it for less than that."

I chuckled. "You sound like me in a dress shop. I love how deep the shelves are, too. I could probably fit all my crystals on it and still have room to grow."

"I wish I could get it for you, but maybe I can make—"

"Oh, absolutely not!" I turned away from the shelf. "I just thought it was cool."

We drifted toward the checkout counter. In the line, Jason's hand bumped mine, and my heart rate went up. One casual stretch of my fingers, and I'd be holding his hand. But that would be admitting I wanted more. And I didn't want to admit that unless he felt that way too. We moved ahead once more in line.

My one-to-three scale for relationships started at having sex. So, with his desire to remain celibate, I didn't know where to place him. I never held hands unless I was about to or was sleeping with someone. Would holding hands skip him ahead to a Two because it was more relationship-y? But if all my relationships were based on sex...

Two of his fingers hooked onto mine. And stayed there, his thumb rubbing circles. He didn't look at me, didn't speak. But casually, more of his fingers connected with mine, electricity shooting to my core as he gently played with my fingers. My heart pounded. I returned the gesture, all of my attention focused on the places where our fingers met. Just as he scooped up more of my fingers and ran his thumb softly over the back of my hand, it was his turn to check out. He clasped my whole hand as he took the step forward, pulling me gently with him, and then squeezed my hand once before placing his glasses on the counter.

I folded my arms, unsure of what to do with my hands now that we had held hands. My heart jittered as I did careful relationship math in my head. What were we? What was this? Because the idea that Jason Soniat could be interested in me, even if sex was off the table, was too ridiculous to be true.

But as soon as he signed his credit card receipt and took his bag, he gave me the loveliest smile, slipped his arm around my waist, and led me from the store.

Once on the sidewalk where we finally had breathing room from the crowds, I let my hand swing free as we walked toward the back of Seaside to where wooden shops clustered around an open courtyard. He pointed toward Rudolph's Christmas Shoppe. "Can we go there? I'm so excited to get a big-ass tree this year, and I barely have any ornaments." He smoothly slipped his hand into mine.

It was hard to form words, the way his thumb caressing my hand was waking up far more intimate parts of my body. Would I survive a sex-free relationship with Jason? Would he give in? How horrible was I that I wanted him to compromise his morals?

"Sure," I said. "And then don't forget you promised me a bookstore *and* a record store." I risked a glance up at him. He was grinning down at me.

"Of course! I like making you smile."

My smile got so much bigger.

Rudolph's was a Christmas wonderland. They'd divided the shop into themed rooms, one filled with blown glass ornaments, a whole room of Santas, and a whole section for ornaments celebrating southeast states. Jason's wide-eyed wonder was infectious. "Can we just stay here for the rest of the trip? Oh wow, look at this Santa."

Within a few minutes he'd collected so many ornaments that I went to grab him a basket.

"Thank you. Can you tell I love Christmas?"

"No." I kissed his cheek. "It was not at all apparent."

I followed him around a corner, and he stopped short. "Girl. There's an upstairs?"

I laughed. "Come on, you big kid. Let's go see what they have."

The upstairs was full of mini Christmas villages, Halloween decorations—where I immediately diverted to—and a whole section of Christmas greenery. Heather, Abby, and I used to put up a Halloween tree when I lived with them. We made cool crystal ornaments, hung up spell sachets and other witchy things. I missed those days. Maybe I'd put my own tree up this year.

"Hey Rose." Jason's voice was at my ear as I checked prices on two witch ornaments that I really, really wanted.

"Yeah?"

He cleared his throat, and I tore my eyes away to look at him, then at the mistletoe he held over his head.

I grinned. "You're an adorable dork. Do you know that?" A family of four passed us on their way down the stairs, and no one else was around. I set the ornaments down and reached my hand up to cup his face, and he leaned down to kiss me.

And oh, what a kiss. Tender, slow, so much yearning I was unsteady on my feet. I rocked softly into him, my hand on his chest, his hand on my lower back. The world was cinnamon, pine, soft jingling, and stardust.

"Eh-eh-ehm."

We broke apart with a *smack*. An older woman stood with a fist on one hip, her other hand pointing at a sign on the wall that read, "you kiss under it, you buy it" in old timey red and green letters.

"Yes ma'am." Jason smiled. "We were just trying it out to make sure it was legitimate, kissing-under mistletoe. It satisfied all my requirements. You, Rose?"

I gazed starrily up at him, only able to nod after a kiss like that.

The woman smiled indulgently at us. "As if I'd sell anything less." She pointed to the basket at Jason's feet, which was nearly full. "Would you like me to hold that at the counter for you?"

"Yes please." He lifted the basket, dropped the mistletoe into it, and passed it to the woman. "Don't let anybody else buy that mistletoe." He turned the full force of his dimples on her. "I mean it. That particular one is the only one I'll have."

"Wouldn't dream of letting another soul have it." She winked at me before heading back down the stairs.

Dinner and less than ten minutes of a movie at the condo led directly into making out on the couch again, him half on top of me, but with his pelvis not touching me. I didn't mean to be that person who couldn't have a relationship without sex, but he had me desperate only with his lips on my mouth, my neck, my jawline. I dove my hand down the back of his shirt, stroking the hard muscles of his back and trying to shift my body more underneath him. I wanted this man. No, I needed this man, and I needed him now. Had I ever been so desperate to show a man with my body how crazy he made me?

But what satisfaction couldst I have tonight?

None, as long as he planned to remain celibate. I loved sex. I was good at sex. But maybe I needed to let a better person than me teach me how to be patient.

Or maybe he just didn't like me enough.

His thumb's circles on my bare thigh went up three more inches as he sucked kisses at the crook of my neck. I whimpered. "Just when I think you've hit my Achilles heel, you find a new spot for your magical mouth to tease me."

He chuckled and kept at it.

Irredeemable, incorrigible, wanton. And still somehow defective. That was me. I'd throw out one last invitation.

"Jason, I respect your journey through celibacy, I really do, but when you're ready, I want you to take me so hard and rough that neither of us can walk for days. Respectfully."

He groaned, and his hand left my thigh to hover over my breast then fall to my stomach. "You're the sweetest torture."

My heart sank. My panties were soaked, all my blood was pooled between my legs, and my nipples were so peaked they stung. "Jason, I don't want to stop kissing you, but I need to go take care of myself because wanting you is physically painful."

I skirted out from under him and went toward the bedroom.

"Don't leave me," he begged, turning toward me with puppy dog eyes.

But I closed the door anyway and pulled out my new favorite vibrator. I threw everything off the bed, switched on the lamp and off the overhead light, eager to run my hands down my own skin since Jason wouldn't.

Finally naked, I pulled back the covers, fighting the tears springing to my eyes. He didn't like me enough. That had to be the reason, and it sucked. Sex was emotional for him, and he wasn't about to give up his celibacy for someone he didn't really care about.

I respected the hell out of that, and it was for the best. Because...I liked him a lot. He was such a cool person. Kind, talented, and smart. Not to mention funny and caring. Not that it mattered. I could enumerate all his wonderful qualities, and it still wouldn't mean—

"Rose?" His voice came from just outside the door.

"Jason," I replied, wiping under my eyes.

The door opened. I turned. Jason strode toward me.

Completely naked.

My eyes went down of their own accord. "Holy smokes, Deck Daddy is *hung*."

He took my face in his hands, standing so close that his hefty, erect cock pressed hard and warm against my belly. My entire body short-circuited.

"Rose, I can't wait." His dark eyes soaked into my soul. "I don't want to miss a minute of us." He kissed me hard, possessively, and I grabbed his waist, kissing him just as fiercely.

Us?

His hands traveled down. His hand on my breast caressing, his hand on my bottom pulling me tighter to him even as he pushed me back against the wall. But I could never be close enough, no matter how my hands scrabbled at his broad shoulders, dug into the curls at the back of his neck, and pulled his face closer, his whiskers scritching my palms. His kisses claimed me, pulling me away from shore, but he was an ocean I wanted to drown in.

He pulled my arms over my head, threading the fingers of his one hand through both of mine and pinning them to the wall. "You want me to be in charge?" he asked with a cocky smile.

"Until I say so," I dared.

He swept his tongue inside my mouth, then his lips and tongue ran hot down my neck. I arched my back, and he took the bait, capturing my breast in his mouth. *So good.* My whimper bloomed into a moan as his hand slipped between my legs, his fingers dipping in, stroking me, circling me with devastating gentleness. My knees went weak. Did my pussy write that book he was reading?

His thumb circled my clit, and his fingers slipped inside. With his tongue flickering fast across my nipple inside his suckling mouth, I was overwhelmed by the sensation of *him*. My orgasm came fast and hard.

He let my hands go, and I grabbed his face to bask in the onslaught of his claiming kisses on my mouth. Then his hands and tongue and teeth teased my nipples and skipped warm exclamation points down my belly.

Kneeling down, he pushed my legs apart and glanced up at me with a wicked smile. He tugged one of my thighs over his shoulder and split my sex open with his thumbs. And then he buried his face in with a lusty moan.

The hot, overwhelming pleasure of his mouth consumed me, and I whimpered his name. I dug my fingers in his curls and pulled his sucking, probing mouth closer. I ground against him, but he braced his free arm across my hips and pinned them to the wall. A couple minutes in, I stopped struggling for control. He wanted to take his damn time. What if I let him?

Slowing down as if he was savoring me, he edged me with a mind-numbing attentiveness, like he could do this all day and night. Like he wanted to. The long, flat licks inside the hot suction of his mouth and the slow, leisurely explorations of his lips and tongue had me gasping his name with every breath.

For long minutes, his mouth stroked and lapped me into languid ecstasy, warmth stealing through all my limbs until my whole body ached with the need for release. My every exhale was a whimper. But then his lips sucked against my clit, his tongue swirling unmitigated tension into my every cell. His thick fingers slipped inside me, and I cried out, an orgasm tremoring through my whole body.

While I struggled to stand, his tireless tongue traced all the way back up to my mouth, probing inside and making me taste myself. I grappled at his back, lifting my leg along his hip, rubbing every smooth expanse of his skin I could reach until my hand closed around his cock. I pumped him once and my feet left the ground.

"Do you want me inside you, Sweet Rose?" he murmured in my ear.

"Yes," I gasped. "God, yes!" But guilt ate at me. "Jason, are you sure? I shouldn't have rushed you."

"I'm sure." He leaned in to kiss me, but I pressed my hand against his chest to stop him.

"Okay, but if we're doing this, I need you to be exclusive for as long as we're, you know, doing this."

His brows came down as his eyes burned into mine. "Absolutely. I'm only yours." The heat of his gaze warned me he meant more than physically, but I needed him too badly to heed that now.

The fat tip of his cock pressed between my labia. "Are you sure you want me *bare*?" His hoarse voice cracked on the word, gruff, full of need.

"Yes, *please*," I panted. "I'm sure. Give me *everything*."

His first thrust filled me completely, so full, so good. We swallowed each other's moans as he ground against me in a rhythm. "Talk to me, Jason, tell me—"

"You're so hot, so tight. Christ, Rose, I've never..." he thrust deeply again, and paused, his words quivering out desperate, thoroughly undone. "So good. So...*ah*...so good."

"Fuck me, baby, fuck me so good," I begged.

He ground so deep, and I mewled against his mouth with my hands digging in his hair.

"Is this what you wanted? Is this what you imagined when you slipped that vibrator inside your pussy?" He pulled out a little, then thrust himself in to the hilt, filling me to the brim and staying there. Pivoting his hips in tight circles, he devoured my mouth.

"Yes," I moaned. Completely overcome, I slapped softly at his shoulders and sucked at his lips, bucking my hips. "Just like that, just like that."

He shifted his angle, growling at the back of his throat. "Tell me how you like it, baby. Tell me and I'll give it to you. I'll give you everything."

"Deep and hard, so hard," I whimpered. My fingernails were at his neck and down his back.

His tongue dove into my mouth. I wanted all of him inside me. His tongue, his cock, his fingers. I could be the goddess of taking him into me. I wanted him to fuck me into divinity. I squeezed his cock inside me and he cried out, never stopping the sublime grinding that had me barreling toward transcendence.

"Oh my God, you feel so fucking good, Rose."

He shifted me lower on his hips, grinding against a new place no lover had ever tapped. I cried out.

He stopped moving. "Am I hurting you?"

I almost shouted. "No! Don't stop! It's perfect." I gripped his shoulders as he committed hard to those deep-inside-me perfect grinds against that perfect spot and kissed me like he'd eat me alive. He brought me higher and higher, then I broke loose. Stars sparked behind my eyes as I embraced the cosmos, elevating to another plane of being. I came so hard, I squirted.

"Oh, Christ, Rose, I can feel you coming, so hard. Baby, you feel so fucking good." He drove harder, rougher. My breasts bounced against his hard chest as he prolonged the divine contractions deep in my body. He became a primeval god of thrusting, crying out as his release throbbed inside me. He ground slowly and deeply until it ceased.

With his arms still tight around me, he pulled me away from the wall. My feet gently touched the ground. Our hungry kisses turned to smiles and searching gazes.

"Goddamn," I panted. It was all I could manage. I laid my head against his sweaty chest and wrapped my arms around his middle, my legs trembling.

"Fuck, never in my life," was all he could say, breathless as me. He pressed a kiss to my head and pulled me with him toward the bed.

"Wait," I said, "I need to pee."

His eyes focused on me, and he kind of laughed. "What?"

I pushed him toward the bed. "I'll be back. I want to prevent a UTI."

He chuckled and playfully slapped my ass as I went to take care of myself. When I came out, he was sprawled out across the bed, gloriously naked.

"Goddamn, you're beautiful." I ran my hands up his hard body before curling up in his arms, my blood pounding through my veins, the air conditioning cooling my skin even as it stuck to his. I felt powerful. Irresistible. Radiant. Desired.

"You're a goddess." His fingers caressed my side, and he chuckled. "Best sex of my whole life, and you're going straight to pee right after."

I laughed too, nuzzling his neck with my nose. "I'll thank myself later when it doesn't burn when I pee." I fixed my eyes on his. "Jason, you were so goddamn good, you made me squirt. I've never done that with a partner."

His eyebrows went up as if he was amused by my frankness, but he held my gaze and threaded his fingers through mine. "So...best sex of your life?"

I nodded, slipping my leg up over his thigh and running my hands across the glory of his skin over the drum of his heart. "No competition. Are you just naturally designed to pleasure me, or did you learn a lot from that book?"

He chuckled. "I'm only halfway through it."

"Hoooooly smokes," I whimpered.

He laughed, and we were silent for a long moment. Long enough for me to start questioning everything. What if he hated me for tempting him too hard to get physical?

"I'm sorry I made you break your celibacy," I said softly.

"What?" He pulled back and took my face in his hand. "You didn't make me do anything. I'm not sorry at all. I needed you, Rose." His soft, sweet kiss on my bruised lips made sunshine beam through my body. "I think I was waiting for you." His big brown eyes searched mine, filled to the brim with...emotion?

He pressed a long kiss to my forehead, then soft, indulgent kisses to my lips. I could kiss him forever, my hands traveling along his skin, grabbing his face, his arms. His eyes fluttered open, sparkling with the curve of his smile. Then he planted kisses in the crook of my neck, nudging his hips—and his erection—against me.

"Holy reset, Batman, are you ready to go again? Maybe we should break out the Bat Cuffs," I joked.

He chuckled, nuzzling my breast with his nose. "You're gonna tie me down? Sounds hot." He lapped and sucked at my breast, and my whole body was lit again. It was like the last three orgasms hadn't even happened. "Now you've given me the taste for it, it would definitely be a distraction from my meeting in the morning."

"Don't tempt me, Deck Daddy. I could distract the hell out of you." I latched my mouth onto his and pushed him down to the bed, straddling him and nestling his cock along my sex. I ground against him, and he resumed his careful attention to my breasts. I couldn't trust words any more than I could trust my heart. But sex with my ideal Level Two man? That I could do. All. Night. Long.

Chapter 11

Aftermath

Jason

The view from the top of the world was amazing.

My conversation with the COO of Big Dick Tools, Faduma Abdi, had been going on for about an hour, and just like Rose said, she'd seemed more interested in chatting with me and answering my questions than asking me any.

"I'm so glad you were able to come in, Jason," Faduma said, brushing her braids back over her shoulder. "It was great getting to know you today."

I smiled, nodding. "Absolutely! Thank you for having me." I sat up straighter, more confident than ever that the gig was mine.

"We'd definitely like to offer you some paid ads with Big Dick Tools, but talking with you today makes me feel like you'd be a better fit for our newest endeavor: StudFinders."

I was smiling and nodding as Faduma sifted through some papers in the folder in front of her on the conference room table, but my heart rate had gone up as soon as my solid ground disappeared. Paid ads would be a great avenue of income, but they weren't the big money like their email had mentioned.

"So StudFinders…" she handed me a glossy color paper with a logo and app screen mockups on it. "Is an app-based recommendation service for finding handypersons all over the country. Similar to Angie's List, but with our own kooky spin, of course."

"Okay." I rubbed my beard, barely taking any information in from the paper except bright reds and yellows.

"And you would be perfect in our video and print ads. You already have a rabid fan base, and your single hottie on his own, 'he could be yours but he's not anybody's' mystique is perfect for our brand."

Single hottie on his own?

Now Faduma was talking about a contract and the incredible sums they were willing to pay me to be the face of this new enterprise, which were even *more* than the email had mentioned. It was everything I could've dreamt of, but the details flowed through my brain and into the *oh shit* bucket where I kept information that overwhelmed me.

She wound down her sales pitch and looked at me expectantly. "So tell me, what are you thinking? What questions do you have?"

"Wow," I chuckled. "Um, a lot. So…help me out. You said something about being single? Do you mean that I couldn't have a girlfriend while I was under contract?"

"Of course you can. We can't dictate that. But you'd have to keep the relationship under wraps to embody StudFinders's branding. At least for the duration of the contract."

Well, fuck. "I see. And…how long did you say the contract is for?"

"One year to start," Faduma supplied, "negotiable for more if both parties agree. I'll send you the contract to look over later today, but what do you think?" she asked, her brown eyes lit with excitement. "How would you like to be the face of StudFinders?"

My mouth opened, but nothing came out. All I could think about was the amazing woman I spent last night with who was back at the condo waiting to hear how my meeting went. Who was probably going to bolt the moment she heard about this.

Faduma laughed. "Did I make you speechless, Jason? I know it's a lot to take in, and I did pull a switcheroo on you."

I laughed along. "Yeah, it's definitely...a lot. Can I think about it?"

The corners of Faduma's mouth turned down in what looked like puzzled surprise. She didn't expect that. Shit. Would she rescind the offer?

"Yeah! For sure. I get that it's a big ask for a young guy like yourself, and of course you haven't even looked over the contract yet. I'll email it to you this afternoon. How does that sound?"

"Sounds great."

"Great!" Faduma stood up from her chair, and I followed suit. "I have to get to another meeting, but it was great meeting you. Let me walk you out."

She scooped up the Deck Daddy shirt I'd brought her and herded me toward the door with promises of more information to come. I walked out with her and ended up on the sidewalk outside with little idea of how I got there. But the heavy dread in my chest suggested I'd messed the whole thing up. Maybe she wouldn't send me the contract at all. Maybe people didn't usually ask her *can I think about it?*

I looked up and down the street, oriented my feet toward my car, and obsessed over every detail of the meeting and every implication of the contract she wanted me to sign for the hour-long ride back to the condo.

Back to Rose.

When I got there, I went up to the condo with a black cloud trailing over my head. Rose opened the door just as I fit the key into the lock.

"Hey!" She threw her arms around my neck before pulling back, her face an excited question mark. "How did it go? Tell me *every-thing*." She pulled me inside and shut the door.

"It went great, I think." The dryer hummed in the background, the plastic was back on the sofa, and Rose's packed bags sat near the door. "Wait—we can go home?"

"Surprise! Power's back on at your house! I'm finishing up washing our dirty sex sheets right now, but we can go whenever you're ready and that's done." She sat on the sofa, and I sat beside her. "What happened? I've been dying over here. I thought you'd maybe call me when you were leaving."

"I'm sorry." I squeezed her hand. "I absolutely should have. She kind of dropped a bomb on me, and I wasn't thinking."

"How do you mean?"

I looked around the condo. I'd driven all this way, but I was antsy to get on the road and see what was going on back home. "You know what? Let me tell you while I pack up."

An hour later we were cruising on the interstate toward home, and I'd told Rose all about my meeting. Well, almost all about it.

"Spokesmodel Jason!" She clapped her hands in excitement. "I knew they'd love you! You told her yes, right? It's a fantastic opportunity."

"And so much money. I could turn the community room into a frickin' mansion with that kind of money."

She raised her eyebrows and lowered her head, holding my gaze. "So...what did you tell her?"

I returned my eyes to the road, sighing. "I...asked her if I could think about it."

"What? Why?"

I sighed as I took a fork in the interstate. "They have a stipulation in the contract I'm not crazy about and didn't expect." I glanced at her. Her face was neutral, waiting. I rushed it out. "They don't want me to date anyone publicly for the duration of the contract."

Her brows lowered in a frown. "They can actually dictate that?"

"Apparently. I haven't seen the contract yet, so I'm not sure how it reads. I mean, she said I *could* date. They can't dictate that. But if I dated someone, I'd have to keep it 'under wraps.'" I took my right hand off the steering wheel to put the last two words in air quotes.

"For how long?" Her voice was soft. She was looking out the window now, her posture pulled back from her earlier in-my-space excitement.

My heart sank. I couldn't bear to let this scare Rose off. "A year. More if they still want me and I still want to do it." A deep breath in. "So…I asked to think about it to buy time."

She nodded but said nothing. Long minutes went by.

"I'd give almost anything to know what you're thinking over there," I said.

She smiled, but her smile lost its steam. "Well, neither of us shut down rumors from the sewing video, so you'd have to do that. And…I don't know."

If she said *we might not even be together a year from now* I would be devastated. Surely we were both thinking it, but I didn't want either of us to voice it.

The air conditioner blew her long hair back, and she fooled around with the vents for a minute. I'd want her in a year, I'd want her in thirty years. Maybe I was a complete and utter imbecile to feel this way so fast, but denying my feelings had gotten me into too many bad situations in the past. I wouldn't do it again.

"Say the word, and I'll say no," I blurted.

Her head swiveled to me. "Jason! No way! I would never ask you to do that. That's—no. We only slept together. A few times," she conceded. "You can't make life decisions based on how they affect me."

Dread sank through my body into my feet leaving my stomach cold and nauseated. She thought all we were was one night of sex?

My heart raced. I swallowed hard, training my eyes on the road and willing myself not to get light-headed with anxiety. "I kinda thought…I was hoping we were more than a one-time thing. But if that's not how you feel, I'll—"

Her hand landed on my thigh in a squeeze. "No, no! That's not what I meant at all. I don't think we're a one-time thing."

I exhaled with relief and took her hand in mine. "Cool," I blurted stupidly.

She smiled. "Cool. All I meant was that I think you have to make decisions that are right for *your* life. And if they want you to appear single…I don't know."

"We could...keep things under wraps." I cringed as it came out of my mouth.

"You mean keep us a secret? From them, from social media, from the public?" She huffed a small laugh. "'From the public,' like we're celebrities. I mean, you *will* be." She squeezed my hand once and took hers away. "You kinda are already."

She didn't seem angry, but the sad look on her face hurt my heart.

I briefly squeezed her thigh. "All I know is that I'm excited about us."

She glanced at me and smiled. "Me too."

"And I'm also terrified to find out how many trees came down on my house and how many thousands of dollars of damage I have that I can't afford."

"That you can't afford *yet*," she said softly. She pulled out her tablet. "Let me know if you want to switch out. I don't mind driving."

"That's okay. I'd go crazy sitting there with nothing to do."

"You could design my mom's dress for me. I'm sure she'd love to see your ideas."

I huffed a laugh through my nose. "Yeah. That wouldn't be a disaster at all." I turned up the radio and applied all my thoughts to the road. Literally and metaphorically, I didn't know what lay ahead.

It was almost 6:30 in the evening when we made it to New Orleans. The closer we got to home, the more torn-off roofs and stranded cars we encountered. Standing water blocked the interstate down to only the left lane at one point, and a detour onto Airline Highway bypassed the Pontchartrain Expressway, which was still underwater. And everywhere, downed trees.

I rubbed my beard, more nervous than ever when we got into our neighborhood. Everywhere, people were out cleaning up branches and leaves, throwing out wet carpet. Trees were uprooted on every street. "I don't like this. I'm gonna find all five of those oak trees near the church, *inside* the church."

Rose rubbed and squeezed my thigh. "Whatever we find, it'll be okay. Nobody was hurt, and anything else can be fixed."

"You're right, but Rose?" I looked at her sideways through narrowed eyes. "How is turning me on supposed to help at this point?"

She laughed and slipped her hand under my shorts, rubbing her fingernails gently up my thigh. Higher. "Oh, this is turning you on? I had no idea it would do that."

"Yeah, and I'll show you how much later on." I grabbed her hand and kissed it. "But right now we're about to learn our fate."

I made the final turn onto my street. Everywhere, people were picking up leaves, cutting up fallen trees. An Entergy truck was down the block, a man in a cherry-picker repairing something on a utility pole.

Then there was my property. Three trees had fallen over that I could see, their shallow, mud- and grass-covered roots perpendicular to the ground, tipped over from their bed in the lawn. One in the front yard, two in the parking lot, but none on the church. "Oh thank God." I pulled as far as I could into the parking lot, inspecting the roofline. So many missing shingles. "Damnit, I'm gonna need that new roof sooner than later."

We got out of the car and started walking toward the church.

Rose went around a branch I'd stepped over. "But insurance should help, right?" She gasped and grabbed my arm. "Jason."

I followed her pointing finger. One of those goddamn water oaks had fallen on the rectory—right into Rose's apartment. "Shit."

The whole thing had tipped over like the others, its massive root circle taller than the roof, and the 60-, 70-foot trunk had fallen directly across the building.

I eyed the side of the house as I followed her to the kitchen door. "Damnit. Rose, that's your bedroom. *Fuck.*"

The kitchen was eerily damp and covered with leaves as we made our way into the house. But one look down the hallway showed where the real damage was. The trunk had sliced through the roof and fallen to one side of Rose's bedroom.

"Oh my God!" She stepped forward gingerly, but I reached out and grabbed her.

"Don't go over there. We don't know how secure that thing is."

She pulled back, both hands over her mouth. "I can't even—Jason, I'm so sorry this happened to your property."

I pulled her into my arms and cupped her face, kissed her forehead. "My property? Thank God you evacuated with me. What if this happened in the middle of the night, and you were sleeping in your bed?" I pulled her tight against my chest. "You know what? Never mind, because I can't think about that."

She hugged me back, pressed a kiss to my neck. "But all of your beautiful, hard work in these rooms, your roof—oh jeez, thank you so much for making me put Becca's dresses in the church. But all my stuff's probably ruined. Maybe all my other dresses. And I don't even have a place to sleep."

"You lost all that, and your first words were worrying about my hard work." I kissed the top of her head again. "Sweet Rose. Maybe your stuff will be okay. But look on the bright side. You can sleep with me." I released her but kept my arm around her. I couldn't begin to think of the repercussions of that invitation. "I don't even know where to start. Let's just go back to the beach." I turned her around with me and started walking.

Her laugh cajoled a smile from me. "So tempting. But maybe you should take pictures for the insurance adjuster while it's still light. I'll throw away all the spoiled food from the fridge."

"Yeah, that's probably more productive. Then let's see what we can get out of your room."

It took us till nearly 10 o'clock to take photos, move everything we could get to of Rose's belongings into the church, and clean out our fridge. I was going to have to move that into the community room tomorrow where there was a tiny, outdated kitchen area we could use temporarily. Thankfully most of her fabrics and all of her sewing machines and tools had been in the workroom and were unharmed. But the tree was completely blocking access to her room. I jimmied open the bathroom window to see what I could reach from there, but all I could get to was her packed bag of clothes that I hadn't taken with us, two cardboard wardrobe boxes, and a plastic bin of shoes. So much of her stuff was trapped under the tree, and it didn't look safe to go closer.

With all the grocery stores in the same boat as our fridge, I braved the super-long line at Lee's Hamburgers, one of the only food places open for business. After dinner, I sat at the dining room table in the church as Rose washed all her clothes she could salvage—thank God I'd moved the washer and dryer into the main building last spring. I'd called in all the favors I knew to get that damn tree off the roof, but I'd still come up empty.

"Alright, Ryan. I appreciate you trying. Take care. Bye." I hung up and rubbed my eyes.

"No luck?" Rose asked, sitting a laundry basket full of her clothes on the floor by the table.

"Nope. He didn't know anybody either."

She stopped and stared at me as if there was some obvious truth I wasn't seeing. "I'm a dumbass. Let me call Heather. Her dad owns Aucoin Construction. I bet he can get us somebody to help."

"Really? That would be amazing."

"I'll send her the pictures I took of it. If anybody can make the impossible happen, it's Heather."

I pulled her to sit in my lap, wrapping my arms around her and leaning my head on her shoulder as she texted. She hadn't complained once today, working hard right alongside me. Helping me take pictures of the damages, carting her things out of her living space, reassuring me when I got too overwhelmed by the damages. She hadn't batted an eye when I told her my idea to set up a temporary shower for us with hoses in the old community room bathroom. We worked smoothly together in a way I've never experienced, as if she was really my partner. It thrilled me to find yet another way, especially back from the cocoon that Florida had been, that we were so well suited for each other. She was my rock today, and just having her in my arms calmed me.

"Were you able to salvage a lot of your clothes and your dresses?"

"Kind of. The box of my wedding designs was so moldy, I didn't think anything survived. I somehow only lost four of the twelve dresses in it, but then I lost over half of my favorite things. Like, the clothes I actually wear." Her outgoing text swooshed, and she laid her phone down on the table, wrapping her arms over mine and leaning back against me.

"I'm so sorry, Rose. This is all my fault. I'll bring you shopping and pay to replace everything."

She turned in my lap to face me. "What are you talking about? The hurricane was in no way your fault."

"I should've prioritized taking down all those water oaks. If I had, none of your things would've been ruined."

"As my old therapist used to say, 'don't *should* on yourself.' The trunk was humongous. It was an old tree that withstood decades of hurricanes. Who would've thought it'd come down with this one?"

"Me," I insisted. "I've been worried about it since I bought the place. I'm so sorry about your stuff and your apartment. What if you'd been—"

She took my face in her hands and pressed her forehead against mine, looking into my eyes like a sexy cyclops. "This. Was not. Your fault." A kiss to punctuate.

"If you say so. But look." I slipped my hand up her shirt to rub her back. "If you don't have enough clothes, and you need to walk around naked, I won't stop you."

She laughed and looked down. "Jason, we're really...new. If you feel weird about me staying with you, I can probably stay with Heather and Abby until I have a roof again."

My stomach fluttered, and I dropped my hand to her waist. "But I thought you didn't want to move in with your friends."

"Yeah, but that was when I was looking for a place to *live* live. Staying for a few weeks is different. I could do that."

Maybe she was trying to give me an out, but I didn't want one. "But I'd miss you." Unless she wanted an out?

"I'd miss you, too."

Her steady smile reassured me, and I wet my lips. "I know we've only been together a few days. And under normal circumstances I would never ask you to move in with me this fast. But...I got spoiled in Florida, having you around all the time. I want you to stay with me." I twisted a finger in one of her curls. "I'll make a place for you to sew in the church. You can sleep with me upstairs in the choir loft." I cupped her face, moving in for a kiss. "I could make it worth your while."

She kissed me then studied my face for a long minute. "Okay. I can try that. You know, in the car earlier you promised to show me later how much I was turning you on. Is it later yet?"

"I'm bone tired." I pulled her hips closer to my arousal. "But I'm desperate to get you into my bed."

She laughed and squirmed out of my arms, jogging toward the choir stairs. I took off after her, letting her get ahead of me until she was in my bedroom. I caught her around the middle, and she threw her arms back over my neck, laughing.

"You don't need this shirt," I muttered, pulling it off over her head. "You definitely don't need this bra." I snapped it open in record time and pulled her back to me, filling my hands with her breasts, gently pinching her nipples. She ground back against me. I skimmed my hand down her stomach and slipped my fingers into her panties and into the velvet wetness waiting for me, circling her clit with the softest touch. She sagged in my arms, moaning.

"Is this what you want?" I murmured against her neck.

"Yes," she breathed, squirming her ass against my cock. I think I growled as I flipped her onto her back on my bed and stalked over her, pressing her body down as I kissed her luscious mouth. Her legs wrapped around my waist, and her hands tangled in my hair before moving down and scratching my back.

"What are you gonna do to me, Deck Daddy?"

I kissed my way to her ear. "I'm craving the taste of your pussy." She whimpered as I ground my cock against her shorts.

"You like it?" she panted.

"I want to eat it for breakfast, lunch, and dinner."

Fskfsk she sputtered, shimmying out of her shorts and panties. "Jason, I'm open twenty-four-seven for your convenience."

"I love your hours."

"I love your mouth." She gasped when I suckled her breast, teasing my tongue around the peak of her nipple. Threading her fingers through my hair, she thrust her hips against me.

I pulled off my shirt and settled my chest against the divine heat of her core. "Grind that hot pussy on me, baby." And oh god, she did, spreading her legs wider, whimpering and writhing her wetness against my chest until I couldn't wait any longer to taste her.

I dragged my tongue between her breasts, straight down the center of her belly, and pushed her thighs apart. She watched me, her eyes dark and her lips parted.

I feasted my eyes on the soft folds between her legs—the perfect pink, glistening, just for me. "Christ, Rose, look at you." I pulled her ass to the edge of the bed then knelt before her like the queen she was. I licked a hard line from her opening up to her clit and latched my whole mouth to her, sucking the sweet, transcendent fucking taste that was all her. She cried out my name and her hips went wild, but I hadn't had my fill. I pulled her tight against my face, almost drowning in her nectar. Lapped my tongue in circles around the sweet bud of her clit.

Leisurely, I savored the feel of her sex in my mouth. The hot as fuck noises she made as I pleasured her made me so fucking hard I could cry. The desperate way she moved her hips and whimpered my name. Her eyes were closed, her curls tossing across my sheets. Goddamn I loved overwhelming her with pleasure in my bed. One of her hands caressed my head, holding me deeper against her, and her other grasped her own breast, teasing herself. My cock throbbed with need. I reached up to gently roll her nipple with my fingers. She cried out my name, begged me not to stop.

So I slipped my fingers inside and went in for the prize.

"Oh fuck, Jason! Oh my God!"

Her release squeezed and released my fingers, and she laid there for a few seconds panting. Then her eyes fluttered open and focused on me. With a determined smile, she got up, grasped my shoulders, and pushed me down to the bed. She kissed my mouth, then I grasped and caressed her body wherever I could reach as she left a trail of kisses down my chest and stomach, licking a swirling line down the sensitive skin of my groin.

"Rose," I breathed.

Holding my gaze, she ran her tongue up the underside of my cock. Shivers erupted through every cell of my body. I moaned out her name again, my stomach muscles shuddering as I fought barreling over the edge.

She *mmmed* as if she enjoyed my taste. Then her mouth slipped like velvet down my length until I felt the back of her throat. I dug my hands into her loose curls, pulling them out of her way and gently tugging once they were wrapped around my fists.

Her moan vibrated around me, her beautiful face solemn with determination. Watching and feeling her at the same time was taking my breath away.

She fisted the base of me, sucking me almost whole and torturing me with her ravenous tongue. Grinding me so deep. I panted her name and barely held onto the edge, twisting my hands in her hair. I was afraid to move my hips and spend my load before I buried myself in her body.

Fuck, no more. I sat up abruptly, pulling her up. My cock popped out of her mouth, and she scrambled onto my lap. She stuck her tongue down my throat and swallowed my whole cock into her tight heaven with one downward thrust. I gently palmed the back of her neck to hold her in place as she ground against me, and my release gathered in my spine. I begged my body to hold on, but I erupted deep inside her, her release following mine.

Even then I couldn't stop kissing her. Touching her. Running my fingertips along each eyebrow and weaving my fingers through hers. How did she become everything to me so fast?

Rose

Welp, I'd just confidently sewn this skirt inside out.

I turned off my sewing machine, rubbed my stinging eyes, and sank to the living room rug where I curled into a ball. I'd been at this for four days, and my progress wasn't fast enough. Dread uncurled in my chest. I couldn't do this. It was already September, and I wasn't finished with Becca's dresses. I hadn't even started Mom's. My back ached, my fingers were sore. I was going to let my mother down, and my dream was a nightmare.

My heart jangled in a familiar rhythm of panic. No. Not now. I curled up tighter when the tears started. Why did I think I could do this, especially after losing all that time in Florida? I should've brought my sewing machine, should've set up camp on the condo's table and locked myself inside to work on Becca's dresses. But then I would've missed all that golden time with Jason that I was paying for now.

I couldn't stop shaking and crying, loud sobbing that echoed through the empty church. My arms felt cold. I was the worst human. I was such a burden. I couldn't...I just couldn't do it. I couldn't do anything.

The front door opened, and I gasped my mouth shut, squinching my eyes closed. If Jason found me like this, he'd think I was ridiculous. He'd send me away. I was ridiculous. And so stupid to think—

"Honey, I'm home!" Jason called out. "They had the thread you wanted, and I couldn't read my handwriting on the zipper length. So, I got a 20-inch and a 22-inch. If that's wrong, I'll go back...Rose? Baby, where are you?"

My sob came out like a hiccup. I couldn't hide now. "I'm here," I wailed miserably.

His footsteps came closer, and then he was on the floor beside me. "Hey, what's wrong?" He kissed my head and rubbed my back.

"I can't do this, Jason. I thought it was what I wanted, but—" I hiccuped a sob and gasped for air through my mouth since my nose was completely blocked. "I just sewed a dress inside-out. Do you know how embarrassing that is? I'm so bad at this. Now I have to rip all those stitches out and do it again, and I can't—" I took in a shuddering breath. "I don't know why I thought I could do this. The dresses are a mess, and I'm gonna let everybody down. I can't have a business like this. What was I thinking? I'm...I can't..." I started sobbing again.

"Aw, baby," he murmured. "Come on. Let's get up." He helped me to my feet then carried me bodyguard-style to his deep, cushy sofa. He draped a throw on me and handed me the tissues from the coffee table. "I'll be right back."

He dropped a kiss on my head then hurried off, leaving me to sob and blow my nose. I was a useless burden. Living in his beautiful house and not even paying half the bills. He built me a table and even went and bought stuff for me. I had nothing to offer him, and he was going to realize it. I blew my nose harder—so much snot. He must think I'm so disgusting.

He settled beside me and handed me my purse. "Do you want your medicine? Would that help?"

I nodded, crying harder. Here he was being so good to me, and I didn't deserve it. He pulled out my wallet and peered inside my purse, bringing forth the pill bottle. "Is this it?"

"Yeah."

He handed me a little white pill and a water bottle, and I drank my medicine down.

"Here..." He snuggled up against me, laying us down face-to-face along the sofa.

"I'm sorry I'm such a burden," I sobbed. "I'm sorry. I don't know why I can't stop crying. I'm a mess."

"Baby, you're not remotely a mess. You're not a burden, and you don't have anything to be sorry for." He pulled me tight into his arms, and I nestled closer to his chest. His strong heartbeat against my ear centered me.

"I'm just so tired."

"Of course you're tired. You've been up late and early trying to make everything perfect. Yeah, maybe you took on a lot, but I don't doubt for a minute that you can do it. But you need to rest, now." He kissed my head and rubbed my back, then pushed my hair back from my face. "You're so talented, and so smart, and you care so much. I'm sorry it's so hard for you now, but you are *amazing* at what you do, and you couldn't let everybody down if you tried. You're gonna get everything done."

"Please don't leave me. I need you." I whimpered, his caresses calming me down. If I could just escape my brain for a while. I needed to escape for a while.

He squeezed me tighter and settled in closer. "I won't leave you. I got you. Let's rest, right here. You and me." He rubbed my back and kissed my head. "I've got you. Sometimes you just need a good cry and a good nap, and the Xanax ought to help you relax. I've taken it before, too. Does it make you sleepy, like it used to make me?"

I nodded against his chest and breathed through the anxiety. It felt like he was holding me together. I pulled him tighter. He was right. This was an anxiety attack. No matter how many I've had, it was still hard to recognize them when they came.

Long minutes went by. After a while, my heart stopped banging out of my chest. My viselike grip on him relaxed. My meds and his warm, steady presence topped out the fight-or-flight chemicals surging in my body, and now they were subsiding. Birds chirped, Jason's wind chimes sang gently from the courtyard. Somewhere in the distance, somebody's lawn equipment whirred. The dreamy afternoon sun through the stained-glass windows soothed me, but not as much as Jason holding me close and rubbing my back. I snuggled against him. Every so often he murmured, "I got you," and pressed a kiss to the top of my head, his breathing even and soft.

The spicy scent of tacos woke me. I was still on the sofa under a blanket, but Jason was gone. The church lights were low, dreamlike, and the world outside the stained-glass windows was dark. I yawned, stretched, and went to find the tacos.

The dining table was set for two with a bowl of chips and salsa sitting beside a covered dish of steaming taco meat and a whole bowl of shredded cheese. "Oh, hell yeah." I scooped a heaping spoon of shredded cheese onto my plate. Shoveling it into my mouth, I sat down then dipped a chip in the salsa.

The door opened, and Jason came in with a platter of hard taco shells. "You're up! I was just warming these." He set them on a trivet on the table and leaned in to place a kiss on my cheek.

I wrapped my arms around his neck and wouldn't let go. "Thank you. You're the best."

"You're very welcome." He squeezed me back and dropped into the seat beside me at the head of the table. "How're you feeling?"

"So much better." I scooped meat into a shell, sprinkled a generous amount of shredded cheese on top, and crunched off the edge of it. "M*mmm*. Rrr a eely gook cook," I said around my food.

"Thank you. I'm glad the groceries are starting to open back up." He slid his hand onto my leg and ate with his other, as if needing to touch me.

I took a long sip of my Diet Coke, eyeing him up. He was minding his own business. Eating his tacos. As if he hadn't talked me down from a cliff before making me a home cooked meal. As if he wasn't the first guy to be so caring to me. Definitely the first one to be so fucking beautiful. I wanted to draw him. That jawline, those long lashes.

He caught me watching him and smiled. "What?"

"You're really good at this boyfriend thing."

His eyebrows raised, and his face lit up. "Boyfriend?"

My heart thudded. The word was bigger with Jason, but I didn't want to take it back, even with Big Brother StudFinders watching. "Yeah." I bit my lip. "Unless you're not there."

"Oh, I've *been* there." He slipped his hand into mine and halfway stood to kiss my cheek with that beautiful smile. "I'm just excited to hear you say it."

What did I say now? I stuffed my mouth with another huge bite of taco to take speech off the table. I was...I was living with my *boyfriend*. This was new territory, a Level Two I hadn't explored yet. A level I'd never even considered. Was I still disoriented from my nap, or did this just kind of sneak up on me?

Maybe I'd change the subject. "What have you been up to while I was napping?"

"I wanted to stay close by, so I caught up on all my emails and posts I've been avoiding since I got home. I had three requests for custom furniture quotes waiting for me, which I was pretty excited about. And Faduma sent the StudFinders contract. I let her know I got it, but that I was dealing with hurricane damage and I'd have to get back to her. I still don't know what I'm going to tell her."

"Does it read like you expected?"

"Yeah. They don't want it to look like I'm dating anyone for the duration."

"I still think you should take it." We'd been over and over it for the past several days. But I knew he'd regret not taking it, even if I didn't like the idea of hiding our relationship.

"Maybe," he said. It was how that conversation had been ending, every time.

We kept eating, chatting about my progress on the dresses and his ever-expanding to-do list of custom furniture, social media responsibilities, and the merch orders he was behind on. I offered to help him pack them up and bring them to the post office. Getting out of the house sometimes might do me some good.

My phone buzzed on the other side of the table where I'd plugged it in earlier.

"It's been doing that a lot," he said. "You might want to check it."

When I'd downed my last taco, I unplugged my phone and pulled it to me. Missed calls and texts from Heather, Abby, and a number I didn't recognize. I tapped into Heather's text first.

> Hey sexy, Dad's still waiting on the crane, but I sent your Insta to Sam, and PJ fell in love with your designs. Guess who she wants to design her bridesmaid dresses and maybe even her wedding dress? SWEET ROSES BRIDAL! I hope it's okay I gave Sam your number.

> Fair warning, PJ's a raging bitch, but she has impeccable taste. SO EXCITED

Instant heartburn. "Oh my God." I clapped my hand to my mouth.

"What's wrong?"

I couldn't take in enough air. Tears sprang to my eyes, and before the worry on Jason's face could reach critical mass, I handed him my phone. Stared at him with my hands over my mouth as he read it, his eyes and mouth going wide.

"Girl," he said.

"I know!"

"GIRL," he said again.

Hands over my face, I started crying. His arms came around me. "Congratulations! Baby, this is huge! You can't get much higher-profile than PJ Lane and Sam Cooper! Hey..." He knelt beside me and dabbed at my face with a clean napkin. "You're officially a designer to the stars. How does it feel?"

"Terrifying!" I cried. "How am I going to do this? I'm already so behind!"

"I think you need more information. They can't be getting married next month. Has he even called you yet?"

I took a shuddering breath and took my phone from him. The unknown number. "A text and a call." I played his voicemail on speaker.

Sam: Hey Rose, this is Sam Cooper. Heather Aucoin sent me your beautiful dress designs, and I sent them to my fiancé, PJ Lane? She went nuts over them. We set a tentative date for July. I hope that's enough lead time. Heather said you're already really busy, so if I can help by hiring a team to help with PJ's dresses, I'm happy to do that. So, give me a call back when you can, and maybe we can set up a time to meet at your studio? Looks like I'll be relocating to New Orleans for a while with work, so I hope we can work it out. Thanks!

"Jason, this can't be real life." Something like impending doom settled on my shoulders. "How am I going to do this? I have three dresses to finish for Becca. I haven't even started Mom's." I gestured wildly at my phone. "He thinks I have a studio. Like some kind of professional."

"You *are* a professional." He kissed my forehead and tucked my hair behind my ear. "It's okay. We got this. Let's focus on one thing at a time. You have two weddings to finish now, but Sam and PJ aren't getting married until July. It's only September. That's like...ten months away. Tell him you're booked through October—it's not a lie.

Then you don't even have to think about PJ until after your Mom's wedding."

His smile steadied me, and I smiled for the first time with this news in my life.

He wrapped my hands in his. "Meantime, we need to get all those dresses we talked about photographed and beef up your social media presence before this news drops. Baby, you're going to have more requests and offers than you know what to do with. Own this. You deserve this success."

Happy tears welled in my eyes. My boyfriend was...amazing.

He squeezed my hands and leaned his head against mine with an excited little *ahhhh!* "Now I'm all hyped to take pictures of you in your beautiful dresses. Tomorrow I really have to make progress on some custom pieces I'm behind on, but I'll scout some locations in the afternoon. It might be kinda hard to find places not affected too badly by the storm, but I'll find them."

I grabbed his beautiful face and kissed him, hard and long, sinking down to straddle him. He adjusted, stretching his legs out long and settling me on his lap. His hands and arms snaked around me, pressing me close at every point like I was lovingly ensnared by a hot octopus.

After a minute, he came up for air with a smile. "Damn, woman, what was that for? You're making me want to throw you over my shoulder and carry you upstairs."

"I can't tell you how much your support means to me. I've never had a boyfriend who cared about my dreams enough to help me with them."

His smile widened, dimples engaged. He kissed me softly again. "How can I help my girlfriend tonight with these dresses?"

I laughed. "You want to help me sew? Do you even know how to sew?"

"I'll have you know I once sewed my own button back on a shirt by watching a YouTube video. You might say I'm a master seamstress. Seamster. Sewer?"

"Sewer looks weird written down, but it works orally." I raised my eyebrows at him suggestively.

He chuckled. "I see you, trying to skip ahead to the good stuff. What's the next thing you need to do on Becca's dresses?"

I smoothed my hand down his T-shirt. Sure, I wanted his help. But being this close to him was turning me on. I tried to focus on my work. "I have to rip that skirt apart and put it back together the right way. Ummm...oh! How do you feel about learning to make ribbon roses? I need a shit ton of ribbon roses."

"Is that a US shit ton or a metric shit ton?" He shrugged with a smile. "You know what? Either way I'm in."

"Awesome. But there's one problem." I went back to kissing him, but with more tongue and hip action. I ground against him and found hard evidence that he was into it too. "You being all helpful, and sweet, and hot has me too turned on to do anything but you."

He chuckled and gently slapped my ass. "C'mon then." He coaxed me up, took my hand, and led me across the dimly lit church to the plush rug before the fireplace. I unzipped his shorts and pulled off his shirt and undies, and he made quick work of my clothes, too. Standing naked face to face with him, I reached between us and grasped his erection—already hard and needy.

But he took my hand away, slipping his fingers through mine and placing his other hand at my waist. "Dance with me." He leaned in at the hips to press against me as he began to move under the muted colors of a streetlight through stained glass.

"But there's no music," I giggled.

"I'll sing for you." He took a few steps with me with an *ummm*, as if searching in his head for something to sing. "It had to be you...it had to be you," he sang, dancing slowly with me. "La la la la laaa, and finally found...somebody whoooooo...I don't really know the words to this." He dipped me as I laughed, my long hair hanging down. "La la la la..."

Skin to skin, Jason danced with me, his not at all bad voice echoing through the big room with *la la la's* and snippets of words he remembered. His dark eyes twinkled and never moved from mine. It was deeply romantic, maybe the most romantic moment of my life. He pressed his forehead against mine, and I hummed along with him.

"It had to be youuuuu!" He ended the song with another dip.

I laughed and grasped his erection. "I'm ready for that big finish."

He pulled me with him to the rug with hungry eyes and laid me down beneath him. Fluffy softness at my back and his smooth, hard body in my arms. I spread my legs wide to welcome him and kissed him with my whole heart.

One muscular arm planted on the floor beside my head, and the other pulled my thigh tight against his waist. I slipped my hand between us and grasped him, sliding his tip around my clit in circles as he moaned into our kisses. I positioned him at my entrance, and he didn't wait. One deep thrust, and we were moving together. His deep, dark eyes fluttered, searching mine as he ground into me.

I'd never get tired of looking into his eyes. This was what he had meant. This connection. Sex had never been this deep for me. I'd never been touched so emotionally while being fucked so thoroughly. He laid down devastating thrusts while he kissed me so gently, ground so hard and deep while he gazed adoringly into my eyes and pressed his forehead to mine. Best. Sex. Ever.

I was lost in him. In his scent and his warmth. In the reverent way he touched me and his fervent kisses at my breasts. My hands explored his hard body with caresses, my mouth with kisses and soft bites at his lips and neck. Pulling against his ass to bring him deeper into me.

His slow, soft, breathy grunts at my ear drove me wild. "I love being inside you," he breathed. "Say my name, Rose," he pleaded. "Say my name."

"Jason," I whimpered against his ear. "Oh, Jason...I love how you fuck me."

His eyes gazed deeply into mine. "I know how my girlfriend likes to come." He swirled his tongue inside my mouth. "I wish I could slide my tongue around your clit while I fuck you." And then his fingers slipped between us and did just that.

He overwhelmed me with desire, filled my cup to the brim and over-flowed it, my orgasm radiating in strong, languid waves. He throbbed deep inside me with a moan in my mouth. And he didn't pull out when it was done. I held him tight with all my limbs, running my hands across his broad shoulders. I'd never be tired of kissing him. He laid in my arms, his heart pounding against my breasts.

Jason

Flipping through my camera at all the photos I took of Rose today made me even more sure that my girlfriend was the most beautiful woman alive.

This one of her on the porch of a tattoo parlor was one of my favorites. In a pink bridesmaid gown, Rose was radiant sitting on the railing, her tattoo on display against the sign with a carousel horse on it. The series at City Park was amazing—on the carousel, in the Besthoff Sculpture Garden, on the steps of the museum.

I straightened my tie, ready to pose as her groom for a last set of photos inside the church. Adjusting the lighting one last time, I perfectly illuminated the velvet chaise lounge against the brick wall with the basic lighting I used for my furniture.

Only one bouquet of the few she made last night hadn't wilted over the course of the day's photo sessions. I pulled it from its bucket of water and dried its stems off so it wouldn't drip on her dress.

"Okay, I'm ready," she announced.

I turned at her words and the clicking of her heels on my wood floor. *Holy shit.*

A lace gown nearly the color of her skin hugged her every curve. From the deep V that exposed the center of her breasts to the outline of each leg as she walked toward me, she seemed naked but was fully clothed in sparkling, clinging laces. The stunning contrast of her dark hair, deep red lips, and dark blue eyes against the creaminess of her skin and gown and veil made my breath catch in my chest.

Whatever she saw on my face made her blush and smile. "Does it look alright?" Her gaze raked me down and up again. "Damn, you're hot in that suit."

I blinked and shook my head. "It looks...wow. You're almost too beautiful to be real."

Her blush deepened as she waved me off and looked down. "Oh, you sweet talker. Where do you want me?"

My heart thudded. *Walking down the aisle toward me in front of our friends and family.*

Oh wow. Was that what I wanted? I was like a character in a movie whose ears were ringing after a bomb went off.

"Um, here. On the chaise."

I barely heard her comment on the set-up or her thanks when I handed her the bouquet. I chuckled along with her joke about making sure her nipples weren't showing. But my eyes kept returning to the fake wedding ring set we bought her yesterday. It sparkled on her left hand in the low light, rubbing a spot in my chest I'd forgotten was raw. The month before I confirmed Kasey was cheating on me, I'd been shopping for a ring for her. Like a fucking dope.

Rose settled herself on the chaise and smiled at me before arranging her train.

That spot in my chest wasn't as raw as it used to be. Kasey didn't matter anymore, and it was time I stopped letting her take joy away from me and my life with Rose.

My life with Rose. Goosebumps—I had literal goosebumps thinking about it.

I took photos of Rose reclining on the chaise and standing in the late afternoon light coming through the stained glass.

In the golden hour, I brought her into the courtyard, took photos of her by the fountain, under the brick arches dripping with white crepe myrtle flowers. And as the sun sank, I brought her back into the church.

"Come over by the sofa. I have the cameras set on interval timers. They'll take a photo every three seconds from these two angles, so as long as we stay between the area I have taped on the floor"—she looked down, marking the spots—"we'll be in the picture." I flipped through one of the wedding magazines we bought last night to one of the bride and groom poses we'd marked. "Here. Refresh your memory on the poses while I get my suit jacket on."

After last minute checks and adjustments on the cameras, I started them both and stepped up beside her. I whirled her around, settling her train in an aesthetically pleasing pool at her side. "Let's start with the back-to-back pose."

I smiled slightly, my head turned toward the camera, my eyes downcast and back toward her. I hooked my hand into hers and adjusted the class ring I'd slipped on backwards to look like a wedding ring, and we went through a silent dance of poses, punctuated by the snapping of the camera's shutter. Me standing behind her with her arm out and my hand on her hip. Me standing closer behind her as if I were about to kiss her cheek, which I then did, which made her breathe out a soft laugh. Her turning to me, adjusting my tie. Her hand on my shoulder, mine on her waist as she pressed her forehead to the bridge of my nose.

She was a vision in lace. Her dark eyes were fringed in black lashes, and her soft lips begged to be kissed. We moved closer, lips nearly brushing. She pushed my jacket off my shoulders slowly, letting the snapping cameras have their fill. She held my gaze as she loosened my tie, pulled it off me, and unbuttoned my shirt. Rose untucked the shirt and turned her back to me, pulling all her hair aside and baring her neck as I leaned in to kiss it. I splayed my hand across her belly and pulled her tight against me so she could feel what this was doing to me.

We'd planned all these shots, and I expected it to turn me on. But I wasn't prepared for how it felt for Rose and me to playact our wedding night. She turned to face me, all seductive eyes, her face almost solemn, and pulled my shirt off the rest of the way.

"I want to kiss you so bad," I murmured against her ear.

"But you can't mess up my lipstick," she said, smiling. She pulled me toward the chaise lounge. "Let's finish up with the seated photos."

I lounged on the chaise behind her, not even acting as I gazed adoringly at her as she stood nearer the camera. I arrayed her gown onto the sofa and leaned partly around her from behind as she sat like a queen. I got out of the way and adjusted the camera before setting her up for a solo photo kneeling against the side of the chaise to catch the creamy skin of her bare back in the gown. And finally, I adjusted the camera to point toward the floor where I had her sit on sumptuous fabrics as I laid with my head in her lap, gazing adoringly up at her. Which again, wasn't hard to do.

I sat up and leaned in. "That's all the poses. Can I kiss you now?"

"We deserve it after all our hard work." She pulled my face closer with a hand cupped against my jaw, and kissed me. The cameras snapped.

"What if we turn off the cameras before this gets too hot and heavy, and we maybe go upstairs where I can take this dress off of you?"

"Mmm, I love that idea. But also, a camera sounds kinda hot."

"Next time," I chuckled.

She shrugged and slipped off her heels, and we went hand-in-hand up the stairs to the loft. It was surreal unzipping her wedding gown with a ring on my fourth finger. Surreal to watch her, nude except for the flash of her fake diamond wedding set sparkling in the dim light as she unbuttoned my pants.

This felt real, like it was our wedding night. It was too soon to feel this way about her, wasn't it?

"Wise move not to tell me you weren't wearing underwear under this gown," I murmured against the soft, peaked tip of her breast. "Or we'd never have made it through the photoshoot."

"Mmmm, have you been imagining all the different ways you could defile me?"

"Most definitely."

"Show me all of them."

"Only if you show me where you keep your toys," I dared.

Chapter 12

Pocketing and Flashpanning

Jason

I woke up on the edge of my bed. I shifted carefully to my other side to see why: the most beautiful woman I've ever known had snuggled up against me all night until she'd nearly pushed me out of bed. Warmth expanded my chest and spilled into a sappy smile.

Rose was still asleep, and the sunlight streaming through the stained-glass window cast blues and yellows across her face, shoulders, arms, and breasts. My fluttering heart felt full to bursting when I looked at her. I kissed her forehead and smoothed a lock of her hair from her brow. She smiled, eyelashes fluttering, and slept on with even breaths.

She giggled in her sleep. I tried to hold back a laugh, which was apparently my first reaction to unbearable cuteness, but my breath out through my nose roused her. She blinked once, laid eyes on me. I scooched closer to her, slipped my hands under the covers, and ran them along the velvet of her hip and back. She wrapped her arm around my neck and pulled my head against her chest.

"Morning," she murmured, her voice laced with a sleepy smile.

I pressed a kiss against her breastbone, right over her beautiful heart. "Morning. You were giggling in your sleep. It was the cutest damn thing I've ever seen."

She giggled again, rubbing my back and squeezing me tighter. "I was dreaming about you."

This. This moment. This woman. She was everything I've ever wanted. "I love you so fucking much," I murmured, burying my face against her skin, breathing in her scent.

She stiffened and my heart kicked into my throat.

She pulled back and peered sleepily down into my face. "What did you say?"

I paused, fear spreading from my heart to my toes. Rose wasn't the marrying type, but was she up for commitment? I threaded my fingers through hers, twisting the rings still on her finger from last night. She was what I wanted. Why not tell her?

I gulped. "I said, 'I love you so fucking much.'" I studied her wide eyes. "And I meant it."

She parted her lips, a deer startled in the woods who was clearly not ready to hear those words from me. Seconds ticked by as she studied my face intently. I bit my lip to stop myself from taking them back. Because they were true. I felt them down to my core.

She tucked her hair behind one ear, fake wedding rings flashing in the morning sun. "Jason, I don't know..."

"It's okay." I smoothed her hair from the other side of her face. "You don't have to say it back. You don't have to feel it back." Even though each of her silent seconds was a little death.

"Kiss me," she murmured.

So I did. She climbed up, pushing my back to the bed and straddling me. If we were only physical to her, surely she wouldn't be licking the inside of my mouth like this right after my declaration, rolling her hips against my sex. If she wasn't open to more, surely she would've just run from my bed in horror.

Right?

She wouldn't be holding my face like this and kissing me like I meant the world to her unless she felt something too. Whimpering, she threw her head back and tipped her rosy nipple against my lips. I captured her breast in my mouth. If she didn't want me to tell her how I felt about her, I'd show her.

Rose

Jason loved me, and all I wanted to do was cry. From the bliss and beauty of making love, the wildness of our release, the raw emotion surging in my chest. And afterwards, he kissed the top of my head and squeezed me, and I almost broke.

Jason loved me. And I didn't know if I loved him back.

I murmured my thanks as he set a mug of coffee and a legal-sized pad beside his laptop where I was viewing the photos we took yesterday. I picked the mug up gratefully. Of course he'd fixed it exactly the way I liked it, and Lord knows I needed the caffeine.

He sat down beside me and smiled shyly, reaching past me to grab a pen with a ringless hand. He'd taken the fake band off before his shower, but it'd been there the whole time we made love. Mine too.

My heart thudded. Jason loved me.

Or...did he? He probably didn't *mean* it, mean it. Of the few men who'd ever said it, most of them just wanted to get me into bed or keep me in bed. Of the infinitesimal number who may've meant it, zero of them meant it for long.

Maybe the problem wasn't that Jason loved me and I didn't love him. The problem was that he was a man, and I didn't believe him *capable* of loving me. So how could I really love him?

Sipping from his own mug, he sat and leaned into my space with his arm around my chair. "What I like to do is make a list of my favorites, and then start writing down what the posts can be about. Wow, those are gorgeous."

"You did such a great job. I think you'd give Lily a run for her money."

"Nah, it's not my photography skills. It's the beautiful subject." He pressed a kiss to my temple. "Finding a lot you want to use?"

I'd never known a man to be as affectionate as him, especially when he wasn't actively trying to get my clothes off. A definite point in the *he might actually love me* column.

"Yeah! I think we got at least one to three good ones for each dress, which is amazing. I wish my other wedding dress had survived the storm, but I do still have that photo of Leslie's gown to post."

"And Becca's, after the wedding. Ooh." His index finger lightly poked the screen. "That one of you in front of the tattoo parlor is gorgeous."

"That one's great, but look at this hot one of us kissing here in the church."

"Oh wow." He reached across me and double-tapped the photo so that it filled the screen. "That's my favorite." He leaned his head against mine.

"It's perfect. We both look amazing, and the gown—look at the fall of the lace, the way you can see the back of it." I imagined the StudFinders contract unrolling between us like a royal proclamation.

He moved away and rubbed the back of his neck. "Can we not...post that one?"

My heart sank. "I guess Big Brother StudFinders wouldn't like that." I tried to say it flippantly, but even I heard the hurt in my voice.

"Not if I take the job." He took a big breath. "And I wanted to talk to you about Becca and Brad's honey-do shower tomorrow night."

"What about it?" Weird thing to bring up at this moment. I didn't get the connection, but I didn't like where it was going.

He bit his lip and for a minute, wouldn't meet my eye. "Do you think we can...not let everyone know we're together when we go?"

What the fuck? "Why? Are you...embarrassed of me?"

"No! God, no." He rubbed his hand down my arm. "I could never be embarrassed of you. It's just..." He took and released a deep breath. "My cousin Ashley will be there, and she's gonna be taking a ton of photos for Becca and Brad's wedding Insta." He rubbed his beard, shifting in his seat. "She'll tag us all in it, and well..."

"So I guess hiding us from StudFinders is going to be more pervasive than I realized."

He breathed out heavily. "It might be."

Did this mean we couldn't go on dates like a normal couple? Be seen out together in public at all? But he hadn't acted weird when we were out and about town taking photos yesterday. The term *pocketing* came into my mind from a magazine I'd flipped through in the waxing salon, where one partner hides the other from family and friends because they're embarrassed or not monogamous. Toxic as fuck.

I twisted my lips. "Are you sure you're not embarrassed of me?"

His mouth dropped open, and he leaned in. "No," he murmured, kissing my cheek. "I could never be embarrassed of you. Ever. I don't *want* to keep you a secret." He smiled. "I told Alex."

Okay. That wasn't nothing.

"Did you tell anyone about us?" he asked softly.

My eyes snapped up, a twinge in my chest. "I haven't really talked to anyone." Although, I'd been texting with Abby and Heather since we'd been back from Florida and hadn't told them. I guess I hadn't been eager to tell the world, either.

He nodded but didn't ask me why. If he suspected I was a serial flashpanner who leaves when things get serious—another term from that article—he didn't call me on it now. Maybe I was the toxic one.

"But we can post the ones of us together where we're not kissing, where I'm just a prop—I mean, I'm just a prop through the whole thing. If you post those and tag me, my followers will hopefully follow you too and build your numbers. Remember how crazy they got with our video?"

"And StudFinders won't hate that?"

He shrugged. "We can't control speculation."

"So tomorrow night at the honey-do shower, we're just gonna...drive there together and then act like you don't free willy into my vagina at least twice a day?"

"You have a way with words. But yeah. I guess."

He was trying to follow his dreams, and I was making this about me. I wasn't nuts about being kept a secret, but it would hold him at some emotional length, which made me less anxious. And honestly, being welcomed into his family as his live-in girlfriend was premature, especially as weird as I was already feeling about it.

"Okay. I'll be on my best behavior." I pecked his lips and returned my attention to the laptop, pushing all my unease down my throat. "Now lead me out of the land of the confused with these photos. How do I even start building these into posts?"

Chapter 13

Party Business

Jason

My stomach was in knots as we parked outside Misty's parents' house for the honey-do shower. I was only here for my sister, otherwise I wouldn't step foot into that house for any money. Just how disrespectful would Misty be tonight?

Too bad I was too chicken shit to tell my mom about me and Rose, or having her on my arm might be a deterrent. Not that I'd lied to Rose about tonight—the StudFinders contract was the main reason I didn't want us to appear as a couple, and Ashley definitely would be posting photos of tonight online. But it wasn't such a bad thing to put off telling my mom I was dating Rose, either.

Rose leaned toward me from the passenger seat. "Wait, let me straighten your tie."

This amazing woman entering my personal space would never stop taking my breath away. I slipped my hand into her dark hair and kissed her. I dreaded walking inside the party and acting like Rose wasn't my whole world, dreaded how I'd eventually have to tell Mom that I'd fallen for one of the women she disliked the most.

She pulled back. "Someone'll see us. But I have a surprise for you." She held a small, black remote out to me. "Put this in your pocket."

I took it from her. "What's this?"

She smiled mischievously. "A remote control. When we go in there, we can't act like we're together, but..." She leaned her mouth close to my ear. "Every time you press that button, you make my vibrator pulse for thirty seconds. I want you to go through this whole party thinking about how wet this pussy is for you." She nipped my ear and got out of the car.

Annnnd I was instantly hard. "This is your *best* behavior?" I called out. I sat for a minute studying the controls on the remote. How did I get mixed up with such a damn siren? She got our gifts from the back and walked around to where I was still sitting in the driver's seat, reeling with excitement.

She tapped on the window. I put it down, and she leaned in, her low-cut dress displaying breasts I wanted to bury my face in. "Are you *coming*? Or not?"

"*You're* definitely coming." I shooed her out of the open window and exited my vehicle.

On the sidewalk, I reached for her hand, then pulled back. I couldn't let anyone see that. I was absolutely being a coward for not telling my whole family about her yet, but she'd been talking to Lily, to her mom, her friends. Why hadn't she told anyone about us? It'd been over twenty-four hours since I told her I loved her, and she still hadn't said it back.

Her rose-colored dress hung in all the right places, and her smile pulled on all the right pieces of my heart. Too bad none of that would appease my mother.

I leaned closer to her as we walked. "You look beautiful," I told her again.

Her face lit up. "Thank you."

As she pressed the doorbell, I pressed a button on the remote. Her head snapped to me, lips parted. I leaned to her ear and murmured,

"Every time you feel that, I want you to know that I wish it was my mouth."

Rose turned bright red with wide eyes, as if just realizing she'd put herself in a lot of trouble. I raised my eyebrows at her and smiled.

A maid answered the door and let us inside the Hopes' very fancy house well-kept by housemaids. Tonight it was full of people, most of whom I didn't recognize. Rose was completely silent and still wide-eyed. Could be her sex toy, or maybe she didn't know anyone either.

"Rose!" A woman behind us called out. We both whirled.

The brunette who squealed and wrapped herself around my girl-friend was familiar, but the blonde who hugged them both wasn't.

"Heather! Abby! I missed y'all so much!" Rose said.

"I missed your face!" Heather planted a kiss on Rose's cheek and left a lipstick stain, and Abby tutted and wiped it carefully off. New arrivals moved through the foyer, and the four of us shuffled deeper into the living room. Heather's keen eyes darted between me and Rose. *Shit.* I was sticking beside Rose like we were a couple instead of going further in the party to find my family. Rookie mistake, but I'm glad it only happened in front of her friends.

"Jason Soniat, as I live and breathe." Heather smiled, looking me up and down and coming straight in for a hug. "How much algebra have you done since we last met?"

"A lot," I laughed. "Where were you at when I was in college? How've you been?"

"Great!" She wrapped her arm around Rose's waist and pulled the blonde closer. "This is my friend and plus-one tonight, Abby Lalumandier, like the luxury cut flowers."

"Her family owns the business." Rose added.

"Hi." Abby shook my hand. "I've heard a lot about you."

"Nice to meet you, Abby. Hey, you know I'm pretty sure Becca's bouquets are Lalumandier."

"Oh, that's so nice! I hope she loves them." She smiled and tucked her hair behind her ear, her gaze darting to her friends.

"By the way," Heather said, "my dad can get a crane for your tree situation. It's still pretty hard to get through the streets, and he's prioritized people who work for him. Is Thursday okay?"

Relief infused my chest. "Yes, wow. Thank you so much. Whatever day he can send it works for me."

Mom called my name. I looked over the crowd and spotted her in the back by the sunroom, waving me over.

"Good to see you Heather, and nice to meet you, Abby. I have to go. Mother of the bride's calling me." I pressed the remote, smiled at Rose's fluttering eyes, and went toward Mom.

Mom was near the sunroom with...well, shit. Misty and her parents.

"Hi Hopes." I shook Mr. John's hand and hugged Mrs. Rebecca, but put a hand up to wave at Misty. She fiddled with her earring, her brown eyes gazing at me with something akin to a dare.

"Jason, sweetheart," Mom said, "I was just talking to Misty about the walking order for the wedding. Wouldn't you love it if Becca could change the bridal party pairings so you and Misty can walk together?"

I lowered my brows at Mom, dread rising up my spine. "Why is Misty standing in the wedding?"

"Becca's pregnant friend with the two children—what's her name? Kimmy? Her obstetrician confined her to bedrest, so I suggested Misty take her place. She and Becca have been friends since they were in diapers."

"Is Kimmy okay? And you have to tell Rose." I pointed my thumb back toward the foyer. "She's almost finished with the dresses."

Mom laid her hand on my arm but looked at the Hopes. "He's such a sweet boy. Yes, Kimmy's fine. It's just a precaution. And since Kimmy is taller, and with her pregnant belly a good bit wider, I'm sure it'll be easy for Rose to alter the dress down to fit Misty's petite frame. The two of you would make such a handsome couple walking down the aisle together."

My heart sped up. I'd nearly forgotten I'd be walking with Rose down the aisle. I shook my head. "I wouldn't mess with Becca's plans,

Ma. You remember how she had us all line up by height. I'm not rocking the boat."

I couldn't unpack how standing with Rose made me feel right now. She was in the corner animatedly talking and laughing with her friends. Heather held her hands apart, palms facing, a clear gesture of an obscene measurement. Rose shook her head and pulled her hands out wider. Abby pulled both of their hands down, and they all laughed harder.

Three guesses what they were talking about over there. My face went hot even as my male pride swelled. I hit the remote again. Rose shut her eyes and grabbed Heather's arm, and I turned away before I lost composure and laughed out loud. I pulled out my phone before Mom could follow my gaze.

"Do you have Rose's number?" I asked Misty. "Make sure you talk to her tonight." This was so unfair. Rose was already stressed enough trying to get those dresses done without having to alter one she'd already finished.

I gave Rose's number to Misty. When I looked up, Mom and Misty's parents had disappeared, leaving us alone in the little area off the sunroom.

"I think we're being set up." She sidled close enough that the wine on her breath carried to me. "You look so fine in that suit."

"Thanks." I stepped to leave.

She grabbed my arm. "I haven't seen you in a couple weeks. Has anything changed with your..." her eyes dropped below my belt. "Resolution?"

I roughly peeled her hand off. "That's—wow. I'm gonna stop you there. I'm not interested in anything you're getting at."

She stepped closer, and I stepped away, my back hitting a column. She moved in. "So," she said quietly, "if I wanted to pull you into a closet and suck what I bet is a big, fat dick—"

"Jesus Christ. No." I took her by the elbows and kept her at arm's length as I stepped away from the column. "I'm not interested."

"I promise you'll like it," she giggled, trying to press closer.

"I promise I don't want it. Don't talk to me again." I released her elbows and walked away.

Rose

Jason left me almost the moment we got here. The bastard pressed the remote and then went off to talk to beautiful Misty who was wearing a tight orange dress.

Heather leaned in toward me. "You're totally doing it with Jason," she said quietly.

"Heather!" Abby mildly chastised.

I threw my head back with a laugh. I'd missed this dynamic.

Heather raised her expertly groomed eyebrows. "Where's the lie?" She spoke at her usual volume now, and before she could say anything else, I pulled them both a little farther from the people around us.

"Okay, yes, you're right."

They both squealed, but I shushed them.

"But you can't tell anyone," I pleaded.

Abby's lips were a line. "Why?"

"Because. It's...complicated."

"So uncomplicate it for us," Heather said.

I filled them in on the contract elephant in the room and the cousin who could blow our case wide open on the internet. "And it's fine, honestly, because I'm not sure I'm ready to meet the parents, so to speak, even though I already know them."

My friends exchanged looks, and Abby spoke first. "Okay. If you're okay with it, I'm okay with it."

Heather eyed me for a minute then smiled, a devilish light twinkling into her eyes. "Okay. But you have to tell us *everything*. Is it good?"

"*Fuck yes*," I murmured. Our heads came together as we laughed. All the months we'd been apart melted away as Heather and I went through our usual comparing sex-notes talk, and Abby, the school librarian she was, pretended like she was too polite for such conversation but listened attentively and laughed all the same. I'd missed my Dream House Girls.

Heather eyed Jason up and down from across the room and held her hands out in a decent measurement. "Does he have a big dick, or does he just know how to use what he's got?"

I grabbed her hands, pulled them wider.

Abby grabbed our hands and pulled them down laughing. "I can't take you two anywhere!"

"So much both," I whispered to them. "He loves giving oral, and he's—" The vibrator buzzed against my clit and in my vagina, and I grabbed Heather's arm reflexively. "*Motherfucker*," I murmured.

"You okay?" Abby asked.

Heat shot to my face. I leaned in toward her ear. "I gave him a remote."

Abby's pale cheeks blushed, and she gasped with a big smile like one of her students might do after overhearing a dirty word.

Heather cackled, no blush to her even tan. "Yes, ma'am! You get what you can from that sexy man."

The vibrations stopped, and even though Jason was hardcore edging me, I managed to regain my composure. "Look him up on Instagram."

Heather's phone was instantly out as Abby looked on. "What's his handle?"

"Deck Daddy."

Abby giggled and Heather guffawed, attracting the attention of three older women nearby who frowned at us and walked away with their noses in the air.

Heather stuck her tongue out at their backs and tapped at her phone before going perfectly still. "Holy fucking shit."

"Oh my," Abby said appreciatively.

Heather turned the phone toward me. "This is who you're sleeping with?"

In the photo, a bare-chested Jason was lifting a cabinet against the wall to nail it, his shorts slipping down around his hips. I nodded solemnly, excited to have someone to talk to about Jason. I didn't tell Mom because she'd get weird about me living with him, and I couldn't tell Lily because swearing her to secrecy was a worldwide broadcast.

"Goddamn," Heather murmured. "Look at that delicious man."

"So how did this happen?" Abby asked.

"I remember your epic crush on him in middle school," Heather said, "but were y'all together before you rented his apartment?"

"No." I launched into a breathless summary of digging up his yard through this morning, when, after answering *ten minutes* to his question about how long it would take me to finish the zipper I was working on, he kissed me within an inch of my life and said, *I'll be in the loft. When you're finished, come sit on my face.*

It only took me five.

Why hadn't I connected with my amazing friends earlier? Even though I omitted the part about him telling me he loved me, they completely understood where I was at with Jason. Heather never made me feel like a horny little freak for loving sex because she loved it just as much. And even though Abby was a little shy about sex talk, she was always so supportive.

"So I'm trying not to jinx it," I finished, "but he's a strong Level Two."

Abby's eyebrows lifted. "Really? Do you think he might progress to a Level Three?"

"I'm not stupid," I insisted, although I felt like I was holding a knife with Jason's blood on it. "I'm just enjoying being with him."

"Heather! Rose!" Becca appeared from nowhere, launching herself first into Heather's arms, then mine, then shaking Abby's hand as they were introduced. Becca and Heather fawned over each other. I glanced at Abby, who smiled but said nothing. Did she feel like me, back in high school and standing on the outskirts of the cheerleaders? At least now I wasn't not-pulling-off black lipstick and combat boots. *Now* I was wearing a feminine, slinky dress of my own design. So...progress?

Becca turned to me. "I'm so jealous of your dresses, oh my God."

"Isn't she so freaking sexy?" Heather slid her hand down my side and playfully slapped my butt.

"Stop," I laughed. "You look beautiful, Becca."

She beamed. "Thank you! Before I forget, I have a big favor to ask. Kimmy got put on bedrest and had to step out of the wedding. I asked a friend of the family to step in—Misty. That's her, in the orange dress."

My heart sank as she turned and pointed to Misty, her sleek blond updo like a divine halo blessing her beauty. I maintained my smile, but my insides melted in the sick realization—I was going to have to redo a dress.

"My mom said she'll pay for the alterations to Kimmy's dress."

"Sure, no problem." Shit on a stick, this sucked. "I'll talk to her."

"Thank you!" She grabbed Heather's arm. "You'll never believe who else is here..."

Their voices blended in with the rest of the crowd as Becca dragged Heather away from me and Abby, Heather mouthing *I'm sorry!*

The doorbell rang, and Mrs. Betty opened the door to Mom and Lily. "Dahlia and Lily!" she exclaimed, "Welcome! Come in, come in."

Mom and Lily hugged her back, then they were all looking at me.

"Rose, dear, I didn't see you come in." Mrs. Betty floated over to us and hugged me as I introduced her to Abby. Now that I knew her son so intimately, I saw some of his features in her. His nose was nearly the same nose and his eyes a similar color, although his didn't have the crow's feet or the dark circles.

She touched Mom's arm. "Your daughter is so talented. Has she shown you the designs she came up with for Becca's dresses?"

Jason hovered nearby, watching us warily as if he thought about joining us. Our eyes met, and he patted his pocket with a smile.

That sexy son of a bitch.

"I saw them," Mom said, "and thank you. I'm so very proud of her. It's a good thing Becca caught her before she goes viral. Soon she'll be too busy to take on local weddings."

Mrs. Betty looked quizzically between us. "Oh?"

I laughed and laid my head on my mom's shoulder for a second. "Let's don't get ahead of ourselves. PJ Lane wants me to make her bridesmaid dresses, maybe even her wedding gown."

Mrs. Betty put both her hands over her heart, her mouth open wide. "That's amazing! What a high-profile client!"

Jason inserted himself into our group, saying his *hellos* to Mom and Lily. He pulled out his phone. "Yeah, Mom, she's about to be a rock star of wedding gown designers. I've been helping her with her Instagram. You should follow it too! Look at these pictures I took of her in her dresses the other day."

Mrs. Betty nodded and smiled as she looked at whatever photos he was showing her. He must've had a carefully curated selection.

"Oh, this one, Rose dear, of you on the sofa in that bridal gown—simply beautiful. You do beautiful work. So talented and so lovely."

"Thank you. That's so kind of you."

"That reminds me." She turned her head back and forth until she located her quarry. "Misty! Come see, dear."

As Misty made her way over, her gaze caught on someone walking. I glanced to see who on instinct, and it was Jason walking away from our group. I smirked. I couldn't blame her. My boyfriend was hot as fuck.

"Rose, you remember my good friends' daughter, Dr. Misty Hope. She's stepping in as a bridesmaid to replace Kim."

She stuck her hand limply out to me with a snooty smile. "Nice to meet you," she said, as if we hadn't met before. Her voice and vapid disinterest were like that of every dance team girlie who'd been a bitch to me in high school.

"Will you have time to rework Kimmy's dress to fit Misty before the wedding?" Mrs. Betty asked.

No, but that wasn't the right answer. "I'll make it work. Can you come by tomorrow so I can measure you?"

"Sure. I'll come by before church. Here, let me text you so you can send me your address." Her fingers flew over her phone. "Jason gave me your number."

"Where's Becca?" Lily cut in.

"And where do the gifts go?" Mom held up a gift basket swathed in opaque crinkle-wrap that I hoped didn't contain a bunch of sex toys. Although I had to admit that a "honey-do" shower was the perfect opportunity.

"Forgive me," Mrs. Betty said. "I'm a terrible co-hostess. This way."

Mom and Lily followed Mrs. Betty while Misty walked away calling someone else's name.

I turned to Abby. "How have you been?"

Abby took a breath, but a voice beside us spoke first.

"Hi ladies. Friends of the bride, or friends of the groom?"

We turned toward the voice. A kind-faced man not far from our age approached us.

"Bridesmaid, dressmaker, and...close friend of Jason's," I said.

"Plus-one of a friend of the bride," Abby said. "How about you?"

"I'm a friend of Jason's too." He stuck out his hand. "Antoine."

"Abby. Nice to meet you."

"Hi. I'm Rose."

He took a sip of his beer. "Actually, I was invited by the daughter of the family giving the party. I'm in her singles' group at church."

"Oh, the prudish, 'sex is evil' group?" I blurted it out then felt my face go hot as Abby murmured *Rose!* "I'm so sorry. I didn't mean—"

But Antoine was laughing, pink tinging his brown skin. "Yeah, that's them. Jason and I both got suckered into it—well, he stopped going before the hurricane. We joined a group to build some stuff for old folks and then Misty engulfed our group with her singles' group." He scratched his forehead between his glasses and pushed them up. "Jason must love his sister a whole lot to be here tonight."

Abby and I exchanged glances. "Oh really? Why's that?" I asked.

"Are y'all friends with Misty?"

"I barely know her," I said as Abby shook her head no.

"Between you and me, no matter what that girl says on Sundays, she doesn't know the meaning of the word no, especially when it comes from Jason." He looked into the bottom of his bottle, as if judging how much he had left, then turned his head to look at the partygoers. "Look at her ogling him."

Abby and I searched the crowd. Misty was by the bar drinking wine, and her eyes traveled up and down my boyfriend's body where he stood laughing with Alex and taking no notice of her. Was she the reason for his rough night at that meeting? Super looking forward to working on her dress, now. Maybe I'd leave some pins in it or sprinkle itching powder into the seams.

Antoine shook his head. "She's barking up the wrong damn tree."

"Why do you say that?" Abby asked.

Jason's eyes met mine. He winked, and my vibrator went off again. My whole body went rigid, and my cheeks went hot. I tested this fucker to make sure it was quiet, but was it my imagination, or could I hear it?

Antoine finished out a long drink of his beer and grimaced. "Jason isn't interested in a relationship."

The vibration ended, and I looked at Antoine sideways. Earnest, I-love-you Jason not interested in a relationship? Antoine had to be mistaken. Or maybe things had changed?

Abby's hand snuck into mine, squeezing in apparent solidarity.

"Why not?" I asked.

"Well—he tell you about his ex?"

I nodded. "Yeah. She was a real asshole."

He pointed at me with his beer-holding hand. "Precisely. He's been working so hard to make it up to his family—especially his mom—after being away for so long. I think things are finally turning around for them, but his mom's got him walking over hot coals trying to please her. It's gonna be a while before he wants to be in a serious relationship again. And I'll tell you what else. Whoever Jason does end up with is gonna have an uphill battle unless she comes mom-approved. And that's the God's honest truth, there."

I blinked at him. Was Jason keeping me a secret from his family...on purpose?

Abby cast wide worried eyes at me and asked Antoine a question. I had no idea what.

Jason was keeping me a secret from his family.

I hadn't even realized how closely I'd been holding the tender things Jason said to me until Antoine's words upended them onto the floor, suddenly worthless as the scratch-off tickets littering the parking lot after St. Dorothy's spring fair. Mrs. Betty didn't seem to even like me. She would never approve of me dating her son.

Jason was across the room talking to his brother. Laughing with him as if my heart's hands weren't sifting through the litter, both desperately hoping to find and not to find an accidentally discarded winning ticket. Maybe he'd said those things to Antoine before we met. He'd been through a lot with Kasey, and it made sense that he'd be gun shy and worried about pleasing his mom.

Maybe we didn't even have a chance.

Or maybe I was jumping to conclusions with very little information.

I excused myself from Abby and Antoine to get some water and center myself. Jason was a Level Two. I didn't need the parental approval of a Level Two man. Level Two men were about friendship and fucking.

So why was my heart beating out of my chest?

The vibrator buzzed again, and I paused to let it pass, pretending to admire a hideous black and gold sculpture of—what in the fuck were these? They kind of looked like tall, spindly unfortunate souls from the animated version of *The Little Mermaid*.

Whatever. I was so wet and aching with need, how were my little lace panties even holding the vibrator in place? Maybe I just needed my Level Two boyfriend to fuck me in a dark corner, and everything would be okay. A server passed with a tray of champagne flutes. On a whim, I grabbed one and quickly sipped the whole thing down.

Whoof. Tingly. I shivered and dropped the glass on an empty tray. Let's get this party started.

Jason

All I wanted was to go home, give my girlfriend the leg-numbing orgasms she deserved, and then curl up on the sofa and make more ribbon roses for her. But this party felt never-ending. At least Becca and Brad were finally about to open their gifts.

Rose walked by with her mom and sister near where I was helping Mom plate up an appetizer.

Ms. Dahlia looked between her daughters. "Did you both set your intentions for the full moon in Pisces?"

"When is it?" Lily asked, sipping her drink. "And remind me what this moon's for?"

Rose's easy laugh sounded a little off. "It was Thursday, Lils, but I always sneak 'em in late anyway. What's it gonna hurt?"

"Pisces is about being in touch with your feelings and intuition," their mom said. "Do you have aquamarine and fluorite?"

As the three of them walked away, Mom leaned into me, rolling her eyes. "I'm so glad our family won't have to see the Guidry girls much after the wedding. I've had my fill of their pagan nonsense."

"Rose is still my renter, Ma." Maybe I could soften her up on Rose to make the bomb I'd drop later less painful. "And different people are allowed to have different beliefs about God."

She dramatically dropped both shoulders and hands. "Jason, honey, you need to be more careful, having that girl living on your property.

Making that table with her, taking all those photos with her—she's going to get the wrong idea, and so is everybody else."

My heart sank. "I'd be flattered if anybody thought we were together. She's beautiful. A fantastic person." Mom's face betrayed nothing. "And her family's always been good to us. You used to feel differently about them. Remember? And you just greeted all three of them like they were family less than an hour ago."

"I'm sorry I haven't been around yet to see the damage to your property up close," she said, completely ignoring me. "I drove by last week on my way to Charlene's to try out a new hairstyle for the wedding. It's just terrible. The damage, not the hairstyle. What part of the rectory did it fall into?"

"Right through Rose's bedroom," I said, completely forgetting I was supposed to be distancing myself from her.

Mom's face went pale. "Where is she sleeping now?"

"Spare room behind the chapel." The lie unwound from my tongue more naturally than I was comfortable with. This wasn't me. I had to stop lying to her.

Mom nodded. "Good. Keep that distance, and don't let her needle her way in. You're such a sweet boy, and I'd hate for you to be taken in by a girl like that."

I rolled my neck. "Jesus, Mom, don't be like that. They're good people, and you know it. Besides, aren't you supposed to love thy neighbor?"

"Jason Colin Soniat, are you quoting Scripture to try and win an argument with me?"

I grinned at her. "Maybe. Come on, though. Can you please make an effort to stop being so ugly to them? I've gotten to know Rose really well. If you did, you'd love her." *Too*, I wanted to add.

Mom sighed heavily and turned toward the oven. "I'll try, Jason, but I can't promise anything."

I caught Rose's eye from across the room. She smiled at me, and my heart skipped a beat as I winked at her. I pressed the button again, and

Rose's smoldering eyes stared me down, her gaze clearly drifting to a doorway.

My blood heated straight through my body. Yeah, I had it bad. And I would break Mom's heart if she didn't get past this.

"Tell me, love, how did you like seeing Misty again? You should ask her out."

"No." I said it too loud, and several partygoers nearby jumped and looked at me. I lowered my voice. "That's not happening."

"But why not?" she asked quietly. "Look at her! Who wouldn't want to go out with a beautiful professor of geology?"

"There's so much more to a woman than looks and smarts, like a good character."

"Don't be silly. She has a wonderful character."

I rubbed my hand over my eyes. "Mom, I don't know how to tell you this without making you uncomfortable, but after you walked away earlier, she propositioned me."

Her mouth dropped open, and she pulled me away from the closest other people. "No she didn't."

"I'm not making it up! She wanted me to go into a closet, and I'm not gonna tell you what she wanted to do in there."

For a second, she looked like she believed me. But then her face turned sour. "A nice church-going girl like that would do no such thing. I'm sure you heard her wrong."

"Yeah, well, agree to disagree, because I know what I heard. Not that sex is dirty," I pushed, surprising myself at my frankness. "But I told her I didn't want to get physical with her, and she's still completely ignoring me. I'm not getting involved with someone who's blatantly disrespectful like that. You have to stop pushing women at me, Ma. I'm perfectly capable of finding a good partner on my own."

"Well, have you?" Her eyes interrogated me. "Have you found someone on your own?"

This was my chance. My mouth opened...but nothing came out. Again.

"That's what I thought," she said, her tone weary and disappointed. "If I leave it to you, you'll bring home another Kasey."

"No I won't—" The rest of my sentence was drowned out by Lily calling everyone over to watch Becca and Brad open gifts. Mom hurried off toward my sister, who was opening Rose's gift—a quilted Christmas tree skirt that I have no idea when she had time to make.

Fuck. I bit back my frustration and smiled at my sister hugging Rose. Me, Becca, and Alex—three out of six Soniats liked Rose, and I'm sure Mark would when he came in town for the wedding and met her. Even four wasn't a bad start, but what kind of relationship could I build with Rose if I couldn't stand up to my mother about her?

Rose dropped back and made her way toward the doorway she'd pointed out to me with her gaze and then stopped, looking back at me. A clear invitation. I pressed the button again, and she slipped from the room like a ghost.

I made my way through the crowd, and when I got close to Becca and Brad, I nudged my gift toward her feet.

She looked up at me and laughed. "Okay, I get the hint." She and Brad pulled the tissue paper from the big bag and withdrew a patio cushion, the ones she'd been heavily hinting at to go with a patio set she'd been begging me to make for her for the past year.

Brad looked confused, but Becca squealed. "Ahhh! Does this mean what I think it means?"

I smiled and nodded, commanding my feet to stay put until their attention went to the next gift. "Yep! It'll be on your back patio when y'all come back from your honeymoon."

She got up and hugged me with several *thank yous*, and slipped back into her chair as Brad began opening the next gift.

I backed away from the crowd. Good. Hopefully now nobody will be looking for Rose or me for a while. I covertly grabbed a handful of napkins, stuffed them into my pocket, and slipped out the same doorway that Rose had gone out.

She was at the end of a long hallway, studying paintings on the wall. I gave her another vibration. She looked straight at me, then took off down another hallway. She may've been the one with a vibrator in her panties, but my whole body was tense. I was angry at myself, and that wasn't a feeling I'd had a lot of since I left Kasey.

Why couldn't things be easier for me and Rose? Why couldn't my mom stop being so difficult? Why couldn't I stand up to her? And why couldn't Rose tell me she loved me?

I didn't even care that I was sex-stalking my girlfriend through someone else's rambling mansion. Rose and I weren't only about sex, no matter how phenomenal that was with her. This easy partnership, this pure bliss at existing together. We were more. We had to be more.

I took off across a long hallway. This house was really two houses the Hopes had bought and built together into one monster. Every time I'd see Rose go around a corner or down a hallway, I'd press the button, and she'd take off again. Cat and mouse, erotic hide and seek, far from the party.

After the fourth spot-and-chase, I pressed the button repeatedly, following Rose into a dark room with old furniture piled in. I shut the door and locked it. Double-checked the lock.

She was against the far wall, glaring at me with fluttering eyes, bathed in the streetlight coming through a high window. Her long hair curled sinuously down her arms. Her full, rosy lips turned up at the corners. That delicious mouth always built me up with sweet words and soothed me with laughter. Her talented hands beckoned me closer, kind hands that helped me and surprised me, every day. The enticing swell of her breasts rose up and down in a pant. Underneath her glowing skin was the sweet heart that gave itself in service to me as easily as I gave myself to her.

She was it, for me. I was hers, and she was mine. She had to be, or my heart would truly break.

I took the remote out of my pocket and held it up with a smile as I pressed it again. She threw her head back with a whimper and pressed her hand between her legs. I was so hard, my dick could've cut glass.

I stalked her as I undid my pants and freed my erection. I turned her around roughly and pressed my cock against the perfect curve of her ass. She wiggled back against it as I gathered her dress up the front with one hand and wrapped the other gently around her throat.

"Yes." The citrusy aroma of champagne whispered out with her gasp. Her hands grasped at mine and helped me pull up her dress. "Be rough, baby. Take what's yours. I need you so bad."

Something primal took over my body at her words echoing my thoughts. "Goddamn right, you're mine. Is this the game you wanted to play?" I fished the vibrator out from her panties and brought it to my mouth, making sure she watched me suck her divine taste off it before I bent her over the padded back of a sofa. The little vixen spread her legs and perked her ass up at me.

I tore her lace panties apart. Thrusting myself in so easily, so deep—her needy, wet heat nearly made my knees buckle. She whimpered out my name, grinding back against me. I dug my fingers into the flesh of her thighs and sealed her body tight to me as I ground into her. "This pussy is mine, this ass is mine..."

Her orgasm shuddered around my cock, and she cried out, "Jason, more."

Each contraction of her body made me more feral. Nothing had ever felt like this.

"That orgasm was mine," I rasped, "and every moan that comes from your pretty mouth is mine. You're not ready to say you love me, and that's okay." Amid my grinding thrusts, I took a deep breath to get my emotions in check. "But don't you dare for one goddamn second think this is only about sex." With my knee, I brought one of her legs up onto the back of the sofa for better access, and I thrust deeper as she cried out soft sobs of *yes*, and *please*, and *harder*.

"Because this cock is yours. I want you twenty-four hours a day. This mouth is yours, anywhere you want it, anytime you want it." I slipped my fingers around and circled her clit, and she ground harder back against me. "These hands are yours, to please you and serve you. And my heart..." I swallowed hard. "My heart is yours, baby, it's yours, and I'm not taking it back."

She gyrated against me, moaning. I went faster and harder. I was spiraling toward my release, but I wasn't done. "I love you, Rose. Tell me—tell me we're more than sex."

"We're...we're more than sex," she panted, her voice hoarse and her hands clawing for purchase on the sofa seat against my onslaught.

"Tell me again. Promise me." Her tight, divine heat and soft cries had me so close. But I was going to make her come first.

"*Fuck*, Jason. We're *more...oh God...oh God...*"

The contractions of her orgasm popped me off like a champagne bottle deep inside her body, wringing me dry. I slumped against her, sweat cooling. My whole body trembled. I withdrew and pulled her up from the sofa.

She fell into my waiting arms, kissing me like she might die if she didn't, grasping my face in her hands as I delved my tongue into her champagne mouth. "We're more." She pulled back and looked at me, and whatever she saw on my face made hers crumple in concern, her welling tears catching the scant light. She swallowed hard and nodded again, searching my eyes and caressing my face. "It's okay. We're so much more, baby. We're so much more. I promise. I—I *really* care about you. So much." She pressed her lips to mine, and I kissed her again, and again, and again.

I gasped in a shaky breath, roughly wiped a tear away, and pulled the party napkins from my pockets. She silently watched me wipe my spend from her thighs.

"Sorry about your panties." I shoved them into my pocket and pulled her dress back down around her knees. "I'm keeping this." I shoved her vibrator into my pocket, too, and picked up the remote from where I'd dropped it on the floor. "Let's get this party over with so we can go home, yeah? I saw a bathroom a few doors back down the hallway."

I grabbed her hand to walk away, but she held me back.

"Jason?" Her big eyes were bright and wet. "I've only said it once. Before I knew what it really meant, and I—I got *trampled*. It's hard for me to say..." She swallowed hard and pressed her hand to her chest. "But you know I feel..." She blinked and tears came down her face.

I nodded, trying to smile through the ache in my chest. "It's okay, baby."

She threw her arms around my waist and buried her face against my chest, hugging me so tightly. "Mine," she whispered fiercely.

A huffed laugh escaped my lips, and I crushed her to me, kissing her head. "Mine."

For as long as she would have me.

Chapter 14

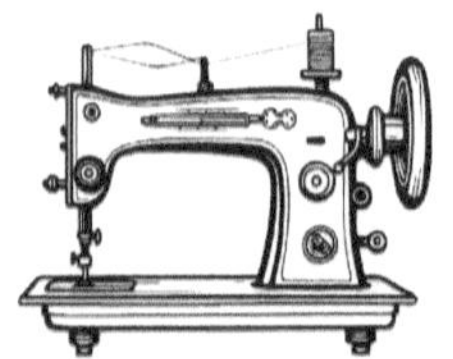

Under Her Thumb

Rose

"Here, can you catch the detail on the side?"

It was hot as balls, but when Jason asked me to help him shoot the tail end of a video on his phone, I couldn't say no. And not because of all the photos he'd taken for me and all the orgasms he'd given me last night *and* this morning.

Nor was it because of the anguish on his face last night, his eyes full of tears, after he begged me to tell him we were more than just sex.

Although that would live rent free in my head until the day I died.

I couldn't say no because his happiness was important to me. Because if I could help him, I wanted to. Because we weren't just sexually explosive, we were *good* together. We were...partners.

I curtsied playfully. "I'm happy to be your lovely assistant once again."

"Awesome." He pulled off his shirt and tossed it somewhere behind him. After whatever had gone through his heart at the party last night, he was back to his golden retriever self when we got home, sexing me up in a shower romp and curling up around me afterward to sleep.

And today, it was like nothing had happened. But everything had happened. He'd gotten me to admit the truth, and now I had to face it.

Jason wasn't a One.

And he wasn't a Two.

He was so much more. I'd been too late to shut the door to my inner heart. Jason had vaulted into that dangerous territory right under my nose, and there wasn't shit I could do about it now.

He adjusted his shorts to hang a wee bit lower on his hips. His legions of internet fans ate up every extra inch of my boyfriend's body they could see. But I wanted him to be all mine, like he said he was. And that jealousy was in a four-way fight with my firm belief in his personal autonomy, my unease that his reluctance to reveal our relationship to the world might not only be about StudFinders, and my turmoil over quantifying what I felt for him.

Maybe I could consider him a Two-and-a-Half?

He caught me watching him, and his smile warmed me straight through.

Don't be a stupid coward, Rose. I knew what his number was.

"Okay. I'm ready," he said. "Start it up."

My finger moved toward the screen, but a text message popped up.

"Wait, hold on. You got a text from...'Do not answer'?"

It began, *Hey, it's Misty.* My lips twisted. "From Misty. Oh shoot, how did it get to be this late? She's coming with your mom before three o'clock mass so I can measure her. Can we—"

"Goddammit," he muttered to himself, putting his things down and walking toward me.

Two more messages popped up. They began, *And maybe after church you can show me...* and *The closet offer still stands an...*

I handed his phone to him. "Something about a closet?"

If looks could kill, his phone would've disintegrated. "This is what I get for agreeing to go to church with my mom. And now she's coming here."

"What's wrong? Are you mad at me? I have to measure her." My voice was defensive.

"No, no. I'm not at all mad at you." He breathed out hard, then shook out his arms and wrapped them around me, kissing my forehead. "I'm sorry. I'm mad at my mom, and I didn't mean to take it out on you." He stuffed his phone in his pocket and grabbed his shirt from where he'd dropped it, putting it on with jerky movements. "She should never have talked Becca into putting Misty into the wedding when you already had enough work to do on the dresses, and now she's bringing her to our home."

My heart thudded once then melted all over my insides. *Our* home?

"I told her I don't want anything to do with Misty," he said vehemently, clearly not noticing the Rose-heart-shaped puddle on the ground. "I told Misty to never talk to me again, and I told my mom what she said to me last night. But of course she didn't believe me."

My heart sucked back into my body and solidified, only a few pieces of grass and dirt assimilating into its new form. Grass and dirt of *our home*. "What did she say to you?"

"I'm not even going to ask you not to get mad, because you have every right to get mad." He settled his hands on my shoulders and slid them down my arms, taking my hands. "Not long after I broke up with Kasey and came back home, I went out with Misty. Just once."

"Yeah. I remember."

"The date started out okay, but then the nightmare started. I told her I was celibate, but she was aggressively sexual and disrespectful. I didn't want any kind of relationship with her, and she gave me so much shit over it."

Itching powder it would be.

"So I never called her back. After Kasey, the last thing I wanted was another person telling me how to live my life."

I bit my lip. "To be fair, I wasn't as respectful of your celibacy as I could've been. My bad."

He frowned, wrapping his arms around my waist. "No, no. Don't apologize. You *were* respectful. You never belittled me for it, and you didn't push yourself on me. I'm the one who couldn't control myself around you." He chuckled and rubbed my back. "It's not your fault you're so damn irresistible." He kissed my forehead.

"So...what did she say to you last night?"

He shut his eyes, looking pained. "She...offered me a blow job."

I backed up a little. "She what now?" Itching powder *and* a few stray pins.

He rolled his neck. "She offered to—"

"What did you tell her?"

"I swear, I told her no and to never talk to me again." It rushed out of him, like he was scared I wouldn't believe him.

I squeezed his arms. "I believe you. What did your mom say when you told her?"

His shoulders relaxed. "She thinks I misunderstood her. But I did *not*. Look at this shit." He held his phone up and showed me the entire text string from the *Do not answer!* contact. "The only reason I didn't block her was because she was coordinating the community service our group was doing."

> Hey, it's Misty. I'm on my way to your house to get measured for my bridesmaid dress.
>
> And maybe after church you can show me what you've been hiding in your pants
>
> The closet offer still stands an I promise I'll be a good girl and take it all. U won't regret it

"Goddamn, she *is* aggressive. Show this to your mom. She'll believe you."

"This isn't the kind of thing I ever want to talk to my mom about." He stuffed his phone back in his pocket. "We'd better go pick up. They'll be here any minute."

He crossed the courtyard on a mission. Barely keeping up with his long strides, I followed him into the church. "Pick what up? The house is pretty clean."

"Can you grab your clothes from upstairs and bring them to the community room? I'll set up that little alcove to make it look like you're living in it."

I stood fixed to the spot. "Wait...what?"

"Mom doesn't know about us, and I don't want her to find out like this." His voice faded on his way into the hallway toward the community room.

My chest constricted. He didn't want her to *find out like this*? This confirmed we weren't only hiding from StudFinders. I didn't realize dating me was a shame or a tragedy. I mean, his mom didn't seem to like me *that* much, but...

Whatever. I swallowed hard and ducked my head, but I did as he asked. I ran up the stairs, grabbed my duffle bag and a laundry basket I hadn't folded yet, and rushed back down. Jason was in the alcove directly behind the altar putting sheets on an air mattress as it inflated.

None of this sat right with me. "Why do we have to lie to your mom? Plus, if we tell her we're together, then Misty would back off." I dropped my things on the floor. "Is it about us living together?"

"That's a big part of it." The sheer panic on his face as he worked told me everything I needed to know. This weekend was giving me whiplash. First it's all *you're mine* and *tell me we're more* and *our home* and then it's all *pretend you're living in this shitty little alcove full of boxes of flooring*. This man not only didn't want his mother to know about us, he was terrified she'd find out.

I straightened up the area, trying to force the tears in my eyes to stay there. "Jason, do you think there will ever be a time when you're not embarrassed to tell your mom you're dating me?"

"I'm not embarrassed of you, baby, I just need more time. After the wedding. When I can sit down and talk to her first. Okay?" In between setting the room up as if I'd been sleeping in it, his puppy dog eyes went up to me.

"Sure. Okay." *I love you so much?* No, if this man wasn't serious enough about me to stand up to his mom, maybe he wasn't as serious about me as he claimed.

My heart thudded. And if he was willing to lie to his mom, couldn't he just lie to me, too?

I didn't know anymore. I left him to his last-minute treachery and went to the garment rack in the living room. I'd just...keep an eye on things. Maybe I was wrong. Maybe, I was wrong. Maybe. I. Was. Wrong. If I said that enough, maybe my stomach would stop threatening to expel the grilled cheese I had for lunch.

I flipped through the finished dresses until I got to the one that would now be Misty's. I pulled out a stool and sat it beside my sewing table, placing my pincushion and my shears beside me. Super excited to work on a dress for the woman who wanted to blow my boyfriend, the boyfriend who couldn't admit to his mom that he was dating me. This wouldn't be awkward at all.

Was itching powder available locally, or would that need to be an online purchase?

The doorbell chimed. Jason hurtled himself down the stairs wearing slacks and buttoning up a short-sleeved shirt. "You ready?" he asked, his face tense, as if hordes of goblins were at our door instead of two normal-sized women.

I nodded as the handle to the front door shook, followed by knocking and his mother calling, *Hello?*

Jason unlocked the door and opened it. "Hey, Ma. Y'all come in."

The two women chorused their hellos.

"Jason, you still haven't made me a key." Mrs. Betty said. "You might need me to come check on things sometime."

"I keep forgetting. I'll try to get that soon."

That's all we needed: Mrs. Betty to have a key and walk in on us going at it in the choir loft. Or the living room floor. Or on the sofa. Or the steps to the old altar. Or bent over the dining room table. Or the choir steps. Geez, was there any place we hadn't done it yet?

Mrs. Betty and Misty walked past the foyer into the main living area. I stood awkwardly by my sewing table as they came in. Mrs. Betty made a big fuss over Jason's progress in the church, but Misty just eye fucked him the entire time.

"Rose, dear, it's so good to see you." Mrs. Betty came in for a hug. "You remember Misty, of course."

I uncurled my hands from fists and exchanged awkward waves and hellos with Misty. Today she was wearing a brown sheath that hugged her tight little body.

"I have the dress right here, if you don't mind slipping it on?" I handed her the gown. "There's a bathroom in the foyer."

"Oh, this is exquisite!" Misty held the dress up, apparently admiring how the chiffon flowed. "You're so talented. It looks completely finished. I'm sorry you have to alter it."

You and me both, you boyfriend-propositioning bitch. "That's okay. Anything for Becca."

"And the extra money doesn't hurt either, does it?"

And now Mrs. Betty had reduced me to hired help with just a few words. Jason pinched his nose and pleaded with me with his eyes.

"Let me show you where that bathroom is," I said, eager to get away from mother and son. I settled Misty where she could change then walked back to my sewing table into a very awkward conversation.

"Jason, you look so flushed and extra healthy today. Did you go for a run this morning?"

I adjusted my wrist pin cushion and acted like I didn't exist.

"No, but I got some exercise in."

I smirked with my back to them, recalling Jason's energetic thrusting from this morning.

"Well whatever you've been doing, keep it up. I haven't seen you so happy and healthy in a long time."

I raised my eyebrows at him and nodded toward her, but he just looked pained and said nothing.

His mom went right on, and his opportunity passed. "I wanted to tell you. After you left,"—she lowered her voice to where she clearly thought I couldn't hear—"I had a nice heart to heart with Misty. You were mistaken about what you thought you heard her say."

"No I'm not, Ma. She explicitly said she wanted to suck my dick."

"Jason!" Mrs. Betty exclaimed, hand over her mouth as if she'd been the one to say it. "You can't have heard her right. Misty's not the villain you keep making her out to be. Why don't you ask her out today and give her another chance?"

"Mom, no. That's never gonna happen."

I slammed back my water bottle, wishing it was vodka, and promptly choked on it. I coughed until my eyes watered.

"Are you okay?" Jason asked, his eyes trying to communicate so much.

I waved him off. "Sometimes I forget I'm not a mermaid."

Mrs. Betty looked up toward the front of the church. "Here she is!"

I never thought I'd be so happy to see a rival for my boyfriend's affections enter a room. Damnit, she was so pretty, holding the oversized dress up to her body, her hair in a messy bun on top of her head. Beautiful, smart, mom-approved, and clearly into fellatio. Why was he with me, again? Although he certainly couldn't complain about the amount of fellatio he was currently receiving.

Mrs. Betty clapped her hands together in delight. "Oh my, you look so lovely. Doesn't she, Jason?"

But Jason had his back to us already, on his way out the back door. "I'll be outside."

"Stay," Misty implored.

But Jason kept walking without a word, leaving me alone with them.

I swallowed down every feeling I had, directed Misty to stand beside me, and began pinning the bodice for changes. I'd have to take several inches off and redo the chiffon overlay on the bodice altogether, since now the darts I made for Kim wouldn't lay right over Misty's smaller breasts.

I needed to find my happy place before I had an anxiety attack to deal with, too. *Deep breath in.* I'm snoozing on that Florida beach in Jason's arms, right now. We're laughing in the waves as the golden sunset lights up the horizon. We're kissing in the moonlight. We're cuddled up watching movies late at night and laughing together, always laughing together.

Misty's smile at me as I directed her where to stand was a straight pin popping the warm reverie over my head like a cartoon bubble. I adjusted her position more forcefully than necessary.

Mrs. Betty pulled a little package wrapped in tissue paper from her purse. "Rose, could you do one other small thing for me?"

I warily watched her unwrap the paper. "What's that?"

She pulled out a blue handkerchief. "My great-grandmother carried this on her wedding day, and since then, all the women in our family have, too. But when I went to get it out for Becca, this part along the edge tore right off."

"Oh no! Let me see?" I took it gently from her. The handkerchief was old, and so pretty. Sure enough, the fine linen fabric was torn and unraveled just inside the cotton lace edging. "It's dry-rotted. That's such a shame. It's so beautiful. They don't make fabric like this anymore."

"Can it be fixed?"

"Well..." I inspected its construction, rifling through options in my head. "I might be able to replace this thin panel and reattach the lace. It might be hard to match the color, but I'm pretty good at dyeing. I think I could make it look like it was supposed to be there. And I can help protect it, so it won't tear in the future."

"Thank you so much! I'll pay you, of course."

No fucking way, after that getting paid comment. Besides, I was a sucker for fabric-based family traditions. "No, that's okay. Consider it a contribution to keeping your lovely tradition alive."

"Thank you, dear. That's so kind." Her voice was warm as she pressed her hand to her heart. "That's just what I want, for future generations to be able to use it, too. I've always wanted to get the names of the brides who carried it embroidered on it, so that knowledge won't die with me. Maybe I'll try and find someone after the wedding. We're all certainly too busy before it."

"I love that idea! The fabric should be able to take it. It might even help keep it strong." I carefully wrapped the handkerchief back up and sat it in a basket on my sewing table.

Mrs. Betty continued talking as I went back to my work. "I'm so excited about Becca's wedding. And after I have my daughter married off, then I'll find a lovely girl for my Jason."

Mrs. Betty and Misty exchanged smiles, and I tried to bite my tongue. Tried.

"Jason's an amazing man," I said. "He won't have any trouble finding a partner on his own."

"That's nice of you to say," Mrs. Betty said. Hands on her hips, she looked around the room as if not quite knowing what to do with herself. She must not come here often. But why not?

"I know you two have become something like friends since you've been renting a room from him," she continued, "but you may not know how he got duped into following his ex-girlfriend all the way across the country, only for her to cheat on him. He doesn't have the best track record for picking girls to date on his own."

I frowned. Where to place the tuck and my verbal barb? "That's not a take I've heard on abusive relationships before, that the victim's to blame for choosing their abuser. You know, people can come in the most beautiful packages but be completely rotten on the inside. And some abusers hide the ugly for longer than others. Right, Misty?"

Her eyes widened as she looked between me and Mrs. Betty. "Uh..."

But Mrs. Betty studied me for a minute, as if she'd never in her life thought of things from that perspective before. "Well. I suppose the good book says we must beware of those who come in sheep's clothing. Kasey seemed like a nice young woman, at first." She walked a little ways away and perched at the end of the sofa, looking uncomfortable in her own son's home. "She sure fooled all of us."

"Okay, I need you on your knees," I said to Misty.

Her head turned to me so fast I almost snorted. "What?"

"Just kidding!" I said brightly. "Step up here so I can pin the hem."

She frowned but did as I asked. "Will you bring the neckline down, too?" She poked at the modest neckline Becca had insisted on.

"No."

"But—"

I met her eyes and poured all my constrained anger into my gaze. "No means no, Misty," I said quietly.

Misty blushed and shut her mouth, looking away from me.

"Can I get you something to drink, Mrs. Betty?" I asked.

"Thank you, Rose. Yes, I could go for some water."

"I'd like some too." Misty's voice was tentative, but I was getting bolder.

I leaned in and whispered harshly. "Go suck somebody else's cock, Misty." That bitch widened her eyes, but she put her head down.

This kind of boldness could go to my head. So, I kept going as I grabbed a water for Mrs. Betty.

"I'm so sorry that you and Jason and your whole family went through all that. But Jason's smart, and he has such a good heart. He's accomplished so much in the past couple of years. He built this amazing home, he has a successful, thriving business—actually at least two businesses." I handed Mrs. Betty her water bottle, then I sat on my little stool and went back to pinning Misty's hem. "The gorgeous custom furniture he does locally plus all the hard work he puts into his social media accounts and online classes."

"But what if it happens again?" she asked. "He's always going to be my baby, and I can't lose him. If I can just find him a girl from a good family—"

"Of course you want him to be happy. But my two cents—he's got to pick the woman he loves, not you. Nobody can make that choice for someone else." I snorted, lost in my work. "I mean, he can't choose the vagina he came out of, but he can sure choose the one he comes into every night."

Fuck.

I held my breath.

Mrs. Betty choked on her water. Misty frowned, her gaze directed off toward the wall.

My face went hot, and an apology to Mrs. Betty was on the tip of my tongue. But her shoulders were shaking. She was laughing. I smiled tentatively, and she laughed harder.

"Oh my goodness, the things you young girls say." She patted her chest and coughed again, looking up toward the ceiling. "Did you girls know I got married in this church?"

"No, I didn't realize," I said.

Misty had apparently chosen not to speak again. Fine by me.

Mrs. Betty smiled and nodded, taking another drink. "A long time ago. I love what he's done here. And I love church weddings. That's what I want for all my babies. I feel so much closer to God in a beautiful church."

"Really? No matter how heavenly churches are built, I feel closer to God outside in nature. Give me a wedding in a forest, or on the beach. Or at least a pretty gazebo in a garden. I can compromise. Spin around slowly?" I said to Misty. Leaning back, I eyed her hem for the full circuit and only had to adjust one pin. "You can change now. I don't want to make you late to church." I glared at her. "I know you have to get to confession."

Misty scuttled off to change without a word as Mrs. Betty went on about how this church looked in her day. But I busied myself organizing my supplies, fighting tears. Just to fit in, I'd contributed my "give me a wedding in a forest" spiel to almost every conversation I'd ever been involved in regarding where weddings should be held. But it tasted different in my mouth today.

Walking up to Jason that day he took my pictures, him in that suit and me in that wedding gown—I kept pushing that memory down before my foolish heart got carried away, especially after his revelation the next morning. But I couldn't deny how seeing him waiting for me by that stained glass window with awe on his face had made my insides magnetize to his smile. How utterly romantic taking those photos with him was. How passionately we made love after, lost in the world of each other. Our bodies and souls entwined. And then his ardent *I love you* the next morning while he twisted my fake rings.

I didn't know about a wedding, but being with Jason made me start to want a marriage. A partnership like that...

No. It was a moot point, anyway. Not only was I not good enough for Jason's mom, but he'd have to keep me his secret shame to make his dreams come true with StudFinders anyway. I would never be good enough for him.

And marriage wasn't for me. Right?

No matter what, Jason would never be happy if he spent his life tiptoeing around his mom. Maybe he needed someone to remind him.

Jason

Somehow, I managed not to sit next to Misty during mass, and oddly enough, neither she nor Mom pushed it. I ignored her the whole time, all the way through mass and until I hugged Mom goodbye before she got in Misty's car.

I stopped at the grocery on my way and came home with a bounty for our kitchen. I put everything away and headed back into the church to find Rose hunched over her sewing machine.

"Hey." She glanced up at me and the vase of pink roses I set at the edge of her sewing table where it wouldn't be in the way. I felt sick about how my mom treated her and having Misty in our home. I should've stood up for her.

I went up behind her and wrapped my arms around her waist, kissing her cheek. "I figured you must like roses."

She patted my arm before returning her hand to her sewing machine. "You figured right. And you sprang for Lalumandier roses."

"You're worth more than fields of them," I murmured, kissing down her neck.

"Pretty sure your mom wouldn't agree."

I completely deflated. "Rose—"

"Make sure you hide them before she comes back over."

I pulled up a stool to sit close to her. "Can we talk about it?"

She sighed, setting her things down and finally meeting my eyes. "You don't have to explain yourself to me, really."

"But I want to. You're important to me."

She rolled her eyes, but I took her hands in mine, rubbing her fingers. "You are! She can be such a chore, I know. But she's my mom. You have to understand how badly I hurt her when I left."

Rose closed her eyes and looked down, bit her lips.

"I barely talked to her for nearly two years. I was almost a different person. I promised her I'd never do that to her again, but it's made her insecure. I made her insecure, and I'm still trying to make up for it."

"I understand that, I do. And I would never, ever suggest that you hurt your mother. And I don't want to cause distance between you. That being said, I think your pendulum has swung too far in the opposite direction. Because what you've made her is certain that she can run your life and pick your wife."

"She doesn't really think that."

"Beg to differ. She's always disparaging your job, and now she's pushing Fellatio Misty at you and not believing you about her? Loving your mom and not hurting her doesn't mean never standing up for yourself. You're a different person around her than you are around me."

"Am I?"

"Yeah. You told me you don't enjoy going to church anymore, but she talks you into it, so you go for show. You're so quick to passionately talk about what you believe, unless she's in the room. She brings someone who has repeatedly verbally, if not physically, assaulted you into your house, and you shut down and beg me to be nice. Well, I did my best. But it's disrespectful of her to keep shoving Misty at you when you've told her to stop. And you just smile and nod, redirect her, or play along. You deserve to do better for yourself than that."

"Rose, she's my mom. What do you want me to do?"

"Be your own person. Disappoint your mother and let her see that you still love her, but she can survive it. Or she'll expect you to live under her thumb for the rest of your life."

A wall shot up around my heart hearing Kasey's words come out of Rose's mouth.

I pulled my hands away and stood up. I'd been through a lot. I needed her to be patient with me, not tell me what to do. "Have you had dinner?"

Her eyes widened. "Not yet."

"I'll go make something." I stood and walked away. Maybe we both needed some space.

"Fergalicious" started playing from Rose's phone. "Wait," she called. "Heather says her dad had someone cancel, and the crane's already nearby. He can have it here in a half-hour. Is that cool?"

"Yeah. Tell her thank you." At least one thing's going my way today. "Eat without me if you get hungry." I turned to leave.

"My mom and Lily are coming over to help me with the dresses later. Is that okay?"

"Of course it's okay." My voice sounded aggravated. I cleared my throat and tried again. "You live here too. You don't have to ask."

She nodded. "Thank you."

As I walked toward the makeshift kitchen for a snack to hold me over, my heart sunk so low I practically kicked it across the community room. I royally fucked up. I fell in love with someone my mom didn't approve of, and I was apparently too much of a coward to face her. It was Kasey all over again, except that Rose wasn't trying to come between us, and Rose—

I froze with my hand on the fridge door handle. Was it that different? Kasey had never loved me. The thought left me desolate. I kept thinking she'd just fallen out of love, or we weren't as compatible as I thought we were in the beginning. But no. She hadn't loved me. Not really.

Was I holding back on telling Mom about us because I was afraid that Mom wouldn't accept her, or because I was afraid that Rose would never love me?

I closed the fridge door and leaned my forehead against it.

What was so hard about me to love?

Aucoin Construction was my new favorite New Orleans business. Not only did they get the tree off the rectory, the men also stayed around to haul out the branches, debris, and molding mattresses from Rose's bedroom and helped me nail plywood and a tarp on the busted-open roof.

Night had fully fallen by the time they left. After sweeping the last of the leaves from Rose's bedroom and setting up dehumidifiers, I was starving and ready to take a shower and crash. But first I wanted Rose to go through her pile of stuff I set aside to see what she could salvage and what I had to trash, and I didn't want to fix something to eat only for myself if she hadn't eaten.

I washed my hands in the makeshift kitchen and grabbed a water bottle. I might never be able to drink enough to make up for what I sweat out today.

I checked my phone. It was nearly nine o'clock, and my stomach was about to eat its way out. As I approached the church, a trio of women's laughter met my ears. I walked in and said hello to Ms. Dahlia and Lily, who were packing up.

"Oh hey, Jason!" Lily said. "Your house is amazing!"

Dahlia put her hand over her heart. "It's stunning, Jason. You really have a gift. If I ever move into a bigger house, I know who I'm calling to help me renovate."

"Thanks! I appreciate it." I sat on the altar steps, guzzling water and trying to cool off.

"There's some pizza left over, if you're hungry." Rose pointed toward the table where a couple boxes of Fat Boy's Pizza sat.

"Oh God, yes." I struggled to my feet. "Thank you." I popped open the top box and gobbled a slice down in nearly three bites.

"Rose, honey, get some sleep. I'll check on you tomorrow," her mom said.

"And don't forget to work on Mom's sketches so we can pick dresses by Thursday." Lily's bossy tone didn't sit right with me. "And I'll help you stay on schedule to make sure you can get it all done."

I grabbed another slice, but I didn't want to sit on my chairs this dirty. I also didn't want to be here for this conversation.

"Jesus, Lily, you don't have to treat me like a to-do list. I'll get Mom's sketches done *and* make her dresses in time for her wedding, but on my timetable, not yours."

"I just meant that—"

"Lily, let her do it on her time," Dahlia said. "Rose, I trust you. Oh honey, I can't believe we've been here all this time and haven't asked you about Isaac. How are things going with him?"

"Oh that's *been* over. Almost since I got back home."

A chorus of "oh no!" and "I'm sorry!" from Lily and Dahlia.

"I mean I'm not surprised, though," Lily said. "It must've been getting serious, for you to break things off."

Ouch.

"Lily," her mom chastised.

"Come on, Mom. That's her MO! Let me guess. He told you he loved you? He saw a future with you more than two months out?"

"No, he was cheating on me. Is that an acceptable reason to break up, Lily, or should I have gotten your permission first?" Rose asked, her voice higher-pitched than normal.

Dahlia hugged Rose. "I'm so sorry, honey, you didn't deserve that. Lily, apologize to your sister."

Lily shrugged. "I didn't know. I'm sorry, but you can't blame me. I can't remember all the names of the men she's dated and bailed on when things got serious."

It was on the tip of my tongue to put Lily in her place, but that would be a shitty thing to do when I hadn't even called my mom out. I couldn't imagine Rose would appreciate it. I popped my last bite of pizza into my mouth. I should go straight and take a shower. But I was rooted to the spot. Why was Lily being so mean, and right in front of me? Did she treat her worse when they were alone?

"Are you seeing anyone new yet?" her mom asked. "You're taking care of yourself, though, right?" She said that more quietly, but sounds traveled in this church. "That bag of toys didn't get destroyed in the hurricane, did it?"

"MOM," Rose balked while Lily cackled.

"Rose," Lily started, "I'm going to need your full sexual history, solo and partnered, with dates, times, and toys used." Lily's voice had taken on the deeper tone of their mother, who then started laughing as Rose muttered an "Oh my God."

"Lily, you know that's not what I'm after. I just want my girls to be happy and fulfilled."

I waved my hand on my way into the hallway toward the community center. "Y'all have a good night!" And I went straight to our makeshift shower, washing away the heat of the day and the emotions in my chest. They shouldn't have said those things in front of me. But also, does Rose really date someone until things get serious, then dump them?

That wasn't what happened with Isaac, but maybe I'm lucky she didn't bolt the second I said, "I love you." She still hadn't said it back.

How would I move on if she broke up with me? I couldn't bring myself to evict her. I'd have to watch other men go in and out of that apartment until she moved out on her own.

I put my head under the cool water, but it couldn't untangle the knots in my chest.

Chapter 15

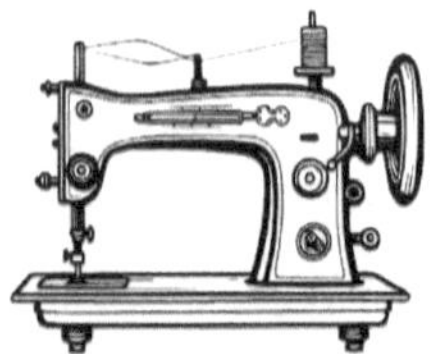

The Cards Don't Lie

Rose

I hung up the Last. Bridesmaid. Dress and stretched my back. They each hung in garment bags labeled with the women's names. All *done*.

And the evening all to myself. I hadn't seen much of Jason since after Mom and Lily left. He'd gone to bed early, completely beat from all the hard work he'd done on the storm damage, and he was up earlier than me to pull out the damaged floors and drywall in what had been my apartment bedroom. After another shower and a quick kiss, he went out with Antoine and a couple of other friends.

Unless I pounced on him tonight, we would have gone our first whole day without sex, and his distance was a pit in my stomach.

It was only seven o'clock. I didn't want to do anything but mope, but our laundry had piled up with everything we had going on, and I guess I had time to watch some guilty pleasure TV.

Lord knows I needed something to distract me. Our first day without devouring each other. When he was in the house with me, however briefly, I kept trying to engage in our regular conversations, but he'd been so surface-level. How was I doing on the dresses? He'd like to get the yard work done before it rains. Would I mind if he went out tonight with friends?

I forcefully sorted our underwear from our colors. He'd been weird ever since I'd confronted him about his mom. But I didn't regret it. I didn't have my mom's expertise, but it was clear to me that he needed to be honest with her. If he was in love with me like he said he was, shouldn't he be willing to have an uncomfortable conversation with her about us?

His words haunted me. *After how I left, I feel like I have to atone forever.* After how he left.

A man who could lie to his mother could lie to me. A man who could leave his mother, could leave me.

I wiped a hot tear from my cheek. The back pocket of Jason's khakis crinkled. I pulled out a well-worn sheet of paper and tossed it on top of the washer to give him later, whatever it was.

Wait—my name was on that paper, written on the outside in Jason's all-caps architect's print. I shoved his pants in the washer and picked up the paper, carefully unfolding it. It was a copy of my middle school bucket list, with a code Jason had added at the top in blue pen: check-mark = done.

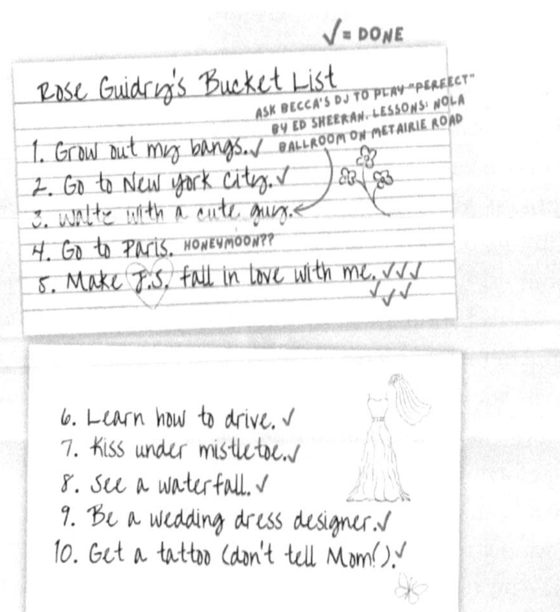

So that's what the waterfall and Christmas shop had been about. He'd been trying to help me finish my list.

Beneath the copy of my bucket list, Jason had started his own bucket list—get a tattoo? Damn, that would be hot. But that was all scratched out, and next to it was a list titled "What I want in a life partner."

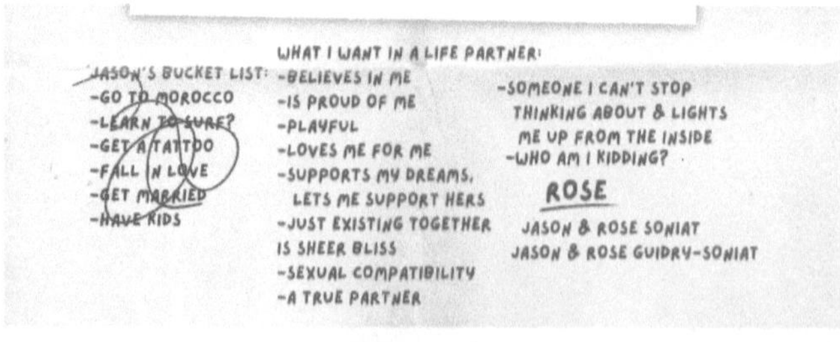

The paper trembling in my hands, I left the clothes and went into the church. Sat at the table. Stared at the paper. How long had he been trying to help me finish my list? I couldn't even figure it out. Because my eyes were stuck on the word *honeymoon* and my name underlined at the culmination of his "what I want in a life partner" list. On our names written together with his last name like he was a lovestruck teen. Exactly what I used to write in my middle school diary. He even added a version if I wanted to hyphenate. What man did that sort of thing?

He told me he loved me. I didn't know he was this serious.

To have a honeymoon, you'd have to be married. Jason would never marry someone he couldn't tell his mom about.

Heather's "Fergalicious" started playing on my phone, followed by the doorbell ringing.

> Abby and I are on your porch, sexy. Is this a bad time for a visit?

The list still in my hand, I went straight to open the door and threw myself into Heather and Abby's arms.

"Baby, what's wrong?" Abby asked while Heather *noooo'ed*. "Why are you crying?"

"How did y'all know I needed you?" I sobbed, pulling them into the church.

They hugged me back while shutting the door behind us.

"Do I have to kick Deck Daddy's ass?" Heather asked. "Because I'm way tougher than I look."

Abby ushered me to the sofa and held and *shhed* me as I cried myself out while Heather rubbed my back and murmured soothing words like "it's okay" and "I will cut a bitch for you."

"Do you want to talk about it?" Abby asked.

I pulled away and handed her the bucket list, grabbing the tissue box off the coffee table.

"What's this?" She pushed her long braid over her shoulder and held the list so Heather could see it too.

"My bucket list from when I was in middle school. He must've made a copy of it after we dug up the time capsule. I can't believe he's had it all this time."

Abby frowned. "Help me understand, love, because this is adorable."

Heather looked around the church. "Is he home?"

"No. He's out with friends." I blew my nose until I had a healthy collection of snot rags on the floor. "I was doing laundry, and I found it in his pocket."

Abby rubbed my back. "Why is this making you cry?"

I spilled the whole story. About Kasey and Jason's mom and how my mom suddenly decided after nearly thirty years that maybe marriage wasn't so bad. I told them about Fellatio Misty and how Lily mocked me, about how I now lived with my landlord who was "in love with me" but also wanted to keep me a secret from the people he *actually* loved.

"How can I trust him? I mean—Heather, you're as commit-ment-phobic as me. Isn't this shady as hell?"

"For sure. But girl..." She picked up the list and held it out to me. "I'm so confused. This is the list of a committed man. Why won't he talk to his mom?"

"I don't know. Maybe none of this matters, anyway. The worst part of Lily's bullying is that she's right. I'm a flashpanner. I always break up with men when things get too serious. But I can't tell if Jason's safe—i.e. not serious about me—or somebody I need to break up with. I'm stuck in this limbo."

"Are those really the only two options?" Abby asked gently. "Stay because he doesn't love you, leave because he does?"

"I don't know. Those are the only two things I know how to do."

"No, no," Heather said. "You also know how to love yourself first and make hard choices when you have to. Maybe consult your tarot cards, pray about it. Get your head straight about what you really want, and trust yourself." She squeezed my face in her hand. "You're too amazing to stay with someone who isn't proud to be with you."

I blew my nose. "What I really want is to go back to playing around and having a ton of amazing sex and none of these Serious Thoughts and Complicated Feelings." I tossed my tissue on the pile. "Everything was perfect before."

Abby squeezed me. "If only you weren't so lovable. Jason never had a chance."

I laughed and rolled my eyes.

"Why don't you come to dinner with us?" Abby asked. "Could you use a girls' night?"

I nodded. "I could. Y'all." I looked between my two closest friends. "I'm so sorry. I was avoiding you and your offer to live with you. I've been so embarrassed that I failed in New York, and I was worried y'all would think less of me. Especially after throwing me a going away party and sending me off with all that money y'all collected."

"Stop right there." Heather leveled her brown eyes at me. "First off, you didn't fail in New York. You rocked your internships. Lovelace Bridal even featured one of your designs in their fashion show! It's ungodly expensive to live in New York, especially as an artist, who are never paid enough. For as long as I've known you, you've talked about having your own label, and from where I'm sitting, you're well on your way."

"Absolutely!" Abby said. "Even if you had failed up there—and you didn't—we love you and will support you no matter what. You're so talented, and so hard-working. The only way you could fail is if you give up. And you're too driven for that."

"Thank you." I dabbed at fresh tears. "I love you, too."

They wrapped their arms around me in a big cuddly hug.

"We know," Heather said. "Now go dress yourself in somethin' slutty." She threw her long, balayaged hair behind her. "And let's make some boys cry because of how hot we are."

Jason was already in bed when I got home. I almost went to sleep on that air mattress out of spite, but I'd missed him too much.

I'd no sooner crawled into bed when he rolled over and sleepily pulled me into his arms, kissing my head. With my back to his front, it didn't take long for simple caresses on my arm and belly to arouse both of us. After a quickie in the dark, we fell asleep in each other's arms.

But he was gone when I woke up. I found him working in the rectory, pulling out sheet rock and refusing all my offers of help. Not even taking advantage of the clear message I was sending with the "Deck Daddy nailed me" tank top I was wearing without a bra.

But he agreed to let me smoke-cleanse the church, at least. So I did it in my tank top and panties just to lure him between my legs if he happened to walk inside. And now the air smelled pleasantly of mugwort and lavender. And since he sadly still wasn't nailing me, I sat down to talk to my tarot cards about him.

I settled onto his plush living room rug at the coffee table with some tea and my favorite deck. Knocking three times on the stack of cards, I murmured, "Tell me about my relationship with Jason."

I shuffled a few minutes more, focusing on my question, then I chose a card and laid it face down on the table. The golden goddess on the back of the card gazed encouragingly at me.

But I couldn't bring myself to turn it over.

The door opened behind me on the side wall. "Jason?"

I snapped my head toward Mrs. Betty's voice. She was three steps in, and my heart banged against my rib cage. I froze. She was about to catch me in my panties in her son's house. It was bad enough I wasn't wearing a bra.

But it was too late to hide. I couldn't reach the throw on the chair without getting up, and it would look suspicious to be wrapped in a blanket with it being ninety-seven degrees outside, anyway.

She breathed in and waved the air, coughing. "What's that smell?" She sat her purse down at the pew by the door and called for Jason again.

I had to admit I was sitting here before she turned and saw me and wondered why I was being rude. "Hi Mrs. Betty," I called out, waving but not getting up. I grabbed my phone and texted Jason.

Mrs. Betty turned toward me then walked forward quickly, a frown on her face as her eyes darted around from me to my tarot cards, to the smoking bundle of mugwort in the abalone shell on the side table. I got up from being cross-legged to kneel on the floor, guiltily pulling down at the hem of my tank top to cover my panties, but that only made it more obvious I wasn't wearing a bra.

"Why are you sitting in my son's living room half-naked?"

All the blood left my face. She was an archangel down from heaven to condemn me.

"Have you been smoking weed?" Her gaze fell to the coffee table, to my box of clearly marked tarot cards. "Why are there *tarot cards* in my son's *church*?" Her voice went up an octave.

"Mrs. Betty, I can explain—"

"You don't have to explain anything. My son does. He should never have rented a room to a godless Guidry girl—" She clapped her hand over her mouth.

"*A godless Guidry girl*?" I echoed. "What's that supposed to mean?"

Jason burst through the front doors. He jogged up, his wide eyes looking in between us.

"Jason Colin Soniat, I came by to see how things were coming here with the repairs," Mrs. Betty said. "And you told me that this girl was living in that spare room after the tree fell in her bedroom, but she's sitting here with hardly any clothes on. Where is Rose living, Jason? Tell me the truth."

He took a big breath, his hand to his cheek. "You're right, Ma, and I should've told you. I'm sorry. Rose is living with me. We're together. Rose is my girlfriend."

Mrs. Soniat went quiet. Fuming. I was sixteen again, caught by my high school boyfriend's mom making out in his bedroom. Except I wasn't. I was a grown woman, and this situation was ridiculous.

"So you moved in, seduced him—"

I stood up. "I didn't seduce him. We're—"

"Can you *please* put some pants on?" She covered her eyes and turned away.

Jason gestured at me like, *woman put some clothes on*. I grabbed the throw and wrapped it around my hips like a sarong.

"Jason, my heart is broken. I can't believe you kept this from me, after everything that's happened."

"Ma, it's not like that."

"And did she talk you into doing these drugs?"

"It's not drugs," I asserted. "It's mugwort, and we weren't smoking it. It's to clear the space."

She turned on me. "Is that some kind of pagan ritual? And to bring *tarot cards* into my son's home—" she broke off, her throat catching. Jason reached for her, but she waved him away from her. His face fell.

"Are you two serious about each other?" she demanded.

"Yes," I blurted, then turned at Jason's silence.

His mouth was wide. He stared at his mom, then turned to me. "I..."

I waited, but that was all he said. One singular personal pronoun.

My stomach dropped. The man I thought I was falling in love with looked between his mother and me and took a step toward her as she went for her purse.

He ran a hand through his hair as his mom walked out the door. "Did you have to be half-naked playing with your tarot cards in the living room?"

And then he followed his mom out of the church, calling for her.

The door shut. For a moment, I stood staring at it, my heart in freefall.

"I don't mean *anything* to you, do I?" I asked his quiet house.

I looked down, flipped over the card. The Tower.

Figures.

My tears fell on my cards as I gathered them and shoved them back into their box. I doused the smoking bundle of herbs in its shell on my way upstairs. I siphoned all my emotions into an imaginary box in my heart and locked it.

After ordering an Uber, I calmly threw three changes of clothes into my bag. I changed my shirt, throwing Jason's tank top onto his bed where we'd made love so many times. Threw on some shorts. Laced up my tennis shoes without socks. Swept down the stairs and shoved my iPad and charger into my backpack. And his mom's handkerchief. I still had to deal with that.

I packed up my sewing machine, hurriedly wrapping its cords and sticking it into its hard plastic case.

As I walked toward the parking lot, Jason stood talking through the open window of my Uber driver. I checked the license plate against my app.

Jason's expression grew panicked as his eyes fell on everything I was carrying. "Where are you going?"

"Home. Where I should never have left." I murmured a hello to the woman who nodded at me, clearly trying to stay out of this drama, and started putting my things in the back.

"Baby, this is your home, with me," he said softly.

The broken tone of his voice made tears fall down my face. "If I can't do what I want in my home, then it's not really home for me, is it?"

"Rose—"

"If you really loved me, you would've told her."

"Baby—"

But I wouldn't let him speak. "I love that you love your mom. I would *never* have come between you. But you chose her anyway." I got in and shut the door.

"I didn't—I wasn't trying to." He put his hands on the car, talking through the closed window. "Please don't leave. Can't we talk about this?"

"No. You want to please Big Daddy StudFinders and your mom? Fine. You do you. Because you sure as hell won't be doing me. I'll send somebody back for all my shit." To the driver, I said, "You can leave."

He called my name as we pulled away, but I didn't turn to look at him once. I pulled out my phone and texted him with trembling fingers.

> This is my official notice that this is my last month renting your apartment.

> As agreed upon, I have given you above three weeks' notice. I will have all of my things removed from the premises and will return the key by September 30.

Jason

The silence of the church was deafening. Burning herbs hung in the air. My hands were shaking. What the fuck just happened?

I sat heavily onto the pew by the door. Rose's tea was still on the coffee table, as if she'd walked away just for a moment.

But that look on her face. She wasn't coming back.

When the tears came, my elbows were on my knees and my head was in my hands. I did this to myself, like all the worst things in my life.

With Kasey, I chose what *she* wanted over what I wanted. With Rose, I chose what *Mom* wanted over what I wanted. What fucking StudFinders wanted, over what I wanted. I'd acted so evolved over the last two years. But treating Rose like that was the opposite of how I wanted to live.

I pulled out my phone and texted her, ignoring her formal notice to leave the apartment.

> I'm so sorry. Please come back. Or can I come to you? Does your mom still live on Wilty Street?

She may not even be going to her mom's. Shit. I'd be screwed if she went to a friend's house. I'd never find her.

Who was I kidding? The way she left, the way she looked at me—she didn't want me to follow her.

Minutes went by, and I couldn't even tell if she'd seen my text.

Hard knocking on the front door.

"Rose?" I dashed to the door and threw it open.

Becca stood on my front porch, arms akimbo. "What in the holy hell is happening? Mom just called, yelling something about you lying and Rose in her panties?" She opened her mouth to say more but stopped, leaned in closer. "Jason, are you crying? Are you okay?"

I roughly wiped my face and stood back, gesturing her inside.

Only a few steps in, she turned to me and put her hand on my arm. "Jason, you've done so much since the last time I was here!" She pulled me toward the couch. "I want to see everything, but first, talk to me."

I took a big breath. "Rose and I have been together since we evacuated."

She smiled and raised her eyebrows. "*Together* together? And be honest, because if you mean *like a couple* together, Lily owes me fifty bucks."

I nodded. "Rose is my girlfriend. Was—she *was* my girlfriend." After my last break-up, I mostly felt numb. But by the time I finished telling Becca the highlights from the moment Rose and I kissed to the moment she walked out, my chest hurt so badly I could barely breathe.

"And you didn't tell anybody because of the StudFinders people?"

I rubbed my eyes with the heels of my hands. "And because I was afraid of how Mom would take it."

"I know." She sighed and rolled her eyes. "She's ridiculous about them for some reason. I think she's never forgiven Ms. Dahlia for giving me a vibrator when I turned eighteen, and it's extended to Lily and Rose."

I shook my head and grabbed her arm. "Stop there and don't elaborate. It's not Ms. Dahlia's fault, it's mine. Mom's disapproved of everything in my life since I came back home. She's been pressuring me to date a woman she approves of, like fucking Misty, and completely ignoring me when I tell her no. And Misty literally propositioned me after I told her I wasn't interested."

"Wait, what did she do?"

I shrugged with my whole upper body. "She's obsessed with offering me blow jobs, for some reason. And no matter how many times I tell her to fuck off, she won't stop. And Mom doesn't believe me." I pulled my phone out and showed Becca the conversation.

Her jaw dropped as she scrolled through it. "That bitch is out of the wedding. I didn't want her in it in the first place. That was all Mom." She handed me back my phone.

"I'm so fucking done with her." I took screenshots of Misty's latest propositions and sent them to Mom. "There. Now Mom'll have to believe me." I set my phone aside and put my head in my hands. "But none of that matters. I fucked up. I hurt Rose so badly, she's never coming back." My voice was consumed by my crying, and Becca hugged me close.

"Jason, my heart's broken that you're so sad. You really love her, don't you?"

"I love her, and I love Mom, and I can't make anybody happy."

She squeezed me tight then released me, wiping my tears and smoothing down my hair. "It's so weird to see you all grown up, crying over a woman when I remember you crying over a Superman action figure you lost. Mom must feel that even more than I do. She always says that having a baby is like having a piece of your heart walking around outside your body. It can make her a little extreme."

"But I did this to her. I hurt her so badly when I left, and I don't think I can ever make up for it. Kasey—"

"Kasey wasn't the whole problem, and neither were you. I'm not trying to downplay what you went through, or what Mom went through missing you. But I was there from the beginning of that whole thing. Mom basically gave you two choices: break up with Kasey or leave with her and try to find some peace and happiness." She shrugged. "None of us hated her at first. But then we all started noticing how you always deferred to her in everything. Your whole personality changed from the lovable, happy goofball we've always known to this somber man who always looked distracted and miserable.

"That's when she started laying into her. The religion stuff was just a scapegoat and what Mom turned to when she was sick with worry, missing you. We were all worried about you. Even Alex expressed concerned emotions and not just jokes, if you can believe that."

A corner of my mouth quirked up.

"My point is that Mom was at fault too. She didn't give you a minute's peace when you were already under enough stress with Kasey. And I'm sorry I wasn't there for you more. I was so wrapped up in getting that new pharmacy started, and Brad was trying to establish his law practice. It's no excuse, but sometimes you don't realize something's a huge problem until it goes critical."

"I wish I'd never left with Kasey. I wish I never even met her. But you're right, I didn't feel like I had a choice. With her always in one ear, and Mom always in the other—and I thought I loved her. I thought Kasey was my future."

"You did what you thought you had to do. I know. And it sucked. But you don't have to atone forever. You have to let Mom take responsibility for her part in it too, or she'll never learn how to talk things out reasonably. You can't be under her thumb forever. That's no way to live."

"Gah, *under her thumb*. That's what Kasey used to say about Mom. When Rose said it to me the other day it made me want to shed my skin."

"You might have some trauma. Have you thought about seeing a therapist?"

"I went for a long time after Kasey. But maybe I need to go back."

She grinned. "So, you and Rose, huh? Lately, you've been the happiest, most Jason-like you've been in literal years. We've all noticed it, but none of us figured it out. Well," she amended. "I had suspicions."

I put my face in my hands. "Me and Rose. It's—it was so good. I love her so goddamn much. We were really partners. We worked so well together." I paused. "We played so well together. We supported each other, and she trusted that I would make good decisions."

"Stop talking about her in the past tense. You had a fight, is all. Do you know how many fights Brad and I have had?" She gestured to my phone, which I'd just checked for the thousandth time since she'd been here. "Did you try calling her?"

I shook my head. "I texted her, but she hasn't written back."

"Maybe give her some time to cool off. In the meantime, you know who you have to talk to, huh?"

I shook my head vehemently. "I'm not talking to Mom."

She shook my knee. "You dumb little brother. Not wanting to talk to Mom is the whole reason Rose left. If you want her back—I assume you want her back?"

"Yeah, more than anything."

"Then you have to pick Door Number Three, the 'stand up to Mom and talk to her about big things' option you didn't take last time."

"But how do I let go of this guilt? I'm just going to let her railroad me again."

"Let her cool off, and talk to her at the rehearsal. Rose'll be there too, and it'll be a chance for the three of you to be adults and work it out."

"I can't bring that kind of drama to your wedding rehearsal."

"Jason, there's gonna be drama with both of them there. You might as well let me set a place card for it. It'll make me feel more in charge." She smiled, but I couldn't.

"But what if she never gives Rose a chance?"

She shrugged with her hands up on either side of her head. "I don't have a crystal ball. But Rose is awesome. Mom'll come around when she sees how happy you are and that Rose isn't trying to keep you away from us. Just because they don't get along immediately doesn't mean they won't ever get along. The important thing is that you're here, you're talking to each other, and you're trying. That's all she wants. That's all any of us want."

I laughed without humor. "You make all of this sound so easy, but it's not. The way I treated Rose, she'll never talk to me again."

Becca ruffled my hair. "You don't know that. Love always finds a way."

If Rose really loved me, that might be true. But did she?

Chapter 16

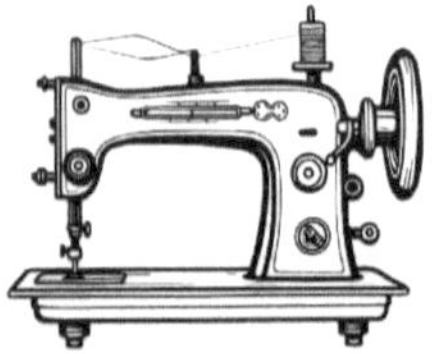

A Coward and a Dumbass

Rose

I wanted Jason. But I didn't *want* to want him. The whole Uber ride, I reminded myself of all the reasons I would never go back.

He got mad at you for being yourself in what he told you was your home. He wouldn't stand up for you. He was embarrassed of you. He couldn't bring himself to say he was serious about you when it really counted. You're not heartbroken, you're pissed.

The driver pulled away as I walked up the sidewalk to Heather's real-life dream house: a gorgeous, old New Orleans mansion. I knocked and waited. If she and Abby weren't home, that would be what I got for not calling first.

Just as I was pulling out my phone to call, Abby appeared through the glass door. Her gaze darted to my pile of things and back to me.

She yelled for Heather as she opened the door. "Rose! What happened?" She threw her arms around me. Heather joined us, throwing her arms around me, too.

I sobbed out Jason's name as I hugged them back. They took all my stuff from me, brought me over to the velvet sofa in the living room, and sank down on either side of me.

"I'm sorry to bust up in your house, but I didn't want to go to my mom's," I said. "And since I stupidly got involved with my landlord, and there's a tree-sized hole in the roof over my bedroom, I couldn't stay there. Not with him."

"Of course, baby, you're always welcome here." Heather grabbed a tissue box off the wooden coffee table and pulled several out, handing them to me.

When I could speak again, I told them both what happened. "He said he loved me, but that was a lie. Just like he'd lied to his mom about us. I'd started to think I was serious about him. That I might...love him." The words tasted both foreign and true on my tongue. "But I could never be serious about someone who treated me like that."

Abby's blue eyes met Heather's brown eyes, and the latter took a long breath to speak.

"I know, I know," I said. "I need to get him out of my mind and move on. It just really hurts tonight, you know?"

Heather shook her head. "No, I don't think you should make any decisions tonight. I'll move your stuff into your old room and make you a bath and the most luxurious bed I can put together. The whole thing's just gonna suck, but you might have a clearer head tomorrow."

"I don't need a clearer head. I need to put him behind me. It all happened so fast anyway. It's not like we were gonna get married or anything." The pictures we took playing bride and groom rose in my mind's eye, and I started crying all over again.

"Is putting him behind you what you really want?" Abby rubbed my back and handed me another tissue. "He—"

My phone started blasting The Bee Gees, "More Than a Woman." I reached over and shut it off. "And he won't stop texting me. 'I'm sorry, Rose,'" I said in an unkind mockery of his deep voice. "'Come back, Rose.'"

"He apologized?" Abby asked.

"Repeatedly. But they're empty words. Like his 'I love you.' He doesn't mean any of it."

Heather grabbed up my phone. "What could he do to show you he meant it?"

I sputtered. "Do something about it. Stand up to his mom. Stand up for me. Take some kind of action to show me he understands how I feel and...that I really am important to him."

She glanced at me and went back to my phone. "All I can see is the preview, but it says, 'I told Becca everything, and I sent screenshots of Misty's texts to Mom. She's out of the wedding. You never have—' and it cuts off."

I laughed unkindly. "So glad I busted my ass to get her dress altered."

Abby shrugged. "But at least he did the right thing. Finally. And you don't have to see her at the wedding."

"Oh, I'm not standing in the wedding. I might not even go. I was supposed to walk with him down the aisle. Can you imagine?"

Heather set my phone face-down on the coffee table. "Where does Jason fall in your levels?"

I closed my eyes, grateful for the shorthand between old friends. "I've been asking myself this since last weekend. He's not a One. I mean, the sex was *transcendent*, oh my God. But we meant so much more to each other than that."

"You'd said he was a strong Two," Abby gently supplied.

I nodded. "We're friends, no doubt. We play together, support each other. We laugh all the time when we're together. Life was just *good* and *easy* with him."

Jason was right. There was *so much more* to us. The look in his eyes when he told me he loved me made me panic. Because I knew deep in my soul, even then, that I loved him, too.

I loved Jason. With everything that I was.

"He's a stupid Three!" I wailed. "How did this happen? I know better than this."

Abby handed me more tissues. "Having a fight doesn't always mean a friendship or a relationship is over. And it sounds like he took some baby steps. If you really love him, you owe it to yourself to get all the information you can about the situation before you make any kind of permanent decision. What if he's the love of your life? You can't just cut him off. Right, Heather?"

Heather sighed. I hated that heartache haunted her pretty dark eyes. Her ex left her at the altar for a bridesmaid almost seven years ago, and I still wanted to punch him in the balls.

"I shouldn't weigh in," she said. "But I do think some time apart from him is a good idea. And like Abby said, don't cut him off cold. He's trying."

Abby nodded. "You went from friends to living together and in love in only a few weeks. That has to be overwhelming for you both. Maybe the distance will help you clarify how you feel about him."

I clutched my best friends closer. Their squishing me was a comfort, but it made me miss Jason even more. I wanted him to comfort me. I missed how hot his body always ran, and how he always gravitated to where I was in the church, even if it was just to sit near me while I read or sewed, or to drop a kiss on my head as he went past. I even smelled like him now, or at least this amalgam of me and him.

Heather and Abby made a big fuss over getting me comfortably situated in my old room and tried to cheer me up with dinner and conversation. But I took my bath and went to bed early. The murmur of my friends talking low in the kitchen comforted me even more than the plush bed Heather made for me. I needed sleep, but first I pulled out my phone. Missed calls from Mom and Lily. Five missed calls from Jason, a voicemail, and a long string of texts. Besides the bit about Becca and Misty, his texts were increasing amounts of groveling, which I perversely enjoyed. I took a deep breath and listened to the voicemail.

Baby, please say something. Anything. I called your mom and Lily looking for you, but they don't know where you are. Now I made them worry, too. If something happened to you because of me—

His voice choked up, and he sniffled, his voice raw. It cut me clean to my heart.

I'm so, so sorry. And I'm sorry if I'm bothering you with all these calls and texts. I fucked up, and I'm so sorry. My mom was so horrible to you, and I should've stuck up for you. I should've made you feel comfortable in your own home. I should've told the whole world how much I love you. Because I do. There's no excuse for my behavior. I know I...I have to make changes to be worthy of you, because you sure as hell deserve someone stronger and braver than me. I love you, Rose, so much. And I just want you home with me. I miss you.

The emotion in his voice felt like someone ripping all the stitches that held my heart together. By the end of his message, I was sobbing. I didn't trust myself to call him and be able to talk rationally. So, I texted him back, texted my mom, and turned off my phone.

Jason

This French Quarter dive bar was the last place I wanted to be. It'd been three days since Rose left. Three days since her last text to me, the night she broke up with me. Sitting alone at the bar, I pulled my phone out to read it—and my response to her—again.

> I'm safe and with my friends. I'll tell my Mom. Thank you for apologizing, but I can't be with someone who's embarrassed of me. I know you and your family have been through a lot, and I would never want you to hurt your mom because of me. But I would've weathered anything for you.

> I would've done anything to win her over. For you. But you didn't give me a chance. I can't stay in a relationship with you where she gets to decide if you love me or not.

> I love you. I'm sorry.

Every day without her was a little more of my soul whittled away.

I threw myself back into my socials, custom pieces, and hurricane repairs, but everything I worked on reminded me of her. Working on my Insta made me go to her profile and check her follower count. I worried about her keeping up engagement because she hadn't touched it in days. I couldn't pick out a wall color for the bathroom because I wanted to make sure she'd love it. I was up late last night working on my plans for the community room for the first time since Florida, and I was out of my chair to bring the plans to her sewing table and ask her what kind of rooms she wanted in her dream house. Then I remembered.

And this morning I called Faduma and turned StudFinders down. She definitely didn't expect it. She did her best to talk me into it, but I told her, respectfully, that I couldn't sign a contract that dictated how to live my life. She was disappointed but understood, and she wished me luck. I may never be able to afford to finish my house, but none of that mattered if I had to hide the woman I loved.

Alex stumbled up beside me at the bar. "Come on, dude—"

"For the last time, Alex, I don't want a fucking lap dance." I pushed my brother back toward the crowd in this godforsaken Bourbon Street strip club.

He laughed at me. "I already paid for it, so I guess it's for me!" He whooped and retreated back into the crowd as my dad sat beside me.

"I see you enjoy this kind of establishment as much as I do." He took a sip of the beer he'd been nursing for an hour.

"It's not my scene on a good day." My eyes flickered back up to the football highlights playing on the TV over the bar. The bass thrumming up through the soles of my shoes was making a nauseating slosh of the peanuts and beer in my stomach. The other bars the bachelor party hit tonight were cleaner than this one, and the streets in between reeked of puke and piss.

My dad studied the TV for a minute. "Saints might have a chance this year, with that new running back."

I shrugged. "Maybe."

"I ever tell you how when I started dating your mother, her parents hated me?"

I frowned over my beer and snapped my gaze to his. He was studying the TV still, the images flickering over his glasses. Alex may've looked more like Dad, but I was more like him. I was more sensitive, usually more open about sharing my emotions. Which is why I was shocked that I'd never heard this before.

"What?" I needed him to say it again.

"They absolutely hated me."

"Nana and Pops love you."

"They do now, after thirty-some-odd years of faithful marriage and giving them four beautiful grandchildren. But back then? They didn't want me dating your mother. They were upset when we got engaged, and..."

"And?" I took a sip of my beer.

"They were furious when I got her pregnant before we were married."

The beer went down the wrong way. I coughed, grabbing napkins off the bar to get myself straight. Son of a bitch. Rose was right. "When you did *what*?"

Dad laughed. "Don't ever tell your mother I told you."

"So, wait. Mark was born out of wedlock?"

"No, your brother was born plenty inside wedlock." Dad shrugged. "He was *conceived* out of wedlock in the back of—"

I put my hand on his arm. "Dad, stop. I don't want to hear any-more. Excuse me," I said, catching the bartender's eye and pushing my half-drunk beer away. "Can you bring me a Sprite?"

Dad shrugged. "All I'm saying is that it took a lot of hard work for us to show your grandparents that I was a good guy who'd do right by their daughter. Our hard work together. You mom seems to have forgotten all that."

"And you're telling me all this...because?"

"Let me answer that question with a question. When your mom asked you the other day if you and Rose were serious, apparently she said yes, but you didn't answer. Why not?"

"Because I'm a coward and a dumbass."

"Son, are you serious about Rose?"

"Yes. I love her. She's everything to me."

"Is she good for you? Do you see a future with her?"

"She's so good for me. Things are just...easy with her. We work together in such harmony. We laugh together, have fun together..."

"I don't want to know what else you do together." He took another sip of his beer.

I laughed, straightening out the plastic straw wrapper, folding it over in half, and folding each end under alternately like Rose taught me with her ribbons. "You know, in Florida, I asked her if she'd de-signed any wedding dresses for herself over the years. And I can't get it out of my head, how..." I pinched the wrapper at the end of the folds and pulled one side so it formed a rose. "The whole time she was showing them to me, all I could think was how I wanted to marry her in every one of those dresses."

Dad pointed at the straw wrapper rose I'd made. "I know you went through hell, but I agree with Rose. It wasn't because you made bad decisions."

"Wait, you talked to her?"

"No. It's something she said to your mom on Sunday, before church. That it wasn't fair to blame you for bad choices when Kasey was abusive."

My face heated with welling tears. She stood up to Mom for me when I couldn't.

"You always were a smart kid with a good heart. And I'm so proud of the man you've grown into. If you love this girl, then she must be alright. And you have something worth fighting for." He took a sip of his beer. "It's not all or nothing, you know, your mom's happiness versus yours and Rose's. I know you're too old for me to tell you what to do, but you can't roll over and give up."

He clapped his hand on my shoulder, and I grabbed it. "Thanks, Dad. I love you."

"I love you too, son." He slipped out of the stool and tossed his head toward the other room. "Brad looks miserable. I'm gonna go see if I can talk his best man into shuttin' this party down. And make sure Alex doesn't go home with a stripper."

I laughed and cleared my throat. "Hang on; I'll come too. I'm gonna say my goodbyes and call a ride. There's something I have to work on at home."

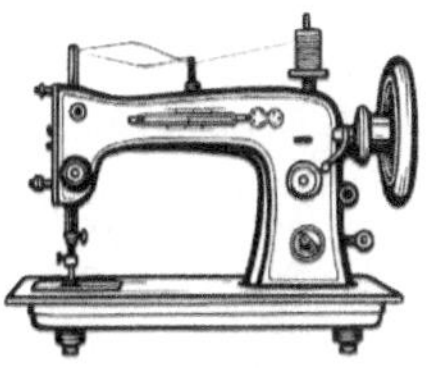

Rose

It had been only four days since I left Jason. Apparently, distance did make the heart grow fonder, because I was only more certain that I was in love with him.

Nothing could keep my mind off of him. I worked on Mom's designs—thought of marrying Jason. I let Heather get Becca's dresses from Jason—soaked up every scrap of information she passed to me. He'd been worried about me and sent along Princess Sleeparella because he knew I had a hard time sleeping without it. The pillow was completely saturated with his scent. The majestic bastard must've hugged it every moment I was gone.

So then I slept on it every night, missing him even more intensely than I had before.

I woke up a little hung over this morning, even though I'd skipped out on going to Becca's bachelorette party in case we accidentally ran into Brad's bachelor party—the French Quarter was small for being so big. So, I was taking it easy today, sipping tea on the sofa and flipping through one of Abby's flower catalogs. Down the hallway, Chris Evans's head Photoshopped onto a naked hunk's body stared at me from the poster Heather brought home from the party. The three of us stayed up too late playing pin the junk on the hunk, and Heather and I drank too many margaritas. Abby put up with us and got us into bed, bless her teetotaling heart.

A key turned in the door, and Heather came in from work. She flopped beside me on the sofa, sifting through mail in her lap.

"Shouldn't you be getting ready for Becca's rehearsal dinner?" she asked.

My stomach flopped. "I already told Becca I wouldn't make it."

"Um, ma'am?" She tried to take my catalog out of my hands, but I pulled it away.

"I don't have time to go. I have to finish something for Becca, any-way." A white lie. I'd finished it this afternoon, but it wasn't wrapped.

"But you have time to flip through a flower catalog? Rose."

I met her warm brown eyes.

"You made a commitment to Becca."

"Yeah, but I don't *have* to go. I mean, if you've stood in one wed-ding, you've stood in them all. I don't need to practice walking down the aisle. Especially since I'm paired with Jason," I added in a small voice. "Do you want to make cookies tonight? I want cookies."

She frowned at me for a moment. "You can't deter me with cookies, baby girl."

The doorbell rang.

"You can't *not* go." Heather got up and went toward the door. "You have to go to this thing looking like the fierce, strong woman you are."

I didn't answer, just kept flipping as Heather talked softly with whoever was at the door. The only way to stay out of the Soniat family drama was to stay away from the Soniats. It was bad enough I'd still have to stand in the wedding. She'd already lost one bridesmaid, and I couldn't bail on her.

Heather walked back into the living room with my mom, who was armed with her "my baby needs me" face.

Well, shit. My hand paused on the catalog. "Hey, Mom." I'd been minimally answering her texts because I wasn't ready for her cocktail of motherly mollycoddling and reasonable advice. But alas, the time had come.

"Hey baby, I came over as soon as I got back in town."

Heather looked between us. "Can I get you something to drink, Ms. Dahlia?"

Mom sighed and dropped her purse beside the sofa, re-fluffing her short, dark hair. "No thank you, sweetheart. I just need to talk to this one."

Heather nodded and left us alone as Mom sat next to me on the sofa and affixed her green eyes on me. The familiar scent of Lancôme Magie Noire perfume wafted into my personal space. "Rosie, why didn't you tell me about Jason?" she asked softly.

I went to flip the page, but Mom sat a tissue box on top of the catalog. I huffed a deep breath. "I don't know. I didn't think it was going to get serious. And then I thought you'd give me shit about living with him so fast. And he didn't want his family to know, so I couldn't tell Lily."

She chuckled. "Well, Becca told her, then she told me. Are you okay?"

I looked into her big eyes. Just like Lily's. I was the odd woman out with my dad's blue eyes. "I'm okay," I lied.

Mom sighed heavily and pulled all my hair away from my face. "You don't have to be brave for me, Rosie. Is this thing between you guys serious?"

All the contents of that locked, imaginary box in my heart spilled out into my blood, and I crumpled into her arms in tears.

"I love him, Mama. I tried not to, but I couldn't stop myself. We've been so happy." I swallowed, trying to breathe. "But he's not serious about me. I mean—" I grabbed a tissue and blew my nose. "I obviously wasn't gonna marry him." That thought only made me cry harder.

"I did this to you, didn't I? Made you not trust men. I can't believe it took me and Steve getting engaged for me to start puzzling it together."

I took a big breath, let it go. "It's just...my whole outlook on relationships was formed at a very early age. You raised us to be independent. Not to rely on men for anything—not love, not friendship, not pleasure. Commitment leads to marriage, and marriage perpetuates the fantasy that married couples are somehow better than couples who don't get married. It keeps women in abusive relationships and thinking that they have to be subservient to men. So many people use it to exclude and degrade people in the LGBTQIA+ community. God, the symbols of the white virgin wedding, and how dads give their 'property' over to the groom. The statistics of married women not living as long as their single counterparts. It's permeated all of my relationships, been one of my core values. Men don't feel love the way we do, and they don't stay. And what happened with Jason proves it."

Mom's eyebrows had gone up higher and higher as I spoke. "Rosie, why on earth do you design wedding dresses?"

My nails bit into my palms. I was tired of answering this question. Frankly? Tired of my own hypocrisy. "Because I love to sew, and I love the way they look. It's the only socially acceptable way to wear ball gowns and princess dresses. Trust me. I tried wearing some of my gowns in New York City as daywear, and the world is *not ready* for that."

"Or do you, deep down, want to be a bride yourself, but you're afraid to be vulnerable? And you're afraid there's something wrong about you that makes men leave?"

My heart cracked at her gentle words, exposing its gooey, shameful center. There was no stopping the sobbing now that she named it out loud. The truth. My truth. My big fear. I'd never told anyone, but nobody knew me like my mama.

I nodded. "How did you know?"

Mom held me through the tears, kissing me on the head. "Because that's how I felt after your dad left. And instead of teaching you to be strong, I gave you my fears. I'm so sorry, Rose. I was wrong. And don't you misunderstand." She pulled back and smoothed my hair from my face to look me in the eyes. She was crying, too. "He and I fought constantly, ever since we met. We were completely incompatible. He left because he and I were a nightmare together. He never came back to see you two because he doesn't care about anybody but himself. Trust me. It was a recurring motif throughout our entire relationship."

She pulled three more tissues for me and two for herself, dabbing under her eyes. "It wasn't your fault that he left. Or your sister's. But after he was gone—" She breathed out, shaking her head. "I didn't want you girls to think of your dad as the monster he felt like to me, so I made all men the enemy. I made commitment the enemy. It was faceless. It would keep you from being hurt the way I was."

Mom had never said a bad thing to us about our dad, but I remembered her scoffing at weddings and Valentine's Days. I remembered her getting hit on in the grocery store and her dressing the man down for approaching her when she was with her two kids. That guy ran off with his tail between his legs, and Mom lectured us on how all men were rude and inconsiderate.

"And you have to remember," she continued. "My dad died when I was a little kid. I barely knew him. I didn't have a clue what a real partnership could be like because the only experience I had was my shitty one."

That's all I'd had too. Shitty relationships built on nothing but sexual compatibility. Which, important, yeah. But only one piece of the puzzle. I learned that as Jason had lovingly fitted together so many more pieces of the puzzle of us. Him investing his time and know-how in my work because I was important to him. Him saving the last fortune cookie from our takeout for me because he knew how much I love them. Us fitting together like two puzzle pieces ourselves, helping each other with big and little things, collaborating to solve problems, and truly enjoying the time we spent together. Even the non-naked time.

"But when I went back to school to become a therapist," Mom said, "gosh, I learned so much. I started seeing all these couples with real problems. But also? With real connections. I thought couple's counseling was all opposition, a last-ditch effort to reanimate something already dead. But more often than not, it's two people who love each other so very much that they'll do anything to make it work. To deepen or rekindle their connections, not to break them. Men as equally as women. And no, they weren't all married. Marriage isn't for everyone, and that's okay. But I'm so sorry I didn't bring what I was learning home to you and Lily.

"Until I met Steve, I didn't know how amazing a true partnership could be. Our life together is built on mutual respect and unconditional love. A commitment with the right partner is life-changing." She laughed. "Even if it's with a man, and he still can't find shit in the pantry if other shit's in front of it. No one's perfect, Rosie. And good relationships still take a ton of work. It's not all chocolate and orgasms. It's both of you choosing each other, repeatedly, over all the other problems. Because you each know in your heart that the other person is worth it."

"How do you know they're worth it?" I sniffled and wiped my nose. "How do you know if your relationship is worth it?"

She blew out through her mouth. "That's a hard one. I think you have to just...feel it. Of course, we're assuming far and above the low-bar baseline of they're not abusive or someone who would cheat. When you're both good people, it's really a personal decision because no two relationships are the same. But intention matters. Compatibility matters. Willingness to say, 'I'm sorry' and not only mean it, but actually do better. That matters a lot."

Jason *had* apologized and gotten Misty kicked out of the wedding, and that wasn't nothing. I closed my eyes. We *were* good together. So much laughing, all the time. Daily life with him was weirdly fun. Even doing dishes. He approached everything we faced as though we were equal partners, even went above and beyond to do more for me. Until StudFinders and wanting to hide me from his mom, I'd never questioned his intentions. He admitted he'd messed up, without excuses, and he vowed to make changes. But would he?

All I knew was that my whole body ached from the loss of him. I teared up again. "I don't know what to say, Mom."

She sat me up and pushed more tissues into my hands, pulling all my hair back again as I blew my nose. "Say you won't judge Jason by anything other than who he is and who you are together. And admit that it's okay that he's not perfect. He's still learning and growing like the rest of us." She pulled out her phone and tapped her way to Instagram. "I went to see what I could learn about this Deck Daddy. Did you see what he posted today?"

I shook my head. The day after I left, I'd gotten one too many pop-ups from his socials and turned off all my notifications.

She started a video and handed me her phone. "Take a look."

My first sight of Jason in days made my breath catch and my heartache intensify. After his cheesy opening sequence of photos of him building and being his goofy self, he appeared. Shirt on for a change, he stood beside a superimposed still image of the video we made together of my table.

"Hey everybody, It's your Deck Daddy, Jason, and today I want to talk about this video." He pointed to it. "Not the video itself, but the woman in it. It's time to set the rumors to rest. Yep, you caught me. This is Rose. And I am"—he pressed his hands to his heart—"hopelessly, completely, *transcendentally* in love with her."

He said that to the whole dang internet? Mrs. Betty and Big Brother StudFinders must be crying into their tea and beers.

"In case you missed it," he went on, "she's the genius designer and seamstress behind Sweet Roses Bridal, and I recently posed with her to help get her Instagram up and running. We've both shared photos from that day, but here's my favorite."

The screen filled with the photo of us kissing that he didn't want to post before. My eyes filled with tears and Mom *aww'ed* beside me. "Y'all are such a beautiful couple."

I'd forgotten how devoted and in love he looked in that photo, his brow lowered, his eyes closed, his hand along my jaw as if loving me was the most serious thing in the world.

"The only thing more beautiful than that gown is that woman's heart," Jason continued. "And while we were evacuated in Florida because of Hurricane Oscar, she saw this cool wall shelf made from an old church window in a shop. She wanted it for her crystal collection, but neither of us had the extra cash. So I made her one to look like the windows in our converted church home."

A corner of my mouth twitched up. Again with the "our home."

I watched the whole video with tears streaming down my face, from him designing the shelf, cutting the wood, bending the pieces to make the curved point at the top. All the little details he poured into it to please me, like the deep shelves and buying me a new set of tarot cards he said he found on my Amazon Wishlist to be sure they'd fit. Becca even came on camera to help him with a portion of it, putting the first coat of the gray paint from the rectory on it—"Diana's Moon," Jason called it—and helping him distress it.

I missed him more and more as the video went along. Then finally, he hung the finished shelf on a wall—with tarot cards on it—in the main living area of the church. Where God and everybody could see it.

Becca stood beside him with a gift bag in hand. "I have a friend in Arkansas who collects hunks of quartz off her land." She reached in and pulled out a gorgeous fat cluster of clear quartz big enough to hold with two hands. "She gave me this a while back, and I've been trying to find a good home for it. Would Rose like it?"

"Ahh, thanks Becca, it's perfect." He took it carefully from her and sat it on the shelf. "I think she'll love it."

Watching Jason and his sister talking so casually about me, hearing Jason call his house my home too...I'd been so certain that what happened between us was the end of it. And so certain that I wouldn't have a permanent place in his life that I grabbed onto his issues with his mom and pushed our relationship away with both hands.

I walked out on him when he needed me. The truth was, we needed each other.

Mom squeezed my hand. "Does being with Jason make you happy?"

I nodded through softer tears. "Blissful."

"So...maybe it's time to follow your bliss?"

I huffed a soft laugh at her choice of words. "Yeah. I think it is."

"Then go get ready. I'll drive you to the rehearsal dinner."

I nodded. "Okay. But I have to wrap something first."

Jason

The hot September evening gave no quarter, even as the sinking sun infused the sky with shots of pink and orange. Sweat tracked down my back, soaking my white Oxford shirt under my suit jacket where I climbed the front steps of Bastian's Bistro. I took another look either way down the street to see if Rose had magically appeared.

But she wasn't walking or driving up the street. I sighed and went into the restaurant.

"Mama," Becca said, phone in hand near the empty hostess station, "Rose won't let me down."

Enough was enough. Becca hadn't wanted me to pull Mom aside at the church, but it was time to move forward because loving Rose was my future.

"Maybe it's for the best if she doesn't stand in the wedding," Mom said. "I'm thinking of her, too, and how awkward it'll be for her to walk with Jason now that they've broken up."

I approached them. "Rose was probably worried about coming tonight because she didn't want to upset you."

Becca pointed at me. "Bingo. She also said she had to finish something before she could come, and that it couldn't wait."

I frowned at Becca in question.

Becca shrugged back with a smile. "No idea," she singsonged.

Mom frowned. "It seems a little rude, is all."

"Ma," I said with all the calmness and respect I could muster. I took a deep breath, symbolically filling myself with the strength of my love for Rose. "I'm sorry. I was completely out of line not to tell you about me and Rose from the beginning. I was afraid to hurt you again, and I own that I messed up. I promise not to hide important things from you just because I think you won't like them. You asked me if I was serious about Rose, and I hate that I didn't answer. I am. I love her. I'd marry her tonight, if she'd have me. I don't ever want to hurt you. But as a very wise woman told me, I might have to disappoint you sometimes, and we'll both have to learn that we can still love each other after it."

Mom frowned back at me, her eyes glossy. "Jason, I've just been so worried you'll get hurt again. You didn't deserve what you went through with Kasey, and I don't want you to fall for someone else who'll take advantage of your good heart."

"But Rose is an amazing, loving person, which you'd know if you'd give her half a chance. You were really rude to her at our house, and I—"

Mom's brows pulled together in a question and her mouth opened, but I kept talking before she could speak. "Yes, I said *our house*. Mine and Rose's. And she has a right to do what she wants in her own house. She didn't do anything to deserve you talking to her like that, and I should've spoken up for her. She wanted to tell you about us. I'm the one who was afraid to tell you something I didn't think you'd like."

Mom's face crumpled, and she took my hand. "I only want what's best for you."

"Rose is best for me," I said.

"I just don't want her to take you away from me."

I squeezed her hand. "Ma, I wouldn't love the kind of woman who would. Never again."

"Hey Rose!" Becca called with a smile. "I'm so glad you made it!"

I followed her gaze to my right. Seeing Rose standing in the same room as me hit my system like a drug. My heart thudded into service like it'd been stopped before, and even more sweat poured down my back. She was breathtaking in a flowery dress with a corset top and her long hair curling down. I could tell from the style and how it hugged her curves that she'd made that dress, and my heart swelled with pride for the talent and beauty of this amazing woman.

And when our eyes met, all the stars that had come untethered in my sky snapped back into place.

"I'm sorry I was late." She stepped forward with a small white box in her hands. "I was putting the finishing touches on this. It's for Becca, but it's also for you, Mrs. Betty." She handed the box to Mom, who looked like she wanted to sink into the ground. "Here, open it."

"Oh. Um, thank you." Mom wiped her eyes and carefully removed the ribbon and top of the box. Behind her, Becca's smile was huge.

I could hardly take my eyes off of Rose, but she didn't look at me again. How much of that had she heard?

"Oh," Mom breathed. She pulled a blue handkerchief from the box. "You fixed it, but you—"

I stepped closer to see it as Rose explained.

"You mentioned how you always wanted to have the names of all the brides who carried it embroidered on it, and I thought, wouldn't it be cool if it was actually their signatures? So, I got Becca to track them down for me, and I embroidered them for you." She twisted her hands. "I hope I didn't overstep."

"I only found Great-Grandma Mary's this afternoon," Becca said, "so Rose didn't have much time to finish it for tonight."

A tear rolled down Mom's cheek. She reached over and took Rose's hand. "It's beautiful, honey. Just beautiful. It's exactly what I wanted, and now the tradition won't be lost. Thank you. It means so much to me that you went to all this trouble for my family."

"Of course. Try and keep it in this archival, acid-free tissue paper. It'll help keep it from yellowing. And I wrote up some instructions to best preserve it." Rose tugged on a card stuck into the box. "There's no reason it shouldn't last until your descendants run out of places for signatures."

Mom stared at the card. "I can't believe you did all this for me after I was so awful to you." Mom placed the handkerchief back into the box and handed it to Becca. She took Rose's hand. "I'm sorry, Rose, for the way I acted and for what I said." Then she took my hand. "And I'm sorry, Jason." She connected my hand with Rose's. I held my breath, afraid to grab hers too fast, but she grasped my hand first. I squeezed hers for dear life.

"I'm sorry I didn't give you a chance, Rose," Mom said. "I'll do better."

"I'm sorry we didn't tell you about us," Rose said softly. "We should've been honest from the beginning."

I wasn't sure where we stood, but I loved hearing "we" and "us" from her mouth.

"Thank you for saying so. And thank you for the handkerchief. It's perfect. More than I imagined." Mom put her hands on each of our cheeks. "Be good to each other." She turned and took Becca's hand, going back into the restaurant.

Rose's gaze met mine. She took my other hand. "I saw my crystal shelf. Thank you. It was beautiful, like everything you make. But...aren't you worried about what StudFinders will think?"

I shook my head. "I already turned them down."

She gasped, her eyes wide. "Why?"

My heart pounded a desperate rhythm, and I swallowed hard, wanting to throw my arms around her, but also needing her to say it was okay for me to. "Because it's not enough to follow my bliss. I want to move forward with integrity. And I love you too much to hide it from anyone."

One side of her smile quirked up as her eyebrows pulled together. "But what about your community room?"

"I'll figure it out." I shrugged. "Like you said—if that wasn't the way, then the right way's coming." I licked my lips. "Thank you for doing that for my mom. That was really cool of you."

"She's important to you, so she's important to me," she said. "I missed you."

A dam broke in my chest. "I missed you, too. I'm so sorry, Rose. I should never have talked to you the way I did, and I shouldn't have let my mom talk to you that way, either. I should've been honest and told my mom how I feel about you. There's no excuse for any of it, and I'd undo it if I could. But I promise I'll do better. If you let me."

She nodded. "Thank you. And I'm sorry I walked out the way I did. Next time we argue, I'll stay and work it out. Because we're everything to me."

The aching in my chest subsided as warm relief stole through my limbs. "We're everything to me, too."

"And I'm also sorry I couldn't say it before...but Jason?" She bit her lip and studied my eyes. Took a deep breath. "I love you."

A full smile broke across my face and warmth like sunshine filled my chest. "I love you too. So much. So...does this mean you're coming home?"

"Um. Just one thing." She busied herself with straightening my tie. "I overheard what you said to your mom."

I closed my hand over hers, over my pounding heart. "I meant it all."

"I know. I want you to know...I'm not sure if I want to get married. I might, someday. But I'm not sure right now. If that's a dealbreaker, please tell me now." Tears sprang to her eyes. "Because I don't want to stand in the way of your happiness, but I selfishly want you to be happy with me."

I slipped my hand along her face. I've always wanted to get married, and even more so, I wanted to marry Rose. But there was something I wanted even more than that.

"I want to be your partner. If I get to do that as your husband or as your boyfriend, either way, I'm thrilled. And I respect your feelings about it. I promise I'll never hold it over your head, and I'll never ambush you with a surprise proposal."

She exhaled and smiled. "Thank you," she murmured, pulling me closer by my lapels. "Now I'm ready to come home." She reached her hand along my jaw and brought my face close to hers, looking deeply and seriously into my eyes. "But I have to warn you." She smiled, her wet eyes starry. "You're never gonna be able to get rid of me."

Tears slipped down my face as I pressed my forehead to hers. "I wouldn't have it any other way." I pulled her closer, breathing in her rosy scent like a parched man who'd finally gotten a drink of water.

She wrapped her arms around my neck. "I'm serious, Deck Daddy," she murmured against my lips. "You're gonna be so stuck with me."

"I want you, I love you, and you can't threaten me with something I want. Weak sauce, Sweet Rose. Weak..." I kissed her. "Sauce."

She pulled my ear to her mouth. "So how long does this shindig last? I desperately want to be reunited with Dick Daddy."

I laughed, squeezing her tight and leaning into her with my hips so she could feel how badly I wanted her. I nuzzled my face next to hers. "Baby, did you name my cock?"

"Yeah." She nipped my ear and pressed back against me. "And it feels like he likes it."

Chapter 18

Four Months Later

Jason

"ROSE, HONEY, WHERE'S YOUR tea?" Mom stood near Rose in our barely functioning kitchen area on the altar, opening and closing doors of the sideboard I'd built.

Collecting dirty dishes at the dinner table, I strained to listen to their conversation over Alex and his new girlfriend laughing with Becca and Brad over who got Mom the best birthday gift.

"Ooh, let me bring out my special Betty collection." Rose pulled a decorative tin box from an antique cupboard she scored at a flea market and presented it to Mom with a smile. "That's where I keep your Earl Grey."

Mom patted Rose on the back with a smile. "You always remember. Thank you, dear."

I grabbed the last dirty plate off the table and added it to my stack, grinning from ear to ear. Watching Rose with my mom spurred the warmest contentment in my chest. They laughed together about something as Rose set the tea kettle on the hot plate and pulled teacups from the sideboard. She set them alongside Mom's birthday cake, which was a king cake from Haydel's Bakery since her birthday was on the first day of the Mardi Gras season, Little Christmas. Rose winked at me as my dad and I passed with dirty dishes and leftovers from dinner on our way to the community room kitchen.

"They sure are getting along well these days, huh?" Dad said. He elbowed me and gave me his best "I told you so" smile and eyebrow raise.

"Turns out you were right yet again. But I'm glad it took months and not years." I pulled open the dishwasher and started filling it up.

Dad covered the leftover lasagna with foil. "I may have reminded her about our uphill battle with her parents. To grease the wheel, so to speak."

"And you know I appreciate it."

"In fact, your mother was telling me the other day about how much she loves the weighted blanket Rose gave her for Christmas, and how thoughtful it was. She's been using that thing pretty much every day since she got it."

"Aw, that's great. I'll have to tell Rose."

The familiar ring of my phone got louder down the hallway, and Mom appeared in the kitchen, handing my phone to me. "Jason, honey, your phone's ringing."

"Thanks, Mom." I tapped the green button and wedged the phone between my ear and shoulder. "Hello?"

"Hi, this is Faduma Abdi from Big Dick Tools. Am I speaking with Jason Soniat?"

Surprise kicked into my system as I put the dish in my hand down and quickly rinsed off my hands in the sink. "Hi Faduma. Yes, this is Jason. How are you?" I shrugged at my dad and held my phone carefully to my ear, striding toward the door to the courtyard.

"I'm very well. Thank you for asking. Do you have a moment to speak? I hope it won't be a bother for you to hear from us after so long."

The door closed behind me, and I walked out toward the fountain, shivering and crossing my free arm across my chest. Winter had finally come to Metairie, and even the rose bushes that'd been blooming at

Christmas were starting to look bedraggled. "No, yeah. I can talk, and it's not a bother at all. What can I do for you?"

"Well, Jason, as you know, we were so disappointed when you turned us down back in September. I say this only to give you context for my call tonight. Of course I've talked about you with our CEO and founder, Dick Goodwin, and we were both impressed with your integrity, and how you turned down the promise of big rewards so you could live honestly.

"I didn't want to look for a new spokesmodel, but I tried. Unfortunately, I kept running into the same problem: none of them had that special 'Jason' quality."

She laughed, and I laughed too. "That's very kind of you to say." A swift, icy wind careened through the courtyard and straight through the thin sweater I was wearing, and I ducked behind a brick arch to try and escape it.

"Well, it's true," she said. "We kept sending each other your new posts, talking about the one who got away. Since we last spoke, I've so enjoyed your new content with Rose, the partnership you two have—it's really sweet to see. So, over the past month, I've been retooling our original concepts with the StudFinders project, and I'd like to extend a similar offer as last time, but with, we feel, some much-needed changes."

"Really?" I said in my best attempt at not sounding overeager.

At that moment, Rose came out of the side door in her coat with a big blanket. She spotted me and closed the distance.

"Yes. So, once again, we'd like you to consider being our spokesperson for StudFinders, but this time with no contractual obligations on your personal life."

My mouth dropped open as Rose reached me. With raised eyebrows and a smile, she draped the blanket around my shoulders. I pulled her close to me, and she giggled. Wrapping her close to my chest with my free hand, I pressed a kiss to her temple and murmured, "thank you."

As Faduma continued talking, Rose's arms wrapped around my middle, and she laid her head against my chest with a contented sigh.

"The StudFinders service was designed to promote the best handypersons in every market. We never intended to exclude handypersons who are married or in relationships, and we started to think our advertising—if it was based on the single hottie prototype—might give the wrong impression. Let's be honest—there's a good chance that the majority of handypersons who will show up at the customer's door will have significant others. So, what do you think? Does this sound like something you might be interested in?"

"Yeah! Definitely. I mean, I'd like to read through the contract."

Rose's head popped up to look at me with a confused frown.

"Absolutely!" Faduma said. "As soon as we get off the phone, I'll send you the contract and some of our concept art for the ad campaign."

"Thank you so much," I said. "That sounds great. I look forward to your email."

"Wonderful! Have a lovely evening."

"Thanks, Faduma. You too." I hung up and grabbed the ends of the blanket, wrapping Rose in my arms. "You're not gonna believe who that was."

She laughed. "I'm guessing Faduma?"

I nodded. "StudFinders wants me again, for the same thing, but this time without the appearing single clause."

She pulled back to look at me with wide eyes. "What? Seriously?"

"Yeah." I laughed. "I guess we'll get to turn that community room into our home after all."

She let out a happy little squeal and wrapped her arms around my neck, kissing me. "Congratulations! I'm so happy for you."

"Be happy for *us*," I said.

"No no, that's all your money and hard work."

"All my money and hard work is for *us*." I kissed her, then remembered something that happened before the party tonight. "Hey. You said you wanted to talk about something later. We're alone now. Tell me what it is, because I can't wait."

She smiled, settling her arms around my neck. "I've been mulling something over for a while, and I'm finally ready to talk about it."

I cocked my head, worried by her words, but reassured by her smile. "Okay. Talk to me."

Her eyes shone in the darkness, and her smile turned shy as she looked down. "So, I've decided...that if you're ever interested..." She huffed a laugh. "God, my heart is pounding." Her eyes met mine. "Jason, I want to marry you."

Her words hit me as if a rainbow had kicked me in the chest with awesomeness. "Really? You do?" I felt my smile take over my entire face.

She nodded, her smile widening. "I do. We belong together in a way I never thought was possible. And in the past few months, you've shown me, over and over, how happy you are to choose us every day. And I'm not afraid of getting married anymore. Not when it's you. When it's you, it just feels...right."

"I want to marry you, too." I kissed her, and her head tipped back to give me deeper access. My heart was full to overflowing with love for this woman, with excitement about our future. I poured everything in my soul into that kiss, and it was a long time before we came up for air.

"I'm gonna need to know what kind of ring you want," I said breathlessly. "And what size. Like, tonight. And then I'm going to propose to you in the most amazing way I can think of, at the very first opportunity."

She laughed and kissed me again. "I'll send you my Pinterest board. And spoiler alert: I'll say yes."

"Are y'all gonna stand out there and make out all night?" Alex shouted from the door. "It's time to cut the cake!"

"Coming!" I shouted back. Then I turned to the love of my life and murmured, "I can't wait to marry you."

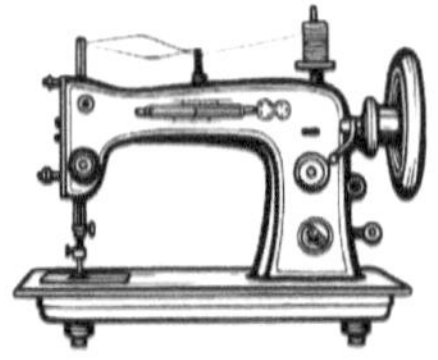

Epilogue: Eight Months Later

Rose

EVEN THOUGH PJ AND Sam had delayed their wedding until the following year, her announcement of intent to have me make her gowns spurred several heavy hitters in the bridal fashion industry to offer me my own lines. I went with Adèle Allais because Adèle herself offered to mentor me to start my own company.

But despite having less time on my hands than ever before, it'd taken me shockingly little time to design my own wedding dress, a corseted blush-champagne gown with draped, off-the-shoulder French silk tulle sleeves and vertical ruffles of tulle over an A-line lace skirt.

And even though these days I had a staff of talented seamstresses to sew everything for me—for which I was still pinching myself—my hands alone were on this dress from start to finish.

At the moment, Jason's hands alone were on this dress, but neither of us would get to finish until we said goodbye to our wedding guests and took the limo home where we had only a few hours to fill with bliss before we had to catch our plane to Paris. We'd already second-lined and cut the cake and done all the things, but we had one more reception responsibility for the night: the bouquet toss.

"Can I have everyone's attention?" the singer of our wedding band asked on the microphone from his place at the head of the Peristyle in New Orleans's City Park.

"Not mine," my husband murmured into my ear where we were making out not far from the band. He squeezed my ass and murmured in my ear. "My wife gets all my attention."

I giggled and murmured back, "My husband is gonna fuck me so good tonight."

His groan went right to my core as the singer boomed, "Time for the bouquet toss! Let's get all the single people on the dance floor!"

Jason reluctantly let me go to the head of the crowd of our guests currently making a mosh pit waiting for me to throw, and Heather approached me, handing me my bouquet.

"I already untied the handkerchief from it and delivered it safely to Becca." She stepped back toward the singer, on the opposite side from the growing crowd of would-be bouquet catchers on the dance floor, which included Abby and Lily.

The singer, who Heather had been flirting with all night, leaned into his microphone. "Aren't you going to participate, brown eyes?"

She put her hand up and stayed where she was. "*Unh-unh*. Not about it."

I winked at her and nodded to the singer.

"Everybody ready?" he called out. "One...two...three!"

I threw the bouquet back up over my head—too high. It hit the concrete rafters of the Peristyle and bounced back, spitting a shower of rose petals on me as it headed directly to Heather.

Heather threw her hands up reflexively to protect her face, and she caught the bouquet upside-down. "What? Noooo!" she lamented. "That wasn't supposed to happen!"

The singer's chuckle echoed through the air as I hugged her.

"Sorry, babe! I swear I wasn't trying to hit you with it!"

She shrugged. "It's a silly tradition anyway that means absolutely nothing."

Heather took a few pictures with me and the bouquet, then Jason grabbed my hand and the mic. He offered it to me first, but I shook my head and pushed it back to him.

"We want to thank everyone for coming out and celebrating us tonight. Thank you to our parents, who all contributed to throwing this amazing party for me and Rose." He grinned. "Me and my *wife*." He kissed me quickly. "Thanks to our wedding party, round of applause to our kickass band, Two of Hearts." The crowd went wild because the band had rocked it. "And...Rose, anything you'd like to add?" He held the mic to me.

"Thanks everybody! But we gotta go! Our time's up in the Peristyle, and we have a marriage to consummate!"

During the laughter and applause, Jason scooped me up body-guard-style. I squealed as he walked me through the edge of the crowds lining up and set me on my feet so we could walk through the line of family and well-wishers sending us on our way.

When the door closed and our limo drove us away, we were already hot and heavy in the back. I twisted the ring on Jason's finger, waiting for my new favorite thing to happen. His face lit up in the middle of kissing me, his dark brown eyes full of love. "I love you."

"I love you, too."

"This dress is the most beautiful thing you've ever made," Jason murmured, slipping his hand up the skirt as he laid me beneath him. "But right now, I just want to taste what's underneath it."

"Truth or dare?" I asked him.

His face lit up. "Truth."

"What was your favorite part of today?"

He kissed me sweetly, then looked deeply into my eyes. "Every minute. When you first appeared at the end of the aisle in this perfect dress, looking like my best dream come to life. When you walked toward me, and I knew today was really happening. When you said, 'I do,' and made me the luckiest man in the world. Right now, making out with my wife on our way to our future together." Jason's arm was around me, his hand cupping my face, his forehead pressed to mine. "I can't believe I get to call you my wife. I love you so much."

His big brown eyes sparkled down at me, and there was no one else in the world.

I pressed my forehead against his. "I love you too, husband."

★ ★ ★ ★ ★

I hope you enjoyed *Follow Your Bliss*. Please consider leaving a review on social media, Goodreads, and/or your preferred retailer to help others find my books!

Next in the Dream House Girls series:

Beautiful, brilliant, and born into wealth, Heather Aucoin is used to getting whatever she wants—except, of course, that time she was left at the altar. Since then, all she wants is meaningless encounters with men, the latest being a hot tattoo artist who she talked into some after-hours fun. It's not like she has time for men, anyway. She's in the middle of leaving a secure career to start her own business, and life is busy.

Tattoo artist Leo Brignac is a hopeless romantic, so his first one-night stand—with a client, no less—has him shocked at his own behavior. Or maybe he's just tired of things never working out, like years of having his heart stomped on by ex-girlfriends and not being able to get a loan to buy his beloved shop, The Flying Horses Tattoo Parlor, after the owner puts it up for sale. You can't get hurt if you expect a woman to leave. Right?

When Leo's offered the chance to inherit the shop by working with a business revitalization expert, he jumps at the opportunity, even when the expert turns out to be Heather, the sexy client he can't stop thinking about. Despite agreeing to keep things professional, neither can deny the chemistry brewing between them, and soon they're involved in a hot and heavy affair. When past flings and meddling exes show up in the shop, it seems like they'll only find success and happily-ever-afters when horses fly.

Also by Holly Rose

Until the Stars Fall
(Interstellar Witches #1)

Falling in love on an interstellar road trip
wasn't part of Gemma's plans...

The Knight of the Trove
(Knights of Mellora #1)

The knight of a dragon's trove, Nesrin would
rather fight off suitors than invite one in.

**A sample of *The Knight of the Trove*
begins on the next page!**

Join my newsletter

https://linktr.ee/writerhollyrose

Chapter 1: Prince Forth Comes to Call

I WAS SACRIFICED IN the usual way: bound to a pole and left for a dragon I was told would eat me alive. I'll always be grateful that the Dread Dragon Adydorrstea offered me a place in her trove instead of a long, excruciating death. But with every feckless prince and hero who arrived trying to "save" me, I wondered if death would've been a mercy.

"Nesrin! Someone at the gate!" Ady called. Her deep voice pealed through the Great Hall as she flew past the doorway to the treasury, the downdraft from her wings fluttering pages in my record book and littering the worktable with an assortment of her feathers. I climbed the ladder against a sandstone bookcase overflowing with gold coins and knickknacks and tried to ignore the pit in my stomach that churned each time we had a *guest*.

The top shelf was a jumble of armor, crowns, and baubles. A crude wooden box under a bronze shield looked as good as any other place to start. I pulled it out, blew the top layer of dust off, and popped it open: dozens of rings. Hooking my arm on the ladder, I tucked the box close to my breast and dragged my fingers through the top layer. Dust motes swarmed in the light streaming through the stained-glass window overhead. Most of the rings were golden and gaudy, encrusted with precious gems and centuries of neglect.

Nes-reeen! Ady called out to me mind to mind, drawing out the last syllable of my name. *We're waiting!*

Can't you deal with him this time? I answered, taking advantage of her dragonian telepathy to steal a few more minutes at my task. I slipped a dragon-shaped ring onto my finger and rubbed off the dust with my thumb. Its miniature golden scales shimmered, undulating around the shank. Maybe Veytian, from the style of it.

Ady's voice popped into my head. *No. It's your job now: I'm the welcomer, you're the defeater.*

Fine, I huffed. I climbed down and tossed the box on my worktable, the rings popping out and *tinking* as they scattered. My leather boots clomped a quick pattern on the stone floor of the treasury and echoed among the columns of the Great Hall as I jogged toward the armory. Once there, I strapped on basic armor, tightened my bandolier, and grabbed my sword. By the time I got to the stables, Ady's magic had my dappled mare tacked, a lance attached to her saddle.

I urged Pistachio gently out of the stables, creeping her one hoof at a time beneath the low canopy as a brisk autumn breeze stirred a mini whirlwind of red and gold leafmeal on the forest floor.

"How dare you disturb the Dread Dragon Adydorrstea?" Ady's professional, man-eating dragon voice resonated through the forest, deep as bronze windchimes.

Stop riling him up! I grouched. As I came around the base of the steep monolith to approach him from behind, the prince's baritone voice carried through the forest.

"I'm Prince Forth of Oprolodas, and I'm here to rescue the fair maiden, Nesrin of Araven!"

He already sounded like a prick—young and privileged, as if he'd come of age, was gifted a fine horse from King Daddy, and immediately set off to abduct me. I peered up through a hole in the pied canopy. Ady held court on the open landing balcony chiseled high into the nearly vertical front face of her mountain, massive, feathered wings tucked in and front legs resting on a balustrade twice my height. She was swift and fiery death on black feathered wings, and she was flickering out a quiet laugh at my expense.

Her voice in my head shimmered with loving mockery. *Should I tell him you're neither fair nor a maiden?*

I approached the line of poplar trees encircling the glade before Ady's front gate. *Since you can't see me, shall I describe the ugly face and hand gesture I'm making at you? You overgrown lizard bird.*

Her appreciative laugh echoed in my head like a pattering of muted bells as she turned her attention back to the imbecile on the muddy clearing. "Welcome to your doom, Prince Fifth!"

"It's Prince *Forth*," he asserted.

"That's what I *said*," Ady replied, setting a small, already-charred tree ablaze with her sibilance. Her intonation was not unlike that of an heiress with sophisticated manners and a questionable past.

I smirked and peered through the trees, close enough to see but not be seen by Prince What's-His-Name to get a read on him before I engaged. He sat tall and dressed in full metal armor atop the requisite majestic black stallion, which was large enough to bear his weight another time over.

"No, you didn't," he argued back.

Actually, that *was* a nice horse. He tossed his mane, and the feathering around his feet fluttered as he stepped high and proud around the clearing.

"Doom awaits you, Prince Third! You have to fight to bring Princess Nesrin away with you."

The prince whipped his horse, coercing it closer to the cave, and my nostrils flared. That stallion was definitely going to be mine.

"I'm ready," he called up to Ady, unsheathing his sword. "Come down and fight me!"

Ady glanced behind herself as if she wasn't sure to whom he was speaking. "Me?" She raised an obsidian talon to her feathered breast. "Oh dear. You thought you had to fight *me*?" She tutted. "You've been misinformed. How embarrassing for you." Her eyes flickered to where I emerged on the ground, twenty feet behind the armored git.

I nodded to her once. I was in position and ready.

"You see, Prince Second, the princess may occasionally take a lover, but she doesn't wish to leave. To make her leave, you'll have to fight her yourself." Ady tilted her slender head toward me, her black and burgundy head feathers dancing around two gently curved horns. The prince turned quickly, startling at the sight of me.

"Princess Nesrin?"

I wiggled my fingers at him in a bored wave. His head bobbled down then up, no doubt taking in the horse clad in armor and the lance captained by a very unprincess-y woman dressed in fighting leathers instead of a flowing gown.

"Can we get this over with?" I tossed my long braid behind my back. "I'm very busy."

As much as I resented this intrusion into my carefully scheduled day cataloging the treasury, I had to admit this was my favorite part. Every man had the same reaction. I didn't have to see this one's face to know what passed across it: confusion, disbelief, then irritation. Hopefully this one wouldn't balk at having to fight a woman.

Prince Forth's eyes darted between Ady and me. "Surely you don't expect me to fight the princess?"

I grimaced. "Look out, Forth!" Urging Pistachio into a trot, I steadied the lance for impact.

Ady's disappointed voice echoed low into the clearing. "Oh, she's got the *lance*."

Pistachio and I bore down on the prince, and he wheeled his horse around. Despite my perfectly-poised lance, he drove the stallion forward and skillfully turned away at the last minute, rushing past me in the opposite direction.

Damn. This one was significantly better than the last one I'd used the lance on. I reset the weapon into its vertical position and wheeled Pistachio around.

"Are you really trying to kill me?" he shouted from across the clearing.

"Ha!" I barked out an unladylike laugh. "It's a jousting lance, metal-for-brains. If I wanted to kill you, I'd have brought the real one."

He brandished his sword, leaning low and spurring his horse into a gallop toward me. What did he expect to do against a lance? He tried pulling his horse aside again, but my blunted lance slammed into his chest, knocking him backwards off the stallion. He clanged to the ground into a bright pile of fallen leaves, and I circled Pistachio around to enjoy the results. The mouth of his visor was twisted open in a lopsided smile, his metal chest dented with the impression of my lance. He rolled almost to his side, but fell back down, unmoving. I was just about to feel bad for him when he got to his feet.

"What's wrong with you?" He pulled off his dented helmet and tossed it aside.

I cocked my head, appraising. This one was rather good-looking—tall, muscular, kind of dashing. His thick dirty blond hair was a curly, sweaty mess, but he had suntanned, chiseled features under an attractive beard, and his blue eyes were—oh dear. Flashing in outrage. Maybe another tactic would work better.

"I don't want to go with you," I said, "and I don't want to hurt you. But this is my home. Tell your comrades: you all need to stop coming here."

Forth stood and picked up his sword from the ground. "You must be under some sort of fey dragon spell." He held his head at an odd angle, his eyes roving all around me as if trying to see the aura of an enchantment. Which wasn't even possible. "I won't give up!"

To his credit, he was brave, running full at me with a battle cry. But I urged Pistachio straight at him, daring him to back down or be trampled.

At the last possible moment, he yelled "Bloody hell!" and threw himself aside into a low part of the clearing that had taken on rainwater, landing with a clanking splash that sent mud spraying all over him and his horse. He righted himself, pulled off both gauntlets with jerky movements, and threw them hard across the clearing in my general direction. He stood and wiped the mud from his tightly trimmed beard, eyes flashing. A vein bulged on his forehead, and his fists clenched at his sides.

I hated when they stayed to fight instead of just leaving. More than that, I missed the good ol' days when Ady used to fight them off for me. She was up there tossing apples into her mouth like a human would eat popped corn, her eyes tracking the fight. She gave me an enthusiastic talon's up.

"Please." I reset the lance to its upright position. "Just go away. Thank you for trying, thank you for your *concern*, but I don't want to be rescued. Today or any other day."

"What have you done to her?" he shouted, looking up at Ady then back to me.

"Oh, for gods' sake." I dismounted and advanced on him with a sword, planning to drive him farther back down the path from whence he came. I punctuated my words with the clanging of my weapon against his. "Go! The! Hell! Away!"

But he was in his element on the ground. Instead of me backing him down the path, he backed me toward the sheer side of Ady's monolith. I parried blow after blow, but he kept coming, his sword meeting mine at every turn. I was strong, but he was taller and stronger. He backed me up against the mountain, our swords straining together.

His eyes were bright and intense, and his strength was crushing me. I pushed harder, determined not to break, but I was folding.

Unless.

I blinked and shook my head, breaking eye contact and letting up *just a little* on my sword. I looked at him and around the clearing, as if seeing it all for the first time. "What's happening? Who are you? Please don't hurt me!"

His face changed from fury to concern, and he loosened his pressed sword.

Ignoring Ady's snorting laughter in my head, I let him take my weapon. I cowered away from him with my back against the rock. "Please sir, don't hurt me!"

"I won't, Princess! I won't." He threw our swords aside and held his palms out, backing away from me a little. "See? No weapons. You're safe now."

He glanced up at Ady, and I chambered my thigh, delivering a front kick to his face just as he turned back to me. His head spun sideways, and he wobbled off balance as I followed up with a rear-legged kick. He dropped to the ground. I raced to Pistachio, grabbing my secret weapon from a scabbard on her side: Steelbane the Sword Slayer—Baney for short. Forged in dragon fire, Baney lived to break lesser swords.

I whirled around to see him recovered, holding both our swords and advancing on me.

His face was red and twisted. "That was a dirty trick! I came here to help you."

But that was a lie. No one ever came to help me. I learned that lesson at a very young age.

"No, you didn't," I spat at him. "You came here to kill my friend and take me against my will. You'll get what you get!"

I advanced, a battle cry erupting from my lungs. My first hard strike broke his sword off at the hilt. He cursed and flung it away, drawing my sword up to fight with wide eyes.

I pulled Baney back but hesitated. "You're going to make me break my own sword?"

"I didn't come here wanting to kill anyone!" he shouted back. "I thought you were in danger!"

That only pissed me off more. Where were his people when I was *actually* vulnerable and alone, when I was held against my will in my own home? No-fucking-where.

I growled and struck with enough force that Baney broke my sword he carried off at the hilt. I'd liked that one, too. He threw himself sideways, slipping in a patch of mud and falling to his back, floundering. His eyes were wide, and he held one hand up in supplication. Baney had that effect on people.

"I yield!" Forth struggled to his feet and held his mud-streaked palms toward me. "I'll leave you alone. Stormbreaker." He stretched one hand toward his stallion.

"Stormbreaker's mine now." I shrugged. "Spoils of battle and all."

"But it's," he huffed, "a very long way back to Oprolodas."

"You should've thought about that before you came to abduct me. Now go before I change my mind and slice off your head." I whirled Baney around in a flourish for emphasis, its notches catching the sunlight.

His face blanched, and he glanced up at Ady. She drew a talon across her neck and waggled her feathery eyebrows at him. "Oh, no, Nesrin," she deadpanned, just loud enough for us to hear. "Don't do *that* again."

"I'll go." He stepped toward his horse then stopped to look at me. "At least let me get my things."

I nodded once, slowly, like a queen granting a boon.

He bowed then unfastened three saddle bags, arranging them on his shoulders. A couple of times, he took a quick breath and looked at me, as if he had something to say. But both times he closed his mouth and returned his attention to his bags.

Most men took their defeat and left without a fuss. It'd been a long time since I'd cared about what people from the outside world could tell me or thought of me. But for some reason, whatever this was bothered me.

"It's a shame you're so eager to get rid of me." He shouldered his last bag. "We would've made a hell of a team on the battlefield." He pressed his nose and forehead to Stormbreaker's long nose, patting his cheek.

"What battlefield?" I demanded, trying to ignore his kindness to the horse and maintain my anger. But a cold wind snuck down the back of my tunic and chilled a dripping bead of sweat, sending shivers across my skin.

He pulled away and met my eyes, his face softening. "Oprolodas and other nations are joining forces. We're marching against Galter Velius."

I recoiled. That name was a punch in the gut. Frowning more deeply at him, anything I could have said died on my lips.

He shifted his burdens and spoke gently. "I thought you'd want to know." He bowed to both of us. "Dread Dragon, my lady, I'll spread the word that you're happy here and not in need of rescue." He gave me a pained look—was that *pity?* Then Prince Forth of Oprolodas turned toward the forest and walked away.

Dropped that on me and walked casually away, the back of his armor glinting in the nearly-setting sun. An old anger edged with panic rose in my gut. I ceased to see the golden trees, Forth's retreating back. Instead, I saw my uncle's army breaking like a wave against the palace. Saw my eldest brother, Talon, through the iron bars of a dungeon cell, bruised and bloodied on the filthy floor, barely clinging to life. Galter stood beside me. His cruel hand, fresh with my brother's blood, gripped my arm like a vice. *That's what'll happen to you if you don't comply.*

Nesrin. Ady's voice called me back, and the spell of his words broke. A cold breeze careered through the clearing, chilling my sweaty skin and the tears tracking down my face.

I whistled to Pistachio and collected Stormbreaker's reins. I patted the stallion's nose, thinking of how Prince Forth had put his head against him and trying not to feel like an asshole for taking the man's horse.

"C'mon Stormbreaker. You don't have to live with that mean ol' man anymore. Let's find you some fresh apples, hmmm?"

After I'd settled the horses in the stables and put my weapons and armor away, I found Ady sitting in the dragon-sized settee in the treasury. Her tail was curled around its carved feet, and she was painting her talons by the cheerful fire roaring in the hearth.

Her black eyes assessed me from beneath raised eyebrows, a black talon half-painted blood red poised in front of her. "You're no fun anymore," she said, gesticulating with the foreclaw that held her nail brush. "When I first brought you here, I used to at least entertain you when I defeated your suitors. I passed that torch to you because you're capable of defending yourself now, but would it kill you to learn a little showmanship?"

Want to keep reading?
Scan the QR code to go to the retailer of your choice.

About Holly Rose

Holly Rose is a romance author who lives in Louisiana with her husband, two sons, and two cats, Loki and Olivia Newton-John. She eats too much cheese fries, loves stargazing, and writes books about people falling in love.

For the latest information about my books, join my newsletter. As a bonus, you'll get a free ebook, the prequel chapter to *Until the Stars Fall* titled "Two Days to Liftoff." Scan the QR code below to get started.

Acknowledgements

I would never have written this book if my sister and I hadn't played with Barbies when we were little, and if I didn't have anxiety. My big sister was done playing Barbies way earlier than me, and as I grew up, it always bothered me that my Barbies—fully fleshed out characters—never had their stories finished. So when I was older and far from home (and struggling HARD with anxiety), I started telling myself more grown-up stories about my Barbies to help me fall asleep at night. Rose, Heather, and Abby were my three favorites. In fact, the original Rose, a Sweet Roses PJ doll, is pictured above.

Thank you SO BIG to Despina who selected me as her 2024 KissPitch Mentee for *Follow Your Bliss*. I cannot express how much your edits improved this book, how much I value your opinion and input (you were right literally every time), and gosh, how darn thrilled I still am that you picked MY BOOK and ME to mentor. You are brilliant, I've been so lucky to work with you, and I love you!

Thank you to my Mom and Buddy for buying us Barbie dolls, and thanks to you and Papa for all the support!

My beautiful, brilliant, loving sister, I love you forever, and you're in all my happiest childhood memories. I invite you to remember reading Hardy Boys Casefiles so our Barbie storylines would never lack for international intrigue and assassination attempts, tossing our Barbies off the shed's roof and into the big swimming pool, and eating French fries on plates sitting on a board stretched across a kiddie pool on the porch while our Barbies floated around the edges. Thousands of Barbie outfits changed, hair brushed, tiny shoes selected, "floaties" getting them up and down from high places, and Barbies going mountain climbing through Grandma and Grandpa's house. Finding the best Barbies at the flea market on Sunday mornings, and, more recently, watching the Barbie movie together because there's no one I'd rather watch it with. (And you were right: I totally stole your Crystal Barbie. In my defense, I was little, and as it was happening, all I knew was that one doll was way prettier than the other, and that was the one I wanted. Whew. I've been holding onto that for a long time. I'm really sorry.)

Thank you to ruisfree for creating the most perfect cover for this book. I've always wanted my own illustrated cover, and what you created for me is more beautiful than my wildest dreams. Thank you for your patience and your kindness!

Thank you to my betas and CPs, Kalla, Marina, Kahlan, and Darcy, and thank you to Abby (Deck Daddy is the gift that keeps on giving!) and Livy who was kind enough to be excited when I asked her if she would read and blurb my book (thank you so much!!). Thank you Skyla for your encouragement. I love all my Hex Quills. Thank you to my dear, brilliant Owls who took me under their wings and continue to teach me so much every day. You are all a fucking delight, and I love you all. Thank you to my Starry Knights for supporting me and my books! Y'all are seriously the best!

And of course thank you and all the love to my sweet husband and my adorable kids without whose support I would not be able to write anything at all, and for my cats who love to interrupt my writing time with scratching at the door (Niv) and needing scratchies (Magokes). Also thank you to Mónica whose unfailing support of my writing career warms my heart. She-Ra and the superheroes love you! Thank you to my dear Sarah, who I love and miss every day and who never fails to cheerlead me—you are too damn far away, and I'm ready for our permanent beach vacation. Love you!